SIREN STORMS OF MADNESS

Fabled Quest Chronicles

Book Five

AUSTIN DRAGON

Published by Well-Tailored Books, California

Siren Storms of Madness
(Fabled Quest Chronicles, Book 5)

978-1-946590-10-7 (paperback)
978-1-946590-05-3 (ebook)

http://www.austindragon.com

Book cover design by Humbert Glaffo

Printed in the United States of America

CONTENTS

Once upon a time...

Beyond the Lands of Man and its Seven Empires, there was the legendary marker known as Titan's Bridge--the sole legendary gateway created by the ancient Titans themselves to the realm of the Magical Lands. Men had passed through the gateway for a millennium since its discovery in search of adventure and, later, unimaginable riches. The destination was the fabled kingdom of Atlantea coveted by humans and fae alike.

Long ago, before the dawn of man, fae, and beasts of light and darkness, was the Age of the Titans. They were gigantic humanoid beings of such size that their heads reached high above the clouds into the heavens. According to myth, a Titan known as the Maker of All Mountains was so devastated by the death of his beloved, he walked the entire circumference of Pan-Earth, dragging his fabled weapon, the Star Slayer. He carved a massive valley before he killed himself by leaping off the world into the void of space. This valley, cut through not only the known world but every other realm, was known as Titan's Trail.

Every three years, the northwestern lands of Avalonia became the starting point of the Kings' Caravan. Twenty years ago, the Kings of Xenhelm began this royal ritual journey across the Trail, attracting men—royal, noble, and commoner, farmer and knight, apprentice and warrior—from every corner of the Lands of Man. It was a year-long journey like no other through unimaginable dangers, mortal and magical, by day and night, all for one reason—to obtain the limitless riches of its final destination—the magical kingdom of Atlantea. Most brave men would never risk such a venture filled with danger and death, even with the protection of the Caravan. However, there were plenty of men who would and gladly did so under the auspices of the Four Kings.

But the Kings' Caravan was no more, due to their own treachery. There remained only Titan's Caravan. Under the command of a human, a man called Traveler, was a caravan the likes of which none had seen before—humans, elves, sprites, fairies, giants, other fae races, many magical beasts, and a shape-shifter not from the world of Pan-Earth.

But can the unlikely caravan make it to Atlantea? The Kings' Caravan was no more but the Four Kings, with wretched evil hearts, and their dark allies lived on.

The Fabled Quest Chronicles continues...across the Oceans of Faë-Land Omnis, their oceans greater than all others in the magical lands, straight to the kingdom of Atlantea.

BEYOND THE GREAT FOREST

At the Edge of the Great Oceans

CHAPTER ONE

Trial by Water

Young Quillen had been so fascinated by the icarian, a majestic being, part human, part bird with large, eagle-like wings, large bird eyes, and feathers for hair. He dressed as royalty in a golden-brown tunic, coat, trousers, and sash. Quillen could not tell if the icarian's boots were made to resemble large bird feet or were the fae's actual feet. The icarian's face also had a quality of nobility, with his upper and lower lips pointed like a bird's beak, as his large eyes quickly scanned all around him the moment he flew down from the sky.

Traveler had wished the winged fae well. With a birdlike shriek, the icarian shot into the blue sky and disappeared. With the new silver key in hand, Traveler turned to face the caravan, looking at them with his dark-brown eyes, holding back a smile. Quillen, for the first time, noticed that their caravan master's clothes were different. He wore his magic sword at his side rather than on his back, as he had done for most of their journey. Actually, it was rare to see his head uncovered by his hood, but he never let his black hair grow too long. The answer to his own simple question came to Quillen quickly as their guide spoke.

Traveler said with a mischievous grin, "We made it through the Forest of the Ancients, or what I called the Great Forest of Horrors as a lad. The rest of Titan's Trail to Atlantea is covered by water. Shall we continue on?"

Their caravan master had already changed into the clothes necessary for the rest of their journey—by water rather than land. Other than his head, there was not one piece of exposed flesh to be seen, with skin-tight gloves and boots and a thick garment snug around his neck.

"What of Mr. Bragg and his men, Mr. Traveler?" a man asked.

"They have returned, but they are different," another fae said. "They have aged."

"We will have plenty of time to speak about it and much more. Our ship awaits, and so does our sail through the Sirenic Seas," Traveler responded.

He marched forward with his dog, and the entire caravan followed. He extended his hand with the silver key into the air and turned it. A doorway to a magic realm opened. Titan's Caravan entered, and after the last human, fae, and animal marched in, the doorway vanished.

From inside, none of the caravan knew that in the door's place appeared a splendid flying fish that flew through the air across the black sand beach and dove into the great ocean.

Inside the pocket-realm, the biggest smile flashed on Young Quillen's face. He ran through the crowd to be right behind their caravan master. The realm had chest-high, thick grass leading to a small lake, where their magic ship awaited. A greenish sun hung in the sky with not a cloud to be seen. Titan's Caravan had made it through the Great Forest. There had been loss of life, which the boy had diligently recorded in his book, but there remained only one more leg of their journey before reaching their final destination—the fabled kingdom of Atlantea. Now, they marched toward the ship before them, soon to set sail. No human or fae was without a smile either. Quillen was certain that even the surly väki were smiling as human, fae, and animal moved forward in three columns.

The enjoyment and excitement did not last long. The sun disappeared in an instant, plunging them all into darkness. A single door swung open on the ship lit like a beacon in the night, enough for them to see the vessel clearly. They boarded the ship—one that appeared strangely unremarkable at first glance, more like a vessel suited for the Lands of Man rather than the titanic oceans of the magical lands—stepping through the door into an open cargo area within the hull.

Traveler gestured them all in. No one realized until he closed the ship's hull that neither he nor his dog had followed them inside. The illumination vanished, then the ship plunged.

Many screamed on the way down, an extreme sensation of falling and one's insides rising toward one's throat. But most did not even have time to comprehend what was happening to them. As terrifying as the falling was, it ended with a loud crash into freezing water. Quillen flailed about in shock; his mouth filled with water.

Screams of men and beasts and the thrashing of many in the water, including two thousand giant lizards and their human minders, echoed in the dark. But the loud pandemonium didn't last long as men settled down and began to yell out, asking if anyone was injured or needed aid.

"I have you, Mr. Quillen." Lady Aylen pulled the coughing boy out of the water with one arm.

He felt his body land on something soft but solid. He coughed out the excess water and was able to breathe properly, then opened his eyes—another realm. He could tell from the new orange sky, though visibility was poor, as if it were dusk. Their ship was a sinking wreck in the center of very dark waters. All around him were the members of the caravan and their beasts. King Aereth lay next to him on his side, shivering. The boy realized that he too was shaking. His eyes returned to the crowd. Lady Aylen was leaping from water to land, rescuing people. The noblewoman was not alone. Pangolin, ever clad in his earthen armor, and many Cut-throats did the same, though not with the same agility as the princess.

"At least some of us are ourselves," the king said.

"I am so cold, sire," Quillen said.

King Aereth forced himself to sit up. The king remained in high regard by the men and fae. He did not travel with his crown anymore, but he was no less a royal. Even with his well-groomed silver-gray hair, mustache, and beard, he was seen truly as one of them rather than apart. "Yes, we must do something," he said.

"Sire, the earth is moving."

The realm itself was indeed moving. They could see that the sky was actually massive windows to the outside world. Giant waves crashed against them, revealing that they were near the great ocean, and their entire realm rocked back and forth like a churning ship due to the power of the tides outside. For many of the men, even if they were not prone to seasickness, they would be now. Random vomiting broke out through the camp.

Before the brownies joined the caravan, the men had become quite accomplished fire-lighters under Hobbs's direction. However, it was as if all their knowledge had evaporated and the brownies were nowhere to be seen. Campfires were finally started by the men but not without great difficulty.

"Where are our fire-shooting väki when we need them?" asked Lady Aylen, who had also taken up the task herself.

The princess joined the campfire where Gwyness and the female half-elves were huddled. Lady Aylen's maiden always wore black, which suited her dark eyes and hair and fair skin. But her normal appearance lacked its healthy vitality.

"How are you all doing, Gwyness?" she asked.

"We are fine, m'lady," Gwyness replied but looked extremely pale.

"You should not be suffering as much as you are." The princess looked at the female half-elves who looked to be in a similar weak state, shivering as much as Gwyness. "I will see to it that we have more fire. It must be this realm. The campfires should be raging. There must be dry blankets somewhere."

Lady Aylen noticed and walked to the new realm's entrance—a door floating in the air near their wrecked ship. Pangolin and the Cut-throats had gathered for a meeting. They saw her and gestured her in.

"M'lady," Pangolin said.

"Is the door locked?"

"No. We've already been outside to explore."

"What is beyond the realm's entrance, then?" she asked Pangolin.

"Another ship, the real one, we believe, and securely anchored to a rocky shore but all within an enclosed cave. Mr. I'wulf and some of his men are searching the area and will return when done."

"Let us assume our caravan master has left us in a place free of any danger." Lady Aylen noticed the magic door had a small viewing port. She stepped up to it and stared across the darkened exterior outside the realm. "Yes, we're in a giant cave adjacent to the ocean. I can hear the ocean and sense it, too, but I don't see a passage to it."

"Yes, we saw no openings either. A very good hiding place."

"Where's Mr. Traveler?"

"He has not been seen."

"I know why he did this to us, but I am not happy about it."

"Our caravan master is not interested in our comfort, m'lady, as much as he is in our survival. I agree with what he did. I know little of the life aboard a ship, but I do know, above all, it is far more dangerous than journeying across a land trail. Better the men and our animals get accustomed to being thrown about by the waters here without any warning than on the real open ocean. Here they can collect their wits and be ready for when it is real."

"It would seem that you, your berserkers, and I are unaffected by this realm."

"Yes, both the men and animals are weak and unable to stay warm."

"Are we in motion too?"

"We are, m'lady. Moving up and down, side to side, like any ship in open waters. But that's not why our people are in the state they're in."

"We wish it were only sea sickness, m'lady," one of the other Cut-throats said.

"Is it better to keep the caravan here, Mr. Pangolin, or leave this realm for the real ship, and maybe find our wayward caravan master, if we're lucky?"

"Remain here, m'lady. If they're this sick now, feeling the full force of the ocean outside will only make them much worse."

"What are we to do? What did Mr. Traveler have in mind?"

"Attend to men—"

"And women."

Pangolin grinned. "And animals. Attend to them until our caravan master returns. He's done this before, m'lady."

"Yes, he has."

"He's making the preparations for us to start our ocean journey. Always to our benefit, m'lady."

"Yes, but we must do our duty and properly scold him for leaving the caravan alone again. Ah, Mr. I-wulf and his men return."

To stare out across the Oceanus Omnis, one would have believed that Pan-Earth itself was made of water alone. Even small waves in the water realm towered far above the tallest castles in the Lands of Man, or in Faë-Land Minor or Major. The darkened sky above was filled with black clouds to give the eerie gray region a palpably sinister atmosphere.

A giant vessel coasted by—a city ship. It moved without oars or sails but traveled swiftly, nonetheless. Traveler knew the ship was searching. He watched it through his telescope from his post tucked in a small realm within a cul-de-sac on the side of the cliffs beyond the Great Forest. He saw no one aboard its deck or compartments but knew that such a ship was packed with a large crew. Water fae were as adept at invisibility as their land cousins. The ship had circled half a dozen times already. They were searching for Titan's Caravan and knew they were nearby. But that meant nothing. They could search for years and never find them despite their determination.

His dog crouched beside him in a form with more aquatic mammal characteristics, such as webbed feet and thicker fur. Traveler playfully stroked the dog's neck with his gloved hand, but he kept his attention patiently on the ship. He dared not risk the use of magic to reveal the ship's occupants. If they had even a mediocre sorcerer, he or she might be able to detect the use of any spell nearby.

A shadow on the deck—Traveler focused his telescope. The figure disappeared, but he had gotten his answer. It was a ship of sea goblins.

Lady Aylen was not a person of patience. She decided to inspect their real ship herself, bringing along Pangolin and some Cut-throats. The vessel was of a design that none of the humans nor fae would have seen before. The craft looked more like a giant supine golem than a vessel, made of a plain dark-silver substance, as strong as any elfin or dwarven metal but, to the touch, felt like skin. Along the hull on both sides were a dozen arms, each tucked in tight and fists clenched. The entire ship of relatively medium size had four decks and could only accommodate half their number, not including their animals, but when using pocket-realms, that did not matter. The Cut-throats imagined the vessel was built for speed with a low profile rather than as a true warship.

I'wulf stationed men on all decks in the passageways. The main deck had a translucent cover of some kind. The ship was tied loosely enough for it to move freely, bobbing strongly in the indirect currents. Daylight appeared through cracks in the cavern ceiling high above but nothing more. Pangolin and about a dozen men stood on the main deck to guard the ladder to the lower decks, passing the time with board games like knucklebones, with newly carved dice, and checkers.

Traveler appeared the next day. For the first time, they saw the dog's new, more aquatic form. Pangolin and the men greeted the caravan master with hugs.

"We see you have your healing bag, sir," one of the berserkers said to him.

"Yes, as I believe my services are needed again."

"That they are, Mr. Traveler. That they are," Pangolin said.

Traveler turned to Lady Aylen with a mischievous grin. "Your favorite, princess."

She laughed. "Shall I guess, Mr. Traveler? Your vapors again."

"Please, Mr. Traveler, restore my lads. I have never seen them in such a state. They seem as if they are close to death," Nirgund the berserker said with a pained look.

"Yes, our animals do especially poorly on the open waters. As Lady Aylen feeds on the power of the great oceans as a water elf, the same waters drain the powers of beings and beasts of land and air, both human and fae. It is not simply the rocking of the ship and the cold," Traveler explained.

"The oceans sap their strength?" Lady Aylen asked.

"It does, princess. But not you, and not any of our berserkers, mole-man fae, or kirins. I should waste no more time then. I trust none here have any concerns with me temporarily putting aside my caravan master duties for my old healer duties."

"None at all, Mr. Traveler," Lady Aylen said.

"Are we likely to receive any visitors?" Pangolin asked.

"No, not while we are here, Mr. Pangolin. However, we cannot stay too long and the moment we do leave, we will not be able to return to this sanctuary ever again."

King Aereth had gone from having the chills to a near-unbearable restlessness, but now he lay under his covers, relaxed. The shivering had ceased. He sniffed the air, feeling the warmth in the atmosphere of the room, and pulled back the covers, squinting. How long he'd lain asleep, he did not know.

The seemingly endless human quarters housed nearly four thousand men. Humans still consisted of the majority of their Titan's Caravan. All rested on their cots arranged row after row. While the ship rocked in the waves, their beds didn't move; they had been bolted or fastened to the floor in some way, or possibly with a simple magical spell.

In a bed adjacent, he saw Hobbs peeking at him. The steward's blanket was up to his nose. On another cot, he could see Quillen sitting up and lying back down, restless. The boy had clearly recovered. The king scanned the room of men again, some sleeping, others talking. The king noticed the translucent heat vapor in the air.

"I don't remember walking here," King Aereth said.

"The Cut-throats carried us here, sire," Quillen said. "We're aboard our new ship."

"Every time we cross from one major magic realm to another, we fall ill. But we have our Mr. Traveler."

The king looked around at their accommodations. The one long room was made of logs, hickory wood, he guessed.

"Is this the ship or another pocket-realm?"

The door of the giant cabin opened, and Traveler entered with one Cut-throat after another, each man with a giant black pot. Men sat up in their cots and cheered. They had seen their caravan master's ex-healer work before. In no time, the pots were set up among the cots on magic rocks glowing orange. When the water boiled, he added mixed powders from his sack. The room quickly filled with more of the translucent vapor.

Men laughed. Others could be heard inhaling it. The king was surprised how invigorated he felt after mere moments. He sat up in his cot. Hobbs did the same.

Their steward, Mr. Hobbs, may have been below average in height, balding, and by no means threatening in appearance, but he commanded the respect of the men no less than Traveler, King Aereth, or Pangolin. He was the first man Traveler had hired those many months ago when Titan's Caravan was first assembled, to manage all non-fighting men. For decades, he had been the master of the household of the Theogar Royal Family before the fall of its kingdom. He'd been as successful there as he was with Titan's Caravan. He commanded respect because he gave respect, overseeing the men with duty, fairness, seriousness, and—rare for someone with his position in a royal house—humility. When he spoke, all listened.

"What would we have even done without Mr. Traveler, sire?"

"Died along the Trail many times, Mr. Hobbs."

"Have you seen, Mr. Gresham, Mr. Hobbs?" Quillen asked from his cot.

"Not since being brought here."

Hobbs smiled as Traveler neared them. The caravan master was greeted by the men as he passed.

"Mr. Traveler, I dare say we are ready for battle," the king said.

"No fighting yet, sire. Humans usually recover quickest when treated with the vapors. I will leave enough of the medicine here and give you the task of keeping the pots boiling and medicine added at regular intervals."

"I will see to it, sire," Hobbs said to the king.

"How long will we need to have these wonderful vapors filling the air around us, Mr. Traveler?"

"As long as we are able, sire. I have other pots outside in the passageways minded by the Cut-throats, which will heat them, primarily, but you all will benefit as well."

"Like sitting in front of a campfire, sir," Hobbs said.

"Mr. Hobbs, also see to the men's new clothing."

"New attire?" the king asked.

"Yes, sire," Hobbs said. "Mr. Traveler had me prepare for the seafaring leg of our journey."

"As long as all members of Titan's Caravan appear well suited for all the royal banners we carry."

"Yes, sire. Our new attire is warm, sturdy of fabric, and worthy of royalty," Hobbs said.

"And if one should find him or herself thrown overboard into the ocean, they will not freeze to death or immediately sink to its bottomless depths," Traveler said with a wicked grin.

"Though it would not save us from the stray sea serpent. Is that what you were about to add, Mr. Traveler?"

"Sire, you're reading my mind again. We've been traveling together for too long."

Hobbs began to stand, but Traveler gestured for him to remain sitting.

"You should hear this, too, Mr. Hobbs. Sire, there will be a change of plans."

"Oh. This close to our final destination? I cannot say it's unexpected."

"How far are we from Atlantea, Mr. Traveler?" asked Quillen, who was suddenly sitting on Mr. Hobbs's cot.

"We're about a month away, Mr. Quillen."

King Aereth closed his eyes with a wide smile. "For the Kings Elder, we are almost there."

"Yes, sire, but we must not celebrate yet, especially when we no longer have a fully functioning crew."

"Crew, Mr. Traveler?"

"Yes, Mr. Hobbs. Titan's Caravan is now Titan's Crew, but we are not even that."

"But you've remedied that, haven't you, Mr. Traveler, with your vapors of medicine and magic?"

"More medicine than magic at the moment. Sire, just as the Great Forest was of magic, so are these great oceans. Unfortunately, its effect on our fae is far more profound than I had expected, even accounting for the fact that they are land fae and not water fae."

"How is Lady Aylen, our resident water elfess?"

"More powerful than ever, sire. But she is among the few exceptions. One never knows how one will be affected on the open waters by its magic. Some take to it; others do not. I've already spoken to the others in the leadership. Our status requires us to make drastic changes to get to Atlantea."

"How so, Mr. Traveler? Were any of the others happy with the news you gave them?"

"Not at all, sire, but they are still bedridden, so they were unable to give much protest. Our caravan of nearly ten thousand is effectively less than twenty-five hundred at this moment. If we divide duties between day and night watch, that leaves only twelve hundred fifty. Only a thousand men to stand guard and fight if needed on these oceans. Ships here are far more formidable than anything you have ever seen. The ships of merfolk can be city ships with crews of hundreds of thousands. And that does not include any sea creatures under their enchanting command. We need a full crew.

"Moreover, the whole point of us leaving the protection of the Atlas turtles and the Great Caravan was to avoid a trap at Titan's Fall. However, as we saw, they also waited for us at Titan's Teeth. And I have already confirmed that we did not destroy all their fleet, so we have no idea of how many will be on the hunt for us."

"Confirmed how?" King Aereth asked.

"From our secure hiding place here, I am able to see through to the open ocean with my telescope. We are being hunted. A single ship has been circling this area since we arrived, undoubtedly looking for us. We must assume, too, our foes have a bounty on us."

"A bounty?" Hobbs asked.

"Yes. They do that here in the magical lands, too, but I suspect the rewards would be far greater than any we would see in our lands. None of you have a full grasp yet of how many vessels sail these oceans. We could not fight off one such vessel in our current state, let alone a dozen or a hundred or more."

"What are our options then, Mr. Traveler?" the king asked.

"First, we get the caravan back on its feet. Then we will abandon this ship."

"Abandon?" they asked in unison.

"But you purchased for this transport from the icarian," Quillen said sadly.

"What does that matter, Mr. Quillen, if we're sunk or captured? Sire, we are known, all of us. On land, we had the protection of our giant lizards, crawling trees, and effective circles of magic. This ship has a translucent covering. The main deck is like a circle to protect us when the deck is open, but protocol on the open waters is for a captain or crew of one vessel to see the other to identify each other as friend, foe, or disinterested party. We are being hunted, so we have no choice. We abandon the ship, or more precisely tuck it into a pocket for later use, while we seek new transport."

"New transport, Mr. Traveler?" King Aereth asked in distress. "How will you find this alternate transport for us?"

"I have my ways, sire."

"But would that not leave us at the mercy of others?"

"Yes, sire, but again, we have no choice. We were a formidable force before, on land, but now, we could not withstand an attack from the smallest vessel. If not for our evil enemy, Oughtred, I would risk it, but it would be beyond reckless, suicidal even, to add to the normal dangers of the open waters with those Oughtred will send our way. We must regain our advantage to get to Atlantea—anonymity. We can only do so as passengers aboard another's vessel."

"I am not sure I like that option, Mr. Traveler."

"Your reservations are no different than the others. Would you like me to tell you who voiced the loudest protest, sire?"

The king managed a smile. "Our princess spoke for me, then."

"Sire, it is dangerous, but far less dangerous than continuing on as if there is no danger."

"Sir, you do seem at ease with all this, as if you've been a true ship's captain before. Have you possessed that title before?" Hobbs asked.

"No, Mr. Hobbs, but I have served on my share of ships. I have knowledge I can use to purchase passage on one of the many ships that travel these waters for us. If we can, we will sneak our way into Atlantea."

"That sounds better, Mr. Traveler," King Aereth said. "You can understand how we all have grown to trust and take comfort in your command of the caravan."

"I appreciate that, sire, which is why I make the decision I do. Whether I command the vessel, or not, I must get us there. We will be their passengers. Therefore, my choice must be a wise one."

Lady Aylen laughed as she walked past Cut-throats in the passageways. Boiling pots of water emitted waves of heat. Her enhanced sight could even see the translucent vapors seeping from under closed doors. "Our Mr. Traveler and his vapors," she said.

The women's quarters was small compared to others. The princess shared it with Gwyness and the five female half-elves alone. The other occupants were their half-dozen tiny owl griffins. When she entered, all the women were wide awake, and the tiny beasts were still groggy but slowly moving around the cot of the main female half-elf who minded them.

"Brenn, your comrades are almost themselves," Lady Aylen said.

"Yes, m'lady. Soon they will be running, and soon after, I expect them to be able to fly again."

In the center of the cabin was a large black boiling pot.

"Well, ladies. Do not let our quarters be without Mr. Traveler's air medicine."

The four other female half-elves jumped from their cots to reach for a nearby sack. They poured more powder into the boiling water.

"You didn't see yourselves as I did. I thought you would never wake or stop trembling. Gwyness, how are you?"

The maiden lay on her cot, revived, but it was clear she was not happy.

"A descendant of Rivermouth's warrior clerics, m'lady? I think not."

"Gwyness, stop that. Most on this ship were incapacitated—humans, fae, elves, all. Do not concern yourself with it. Besides, Rivermouth was in Faë-Land, not here on the greatest ocean of the magical lands. You had good reason."

Gwyness sat up in her cot. "How long will we be here, m'lady?"

The princess sat down on her own cot next to Gwyness's. "Mr. Traveler says we need new transport."

"What do you mean?"

"He says we are in no condition to fend off an attack on these open waters. I wholeheartedly agree. I am unaffected. Our human and fae berserkers are unaffected. Mr. Traveler and his dog too. But no one else. Mr. Traveler spoke of city-sized ships of possible attackers. Tens and hundreds of thousands against our meager numbers."

"But transport from where?"

"Our caravan master is handling it, Gwyness, and we should let him. You must get your strength."

"Are the human men awake, m'lady?"

"Yes, why?"

"I will find Mr. Hobbs. We are to have new clothes for our ocean voyage."

"New clothes?" Lady Aylen looked at the smiling half-elves. "Did you know? I take it from the smiles that you all approve."

"We do, m'lady."

"Then there is nothing for me to concern myself with." She looked at the female half-eves. "None of you are part water elf? Slyviel? Cozira? Iohnia? Oritha?"

The other female half-elves shook their heads.

"Brenn, you clearly have the gifts of a woodland elf. Animals love you."

Brenn smiled.

"Why do you ask, m'lady?" Gwyness asked.

"Mr. Traveler's rules remain. No one is to go anywhere alone."

"M'lady, I will see to our new attire then return to be at your side."

"I wonder if we are allowed to say we are the descendants of the lost kingdom of Rivermouth now that we're on these great oceans. Is it still a secret?"

"We can ask Mr. Traveler, m'lady."

"Yes, but our enemies already know all about us if Oughtred was waiting for us outside the Great Forest."

"But we evaded him again, m'lady."

"Yes, but this time, Gwyness, there is only one path for us to take to get to the gates of Atlantea. All he would need do is wait for us there, or have his dark allies do so."

"Mr. Traveler will outsmart him again."

"I'd prefer Oughtred's death at our hands and to use my mental faculties for other concerns. Perhaps our caravan master will have some thoughts he can share."

For the caravan's one hundred drows, their quarters were small but cozy. Torches lined the walls with their magic fire. All the room's surfaces were of a blackish blue color, including their cots, where they each rested under a blanket.

The off-shoot elf-like race of drows with their dark-bluish skin and purple eyes blended into the surroundings. They might be virtually invisible if not for their white hair. All were men except for one. The drow sorceress, Dr'amal, slept in a cot near her father, the group's leader and king, Dr'as, also fast asleep.

Many of the awake drows were surprised by how weakened their constitution had become in the new region. Most were disgusted with themselves and depressed, but Traveler continued to reassure them. "It is the magic of the great oceans that afflicts you. It is not your fault, or any indication of weakness on your part," he told them.

As he had done before, he had pots of boiling water spreading the vapor through their cabin. For many of the fae, they would be incapacitated longer than the humans for the simple fact that humans were not magical beings. All fae were far more susceptible to the magic of the lands they resided in.

Traveler walked through the aisleways between the sleeping cots. He personally handed out cups of hot medicinal broth to those not recovering as quickly.

The caravan master-now-healer had a few of the Cut-throats helping him with healing duties. One Cut-throat carried a metal pot, and Traveler carefully poured its contents into a cup.

"Sit up," Traveler said to one drow. "Here. Drink this."

The drow complied, slowly drinking the warm medicine.

"I heard that you lived with drows before on your travels."

"I did."

"Where in our lands did you stay?"

"Blue Mist and surrounding villages."

"I know of it."

"You must keep your spirits up. The weakness will pass."

"How could this be? I have been on the sea many times in my life, been on ships for many months at a time."

"But not on the Oceanus Omnis. It is different here. The magic is not the same here. Do not upset yourself. It will pass, and you will be forever immune to its negative effects, as I am."

"If you say, healer."

In contrast, the elfin quarters were much larger, with the clans of high elves, desert elves, woodland elves of the rustic lands, and those of the city kingdoms. The floor, ceiling, and walls were of gray-white stones, as if they were in one of their castles rather than a pocket-realm. Their leopard axexs and magic falcons were in the care of the Tree Shepherds, as were Nirgund's thirteen reptilian hounds. The three leaders, Lyre, Talos, and Chief Ethor, were in a deep sleep of sickness. Shadu-mun, the moon elf leader, was already responding to the vapor remedy faster than the other elves.

While most elves had dark hair, or even blond, the moon elf had snow-white hair to his shoulders. As he was the only elfin leader alert and on his feet, the caravan master approached him first.

"Mr. Shadu-mun, it would seem that you are the elf in charge," Traveler said as he handed him a cup of broth.

"I am sure when you tell them to rest next time, they will not be so quick to disregard your words," Shadu-mun said.

"They will be well again soon. Simply rest. We need all to be as strong as possible when we depart."

"Depart for another ship?"

"Yes."

"But you will not be the captain."

"No."

"No one will like that."

"Let me work on the problem. It may not be as bad as you suspect."

"The thing about you, human, is you are always so calm about what would have caused other older caravan masters to panic. Why so calm?"

"Because I spent so much of my early years in the magic lands being anything but calm. The most important lesson I learned from a caravan master far older than either of us is: always have an alternative plan. No matter how certain your path is, have an alternative for when all goes wrong. I believe the advice was from an elfin caravan master I knew."

The moon elf smiled. "Wise words."

"I would say so. I will leave the elves to your watchful eye. I shall continue on with my healing duties."

A large cabin housed the caravan's gnomes, gnomoids, and fauns. Like the humans, the gnomes and gnomoids responded quickly to the vapor and were, soon up and about in good spirits. The fauns were more like the drows and elves. They would need more time, breathing in the medicinal vapors, over an extended period, to be fully invigorated.

The three races of hooved fae preferred to be in their own quarters. Traveler spent the most time with the deerfolk setting up many smaller pots in their quarters. For the nervous fae they were, he wanted to keep their minds occupied. He would set things up, and the fae would maintain the steady boil of medicine. Vapor filled the air quickly, and trembling, half-asleep rusines, cervids, and elaphines became themselves. Traveler showed them all how much medicine to pour into the pots from the many sacks he left.

Traveler gave a full accounting to their more-than-six-foot-tall leader, Strag. The largest of the elaphines, with huge antlers sprouting from his head, wider than any others in the group, appreciated the news but the good sentiment would not last long. They would soon want even their human healer gone from their quarters so they could recover alone.

The animal men also had their own quarters. It was much larger because they also shared it with their giant animals. Their mole-man-looking fae watched over his comrades. He helped Traveler set up the boiling pots to have the vapor flowing through the room. In their case, many animal men would need to get to their feet quickly to manage their animals, who hated enclosed spaces, and the constant rocking of the ship.

Of most concern, were the caravan's six twelve-foot-tall Antaean giants. Without the earth beneath their feet and with the ocean's draining magic, of all the fae not of the realm, the giants were in the worst state. They appeared deathly sick. Traveler had both brownies and pech in the same large quarters with them, as virtually all of them would be needed to attend to the many, many boiling pots of medicine to restore the giants. The process would not likely be complete for many days.

"We will never doubt you again, Master Traveler," a brownie said to him.

"We thought you mad to have us mix so much of the magical powder on the march. Now we wonder if it will be enough," another said.

"It will be," Traveler said confidently.

The caravan master glanced at the corner and saw the group of fae-blood men, in their black attire and cloaks, sleeping on their cots.

"We will keep an eye on them, Master Traveler," a brownie said. "Though with their kind, you can never tell if they're sleeping or hibernating."

"I did not know wolves hibernated," another brownie said.

"Their kind does. It may happen against their will, their body bringing about the state to protect them from harm."

"We are not on the real ocean yet, are we, Master Traveler?"

"No. We are in a hidden cave closed off to the ocean along the shore."

"If this is the state of us before sailing the oceans, what will be of us out on the open waters? The shortest leg of our journey may be our longest and most difficult."

"Yes, that is exactly what I learned so many years ago. I was on a caravan and it took one year to get from the Lands of Man to the Great Forest, and another year to get across the Oceanus Omnis."

"A year, Mr. Traveler?" the brownie asked with surprise. All the brownies looked at him, as did some of the pech.

"We will not take a year to cross, but our obstacles could be many. Attend to the giants. We need everyone healthy."

Traveler visited the quarters with the four Tree Shepherds—Greenwig, Mossberry, Thornbeard, and Little Root, the youngest. Through a magic doorway in their pocket-realm were open green woodlands surrounding a large blue lake as blue as the sky above it. The caravan's majestic caladrius bird flew in a circle before landing near the lake. Even on the great ocean, the leshy would need the illusion of contact with the flora of the earth. All four of their crawling trees and the soul tree stood together in one section of the woodlands. They had told him the fairy sisters were in a deep magical sleep, hidden away. The three kirins rested in one tree. The group of kilmoulis had their own camp, as did the fenodyree, both sitting around campfires. The desert elves' falcons quietly rested in the branches of another crawling tree, with the leopard axex beasts sleeping around the base.

The caravan master had to use his telescope to see the Diomedian Mares in the far distance huddled together in a pack. Around a large campfire were Bragg's elfin comrades, all asleep.

Greenwig, the Tree Shepherd leader, appeared next to the caravan master. They all had bright-green eyes, white skin, hair and full beards of living grass and vines, and beneath their flowing robes, walked on hooved feet.

"Will you be boiling your medicine here, too, Master Traveler?"

"No, Mr. Greenwig, I think we can use your leshy magic to do better. A ground mist of the vapor to touch every corner of this realm. I brought enough of the powder for you. I will simply dump it into the lake, and you can do the rest."

"A boiling lake." The Tree Shepherd smiled.

"Yes, Mr. Greenwig."

"Ingenious, Master Traveler."

"Thank you. Is both Ursi, the fae-blood, and our Mr. Frog-Dor here?"

"Yes. The woman is in a hidden cave underground. The man rests in a treehouse he created at the top of one of our crawling trees."

"How sick were they?"

"Not too bad, but your vapor medicine will restore them."

"How are the darklings?"

"They are all asleep in their own pocket-realm."

"The väki?"

"Their pocket-realm is locked to all outsiders— even me. That means they are very sick and do not want any of us to see them. They hate the open water."

"Our väki are a bit vain, are they not?"

"Very, Master Traveler."

"I will say hello to Mr. Bragg."

"Were they really aged by the time elemental?"

"No, worse, Mr. Greenwig. They fell through time, into the past. The question is how long did they have to wait until Titan's Caravan came into existence for them to rejoin us?"

"This evil King Oughtred is extremely gifted at assembling dark creatures no one has seen or encountered for ages. Spell-talkers, nemains, time elementals. How is such a human able to accomplish this, Master Traveler?"

"King Oughtred ceased being human a long time ago."

"But his Kings' Caravan was only twenty years old."

"I suspect there is a fuller story, and we will know it in time. Perhaps we will encounter flora and fauna of this realm who can reveal his secrets to us."

"Like the Great Forest, we have no connection to the flora and fauna in this realm."

"But you are leshy, Mr. Greenwig. A Tree Shepherd no less. There are many trees here. They walk, swim, and some of them can talk."

The open blue sky became one filled with thick, billowing yellow clouds. The rain began, and a seated Bragg looked up as the lukewarm water came down. As the water rolled off his face and dripped to the ground, the yellowish vapor rose up to blanket the ground around them.

The dwelf saw the human Traveler approach through the mist.

Every time Traveler saw their great manticore hunter, Bragg Emberstone of the mountain-elf kingdom of the Labyrinth Mountain, he wanted to smile. He felt like Young Quillen seeing a flying unicorn or griffin for the first time. Traveler had heard of dwelfs when he was a lad but never thought to see one, let alone have one as a member of his caravan. Though he was older, he was the same Bragg. He looked like an elf but had a large, brawny, wide frame and was very tall. He had dark hair and wore the same dark-brown leather attire and a belt made of skull fragments. His walking staff with its axe blade lay on the ground at his side.

"I have known many healers in my time, Mr. Traveler, but none who used this particular healing art. However, I learned at my stay at Last Keep about a human boy who lived there for a time, learning all he could from a fae there—including healing arts from one of the realms unknown to your Seven Empires. I was told she was fond of boiling powders, roots, and herbs in large pots of water to create a floating vapor of medicinal powers."

"Yes, I was that boy. The healing sorceress was a woman named Wu."

Bragg smiled. "I knew it was you."

Traveler sat down across from him on the wooded ground. He saw the other elves of their camp begin to stir, breathing in the yellow vapor and sitting up.

"Where is your Mr. Glog? Or should I guess? In the care of our weaponsmaster, Mr. Estus."

"You guess correctly, Mr. Traveler."

"What happened to you and your comrades, Mr. Bragg?"

"How long ago was it that we disappeared to you?"

"Four days."

"What was only days ago for you was in fact years ago for us."

"How far back did you go?"

"Many years, before the Kings' Caravan ever began. We pushed the creature back into its portal of time. The demon was too powerful to hesitate for the briefest moment. He could slow the flow of time while it remained unaffected. The shock of pushing it through the portal distracted it. We did the rest and ripped it apart with our hands, weapons, even our teeth. However, when the deed was done, we found ourselves at the very spot it began. But we knew something was terribly wrong.

"We risked it and went back the same way we came through the Forest. All was different, but you had told us that the Forest moves, that its giant trees and the lands shift. When we reached Faë-Land Major, I knew.

I know the cities and villages there well. I knew one fae in particular who was the landlord of a favorite tavern. I saw him. He had been born the day before we arrived. The fae I knew was graying, had a dozen children, and many more grandchildren. He looked up at me as an infant in his mother's arms. I said nothing.

"My comrades were in as much despair as I. What to do? We had arrived before the formation of the Kings' Caravan and the Kings' Caravan was twenty years before you."

"You found a caravan to take you to Atlantea," Traveler said.

The dwelf smiled. "How did you guess? I was, after all, myself. Bragg, the great manticore hunter. We could not wait twenty years. Maybe we could get our fortune and come back to help you. It was to be one of the many mistakes we made. We traveled to Titan's Fall and found ourselves in the middle of a sea war between water elves and mermaids."

Traveler closed his eyes. "The Siege at Titan's Fall."

"Oh, you know it." The dwelf laughed. "Then I wish we'd had a few conversations of the history of the region. My comrades and I were in the war. We were prisoners of the mermaids and water nymphs. We escaped, and became prisoners of the water elves, who thought we were in league with the mermaids. We were captured again by sea goblins, which we did not know were in these waters. We escaped, only to join in battle again."

"Some of us noticed that not all your elves are returned."

"We lost a quarter of our comrades in the battles. One was a sea battle that lasted nearly four months. Deur died in one of the ship dungeons we found ourselves in. He died from some stomach sickness— for a warrior, a hunter to die in such a pointless way...Mr. Traveler, my comrades and I grew so sickened by the whole ordeal, we turned our backs to it all and returned to Faë-Land. But I could not go home; neither could they.

"Then we began to hear about the tenth great year of the Kings' Caravan moving through the magical lands to Atlantea. Wisely, we resisted the temptation. After all, the demon we battled came from them. Who knew what wizards he had? Maybe ones who would read our thoughts and know who we were and when and where we came from. That would endanger you."

Traveler cast his gaze downward for a moment, thinking.

Bragg saw his expression. "You do not think Oughtred had foreknowledge of you from us?"

"It does not matter, Mr. Bragg. I'm waiting for the good news. And thank you for your note."

"You are welcome, Mr. Traveler. You had no doubt it was me?"

"It was written in goblin, so I knew that to be your kind of humor. Besides Mr. Frog-Dor sensed your presence at the very start of our march through the Great Forest. He described you as members of our party but not us. It could not have been doppelgängers because they never travel in numbers. If you had not warned me, we would have suspected some type of deception, and even our humans are quite good at hitting targets with their heavy weapons. But out with the good news. I know you are eager to tell me."

Bragg laughed as others of his elves joined them.

"Yes, Mr. Traveler. Besides returning to the site to battle the Four Kings' fleet with a bigger and more powerful Mr. Glog, I built over the years, we used our time to give us the advantage."

"What advantage, Mr. Bragg?"

"Oughtred's chief warrior son Wuldricar was at Abacus with an army in search of you. We returned to watch them exit their massive portal. They did not count on the power of the merchant realm's elemental väki. We set out for their fleet waiting for us at Titan's Teeth, waiting with more of his dark allies. Allies, Mr. Traveler. Where does one find the best allies against such an enemy? When you have an enemy above all seeking your destruction, then you must learn of all their enemies. That is where you find your allies."

"Mr. Bragg, Oughtred kills all of his enemies, real or imagined. It is why he has been so obsessed with us, and I am certain this has always been his pattern, though he has hidden it well from most."

"He has, Mr. Traveler. I was not fooled and knew where to look and what questions to ask. I created my list, and I hand it to you."

The dwelf removed a folded parchment from a pocket of his tunic. Traveler took and opened the paper. The caravan master stood as he read it carefully.

"Mr. Bragg, you and your comrades have definitely grown smarter in your old age."

Bragg and his elfin hunters laughed.

"Only a learned caravan master such as yourself would know the significance of the names on that list." Bragg stood.

"I am not quite sure you are completely aware of the significance of the names on this list, Mr. Bragg. You've saved us precious time, time that we will use to our advantage."

"Do you know the names of the kingdoms on the list?"

"I know all of them. This is fine work, Mr. Bragg. It tells us all the water fae caravans not affiliated with Oughtred and his former Kings' Caravan. Those who would be his enemies and his targets. Those who could be persuaded to be our allies."

"We form a new caravan then, of ships."

"An alliance."

"Good."

"There is one other thing you should know since you and your comrades were absent."

"What is that, Mr. Traveler?"

"At our battle where Oughtred was certain I would die, and our entire caravan, he revealed his true plans. The Four Kings and their dark allies plan to conquer Atlantea."

"What? Is that not impossible? You have been there."

"I have lived in Atlantea. It is impossible, which is why I believe it to be possible, if he plans to try."

"Then we need to leave immediately."

"Not immediately, but close to it. As soon as we're able."

CHAPTER TWO

Sail!

For the entire march through the Great Forest, the caravan's musicians, the Brothers Brimm, performed not a single time. Everyone was preoccupied with the fear of being dragged off by a giant spider or eaten by a giant tree or some giant creature out of one's nightmares. Johnter led his comrades to the ship's bridge on the main deck, summoned by one of the Cut-throats.

In the center of the vessel, sat the ship's command bridge. Inside the sizeable structure, their caravan master stood at a large rectangular table covered in nautical maps. The musicians happily greeted him. So many months ago, their caravan master had hired them in the Lands of Man for the journey. He handed Johnter a large wooden case.

"Musical instruments," Traveler said.

"For us, sir?"

"You may be called upon during our ocean voyage, possibly to save all of us."

"Us, sir?" one of the other Brothers Brimm asked.

"How?" Johnter asked, worried.

"Sirens," Traveler answered.

The men looked at each other. They didn't know what to say or do.

"Ignore the fables of men sticking candle-wax-coated cloth in their ears to prevent their dark enchantment. The singing magic of sirens is so powerful, no man, human, or fae is immune. Sirens don't lie about on rocks, unable to move. They run, swim, and fly, something not even merfolk can do. We need every advantage. This case of magic flutes will be our weapons against them, amongst others. You will master them and be ready."

"Will we really be able to fight them with music, sir?" one of them asked.

"Yes. Music against music. Magic against magic."

"But we are men. Would not women be more helpful in this task?"

"No. You are true musicians. That is why you will be able to use these flutes better than me or anyone else in the caravan. You will train in the realm of the Tree Shepherds."

"When might we encounter these sirens, sir?"

"I wish I could say that we could avoid them but it's doubtful. With the majority of our caravan being men, we must be on guard for them at all times because, once mesmerized by their song, it's too late."

"You have encountered them before, Mr. Traveler?"

Traveler had a faraway look as he recalled. "I once saw the entire crew of men dive into the sea to their deaths under a siren's spell. Most drowned, but many were eaten alive by the sirens."

The look on the men's faces loudly conveyed their fear. Johnter grasped the wooden case. Traveler put a hand on his shoulder.

"I know it's a heavy burden, this new task I'm giving you. Just know that when we're through it all and we cross the gates of Atlantea you will be able to reclaim your chosen profession. Atlanteans like humans, especially those who can tell stories *and* play music."

"So that is your secret, Mr. Traveler. You beguiled the Atlanteans with your amazing stories of traveling the Trail and beyond."

He grinned. "Our secret. Don't tell anyone."

Lady Aylen stared at herself in the floating mirror of their women's quarters, a gift from the brownies. Two of the female half-elves checked over the princess's new attire—a battle dress worthy of a royal, made of a dark-blue fabric woven to look like scales of a fish, it was tight-fitting but flexible with gray-blue fur lining the cuffs and neck, and matching thigh-high leggings. She had new brown-hide boots to her knees but no idea of what animal's skin they were made of. She preferred not to have her head covered by her hood but liked her new cloak down her back. They were told that Estus had had a hand in the wide belt around her waist with its secret pockets and compartments, more than she would ever use. For now, their weaponsmaster had fitted it with multiple daggers. The best was the magical straps that securely held her dual war tridents to her back. All she needed to do was extend her hand, and the magical strap would throw a trident into her palm. When the women saw the trick for the first time, they knew that they would practice it for many hours. Finally, each forearm was fitted with a metal guard, also courtesy of Mr. Estus, where a magic triangular shield would appear when needed in battle.

"Here, m'lady," one of the female half-elves said, handing her a pair of gloves.

"Now my new battle attire is complete." Lady Aylen pulled them on. "They feel soft inside but are as hard as metal on the outside."

Gwyness touched the outside of Lady Aylen's gloves. "I wonder if they are strong enough to withstand a blow from a sword."

Lady Aylen clenched her fists. "Probably so." She looked at Gwyness. "Your turn Gwyness, then our royal guardswomen, then our royal owl griffins."

The female half-elves giggled as the tiny beasts flew around, knowing they were being talked about.

Someone knocked at the door.

One of the female half-elves opened it slowly, and Traveler walked in. He, too, was in new attire—his head covered by a cloak of glistening fabric, his chest and forearms fitted with orange-tinted armor. His sword was no longer on his back but on his belt, angled in front of him. The belt also had a variety of daggers and what looked to be individual animal claws.

Lady Aylen was clearly taller, and her increased vigor was obvious with her eyes a brighter blue than ever before.

"Lady Aylen, you are properly dressed for our voyage."

"You appear to be dressed for battle, Mr. Traveler."

"I am, princess, because as soon as we leave our hidden location, we will be. Let's inspect the ship."

Traveler walked through the darkened bridge of the ship with a large torch in hand. Lady Aylen walked alongside him; she glanced at the dog following them.

"I now understand the presence of the women on the journey, Mr. Traveler. They are to guard against sirens."

"Yes, princess, it is the surest way to guard against them. If your crew is driven mad by the creatures, they are the only ones immune. But there are many other ways to defend against them. The elves will use magic to remove their ability to hear all sounds. You are immune not only because you are a woman but because you are a water elf."

"But we aren't heading to the Sirenic Seas."

"No, but that doesn't mean we won't come across one or more of them. For the journey, all the caravan's women will take leadership roles, with you as the royal in charge."

"Me?"

"Yes, the Oceanus Omnis is primarily under matriarchal rule like Faë–Land Minor. For the voyage, I am no longer the caravan master, I am the captain of the ship, even though we will later become passengers aboard another ship."

"I still don't like it, Mr. Traveler."

"You will be the mistress of the ship and be the one who speaks for us, not King Aereth. I hope your elvish has progressed far enough, because you will be speaking a lot of it."

"I'm not sure I like the sound of that either. What if I say the wrong thing? I've never spoken elvish before to anyone, let alone strangers."

"No turning back now, princess."

The ship seemed much smaller than Lady Aylen expected, but she didn't care if it was a row boat, as long as it got them to Atlantea.

"I may have made a mistake, princess."

"Oh my, Mr. Traveler. A man who admits a mistake."

Traveler chuckled. "In my experience, neither of the sexes like to admit mistakes, at least. I think of all the healers and caravan masters I studied under."

"Certainly no female caravan masters."

"Actually, two, princess. One of them was an ugly woman named Bruga, but she was one of those I admired most. They were good, bad, and all in between, princess. Just like the races of humans and fae."

"Undoubtedly, true, Mr. Traveler."

"My possible mistake was sending your Rivermouth followers back to Faë-Land."

"You think they will be needed?"

"I was merely rethinking it since one or more of them may have been mages."

"You told us one can never have too much magic."

"Especially where we are traveling."

"No, I think your reasoning was correct. We did not have the time to learn their true heart or their capabilities. We have what we have on this journey. How soon do we sail, Mr. Traveler?"

"Within the hour. The caravan will remain below deck. You, Mr. Pangolin, and the Cut-throats will be on deck. When we get farther away from the land mass, we will add to the crew—Dr'amal, Ursi, Zefea, and more, including our Brothers Brimm."

"Our musicians?"

"They play a key role in helping us get to safety using their musical talents."

"That is why you hired them, not to entertain us on the Trail."

"Yes, princess. I hired them for this leg of the journey, to battle sirens, if needed, songs against songs."

Lady Aylen smiled. "What of Gwyness?"

"How is she?"

"She is fully recovered, as are my royal guards."

"Princess, if any are swept overboard in battle, with the exception of you, me, Mr. Pangolin, and the dog, we are not likely to ever see them again. It is that deadly, so think carefully about it."

"Are my unknown abilities as a water elf that impressive, Mr. Traveler?"

"Your abilities are not unknown, princess. You have already used them, but you'll no longer need Dr'amal's assistance to reach your full potential. The ocean cannot harm you with its power, and you can breathe underwater. Any creatures of depth will not be able to sneak up on you. You might even be able to mesmerize a few of them. Neither Maiden Gwyness nor your half-elf aides can do the same."

"Where is Mr. Gresham, Mr. Traveler?"

"Why?"

"Of course, we prefer your superior healing abilities, but now that we're setting sail, we'd prefer you back in your role as caravan master or captain. In this case, Mr. Gresham can pour medicine in boiling black pots of water. But no one has seen him."

"Princess, Mr. Gresham has a private task to attend to. He will join when complete, and he can tell you about it himself. You will undoubtedly approve."

"I see. Have you already located our alternative sea transport?"

"I have."

"How? Mr. Traveler, how do you do these things?"

"Because I have done these things before. There are ways captains can send messages to one another across the oceans. I did so and found who I was looking for. We will sail there to find our sea transport. We may be fortunate after all."

"Send messages by magic."

"Yes. You know of the method—a homunculus bird. I created one in a boiling pot of water."

Lady Aylen laughed. "Yes, Mr. Traveler. You and your pots and vapors. How dangerous is sailing to whomever it is that we seek?"

"Very dangerous, princess. Which is why everyone should be below deck except for those I mentioned. We will sail to our destination, not too far, but these waters are not empty. We are likely to be attacked the moment we leave our secret cove."

The only fae not fully recovered were the six Antaean giants, but at least they were awake, and that meant they were eating. Hobbs had everyone in their new thick clothing, and all the warriors were in light armor.

Traveler instructed that close-combat battle on a moving, swaying ship had to be discouraged.

"You do not want to be within reach of any water fae or any creature that travels these waters. They can breathe under water; you cannot. They revel in simply grabbing land walkers, as they call us, and tossing them overboard to drown or be eaten by a giant fish or sea serpent. All those below decks will be armed with long pikes and shields for the forward teams. Keep them from advancing, and push any invaders back until our archers can finish them or make them retreat."

Traveler personally inspected every member of the caravan. All would wait below decks in their quarters but be prepared to assist the Cut-throats guarding the passageways.

"I must say, Lady Aylen, the brownies did an especially impressive job with your new dress," King Aereth said.

"Thank you, sire. They have managed to create worthy royal attire for you as well."

The mole-looking fae had joined the bridge crew but without his carnivorous moose. The strange-looking fae simply sat in a corner of the room. Pangolin and Lady Aylen looked at each other.

"Our special fae is an ally to water nymphs," Traveler said. "You remember, Mr. Pangolin. That may be of benefit to us."

"Yes, Mr. Traveler." The master-at-arms glanced at the king. "Sire, are you sure you are remaining above deck?" Pangolin asked.

"I will be fine, Mr. Pangolin. Mr. Estus has fitted my hand with this interesting gauntlet which he said will do my fighting for me."

"It will protect you with a magic shield, sire," Lady Aylen said.

"Do we not need the same, Mr. Traveler?" Pangolin asked.

"Mr. Estus will be here shortly to fit you with your own. Also, I want to say it again."

"You do not have to, Mr. Traveler," Pangolin said.

"This borders on verbal abuse," Lady Aylen said as King Aereth began laughing.

"Do not, I repeat, do not throw your weapon at any attacker. If you do, you are likely to never see it again. We are on the open ocean, not land. Throw it into a creature and it swims away, then where are you? Never let your weapon leave your hand."

"I will not throw my weapon, Mr. Traveler," Lady Aylen said.

"You've done it before, princess, and I want you to break that reflexive habit here."

"I am not likely to ever do it again after this verbal onslaught."

"Mr. Traveler, I am leaving." The berserker could not leave the bridge room fast enough.

The caravan's weaponsmaster, Mr. Estus, a large, bald, and jovial man appeared at the entrance. "Mr. Pangolin, where are you going?"

"Away."

"Did Mr. Traveler already tell you not to throw your weapon at any creature?"

"And away from you too."

King Aereth was not the only one who wondered how the ship sailed without the aid of sails or long oars, as in times past. The vessel moved by means of magic alone. Traveler stood on the main bridge and navigated not by line of sight, because there was none, but a circular body-length mirror that hung in the air at eye level. With the center mirror he could see ahead. Smaller mirrors on each side showed aft and stern, with another large mirror apart to show the rear. The ship was moving fast and smoothly.

On the ceiling they could see all on the main deck. Pangolin and dozens of Cut-throats guarded the bridge from outside, each man with a long halberd in hand. Even Pangolin kept his axe-mace on his back in favor of the new weapon. The weapons were of the finest elfin metal.

Inside the bridge room was Nirgund and a dozen Cut-throats. I'wulf had many more dozens to guard the steps to the lower decks at the front of the ship. All were ready for battle. Those on the bridge had not seen them in the mirrors yet, but Traveler and the mole-man fae, who stood from his seat on the floor, did.

Pangolin knocked on the door and entered the command room. Their caravan master stood at the large rectangular table covered by nautical maps as everyone looked on. Like his magic land maps, they displayed all that was around them, but the craft and beasts appeared and disappeared frequently, moving at tremendous speeds, and the size of some made them all freeze and look at each other in fear.

"What was that?" Pangolin asked.

Traveler saw the sea beast on the map before it disappeared. "No need to worry, Mr. Pangolin. Our vessel is too small to be of any interest to it."

"But what was it, Mr. Traveler?" Lady Aylen asked. "The size of it."

"A shark, princess."

"That was a shark?" Pangolin's face showed real concern now.

"Everyone, please do not look at the maps," Traveler said. "That's my job and not why we're here."

Lady Aylen noticed the shapes on the magical map moving under the water toward them.

"What are those, Mr. Traveler?" she asked.

Dark shapes appeared on the surface and approached them, moving fast.

"Unwelcome visitors, princess. We are about to be attacked."

Scores of the small boats surfaced from the depths—all of blackened-brown wood, and all empty. However, the vessels moved quickly to the caravan's ship on their own power.

Inside the command bridge, the crew watched the approaching boats on the main mirror. By now, there were hundreds of them.

"Are these Finmen, Mr. Traveler?" Nirgund asked.

"Yes, Mr. Nirgund, but not like those in Faë-Land."

"We should ram the boats," Lady Aylen said.

"The boats are not really there, princess. They're an illusion. Their real boats are invisible and close by. The waters here, near the Titan's Teeth, are part of their territory."

"Can we outrun them, Mr. Traveler?" King Aereth asked.

"Not likely, sire. We must defeat them in battle, then they will retreat."

Boom!

A section on the side of their ship exploded. The bridge crew could see Cut-throats outside scrambling from the sound on the ceiling mirror. Nirgund was about to open the door.

"Lady Aylen, go with Mr. Pangolin. Mr. Nirgund, stay here. Finfolk can also make themselves invisible so take care. This could be a diversion."

Lady Aylen moved so quickly that she opened the door and was gone in almost the blink of an eye.

Traveler's dog turned into a giant cobra-like furry creature with white eyes and encircled the room with its tail.

"Stay in the circle, Mr. Nirgund," Traveler directed.

The berserker did so with his men.

The berserker warrior reached the princess, who stood near the front of the ship. She turned to him. "Did you see where the cannon blast came from, Mr. Pangolin?"

"No, m'lady."

She leaned over the side of the ship. Her eyes fixed on a moving shadow far beneath the water, appearing and disappearing. Her face flush with anticipation of battle as if she were a berserker warrior herself. Her increasing water elfin strength made her feel invincible. She imagined she could crush whatever creatures approached them by her water elemental powers alone with a mere thought.

"M'lady, be careful!" Pangolin yelled, about to grab her. She was leaning so far, her feet were almost off the deck.

She never saw the creature as it jumped from the ocean and grabbed her neck. She grabbed the Finman by the throat as she steadied herself on the deck. The dark fae looked like a human—bald, extremely tall, lanky with a frowning, gaunt face, and mirrored eyes. He looked naked, except he had no genitalia.

"I think not." Lady Aylen threw the Finman back into the ocean with little effort. "What's so formidable about that race?"

A giant human arm from the water grabbed her. Another Finman towered many feet above the side of the ship. Pangolin struck its left hand, resting on the side of the ship with all his might. Everyone heard the bones smash under the power of Pangolin's axe-mace. Lady Aylen broke free from its other hand and fell to the deck.

A giant serpent's head emerged from the depth, and its long neck crashed onto the deck, ramming Pangolin and sending the man crashing into the other side of the ship. The creature's giant humanoid body rose from the ocean too. Cut-throats charged with their pike weapons. A second humanoid Finman appeared, then a third. The sea serpent transformed into a fourth giant Finman.

Lady Aylen jumped from the deck and drove her war trident into the face of one of the Finmen. It yelled, but there was no sound. It fell back into the ocean. She swung at another, slicing its neck. The Finman grabbed the wound and dove overboard. Cut-throats threw their pikes at the remaining Finmen. The giant fae tried to swat them away but they were hit multiple times.

She could hear the noise from the water even without seeing it. When she appeared at the side, she saw dozens of fins racing to the ship, reminding her of sharks.

"We are about to be boarded!" she yelled.

Dozens of Finmen flew out of the ocean onto the ship. They were met by a blizzard of arrows. Lyre, the high elf, and dozens of his men fired nonstop volleys of arrows. Each Finman stopped in midair, their bodies punctured by so many arrows that barely an open patch of skin could be seen. They dropped back into the ocean.

Boom!

Their ship had its own cannons. An invisible Finman ship, as large as theirs, was hit with tremendous explosive force. Its spell failed, and for a brief moment, they could see the creatures' ship—a giant floating conch shell covered with algae weeds. The vessel sank into the ocean.

Pangolin looked at the high elf leader and nodded. They all noticed their own ship moving at an accelerated speed. The scene of their attack was already far behind them. Traveler approached them on the deck with his dog in its aquatic wolfish form at his side.

"Mr. Traveler, I am thankful to our elfin archers. I cannot say we berserkers were all that much help."

"I told you, Mr. Pangolin. Fighting on a ship requires a different set of skills, skills that you and your berserkers will master, as you do with any kind of fighting. But while we escaped the Finmen, I want us to inspect where that cannon damaged the ship."

"We have already retrieved the metal, Mr. Traveler," Lyre said. "Your Mr. Estus and his men are busy repairing the damage."

"The problem, Mr. Lyre, is Finmen ships do not have cannons. They are magical shape-shifters with only one purpose: to abduct captives. If they cannot do that, they flee. They fight without weapons, only using their shape-shifting abilities, and their range, or imagination, is limited. I need to see this cannonball and inspect the damage for myself."

"If the Finmen did not fire the cannon, who did, Mr. Traveler?" Lady Aylen asked.

"That is my question exactly, princess. Who?"

The cannonball attack had shattered the ship's hull on the third deck. All its passageways had been guarded, but none of the cabins or compartments had been occupied. Estus's men were extremely efficient. His team of humans and pech had sealed the hole moments after the attack. Men held torches for illumination as others were still mopping the deck when Traveler entered with Lady Aylen, some Cut-throats, and some elves.

"Why do these Finmen attack, Mr. Traveler?" she asked. "You said to abduct captives."

"They attack for the same reason as those in Faë-Land. They are simply more aggressive here. They kidnap people for slaves, sometimes wives—the Finwomen for husbands."

Lady Aylen had a perplexed expression wondering if their caravan master was serious.

Nirgund nodded. "It's true."

"How successful can this practice be?"

"They are still practicing it after all these centuries, princess, so there must be some value to it for them."

Traveler looked at the cannonball on the ground. He touched the large pieces of metal, then rubbed his finger along it. With a knife he stabbed a metal fragment.

"This is goblin metal."

"Goblin?" Lyre asked.

"There are goblins in these waters, Mr. Traveler?" Nirgund asked.

"Lands and oceans have elves, so too, they have goblins, Mr. Nirgund."

Traveler stood and looked around the empty room. Everyone watched the caravan master scan the area.

He quickly turned to Estus. "Is your work done here, Mr. Estus?"

"Yes, Mr. Traveler."

"Then I suggest we leave everything alone. Toss the pieces of the cannonball over the side. Then we can return to our duties."

Immediately upon returning to the main deck, Traveler marched to Pangolin and gestured for I'wulf to join them. "Recall all your men from the third deck, but double all those on the deck below and above."

"Why, sir?" I'wulf asked.

"When I began my travels into these magic lands, I had always wondered why a goblin attack would later be followed by the appearance of imps, gremlins, or other dark fae skulking around and causing mischief or worse. They are not the only fae who do it, but I learned years ago that goblins like to imbue their projectiles with dark magic, small-realms."

"Are you saying that our ship could have these creatures, Mr. Traveler?"

"I am saying, Mr. Pangolin, that we need to find out, sooner rather than later."

Floating down the corridor, the white mist didn't behave as normal gases did. It pushed through the air like a living thing into every crack, every dark corner. Wherever there was a shadow, the mist occupied and consumed it. All of the second deck was saturated with the white light mist, which then expanded to the third deck.

A noise.

The creature appeared as more a shadow than a flesh-and-blood living thing. It had black claws and fangs. Its eyes were covered with a thin black film. It ran on all fours as it escaped to the fourth and final deck. Soon it disappeared into the deepest, darkest corner it could find. Though the size of a large bear, it moved without sound and easily pressed its body into any size it wished.

The white mist arrived and expanded throughout the last deck of the ship. The creature sensed others. Traveler stepped forward with his magic sword. Shadu-mun, the moon elf, followed then others. Each elf had a sword made of moonlight magic.

The bauk roared, but neither human nor elf retreated. The darkness that the creature hid in was quickly disappearing. It stood in the last darkened corner, ready to pounce on them. With a final roar, the creature attacked. But the creature was cut down in moments by sword blows. It lay on the ground, bleeding and gasping. Even its blood was black to match the shadows it hid in. The moon elves pointed their moon swords at the creature. The moonlight grew into intense, balls of light then dimmed. All that was left of the bauk had been burned away to dust.

"You say goblins do this trick often. What does this creature do?" Shadu-mun asked.

"If it had lived, it would have learned the layout of the ship and could have evaded detection or capture forever. Men would have simply vanished."

"Killed?"

"Devoured, Mr. Shadu-mun. Bauks eat sleeping victims whole."

CHAPTER THREE

Living Islands

The ferocious power of the waves along the shore of the Great Forest had frightened most on their ship. However, the waves towered above them less and less, and the troughs did not plunge as violently the further out to the sea they sailed. The attack of the Finfolk and news of the bauk would be the gossip aboard ship, around campfires in their respective cabins or realms for days.

"Living islands, Mr. Traveler? Do we dare ask?" King Aereth asked.

The bridge crew was as attentive to the watch-mirrors as Traveler. In the distance, they saw three dark shapes in the oceans. As they neared, the three islands grew larger.

"The islands likely will not bother us, if we do not bother them."

The crew burst into nervous laughter.

"Bother them, Mr. Traveler?" Nirgund asked. "Are they sleeping sea serpents?"

"You sail us toward sea serpents after what we escaped in the Great Forest, Mr. Traveler?" Lady Aylen asked.

"True, the landvættir are walking land masses that become part of the land expanse they rest in. What you see ahead are called aspidochelone. Think of them as giant sea turtles."

"They are alive?" Nirgund asked, surprised. "We thought you spoke in jest."

"Mr. Nirgund, no. These giant sea turtles are not as ancient as our Atlas turtles on land but close. Others are more like giant whales. While either can be quite vicious when they need to be, most are quite tame. But they are not why we are here."

"Another ship," King Aereth said.

"Our sea transport, Mr. Traveler?" Lady Aylen asked.

"Not yet, princess, but they will take us to them."

"Their ship is damaged," Lady Aylen said, noticing their destination on the display mirror.

"They must have bothered the aspidochelone somehow," Traveler said.

If Traveler had not told them the true nature of the islands, none would have suspected they were in fact giant beasts. The "islands," four in all, were dense with trees, brush, and vines. The largest had rocky hills rising to a point. The only possible clue to their true nature was the absence of a shore of any kind.

The other ship they saw actually consisted of five. Three of the vessels were badly damaged, as if they'd sailed right into the island or vice versa. The other two ships were undamaged but were much smaller. Watching from their decks were humanoid sailors, each one armed with a weapon—trident, crossbow, or hook.

Once Traveler stepped onto the deck, the translucent covering over the Titan's Caravan's ship peeled back by itself to reveal the open air. The royals followed him, as did Nirgund and his men. Pangolin and the Cut-throat were already waiting. The caravan master had Estus arm Pangolin and all the Cut-throats with crossbows. Berserkers had a code to fight any enemy hand-to-hand and never to use bow weapons. However, it was a code they were happy to put aside while traveling on the great oceans.

Traveler waved to the humanoids in the other ship then took a pouch from his side, jiggled the coins within it, and threw it forcibly to one of the sailors in the other ship.

The one who caught it had fingers like a giant toad. In fact, he was more toad than human in form. They saw him open the pouch, and his comrades gathered around him. They waved Traveler forward.

The dog increased in size as wings sprouted from his back. Traveler casually hopped on and flew his winged dog to them. When they landed, the dog's size grew a bit more as the amphibious sailors looked on.

"Do not worry. He's friendly... as long as you do not try to attack me," Traveler said.

"You, human," the toadoid said. "You are a very long way from your lands. Why are you here?"

"Titan's Fall."

"This is not the Fall."

"I am looking for Nifle."

"The klabautermann?"

"Yes."

"How do you know of him?"

"I just do."

"The eye-bird. That was you?"

"It was I."

"But you know his name."

"He knows mine."

"You know a klabautermann?"

"I worked with him."

The sailors looked at each other, almost confused.

"You cannot speak with him. He is my navigator."

"I am not here to take away your navigator. I need his help."

"He is not here."

"Where is he?"

"He is on the island. We hunt for treasure."

"Do you always crash your ships into living islands?"

"It was an accident."

"I'll wait here for Nifle then."

"Or are you here to steal our treasure?"

The sailors gripped their weapons but their tone quickly changed when the dog growled as its size grew again.

"I told you to be friendly."

"Yes, Nifle will return soon."

The wait wasn't long. More of the amphibian sailors appeared from the center island running to the island's edge, screaming and flailing their arms.

"Something is wrong," the toadoid said.

"Where is Nifle?" Traveler asked.

"He is not with them."

Traveler jumped onto his dog's back, and they flew into the dense foliage of the island.

With a dagger, a kobold slashed at another water leaper but yelled out and grabbed his arm as he was stung by a second. Several kobolds tried to fend off the swarm of creatures—large frogs, the size of small dogs, with bat wings instead of forelegs, no hind legs, and long lizard tails tipped with stingers.

Nearby, another kobold screamed as a muddy blob pushed him into the pool of mud before the entrance of a cave. His comrades couldn't get through the swarm of water leapers to aid him.

"Nifle!" one of the kobolds yelled in desperation.

The kobold's mouth opened, startled, as the water leapers were cut apart by Traveler's sword. The swamp creature stopped as its misshapen muddy face focused on Traveler. It could see the translucent flame on his blade.

"Begone, blatnik!" Traveler raised his sword arm to strike.

The swamp creature laughed as it descended into the muddy pool and disappeared. Traveler pulled a smiling kobold out of the muddy bog.

The kobold started laughing, then he smacked Traveler on the arm.

"Nifle," Traveler said. "Always getting into trouble."

"Young Traveler!" the kobold announced. "But not so young as before. Always there to rescue Nifle." He turned to the other kobolds.

All of them were larger than an average human, hunched over, with ugly faces and missing teeth, especially Nifle. "This is Traveler."

The kobolds greeted him with waves.

"Are you here to help us get our treasure?"

"Nifle, my dog and I will wait here. Get your treasure, but don't get killed. I need you to take me to Tunik."

"He's at Titan's Fall."

"I know that, Nifle, but I need you to take my party there."

"You have a party. Are you a captain these days, Mr. Traveler?"

"No, Nifle. I'm smart enough to know I'm no captain. That's why you'll be taking me to Tunik."

"He'll be happy to see a human even as ugly as you again."

Traveler smiled. "Ugly?"

"Don't you know you're ugly?"

The kobolds laughed.

"The water leapers will come back. Go!"

The kobolds grabbed their mining bags from the mud and ran into the cave. Traveler stepped back and realized that the cave was actually a wrecked ship that had marooned on the island—the creature's back— ages ago. The cave entrance was a hole in its weather-worn side.

The fae treasure hunters were mostly klabautermann, the sub-race of seafaring kobolds, with their big bodies and dark leathery skin in grungy sailor clothing. Similarly dressed toadoids made up the rest of their crew. Traveler and his dog followed them from the dead ship, as they carried bags of precious coins. Like their land cousins, they, too, had a nose for precious metals and gems. Nifle led the group back to the ships, with all the kobolds whistling a tune. Then they stopped in their tracks.

"Look at her," Nifle said with a wicked smile.

Traveler walked to the front and slapped him on the side of the head. "Behave, Mr. Nifle. That is Lady Aylen."

With his big smile, Nifle approached her. She watched him with a smirk. King Aereth and Pangolin stood on either side of her, the Cut-throats behind them with their crossbows.

"Did we go treasure hunting, Mr. Traveler?" she asked. "And with long-lost friends it would seem."

"Mr. Nifle will take us to Titan's Fall."

The royals looked at each other.

"Mr. Traveler, is this wise?" Pangolin asked.

"Mr. Nifle will take us to one of the best captains of these waters."

"Please don't tell him that, Mr. Traveler," Nifle said. "Tunik's head is big enough. How much will you be paying me?"

"Paying you? Don't you have bags of gold coins in your hands?"

"Goblin gold," the kobold said.

"Then why do we need to pay you anything?"

"One has nothing to do with the other, and because, dear human friend, word has spread far and wide that a caravan led by a human with a shape-shifter as a companion travels with a water elfess, elves, drows, giants, sprites, humans, and assorted beasts bound for Atlantea. They are offering more money than any has ever seen in their entire life. You will pay me not to turn you in. Then you will pay Tunik not to turn you in when I take you to him. Then you'll pay us even more to take you to Atlantea. That is why I am so glad to see you, my dear human friend, Traveler."

"Yes, old friend. Tell me something, Nifle. Should I have left you to be buried in the mud by the blatnik?"

"I was never in any danger."

Pangolin noticed Nifle's men move their hands closer to their weapons. The man-at-arms had only to point his crossbow at them for the other berserkers to do the same.

"Yes, I know. That was quite the performance, Nifle," Traveler added. "You do know we humans are not forgetful things, and I did serve with you aboard Tunik's ship for a time. I once saw you punch a sea serpent out of our ship with one arm. I doubt that any pile of living mud like a blatnik would make you scream, let alone drown you in the mud. How far away was I when you caught my scent on the ocean breeze? You must have immediately thought it was your lucky day."

The kobold and human stared at each other a while. Nifle's eyes shifted to the dog and could see the animal's growing size as its eyes became completely black and glistened. The animal made a deep, guttural growl, its teeth now that of a giant piranha.

Nifle returned his gaze to the caravan master and laughed. "Have no fear, Mr. Traveler. You'll pay me because you know my request is fair. I won't double-cross you because I know what you and your dog are capable of, and I plan to live for another century or two. Too much treasure out there waiting for me. Why do you think I went out on my own?"

"Then we have a deal."

Nifle shook Traveler's hand. "As an old friend, human, I have to say, you do know you'll never set foot in Atlantea, don't you?"

The kobold looked past the caravan master to grin at the nervous faces of the royals and berserkers.

Traveler leaned down toward the kobold. "That's exactly what star elves once said to me. But then I did and lived there for years. Their fate was not so favorable."

Nifle's face became serious. "Mr. Traveler, this is not then. I have sailed these waters many years, since before your father's father was born. Lately, I've beheld things I never imagined I'd see even in my dreams. I've heard of things that I couldn't conjure up in my nightmares. You and I are individuals, small, nothing. These matters involve kingdoms and empires. Armies are converging on Atlantea. I know you won't listen to me, but you should return to your lands. All of you should. This is beyond us all."

"Absolutely not!" Lady Aylen yelled.

Nifle smiled and looked at Traveler again. "Your resolve is unchangeable, even though you know they await you, even though you are hunted?"

"Unchangeable."

"Then I'd like to be paid now, please."

Nifle's crew of kobolds and fae humanoids purposely sank their three damaged ships. Then they loaded onto the two smaller ships. Traveler and the royals stood on the deck of their lead ship as Nifle gave the caravan master a sly look and snapped his finger. A tiny flame shot out.

The old wrecked ships exploded with a magnificent cloud of fire and smoke.

"Why did you do that?" Traveler asked.

The islands rumbled, then all could see the massive creatures in full form. The four islands shook from side to side then rose, two larger aspidochelone and two smaller ones—parents and children. The family looked very similar to Atlas turtles but smaller and aquatic. With their heads raised above the water, scores of barnacles, crabs, and fish that had made a home in the folds of the creatures' necks fell into the ocean.

"I wouldn't want any other treasure hunters happening along, poking around the dead ship, looking for riches. They might get themselves killed. I couldn't allow that. You did teach me, Master Traveler, to be more considerate of other life, back when you were our healer."

The four aspidochelone slowly swam by. For beasts of their massive size and with so long a life span, speed was no concern.

"Besides, no force on my ship could ever hurt such magnificent sea beasts," Nifle said. "Are you returning to your ship?"

"I think it best to stay here to keep an eye on you," Traveler said.

"We agree." Lady Aylen watched the kobold with squinted eyes.

"My feelings are wounded. We were shipmates after all."

"We'll stay here, and our ship will follow," Traveler said.

"Has your crew ever seen Titan's Fall?" Nifle asked.

"No."

"Then they are in for a treat."

"Nifle, see to it that our sea convoy doesn't encounter any mer-captains or any other ocean fae. We don't want a battle."

"I'll get you to Tunik without incident. But remember that I did tell you and the others to go back."

"We've been through all that Faë-Land Minor, Major, and the Great Forest had to throw at us. We are not about to retreat now," Lady Aylen said to the kobold.

"With all due respect, water elf, this is not Faë-Land Minor, Major, or the Great Forest. The Oceanus Omnis is a realm far greater than all of them combined. Ask your leader here. He knows."

"How long will it take to reach Tunik?"

"Tunik will reach us."

"What of the pirates that frequent these waters?"

"Pirates? Pirates attack weaklings. None of them sail these waters these days, goblins or otherwise."

"But we have already have encountered them."

Nifle gave Traveler a look.

"They shot a cannon at us," Traveler said.

"Goblins?"

"Yes."

"Interesting."

"And invisible. What do you make of that, Nifle?" Traveler asked.

"I'm not sure." The kobold rubbed his chin. "Maybe I need to get you off my ship."

"Maybe you shouldn't be blowing up abandoned wrecks on islands to alert any invisible ships that may be following to our location."

Nifle smiled. "Have no fear, Mr. Traveler. I said I'll get you to Tunik, and I will. Kobolds can make their ships invisible too."

Back within the main bridge of their own ship, the royals watched the magical display mirrors reflecting the surroundings. Pangolin watched out the windows with his own eyes. They all had their heads covered with the hoods of their cloaks, as Traveler had instructed. The main deck of the bridge couldn't be seen with the ship's magic translucent covering in place. The Cut-throats could see out, but no one, presumably, could see in.

"Do you trust this Nifle, m'lady?" Pangolin asked, his back turned, not taking his eyes from his vigil.

"No, but neither does Mr. Traveler, so I am not as nervous. They served as shipmates together but still he's not trustworthy."

"Bounties tend to do that to men in our lands. We shouldn't be surprised by fae acting in the same manner here," King Aereth said.

"Mr. Pangolin, do you see them?"

Pangolin glanced back for a moment, nodding.

On the display mirrors, the royals could see another sea convoy sailing in the opposite direction. The silver ships had to be at least twenty feet tall. No ports or crew were visible on the convoy of fourteen ships.

"If Mr. Traveler were here, he could tell us what race the vessels belong to," King Aereth said. "But safety comes before curiosity."

"If they decided to fire upon us, sire, there would be nothing we could do about it," Pangolin said. "Only Lady Aylen would be spared as we all sank to the bottom of this great ocean."

"I doubt my fate would be much different, Mr. Pangolin. I may supposedly be able to breathe underwater, but that is not a defense against death. I hate swimming, and I'm still not looking forward to my first encounters with other water elves."

"Mr. Traveler has confidence in you, Lady Aylen," King Aereth said.

She gave a loud sigh. "I truly wish I shared that view, sire. I'm not too proud to say that I fear that ocean, its massiveness, and its depths. I want nothing to do with it. I hope these six days go by quickly so we can be aboard our new sea transport for Titan's Fall."

News spread to all the decks below, and soon humans and fae joined the Cut-throats. The region the sea convoy had reached was enshrouded by mist, which grew thicker and higher in the sky as they sailed. But it was not the mist that drew the crew's attention. A steady rumbling in the distance grew as they neared. The sound had begun four days ago, and each day they grew louder.

"Is it what we think it is, m'lady?" Gwyness asked.

Lady Aylen had left the bridge for the deck. There wasn't enough room for all the crew from the lower decks, but hundreds crowded together, listening and staring up at the sky. "Yes, Gwyness. It can only be Titan's Fall."

"For us to hear it from days away," Gwyness said.

"I heard it five days ago," Lady Aylen said. "Possibly six days, at night, but I didn't know what I was hearing."

"The mist all around us. We can barely see now," Gwyness said. "Can you see the lead ship?"

Lady Aylen shook her head with a pained expression. "I cannot see any of the ships ahead of us."

"If your elfin eyes cannot see, my human eyes will not."

"I wish Mr. Traveler were here with us."

"You do not trust these kobolds, m'lady?"

"I did not trust their land-going cousins. I do not trust these sea-traveling ones."

King Aereth had stepped from the bridge, too, when the princess left. "Ladies, we must trust in our caravan master to see us through this."

Men pointed to the sky. Flocks of giant fish the size of horses with rainbow-colored scales flew above them. The sight brought smiles to both human and fae. Young Quillen already had his magic book open to sketch as he planted his backside on the deck. The flying fish, with their large eyes, circled the convoy.

Men yelled the moment a creature shot out from the ocean. The giant fish was larger than their own ship, and it devoured several of the flying fish in one gulp, scattering the flock. As the creature came back down, they could see its black body clearly covered in porcupine-like quills with jagged teeth, a single eye, and a tail more like a snake's than a fish's. It crashed back into the ocean forcibly rocking their ship and showering it with a huge wave.

They had not seen any sea life in days but now it was all before them at once. Chatter broke out among the men. Pangolin was not amused.

"We should clear the deck," he said to I'wulf.

"Mr. Pangolin, are you mad? That would cause a mutiny."

"But are we sure our magic covering will protect us if one of those creatures manages to land on the deck?"

"On this I must strongly disagree. Let them be. We cannot expect the men to stay below forever with no diversion," I'wulf said.

Pangolin grunted but relented.

"I hate it, too, Mr. Pangolin. Ships are not for us berserkers. We want the earth beneath our feet, not a ship and countless fathoms of water below it. Think of it. When our feet do touch the earth, it will be Atlantea."

Pangolin grinned and patted his comrade on the back.

The flock of flying fish returned in greater numbers above their sea convoy. Another predator fish shot out from the ocean, as did several more.

"Oh no!" I'wulf yelled as the predator fish fell back down after their meal. Two were falling straight toward the deck.

Men ran for the lower deck, but they were packed too tightly. The fish bounced off the magic barrier and into the ocean. Everyone breathed a sigh of relief.

The bridge also served as the dining hall for the royals, Pangolin, the Cut-throat leaders, Hobbs, and the royal guards. The sounds of faraway Titan's Fall were so loud that anyone on the main deck or bridge had to yell to hear each other.

Pangolin ate his meal standing up, watching the window and display mirror. Lady Aylen saw him suddenly drop his plate to the ground and bolt out the door. She jumped to her feet and looked at the display mirrors. Everyone else in the room did the same. I'wulf and the other Cut-throats ran out of the bridge room.

The convoy had been sailing between a group of islands for most of the day, but now one of islands was moving at ramming-speed toward them.

The Cut-throats tried to get as many of the men on the deck below as they could, but when the island struck, the ship careened to one side. Men fell from the deck to the magic barrier. Fortunately, the barrier kept all the men from falling directly into the ocean.

The island revealed itself. Not a colossal turtle, as they had encountered before with the family of aspidochelone, the creature that raised its head from the waters was a real sea serpent whose main body was encased in a rocky turtle-like shell. Its roar shattered the air even with the rumbling of the distant Fall.

Boom!

The projectile hit the side of its snakish head with enough force to send it crashing back into the ocean.

They all held their breath as their ship suddenly rose into the sky with tremendous speed. From the bridge, they could see the other ships of the convoy below.

"The ship will not survive a fall from this height!" Lady Aylen yelled.

The ship stopped in mid-air. Everyone looked around.

"What's happening?" a Cut-throat asked.

"We're not falling," another said.

"Look." King Aereth pointed to the display mirrors.

The sea creature was hit by more cannon fire, each blast erupting in an intense fire ball. The creature swam away faster than they thought possible for its size.

Greenwig, the leshy, and elfin questing knights entered the bridge to see the battle below them.

"A bad aspidochelone that wanted us for a meal," Lady Aylen said.

"A hafgufa," Greenwig said. "They disguise themselves as islands for the sole purpose to hunt prey. Aspidochelone are benevolent beasts. They live their lives as islands. I have always heard of hafgufa, but this is the first time I have seen one with my own eyes. Dangerous beasts."

"This entire route we sail is covered with islands," Lyre, the high elf, said. "How many more might there be?"

"As many as there are islands, Master Lyre."

They all felt the ship move again, descending slowly to the ocean. It gently landed on the water to resume sailing.

Even before Traveler appeared, the bridge heard men greeting him. Traveler entered with his dog.

"We are without injury, Mr. Traveler," King Aereth said.

"Very good, sire."

"Any more sea monsters, Mr. Traveler?" Lady Aylen asked.

"We haven't even begun to encounter sea monsters, princess. Mr. Hobbs, gather the leadership below."

"Yes, sir. Our first meeting on the sea."

"All the fae leaders too."

"Yes, sir."

"Trouble, Mr. Traveler?" King Aereth asked.

"All of you need to know what to expect before we board our sea transport. I don't trust speaking there, so we have to do so here."

"This Tunik is a friend, is he not, Mr. Traveler?" Pangolin asked.

"He is, Mr. Pangolin, but that was years ago. Under these circumstances we must be prepared for anything. Sire, I hope you studied those royal protocol books well because you and Lady Aylen will soon take the lead during this leg of our journey. I won't even be the captain I had planned to be. Instead, I will be the mysterious stranger behind you at all times."

"Mr. Traveler, we have never been here," Lady Aylen said. "How can we take the lead?"

"You both will do fine, as you've been royals all your life. Let's gather quickly. We will reach Tunik's ship shortly."

Humans and fae crowded into the bridge room to observe the leadership gathered around the map table.

For many, it was the first time they had been on the main deck at all. Hobbs had gathered the royals, their aides, the berserkers, both human and fae, elves, drows, and Tree Shepherds. Traveler arrived with his dog and the mole-looking fae. The caravan master squeezed through the men to take his place at the head of the table.

"That was not a nice trick you played on us, Mr. Traveler," Dr'as said. "Something your phooka companions would do."

"Still brooding over our introduction to the realm of Oceanus Omnis?" Traveler asked.

"Training us to get used to such things on our sea voyage, Mr. Traveler?" Lyre, the high elf, asked.

"It is a common practice of the sea beasts in these waters: swim up beneath a ship, using their head, limbs, tails, or tentacles, throw the vessel as high into the sky as possible, and when it crashes to the surface of the ocean, eat all the passengers from the wreck."

"My goodness, Mr. Traveler," Lady Aylen said.

"However, put all that from your mind. We must focus your attention on the affairs of state here. Much of what we encounter will be battles of the tongue rather than battles with weapons and magic. These waters are ruled by matriarchal dynasties older than the patriarchal ones we were born in. Titan's Caravan must be an unflappable unit because every manner of deceit and treachery will be used against us, likely more dangerous than the creatures and sirens we will undoubtedly battle."

"But can we trust this, Nifle?" Pangolin asked.

"No, but I will, to a point. As he said, we must buy his loyalty."

"What honor is there in him, then?" Lady Aylen asked. "You were shipmates."

"And I saved his life, and he saved mine. It means nothing here because obviously the bounty on us is of an amount beyond even a kobold's wildest dreams."

"Master Traveler, what of this kobold you believe can be our captain to Atlantea?" Chief Ethor asked.

"Tunik, I trust. But we'll see. I have also not seen him in years. That is my task, but each of you have your own task. Listen well, because aboard our sea transport there will be many eyes and ears on us so we will likely have no real privacy, which is why we meet now.

"Lady Aylen, in the presence of any of the sea fae, you will take the lead. You will know when because they will ignore the rest of us, the king, humans, elves, drows, all except you. In this role you must speak and carry yourself as if you are the queen of the ship. Maiden Gwyness and your royal guardswomen must be prepared to defend you and themselves at a moment's notice. They must be at your side and guard you at all times. You must be ready to kill with your war tridents in an instant. You will know when, and you cannot ever hesitate. Princess, it's very important. They can be far worse than any marauder or pirate in our own lands. For our elfin comrades, here, think of them as star elves."

The elves grinned and nodded. "No honor," Lyre said.

"Sire, when the situation calls for it, you will be the senior adviser in matters of state, protocol, and negotiation. You must also take a role of deference to Lady Aylen when in the company of female sea fae. Of all the members of our caravan, to them, humans are lowest, even below our animals. Nirgund and his alphyns will protect you like never before.

"Dr'as from this moment on, you are King Dr'as of the D'Shar. As I had instructed before, you and your drows must dress and carry the weapons of D'Shar warriors."

"Not of the kingdom of Nightfire?"

"Outside of me, you, and your drows, no one knows or cares of Nightfire. If there is anything of significance that the sea fae may know, it is of D'Shar, or their allies might know of it, since we know that night drows are likely part of the Four Kings' alliance."

"You believe them to be here?" Dr'as asked.

"Dark magic and the Four Kings are one in the same, so yes," Traveler answered.

"Our clan has the knowledge to fight them."

"Your clan will be fighting them and more. All of us will."

"Dr'amal, I need you to work with Frog-Dor. Time has run out for him. He must be the sorcerer that we all know he has the potential to be, and it must be now. The spell-casters of the Oceanus Omnis are of a magnitude stronger than most of the realms."

"I will see to it," the drowess said.

"Chief Ethor, you are now King Ethor. Sea fae know nothing of the title of chief, or the difference between rustic and city-dwelling woodland elves. You are all elves, Lyre, Taylos, Shadu-mun, Mr. Bragg's mountain and savage elf comrades, even Mr. Bragg. To them, there are land elves, water elves, sky elves, and celestial elves. The greatest asset we have among your elves and the elfin questing knights are the archers. Sea fae do as well, but land elves are better than all. It is an advantage that we must utilize often. Besides, we will not have the aid of our elaphine archers at all during our sea voyage."

Chief Ethor nodded.

Traveler turned to the Tree Shepherd leader. "Mr. Greenwig, the same. You are King Greenwig."

"Are we forming our own 'four kings,' Mr. Traveler?" King Aereth asked.

"And more, sire. Since we will also be without our giants until Atlantea, Mr. Greenwig, perhaps your crawling trees can stand in their place."

"Tree giants? Yes, we can make it so, Master Traveler. However, their power comes from the green nature of the earth, which we are without. Even within the Great Forest we had no connection with its flora and fauna."

"Can Tree Shepherds swim?"

The leshy leader grinned. "Of course, though never in waters of such ancient magic."

"Then we may find out if you can communicate with the flora and fauna of this watery realm."

Traveler stood quietly, looking down at the floor. "The ship is slowing." The caravan master handed Greenwig a parchment. "Do you know the spell?"

The Tree Shepherd read the paper and looked up at Traveler. "Where did you get such a spell?"

"A great leshy."

"We can cast the spell, but it will take all four of us Tree Shepherds."

"I will leave you to it then."

"Do you fear we will find ourselves cast overboard into the great oceans, Master Traveler?"

"It has happened to many a crew many times before. I don't expect it, but we must prepare for it."

"What spell, Mr. Traveler?" Lady Aylen asked.

"Just as on land, we must do the same aboard our sea transport. Our caravan, now crew, must rest within the safety of a pocket-realm strong enough to withstand the dangers of this realm. On land we had circles. Here on the Oceanus Omnis, the equivalent is a sphere."

"Sphere?" Lady Aylen asked.

"Or a bubble, as some humans call it. A magic sphere. If we had our own ship, protection of the caravan would be a simple matter, but aboard another ship—"

"You need say no more, Master Traveler. We will create a sphere of sufficient magic to protect our caravan."

"You will be the gate keepers of that pocket-realm, King Greenwig."

The Tree Shepherd chuckled. "King?"

"Mr. Taylos, you will separate from your elfin questing knight comrades to be at the side of our Tree Shepherds to protect them both with your skill of the bow and your falcons."

"Will night guard be the same?" Shadow-mun asked. "Moon elves and drows?"

"Yes, because it's when both your magic are strongest."

"Will we be joined by your goblins, I mean darklings?" Dr'as asked.

"You'll be joined by them and, many nights, the dog and I as well. Captains get very little sleep on dangerous voyages. Those are our roles. When we board our new transport, the game begins."

"Game?" King Aereth asked with amusement.

"What game, Mr. Traveler?" the princess asked.

"I imagine, Lady Aylen, our game against the Four Kings to complete our fabled quest," King Aereth said. "Do we near triumph crossing the gates of Atlantea, or do we near our death at their hands and the hands of their dark allies?"

"Yes, indeed, sire."

"Do you believe we will complete our quest, Mr. Traveler?" Lady Aylen asked.

Time seemed to freeze. Every eye on the bridge focused on him intently.

A mischievous grin came over the caravan master's face. "We will, princess. No amount of evil will thwart us now, after traveling so far and being so close."

Traveler reached into his cloak and revealed a pouch. He threw it to Pangolin, who caught it. "Equip each of the berserkers with them."

"What is it?"

"They are called talaria."

All the fae gasped. "They know of it, but I do not." Pangolin reached into the magic pouch and pulled out a pair of winged sandals.

"You step onto the sandal, even with your boots, and the wings will magically sprout from your ankles," Traveler said.

"How did you obtain those?" Lyre asked.

Traveler walked to the high elf and patted his shoulder. "I obtained many things from the star elves."

The elves burst out laughing, and they took turns shaking his hand or slapping him on the back.

"What do we do with these?" Pangolin asked.

"You fly with them," Traveler said.

"What about me, Mr. Traveler?" Lady Aylen asked. "I want to fly too."

"Princess, you want to swim, breathe under water, magically command water, throw war tridents, speak elvish, and fly?"

Now it was Lady Aylen, her maiden, and the female half-elves laughing.

"Well, yes," she said.

Pangolin was the first to put on his winged sandals as the berserkers and everyone else looked on. It was as Traveler said. All he had to do was place the sandals flat on the ground, step on them with his full boots, and the sandals disappeared, but dual wings emerged from the ankles of his boots.

"Show us your flying ability, Mr. Pangolin," Gwyness said.

"How do I do this, Mr. Traveler?"

"Mr. Pangolin, relax your mind. Do not think about it. You can fly. Know that you can fly. Imagine it, and the wings will do the rest. Flying with the aid of talaria, for humans, is merely floating on the air. Think of it like that."

Pangolin closed his eyes. His body rose as the wings fluttered. Everyone cheered as their man-at-arms rotated in mid-air several times, then rose to the ceiling, rotated and he was standing upside down on the roof.

"A natural," Gwyness said, smiling.

"Mr. Pangolin, you are behaving in a completely unacceptable manner," Traveler said. "My first time I fell on my face, and the second, and third. Do your home lands have winged sandals?"

"Out with it, Mr. Pangolin," Lady Aylen said. "If not winged sandals, what was it?"

"I like these better than my flying carpet that I had as a boy."

"Cheater!" one of the berserkers yelled, followed by others.

Traveler pointed at Mr. Pangolin, I'wulf, and Nirgund. "I want all your berserkers to master the winged sandals."

"Imagine the fighting force we'll have now, Mr. Pangolin," I'wulf said. "Fighting side by side with our chamroshes."

As the crowd devolved into chatter and horseplay watching the flying Pangolin, Traveler stepped to the mole-looking fae. "You will have a role too."

"I want my animal companion here."

"We cannot have a giant carnivorous moose on the bridge of a ship."

"Then I stay below with my people. Fetch me when we encounter nymphs or undines."

"You know water elementals too?"

"My people are allies."

"Then your people do not live in Faë-Land but here on the Oceanus Omnis."

"We do."

"Do you think that is something you should have shared with me?"

"Why? You are the caravan master, not I. My people are from this realm and maintain our alliances through trade alone. There is no other value to it."

"I disagree, but we can speak of it later. You and I are the only ones in the caravan who have familiarity with Oceanus Omnis, so that alone has tremendous value."

"I will do my part to help my party and the caravan reach Atlantea. You said it many times before. None of us can reach the fabled kingdom alone."

"No, we can't."

Traveler walked to the display mirrors. Already, many of the men had noticed it too, appearing from the thick mist—a ship larger than all the vessels of the convoy combined. The strange ship had an exterior that resembled the exoskeleton of a crustacean. They could see Nifle jumping and yelling to them from his lead ship.

"Our ocean journey begins," Traveler said to himself.

THE OCEANS OF FÄE-LAND OMNIS

The Empires of Mermaids, Ocean Nymphs, and Water Fae

CHAPTER FOUR

Titan's Fall

Aloud, repeating hiss echoed as the giant crustacean ship slowed to a dead stop next to them. The royals watched a door appear on the exterior of the strange ship and a gangplank shot out. Nifle and his men waited on the deck as a new group of kobolds exited and strolled down the plank towards them. The new klabautermann were the same in appearance and dress as Nifle and his kobolds—hunched, large bodies, ugly faces in human terms, dark leathery skin in their grungy sailor clothing. The largest of them, from his swagger, was undoubtedly the ship's leader.

Traveler moved to them, wrapped in his new attire—a dark-blue, hooded robe. His dog followed at his side, no longer gray in color but with blue-tinged fur and webbed feet.

A smile came over the new captain's face. He laughed as he reached out and grabbed the caravan master to give him a bear hug.

"Let me look at your ugly face, human. Traveler. After all these years, my able former healer has returned."

"I am happy to have returned, Tunik."

"I knew if you lived, you'd be much more than a healer, even with your skills. Who's with you?"

Tunik dropped Traveler to the deck and turned his attention to the royals, also covered from head to ankle with identical, hooded blue robes.

"A she-elf," Tunik said.

"Aylen is my name," she said with a nod.

"Aereth is mine," the king said.

"I see the rest of your party hiding in your bridge cabin." Tunik looked back at Traveler, then down at his animal. "Your dog. I heard so much about him. You always had a soft spot for stray animals. Lucky you would find a shape-shifting one from another world."

The dog had not once blinked as it stared at the kobold.

"I don't think he likes me. Traveler, why is that? We're old friends."

"As much as I'd like to stand here and reminisce, Tunik, I'd like to speak privately."

"I already know why. Nifle told me. You were certain I'd be agreeable to taking your party aboard my ship."

"Why wouldn't I? We're old friends. And we have money."

Tunik smiled. "Yes, money." His smile disappeared, and he stared at Traveler, thinking. "Old friend, I am not sure about this one. Last time you were with us, I lost a ship. I don't want to lose this one."

"That had nothing to do with me. If anything, I brought your ship luck, along with my services, which you got at a discount."

"What sea fae would take on a human for a healer?"

"I didn't complain. I got to work aboard a seasoned vessel. You got a healer who knew what he was doing and wasn't squeamish at the sight of blood and guts."

"We were knee-deep in both more than a few times." Tunik cackled, fondly recollecting.

"All we need is passage to Titan's Fall, no farther."

"Do you honestly believe you'll make it to Atlantea? This is not the old days when you lived there or when you traveled with me as a crew member."

"What has changed?"

"If you were able to find me on the open waters, then you know the answer. Nifle told me about your chat."

"You and Nifle seemed to have spoken about a lot for being apart. Why did you let your first mate leave your crew?"

"Who said he did?"

"Nifle."

"You know Nifle. All my men go on the occasional treasure hunt. But we are klabautermann and will always be one crew, even when apart."

"Tunik, we have the money to pay for our passage."

"I heard the first time, but money does me and my crew no good if we're at the bottom of this ocean. It's a very long, long, long way down to its bottom. They say it takes a century to reach it."

"You've never been scared of anything before."

"I have, and many times. You simply never saw me so. A captain without fear out here will soon find himself and his crew dead. Traveler, I'm not sure friendship is enough this time."

"What's out there, then, that so concerns the fearless Tunik I've known? We heard there's a bounty."

"Bounty? Bounties, human. Sea goblins, merrows, mer-captains, and who knows who else are looking to collect. An Atlantea-sized treasure for the capture of Titan's Caravan, a caravan led by a human with a dog shape-shifter, a water elfess, humans, elves, giants, drows, leshy, fauns, fairies, sprites, animal men, assorted fae, and their beasts. Don't bother with your blue robes. They're not worth calling a disguise."

"I didn't need you or Nifle to tell me we are being hunted. It's why I've sought you out for safe passage."

"I am impressed, Traveler. I always knew you had what it took to become an accomplished caravan master. But you seemed to have roused quite the assortment of enemies. I am sure, in your mind, that once you defeated star elves, all else would be child's play in comparison. But you are wrong."

"Tunik, you know full well that I did not pick that battle with the star elves."

"Yes, you have a soft spot for the beasties and misfits."

"I have a soft spot for the bullied and oppressed, you mean."

"Such high ideals from my former healer. Let us cut to the heart of the matter. No."

"That's it?"

"Yes. Why would you possibly want to go there when all the parties seeking you out are either going there, too, or are already there?"

"Because they're looking for our current vessel, not yours."

"It won't work, human."

"Yes, it will."

"It's my ship and our lives if you're wrong."

"Tunik, the city of Titan's Fall is so massive that a fleet could be searching for us for months and not find us. We've been there many times."

Tunik glanced at the dog. It transformed into a bluish fish-scaled, ostrich-like beast with a hooked beak. Tunik returned his attention to Traveler.

"Your bird doesn't like people staring at it."

"No, he does not."

Nifle tapped Tunik on the shoulder. He gestured to the captain, and both kobolds stepped away from Traveler and the royals.

"Your friend Tunik seems even less agreeable than Nifle. Is this a problem, Mr. Traveler?" Lady Aylen asked.

"No."

"What if they don't take us to Titan's Fall?" King Aereth asked.

"He'll take us, sire."

"How do you know?" Lady Aylen asked.

The two kobolds returned.

"Nifle here has gotten me to reconsider," Tunik said. "I might as well. I'm already dropping off another party."

"What other party?" Traveler asked suspiciously.

"No need to worry, human. We rescued them from a sea serpent attack. I supposed I'm doing the same for you."

The kobold extended his hand. Traveler tossed him a bag of coins.

"I didn't forget the kind of gems you like."

Tunik smiled as he shook the bag. "Yes, you haven't. You can bring your party aboard. I'd sink your vessel if I were you."

"We'll handle it."

"Nifle will see your party to the cabins."

"I can join you on the bridge."

"I think not, human. Passengers are never allowed on my bridge. You know that. These days, I keep a nice sea serpent on deck to keep trespassers out. If you don't trust me to get you to Titan's Fall, why set foot on my ship?"

"I trust you to get us there, Tunik. You've done so for more years than I've been alive. I remember that look on your face. What else do you want to tell me?"

"If my ship is stopped by any fleet looking for you, and I have to choose between my ship and you—"

"You need not say it, Tunik. But I know you will not get caught, even with your much larger ship than the one from our days past."

Tunik shook his head.

"What?" Traveler asked.

"It would be pointless for me to try to get you to reconsider your journey. As stubborn as a gnoll, you are."

"Tunik, I appreciate the difficult position I've put you in, but strangely, I trust you more than I'd trust anyone else on these waters. I hope I'm not making a mistake."

Tunik smirked. "I'm coming to the end of my sailing life, human. The Oceanus Omnis was always dangerous, but I knew my way. A good life could be had by captains like me with good crews, but all has changed because of that accursed Atlantea. With the many, many fae who wish to reach its lands or control the waters to get there, it's now become too dangerous for even me."

"Why didn't you say so, Tunik? I understand completely now. You want to retire comfortably, maybe as a city administrator in Titan's Fall."

Tunik burst out with the loudest belly laugh the royals had ever seen. The kobold almost choked. "Me, a bureaucrat? I'd rather be dead."

"You have to do something if you're not going to be sailing these waters."

"I have my plan."

"Good. Get us to Titan's Fall without incident, and we'll part company for a final time. I'll be a passenger for your final voyage. I'll even volunteer my healing services if needed."

"I'd rather you volunteer your sword-fighting skills, but neither will be needed, if we're lucky. You shall be my guest and passenger alone, you and your party. The more I talk to you, I remember that I actually liked you a lot more than I thought. Old age takes away from even a kobold's memory."

"You're not old, Tunik."

"Compared to you, I am. I will get you to Titan's Fall, but you will have to double what you paid me. When we get to the city, you depart immediately. My crew will create a distraction."

"How many are waiting at the city?"

"There was an entire fleet there for weeks. Then they sailed off, but they returned a few days ago. Likely the port will be crawling with agents watching for you and your party."

One of the kobolds spoke to Tunik in another tongue. The captain slapped him.

"Why did you do that?" the kobold yelled, rubbing his face.

"The human speaks fae languages," Tunik answered back angrily.

They all stared at him. Traveler smirked. "I've never heard that dialect before."

"Did you understand what he said?" Tunik asked.

"I don't speak kobold, Tunik," Traveler said.

"I don't speak kobold, Tunik," Tunik mocked. "I know you do, or you understand it."

"I'm a human, Tunik. I can't possibly speak all the hundreds of thousands of languages spoken about these waters and its cities."

"Now, I know you speak kobold. Get your party aboard, human. We leave now, and you're paying me triple."

Tunik waited for an objection.

"Done."

"You're not even going to bother with haggling, human?"

"Why bother? Remember, I worked for you before, so I know. And since I dispensed with the haggling, so will you. A third of the payment now. The rest when we arrive."

"What if I don't like your terms?"

"I will ignore you. Send Nifle to collect the payment. You can get us underway, Captain Tunik."

The klabautermann smiled wide, showing a mouth of missing teeth and teeth sharpened to a dagger's point. "My able former healer has returned, indeed. Yes, Captain Traveler."

As Traveler watched, leaning on the port of Nifle's ship, the vessel of Titan's Caravan sank into the ocean until it was no longer visible. There was a flash of bright light beneath. A magical flying fish jumped from the waters, and Traveler grabbed it. The kobold watched him with amusement as Traveler tucked the magical fish securely in a pocket in his cloak. Nifle led the way. Besides his animal, three others followed behind Traveler. Tunik the klabautermann captain waited on deck, with his arms folded along with crewmembers—kobolds, toadoids, and fish men.

Later, when Bragg the dwelf stepped onto Tunik's crustacean ship, to join them, he too was covered with a bluish cloak, as was Estus, their weaponsmaster, who boarded before him.

"Carefully note the entire layout of the ship and its crew, far different than ships of our lands," Traveler said to Estus as they toured.

"That is an understatement," Tunik said. "I've never seen your human lands, but I'm told your oceans are like tiny ponds and your ships are like floating cups in comparison."

Estus had never before seen these types of animal men. The humanoid fish men especially drew his attention.

"Thanks, Tunik. I missed your frequent insults of humankind and our lands, but at least we're not ugly," Traveler said.

Tunik slapped the caravan master on the shoulder. "It's like you never left, Mr. Traveler."

Estus couldn't stop staring at the fish men. Their skin was lucent green, but Estus's eyes could detect rainbow colors underneath reflecting in the sunlight.

Traveler reached around Estus's neck to place a thick goldish necklace with a large orb there. "See to the realm, Mr. Estus. Mr. Bragg and I will keep my old captain company."

"But not on my bridge," Tunik interjected.

"Mr. Bragg and I would rather accompany your crew. At least they do an honest day's work."

Tunik laughed.

"What cabins do you have for us?" Traveler asked.

"Nifle, take Mr. Traveler's man down below to their cabin. Nothing fancy, Mr. Traveler."

"I'd expect nothing else, Tunik."

Estus scanned the deck as he followed the kobold. He was doing as Traveler had instructed: committing the complete exterior and its crew to memory. The deck was massive and extended beyond his view, not because its length was that long, but because the deck was anything but flat. He glanced back at the bridge area. Tunik, the captain, had not been joking. The structure was indeed guarded by a sea serpent, a blue-green scaled figure, ridged fins along the middle of its body from forehead to its lower half, and no limbs. It appeared that the bridge building sat in the middle of a pool of water. Part of the snakish creature's body was submerged, and the other half rested on the side of the structure and its roof. The sea serpent appeared to be napping.

The same three races of fae made up the entire Tunik crew as far as Estus could see. The main deck appeared to be made of gray wood, but the inside of the hull appeared to be a whitish surface of material unknown to him. Nifle led him down the steps.

"This will be your deck," the kobold told him.

"The entire level, sir?"

"My captain prefers to keep different parties on different levels. See that your party remains on this level alone."

"How many other passengers are aboard, sir?"

"The passageways to other levels will be guarded at all times." Nifle pointed to the end of the passage without answering Estus's question.

The corridor ended in a single doorway about ten feet away.

"There, sir?"

"Your cabin."

"Thank you, sir. I can manage from here."

Nifle watched him closely. "What do you do in this caravan?"

"Weaponsmaster, sir."

"For a human in these lands, that must be a very rewarding profession indeed."

"Very much so, sir."

"Should I open the door for you?"

"Mr. Nifle, is it?"

"Yes."

"Mr. Traveler already informed me of your mischievous nature, so I'm not opening the door until you're gone."

"Did he, now? What did he say? We served together on Tunik's ship before. He was our healer. Imagine that, a human healer aboard a fae ship. But he was good. No one can deny him that. He also didn't vomit all the time like other humans. Actually, I don't think I ever saw him vomit once while we served aboard. You know what I think?"

"What, Mr. Nifle?"

"I don't think your human is human."

"He's human all right, sir. It's due to all the years he spent in the magic lands, including living in Atlantea itself."

"Yes. So he told you that part of the story, too?"

"Yes, he did."

"Don't you want me to show you the cabin? Most humans are not accustomed to the accommodations of a real fae ship."

"Mr. Nifle."

"Yes."

"Do you know what phookas are?"

"Yes, of course. Everyone knows what those infernal creatures are. Why?"

"Mr. Traveler told me that if you did not leave me alone immediately to release our phookas on you."

"Release your phookas on me? You don't have those creatures."

"We have fifty."

"Fifty!"

"Shall I call them."

Nifle vanished. Estus heard footsteps racing up the stairs, but it wasn't just the one kobold. *There were other kobolds hiding in invisibility.* The weaponsmaster laughed, removed the necklace from around his neck, and threw it at the door. The door opened on its own, and a yellow sphere of light pushed out from the compartment. Estus stepped through and disappeared himself.

"Spiders and snakes! Snakes and spiders!" The phookas within the realm cackled in unison to greet him, all in the form of dancing humanoids with ram heads and tentacles for arms.

When Traveler and Bragg leaned over the inner balcony of the ship, the design they saw was not unfamiliar to either. Tunik's ship was like a ship within a ship—a harder outside rocky shell and an inner smooth-shelled ship. Out across the ocean, there was nothing to be seen, no sign of life. A darkened sky seemed to sit atop the rolling oceans. The rumble of Titan's Fall, still days away, was louder, and a sea of mist flying all about them reached into the sky.

"Do you think it's possible to get there without trouble?" Bragg asked.

"I hope so, but I'm not expecting that either. Six days is a long time on these waters."

"We were here years ago, my elves and I. We had to steal a boat to escape. We couldn't wait to get back on land. We wondered if we would ever rejoin you when the right time arrived."

"We're glad you and your men decided to continue on with our quest."

"Our fabled quest. I still want my Atlantean treasure."

"Yes."

"In all our attempts, we never even got within view of Atlantea. I said to my comrades, 'How can we? Our caravan master isn't here yet and is probably just a mere boy.'

Where does this Oughtred obtain these demons?" Bragg asked.

"Did you hear of him back then?" Traveler asked.

"No, but I heard of many strange things sighted—strange ships of sea and air, talk of fiends being spotted. I wondered if the Four Kings were the result of these things or the cause of them."

Traveler felt the tap of his dog lying near his feet. Both Bragg and he turned to see Tunik approaching without sound.

"A magnificent sight, these waters are." He joined them. "The human and I used to do this very thing many a time," Tunik said to Bragg.

"Near dusk was the best time," Traveler said.

"Yes, indeed. Mr. Bragg, I cannot say I've ever met a dwelf before. Tall as an elf, stout as a dwarf, neither ancestor nor co-mingling of either."

"We are among the many hidden races of fae. But a few of us have decided to explore the known magical lands and those of the humans."

"Did Nifle tell you?" Traveler asked Tunik.

"He did," Tunik replied. "An invisible goblin ship in the area. They won't bother us because, if they did, it would be the last thing they ever did."

"I was asking Mr. Traveler if we expect our journey to Titan's Fall to be without incident."

Tunik laughed. "Tall as an elf, stout as a dwarf, dumb as a troll."

"Don't make fun of Mr. Bragg, Tunik. He's an accomplished manticore hunter."

"Really? How many?"

"Twenty-six," Bragg answered.

"That is impressive. I saw one once when I was a boy, and that was enough for me to never want to see another one again."

"I didn't know you were ever a boy, Tunik," Traveler said.

"Actually, I looked exactly as I do now, just slightly shorter."

Traveler and Bragg chuckled. "That I can believe," Traveler said.

"No, Mr. Bragg. Our route is filled with mermen, mermaids, merrows, tritons, and the like—far busier than what your caravan master remembers. It no longer merely holds traveling vessels of commerce and exploration but includes those for war. In fact, will it be only the two of you and the dog on deck?"

"If we are to be traveling secretly, Tunik, it would not be wise for our party to be anywhere near the deck," Traveler said.

Tunik smiled. "Especially elves or a water elfess. Yes, our Mr. Traveler is not as dumb as a troll, quite the opposite. If we are attacked, though, don't look to my men for any help. Mr. Bragg, your Mr. Traveler has his shape-shifter, but even an impressive manticore hunter like you might not fare well in battles against our ocean fae."

"I have a companion too."

Bragg whistled, or his mouth made the motion of one. In moments, they heard footsteps. The crew looked on as the giant ten-foot-tall automaton marched upstairs to the deck and ambled toward his master.

"This, Mr. Tunik, is Mr. Glog," Bragg said.

On the oceans, night and day, dusk and dawn were relative terms. Seasoned crews created their own days based on their needs, not by the disposition of the heavens. Days could be as dark as night because of a nearby storm, and nights could be the brightest a human had ever seen because of the passing of a celestial ship in the void above Pan-Earth.

Traveler and Bragg returned from their daytime vigil with Tunik and his crew. While Glog was left in front of the passage entrance to their realm, the two men stepped through with the dog. Unlike previous realm entrances, they found themselves in a short tunnel and had to step through again. Immediately, two of the Tree Shepherds' nine-foot "tree giants" stood guard. On one side were a camp of moon elves; on the opposite side, one of drows.

"Tunik rarely sleeps when on patrol on the open waters," Traveler said to Bragg.

"But this isn't a patrol for him."

"No. It's considerably more dangerous."

"Are you sure we can trust him?"

"We shall take it day by day. I'm more interested in what other passengers are aboard."

"We've seen no others on deck."

Their pocket-realm was forever dusk, with green plains of sparse foliage, a cool breeze, and three moons in the sky. The caravan's brownies, pech, and gnomes had done a brilliant job of creating a village of taverns, which were now filled with rowdy men, eating and drinking. Outside around the huts were dozens of campfires, surrounded by humans and fae. Most of Titan's Caravan were back together as one group.

"Where are your darkling comrades?" Bragg asked.

"In one of the taverns, of course. Sprites can't resist music and merriment."

Traveler sat at his table eating his nighttime meal. He turned to give half his food to his dog by his chair.

The royals and Gwyness sat with him. The dog snatched the large thigh of meat, and dropped it to the floor to work on it.

The tavern shook with music, dancing gnomes, darklings in the form of black cat-headed monkeys which scampered across the walls and ceilings, chasing each other—humans, and other fae, who drank and joked. At nearby tables both the female and male half-elves, all assigned to be royal guards, watched, laughing and talking.

"How was your day, Mr. Traveler?" Lady Aylen asked.

"Uneventful, princess. Not a ship, boat, island, or creature to be seen."

"Is that normal?" King Aereth asked.

"Extremely, sire. Sailing life can be a lonely one. Weeks or months of not seeing another living thing is common. That's why the danger on the open waters is so often fatal. When it comes, it's fast, and often the victim is unprepared after so long a stretch of the mundane."

"I meant to ask you, Mr. Traveler," the king said. "When we first encountered this Tunik, another sea kobold spoke to him in their language. Tunik slapped him. What was he saying?"

"Do you have a sense of what he said, princess?" Traveler asked.

"No. I don't speak their language."

"But you can sense the meaning of other languages."

"The only thing I sense is that these sea kobolds are not to be trusted."

"But they're your friends, Mr. Traveler," Gwyness said.

"They are. They saved my life, and I saved the lives of several of the crew."

"The bounty, or bounties?" King Aereth asked.

"Or fear, sire. Tunik's ship is formidable, but you have yet to see the war vessels of the other water fae that travel these waters."

"What did these sea kobolds say, then, Mr. Traveler?" Lady Aylen asked.

"He was talking about all the money they'd get for us."

The royals and Gwyness stopped eating.

"What?" Lady Aylen asked.

"Mr. Traveler, we—"

"Sire, there is nothing to do but wait. Tunik is the captain, not his crew. The decision is his."

"But they were talking about double-crossing us," Lady Aylen said.

"Let them talk. That's what a good captain does. He lets his crew talk about whatever they want to pass the time and stay in good spirits as long as the work gets done and they are ready to defend the ship when the time comes."

"Mr. Traveler, you are extremely calm about this," King Aereth said.

"Mr. Bragg and I will keep an eye on them. If anything is to happen, it would be during the day."

"Why not at night?" Gwyness asked as Lady Aylen began to ask too.

"No one does anything at night on the Oceanus Omnis," Traveler said, "not merfolk, water elves, or most water fae."

"Why is that?" Lady Aylen asked.

"The larger and more dangerous creatures of the oceans hunt at night," Traveler replied. "They swim up from the deepest depths, where no one goes. No one risks fighting such creatures, not even me or my dog."

Traveler and Bragg stepped onto the main deck early in the morning. The echoing rumble of Titan's Fall, still days away, was loud enough to mask the sound of Glog following after them.

"Where's your dog?" Bragg asked, half-yelling.

"He's ahead of us. Where's our crew?"

The men noticed that there were less crew members than before, but as they neared the bridge, they saw them—all clustered near one side of the ship, talking amongst themselves.

"We should be careful," Traveler said to Bragg. "But leave Mr. Glog here."

The dwelf heeded his warning as they approached, putting his hand on his weapon fastened to his belt under his cloak. Bragg raised a finger, and the giant metal golem stopped.

Traveler greeted the crew with a smile as human and dwelf approached. "Morning. Where's our fearless captain?"

All of them had stopped talking when they first caught sight of the human and dwelf. The sea kobolds, fish men, and toadoids just stared at them. Then one finally burst out laughing. The entire group erupted in laughter too.

"You should have seen your faces, human," the kobold said. "Did you think we were plotting to murder you?"

"The thought never crossed our minds," Traveler said.

"You are a healer of fae?" a toadoid asked him.

"Yes, I was. Tunik hired me right in Titan's Fall for that purpose. Nifle was with him too."

"Why be a healer out here?" another kobold asked.

"To continue my training."

"But now you're a caravan master?" another kobold asked.

"That I am."

"Where will you go in Titan's Fall?" another asked.

Traveler thought for a moment. "There's a tavern near the eastern part of the city from the shore. It's called the Tommyknockers. It used to be a favorite of elementals. One went there not for drink but gossip, and that gossip was always the best news of all that happened in and around Atlantea. Know of it?"

The crewmen shook their heads.

"I see Tunik's pet sea serpent isn't around either," Traveler said.

"Lovecraft takes the occasional swim when it wants," a kobold said.

"Lovecraft?" Bragg asked with a laugh.

"He *loves* our *craft*," the kobold added with a toothless grin.

"Speaking of news, did anything of importance happen last night?" Traveler asked.

"If anything did, Tunik would tell you."

Traveler looked at the fish men. "Does your kind speak?"

The fish men said nothing.

"They don't speak to outsiders," a kobold said.

"Well, Tunik must be sleeping," Traveler said.

"Yes. He is," one of them said.

"Mr. Bragg and I will wait along the side and take in the view, like yesterday. Tell Tunik that Mr. Bragg and I would like to share a meal one of these days, for old times."

"Tunik doesn't sit for meals," another said.

"Yes, he does," Traveler said, "and he can drink an entire barrel of ale by himself."

Traveler's dog came from behind the crewmen in its bluish-fur, webbed-feet form, away from the bridge. The men seemed especially surprised by its appearance.

"Thanks, men, for the conversation," Traveler said. "Oh, are we expecting a vessel?"

"Why do you task?" a kobold asked.

"Why else would you be waiting here together?"

"A merchant vessel," another kobold said.

"Let us know if we can be of any help. Even though we're passengers, being aboard brings back good memories. I'd like to help out my old captain."

Traveler led Bragg and his dog away from them. Bragg glanced and could see the fish men all staring at them with suspicious, dirty looks.

"Mr. Traveler, may we speak below deck?"

"No, Mr. Bragg. We're going to wait along our spot at the side of the ship and take in the view, like I said. I don't want to let them out of my sight for even an instant."

There was no privacy on deck. Any one of the fae could easily hear their words even with the rumbling of the Fall in the distance. Bragg became a restless ball of energy, never taking his eyes off Tunik's crew, and they never stopped watching him.

"Mr. Bragg, you must learn to relax. You are a seasoned hunter after all. I'd expect your patience to be better than that of a tree person."

"Mr. Traveler, we really need to go below deck."

"Mr. Bragg, we are not leaving this deck. If you would do what I said, you'd see what I see."

Bragg peered out from the ship and saw it—a vessel approaching. The ship was longer than Tunik's but very low to the water's surface. Either most of the ship was underwater, or it only had two decks, a main and lower. The exterior appeared to be simple wood, dark brown, with the wear and tear of many years at sea, with pockmarks, scratches, and repaired gashes.

As the vessel drifted closer, its crew of humanoid fae came into view. They were humanoids with bluish skin and hair and webbed hands. All were men in attire that looked like bluish crustacean exoskeletons.

Bragg turned to see what he sensed behind him. Two humanoid children stood on the deck near the stairs leading below decks. The little boy and girl froze in shock when their eyes met Bragg's gaze. An older girl, nearly in her teens, appeared from the stairs and grabbed the children. They disappeared below deck.

The dwelf's attention slowly returned to the new vessel. "I didn't think children were allowed on vessels such as this."

"They aren't, unless they're with parents who are paying passengers." Traveler's eyes had never left the new vessel. His dog watched them, too, standing on his hind legs with his front paws resting on the upper edge of the ship's side.

Closer to the ship's bow, Tunik was speaking with one of them, undoubtedly their captain. The crew of the new vessel watched Traveler and Bragg like hawks.

"Too bad dwelfs can't fly like kobolds," Traveler said.

Bragg was about to respond but stopped himself.

"Let us see if we can offer any assistance to my old captain." Traveler led them to the parley between Tunik and the new captain. The bows of both ships were practically touching.

"We were talking about you, human," Tunik said.

"I'm sure you were, Mr. Tunik. What kind of ship are you running here? We expect to arrive at Titan's Fall on time. You stop to rescue the shipwrecked, as if that is any of our affair. You stop to gossip with strange fae about the ocean. This is not the service we hired you to do."

"We will arrive at the Fall on time, as promised," Tunik repeated.

"You can forget any additional recompense for this shabby service."

"We will be there on time, human, as promised."

"Who are these fae anyway?"

"I am Ahor. We are a merchant ship, and we will conclude our business."

"Please do," Traveler said. "Queen Anorsa does not tolerate inconvenience."

"You are in the employ of water elves?" Ahor asked cautiously.

"Yes. Who else?"

"I did not know water elves did such things," Ahor said, with a hint of suspicion.

"None of the humans in my mistress's employ are mere humans. We are all wizards of the highest caliber. It is in our blood and we train from infancy. Shall I demonstrate for you? Maybe conjure up a sea serpent to rip your ship apart or have our metal golem merely set the whole thing ablaze." Traveler looked at Tunik. "So that we may continue on with our trip to the Fall unimpeded."

"We sail, then," Tunik smirked.

Bragg tried not to laugh as Ahor and his blue-skinned crew appeared visibly unsettled. The dwelf noticed Nifle stepping out of the bridge room. At the same moment, he noticed Traveler's dog was nowhere to be seen.

Tunik gestured to Ahor, and both fae moved away to the other end of the ship. Traveler and Bragg looked on, as did Ahor's fae. Tunik and the captain spoke quietly. Some kind of magic must have been at work because no one could hear their words, and a translucent haze obscured anyone from seeing even their lips. Their conversation didn't last long. The two fae waved and returned to their respective bridges. Soon, the new vessel moved away.

Bragg could feel the breeze as Tunik's ship sailed away.

"If we don't go below deck this instant to talk, I'll have Mr. Glog drag you, and I don't care what your dog does," Bragg said.

The dwelf felt the entire ship shake with an eruption. The other vessel was visible but far away. It blew up in a fireball so large Bragg winced as he shielded his face from the blast of heat. Then the resulting tidal wave came at the ship.

The magic of the ship easily protected it from the crashing wave, which splashed around an invisible barrier. Wreckage of the other ship washed by and sank below the water's surface.

"Why did you kill those fae?" Traveler yelled.

Tunik's men came to their captain's aid with their tridents, hooks, and crossbows in their hands, standing at his sides and behind. Traveler had his hand on his sword beneath his cloak. Bragg held his bladed walking staff near the face of the closest fae with Glog towering above them. Behind Traveler gathered Lady Aylen, Lyre's high elves aiming their arrows, and Cut-Throats with crossbows, along with Pangolin, who seemed to be moments from throwing his axe-mace into the sea kobolds. More of Tunik's crew swarmed behind their captain, aiming their crossbows.

"I suggest you tell your people to return below deck before they're seen. You know there are many eyes out here on the oceans, even when it looks empty."

"I asked why you killed those fae," Traveler said.

"Did you think your feeble subterfuge would have worked?"

"I know it would have."

"You fooled no one. Queen Anorsa, is it? You pull the name of some wicked witch water elf from thin air. Have you ever met her?"

"I have, which is why my plan would have worked."

"How long do you think it would have taken them to verify your lie?"

"We only need to get to the Fall, not for them to believe the story for all of eternity."

"Tell your people that I saved your lives. Tell them that after you tell them to return below deck. Neither my men nor I am frightened by any of you. You know that. I die, you die. You and your caravan would die a miserable death out here because only I can pilot my ship, but you know that too. Withdraw, my former healer. There will be no battle here on the deck of my ship."

"Did you kill them to save our lives, or did you kill them because you wanted the bounty all for yourself?"

"Think what you want. If you're so suspicion of me and my motives, why not leave now? See how far you get."

Traveler touched Bragg's staff weapon and moved it away from Tunik's fae. He turned to the others.

"Lady Aylen, take everyone back to our quarters."

"This is an intolerable situation, Mr. Traveler," she said. "Either he murdered his conspirators or murdered an innocent crew."

"I'd get used to the viciousness of life out on these waters, elf," Tunik said.

Lady Aylen approached him. "We are well familiar with the viciousness of life."

"Where's your guardian, Tunik?" Traveler asked.

The sea kobold took his eyes off the princess to stare at him. "Lovecraft is nearby. He never swims far."

"Yet we race away from the scene of your crime."

"My crimes? Believe what you want. Shall I stop for you to get off my ship or should I continue to Titan's Fall?"

"Since we've already paid for the trip, and you'll never return our money, Titan's Fall it is."

"I don't take too kindly to passengers pointing weapons at me and my men. If not for our previous partnership, we wouldn't be talking so calmly together now. We'd be killing one after another and tossing your corpses overboard for the fish to feed on."

"If you hadn't been my captain in the past, you'd already be dead."

Tunik smiled. "There. We each made our threats. However, I am captain, not you. Get your people below. A human with a dwelf is no concern, but again I say, what do you think will happen if someone sees an elfess, elves, and humans? Also, they know you have a giant metal golem, so get it off my deck too."

Tunik said nothing more. He turned and stormed off for the bridge. His men watched him disappear inside the building and relaxed their battle stance.

Everyone startled. Tunik's sea serpent jumped out of the ocean and landed on the top of the bridge building. In its mouth was a giant fish. It looked at everyone then shook all the excess water off its skin like a dog before lying down on the roof in its favored pose, half of its body dangling down into the pool around the bridge, as it ate its food.

"We told you he went for a swim," Nifle said.

Everyone relaxed again.

"Lady Aylen, lead everyone back to the realm. Mr. Bragg, Tunik is right, Mr. Glog has to go with them."

Traveler could see the anger in everyone's faces. "Either we do what he says, or we abandon the ship now."

"We are being blackmailed into submission," Lady Aylen said.

She walked off, back to the steps leading everyone down to the lower decks. Bragg reluctantly followed with his golem. The elves, and the Cut-throats led by Mr. Pangolin also followed. Pangolin gave Traveler a look: we must talk!

As they filed back down to the lower deck, Traveler turned his attention to Tunik's crew.

"Let us all behave ourselves for these five days," he said.

"You should stay below with your party," a kobold said.

"I am staying on deck every day until we reach Titan's Fall."

"You do that, human. By tomorrow, with the Fall's mist, you won't be able to see your own hand in front of your face."

Within their pocket-realm sanctuary, the brownies and pech made sleeping huts for all who wanted them. Traveler preferred his standard tent. Inside, he stirred a large black pot boiling over a fire. However, outside he could hear the men and fae had gathered into an angry mob. He had marched through the camp when he returned from his daytime vigil on the main deck so he knew what was coming.

"Mr. Traveler, a word." The king's voice came from outside the tent. The entrance flap lifted.

The dog watched the king, Chief Ethor, the woodland elf, and Dr'as, the drows' leader, step inside. Lady Aylen slipped in right after them with a deep frown, then Mr. Hobbs followed.

"Look at your faces." Traveler dumped the contents of a pouch into the boiling pot.

"What was that you put in the pot?" Lady Aylen asked with a look of surprise. "That looked like a tiny, shriveled up, desiccated corpse."

"He's making a homunculus," Chief Ethor said.

Dr'as laughed. "I don't even know how to make such a creature."

"You should," Traveler said. "I would think the D'Shar would know of this and more."

"We prefer different magic."

"It will be our own flying eye to see better than any human or fae eye could," Traveler said. "Even better than our own Mr. Elman."

"When we were in the Safari Plains of the Great Forest, didn't you admonish Mr. Bragg for using such magic eyes?" Lady Aylen asked.

"Yes, princess, I did. A flying eye is more like a portal back to the user. My homunculus bird is a magical creature that channels what it sees to us, and its detection is far more difficult. Besides, it's a risk worth taking."

"A worthy spy," Dr'as said.

"Mr. Traveler, we must speak about our predicament," King Aereth said.

"Sire, I cannot. This time we must keep it all to ourselves. I cannot take the chance that our words will be heard by others."

"Surely, none could penetrate our protective sphere created by the Tree Shepherds," Dr'as said.

"That is a risk I'm not willing to take. No one must know our plans. I did tell you all this when we were on our own ship. That was the last time we'd be able to speak with full privacy assured until we claimed our own ship again. We are also not free from those creatures who can pull knowledge from us straight from our dreams. This is the domain of water nymphs and sirens. No, not this time. You know how much I prefer to keep the men informed, but we are too close to fail now."

"Well, that I agree with," Lady Aylen said.

"The mist outside from the Falls has grown so thick any vigil of these sea kobolds is impossible," Chief Ethor said to Traveler.

The caravan master pulled the homunculus bird from the pot with metal tongs. "That is what he's for."

"These klabautermann, or sea kobolds, are not a trustworthy race. Even these who were your friends. None of us feel at ease with our fate in their hands," Lady Aylen said.

"Are humans a trustworthy race, princess? Sometimes, and sometimes not. When I was a member of their crew, I trusted them with my life, and the feeling was mutual. But I am no longer a member of their crew, even as a paying passenger. We are mere outsiders."

"That friendship was years ago," King Aereth said.

"Yes, sire. We all change. I have."

"Is there nothing you can say, Mr. Traveler?" Lady Aylen asked. "The concern and fear are justified. They murdered that crew, but we don't know what their true motives were. I personally doubt it was for our benefit, as the captain claimed."

"Trust me, everyone. It is all I can say until we reach the Fall. Trust me."

"Sir, what should I tell the men?" Hobbs asked. "Mr. Pangolin and our returning Mr. Bragg are leading this new unhappy society growing amongst our ranks. They are convinced this Mr. Tunik plots to turn us over to the Four Kings."

"Tunik wouldn't do that. He might turn us over but not in that manner. More like, he'd allow us to be captured."

"Is that meant to reassure us?" King Aereth asked.

"It means, sire, that we can be fairly certain we will get to the shores of Titan's Fall, and equally certain that the moment we step off his ship, our troubles begin."

"I'd say our troubles have already begun, Mr. Traveler," Lady Aylen said.

"Princess, if we hadn't done this, we'd likely still be where we were at Titan's Teeth. The Finmen aren't the only races patrolling those waters."

"Sea goblins?" Dr'as asked.

"That was what I saw, but I'm sure there are others."

"You're certain they were in league with the Four Kings?" Chief Ethor asked.

Traveler set the homunculus bird on the ground to dry. As he did, it began to lighten in color.

"I'm not sure, Chief. Allies of the Four Kings may be in this region, but it is definitely not controlled by them. It is controlled by races who view us and the Four Kings as equal trespassers in their empire. They're very capable of killing either or both of us without a second thought. Let us stay within our realm. I will keep watch. You will all train in your tasks to be ready."

Mr. Hobbs gave a loud sigh.

Traveler grinned. "What was that for, Mr. Hobbs?"

"Titan's Fall is also a city isn't, sir?"

"Yes, the largest any of you have seen yet."

"We don't do too well in fae cities, sir," Hobbs said.

Traveler's smile was gone too. "No, we haven't seemed to have had much luck avoiding danger and possible death."

The homunculus bird stirred. It was a dark-feathered bird with a single giant eye on its forehead.

For the first time in many months, Titan's Caravan gathered together under the three moons of their forever-dusk realm. Human, fae, and animal rested in the green plains that surrounded the village of taverns and tents. The Antaean giants were not fully recovered, but they could at least move about. They walked at a snail's pace and promptly lay down. The Tree Shepherds stood together, the drows in their own group. The fauns sat with the animal men. The hoofed fae sat together behind all others. The brownies, pech, gnomes, and gnomoids sat at the front with the humans. Bragg and his men sat to the side with their incredibly tame, for the moment, Diomedian Mares.

Many of the caravan's animals took the occasion to reacquaint themselves with each other. The darklings ran in circles around the camp, chasing each other in the form of black rabbit-headed monkeys. Even the frowning väki attended, looking as if they had just woken up.

Above the caravan in the sky, a magic window appeared, very similar to what they had seen before when they were camped in the Great Forest.

"Hopefully, nothing will be thrown through the portal at us," Pangolin remarked to his group of Cutthroats, near the human leadership and royal guards, seated on the plains together. After his long absence, their hired healer, Mr. Gresham, had joined them too. He had the stature of a bare-knuckle bruiser, not a healer, with his strong hands. He had let his mustache grow as well as his brown hair at the sides of his balding head.

Young Quillen had his magic book open with his pen in hand. "We can't see anything, Mr. Traveler," he said.

For those who had not seen it with their own eyes, through gossip, everyone knew the mist cloud around the boat was worse than before. From the magic view, the homunculus bird had reached the main deck and hopped along. It stopped. Several fireflies hung in the air, not as a swarm but each of different sizes and different hues of yellow, blue, red, and white.

Traveler took special note of them.

"I take it those are not fireflies, Mr. Traveler?" King Aereth asked.

"No, sire. Tunik did tell us there were other passengers on the ship. They are doing the same thing we're doing."

"Mr. Bragg did say you saw children from one of the parties," Pangolin said.

"Humanoid."

"Mr. Bragg said they were humans."

Traveler shook his head. "Human children wouldn't be running and playing on the deck of a fae ship in the

Oceanus Omnis. They'd be shivering, bedridden, vomiting, or comatose. Humanoids."

"Do you know which race?" Lady Aylen asked.

"There are many, but I'm not concerned about them. I am interested to know who the other passengers are."

"How large is this Titan's Fall for the mist of its falling waters to be seen from so many days away, Mr. Traveler? And it's so loud," Gwyness said.

"Think of a waterfall falling from the heavens themselves. The land region is a giant mountain. The water crashes down from its peak and the city is in the valley below."

"If it is of such power, why wouldn't the city be at the peak?" Pangolin asked.

"It's a port, Mr. Pangolin, and a busy one. A maze of reefs shields the city from the crashing waves, and the city itself is larger than any we have seen so far with its own series of walls and barriers of stone and magic. The top of Titan's Fall is like being in a death storm and pounded with one-hundred- to two-hundred-foot or more waves, and there's the vortex. There's nothing at the top of Titan's Fall but death for any person or ship foolish enough to go there."

"But some do," Pangolin said.

"Yes, you've heard of it."

"Heard of what?" Lady Aylen asked.

"There are some fae races that use the Fall as part of their rite of passage rituals—citizen to warrior, heir to ruler, and some berserker clans, which is why our Mr. Pangolin knows of it. Many fae races in fact. At least a quarter of those that try are never seen again."

"I would like to try someday," Pangolin said.

"Try? You'd be killed," Gwyness said.

Traveler chuckled. "Maiden Gwyness, actually I think our Mr. Pangolin would be one of the triumphant ones based on his entry in the Erymanthian Games in the Giant City of Khury."

"Then, Mr. Pangolin, we are going to command you not to do any such thing," Lady Aylen said. "Though I suspect you'd freely disregard our warnings like our caravan master does when leaving the caravan behind on his many errands."

"I'll say this, Mr. Pangolin, to aid our princess's warning. Whenever those brave souls take on the Fall, they do so with fleets of ships to protect the region and armies to clear the path of any wild creatures. No one ventures to the Fall alone, no one. You should not either."

"Then it will have to be another time," Pangolin said. "When I have a fleet of ship and my own army to accompany me so I could conquer the Fall."

"Mr. Traveler?"

"Yes, princess."

"Have you done so?"

Traveler hesitated. "I did."

Everyone looked at him. "I knew it," Lady Aylen said.

"You did, sir?" Hobbs asked.

"How?" I'wulf asked. "What is the ritual exactly? Scale the waterfall then come down?"

"That is one challenge. The other is to fly your ship to the top of the Fall and dive into it. One must successfully navigate through the torrent and survive the hundreds-of-feet fall to the ocean's surface."

"You did the latter, then, sir?" Nirgund asked.

"I did the latter with Tunik and his crew. I did the former years before. It was the last part of my training with my sword."

The berserkers looked at him with astonishment and admiration.

"How long did it take?" Pangolin asked.

"Over a year. My dog cleared the path of all the gargoyles and other creatures, but he stayed away."

"Why would you do such a thing, Mr. Traveler?" Gresham asked. "The toll on the human body would be devastating."

"It was, Mr. Gresham. When the ordeal was done, I looked like I'd fallen hundreds of feet and survived. I had lost much weight too. But the challenge of the Fall is not the physical. It is the mental. Does one have the mental fortitude to force your body to complete such an ordeal? I did it because, if I couldn't do that, then there was no chance I could do another task."

"What was that?" Lady Aylen asked.

"Lead a revolt and take on a powerful star elfin lord and his entire army of star elves on another world to free my dog's race of shape-shifters."

Titan's Fall could be seen now. A full day's sailing away, the titanic fifth marker of Titan's Trail was visible to the eye without the aid of a telescope or magical means. It was as Traveler had said, a waterfall of such unimaginable size falling from the void of space.

The village that the brownies and pech had created for the caravan was no longer in use. Everyone sat or slept under the magic window to watch the images from Traveler's homunculus bird.

The splendid kirins had returned: King Aereth's horselike beast with its golden fur and scales, powerful muscles, cloven hooves, thick mane, and dragon-like head; Lady Aylen's dragon horse with its lucent-blue fur and scales, a single horn sprouting from his head, and long whiskers like a catfish around its nose and mouth; lastly, Maiden Gwyness's larger dragon-horse appeared—black fur and scales, its head was adorned with full antlers, and a tail not unlike a lion's.

The sight of the three beasts magically galloping in the air many feet above the camp was seen as a good omen. Gwyness couldn't take her eyes off them as she smiled.

"I'm so glad they're back," she said to the female half-elves seated around her as they ate.

The fae humans, Tyfer and Oeric, served the morning meal. Hobbs had been overseeing the daily chores of the men but stayed closed to the leadership. Standing, Traveler sipped his hot brew. His eyes never left the magic window. Many sensed that the final leg to Titan's Fall had some special significance.

"A day away, now, Mr. Traveler?" Pangolin asked.

"Yes. If we have a clear night, we should be able to see the lights of the city, even through the mist."

"Such force," Lady Aylen remarked.

"The Fall can smash a fleet of ships to pieces," Traveler said.

"We have not seen Mr. Tunik or his crew in all these days," King Aereth said.

"Yes, and that's good news. If we had seen them, that would be a sign of trouble."

"What is the plan for when we arrive at the port of the city?" the king asked.

Traveler looked at him with a wicked grin.

"Mr. Traveler, what are you up to now?" Lady Aylen asked.

"Did you royals not hire me to get you to Atlantea?"

"Yes." The princess smiled.

"Then that is what I will do, princess."

"Can we really be heard from within our pocket-realm?" Pangolin asked.

"I am taking no chances, Mr. Pangolin. As the princess would say: we have come too far to fail now."

"Hear! Hear!" Lady Aylen and Pangolin said. The king laughed.

"Look!"

The fairy sisters appeared from nowhere, hovering under the window, with their fluttering translucent wings. The caravan hadn't seen Wildglow or her sister, Sunpetal, in so long. They looked the same as always, the older sister barely two-feet-tall and her sister, half her size. The taller one had two antennae poking out from her short blondish hair, translucent insect wings from her back, and was clad in a muted ivory frock. The smaller sister was clad in her brown half-jacket that had the texture of a woolly caterpillar. With both sisters away and sleeping for a long time, everyone expected the hyper-active fairies to engage in nonstop play and mischief for some time.

"We should fly right up to the top of Titan's Fall," Wildglow proclaimed. Her little sister giggled, nodding.

"Speaking of children," Pangolin said under his breath to Traveler and the royals.

"Mr. Pangolin, always remember that our children are older than most grandparents."

"Still children, and dangerous."

"But on our side, Mr. Pangolin," Lady Aylen said.

"Did we really need to wake them, Mr. Traveler?" Pangolin asked.

"Oh yes, Mr. Pangolin. I did."

Titan's Fall was near. Tunik steered the ship through the water's mist, so thick it was as if giant, billowing white clouds rested on the ocean's surface. The ship wasn't sailing on the waters but flying above the clouds toward the Fall.

Tunik stood on the bridge with Nifle and his crew, all watching the display mirrors.

"Should I get them?" Nifle asked.

"Our Mr. Traveler knows we've reached the Fall," Tunik replied.

"You've decided to be with us?" a fish man asked.

"There's no stronger family than one's crew. Mr. Traveler isn't part of our crew anymore. He was a good human when he was, but that was then."

"Which bounty will we accept?" Nifle asked.

"We take the highest one," a fish man said.

"No, Nifle is right," Tunik said. "We pick the best one and be done with it. We don't want to be anywhere near the Fall when these forces fight each other for possession of Traveler's caravan. We do this quickly before they suspect anything and we can't let either Traveler or that shape-shifter of his get loose. I like my new ship and don't want it destroyed."

"What of the other passengers?" Nifle asked.

"Get your ships, and take them into the city."

"Which bounty, then, are we accepting?" Nifle asked.

"Who can give us the most benefit?"

"Merfolk."

"That's who we turn them over to then."

"When do we turn them over?" a sea kobold asked.

Tunik looked at one of the fish men. "Do it now."

The fish man's eyes glowed yellow for a moment. "It is done."

"It is sad that it must end this way," Nifle said.

"Strange for you to say, Nifle. You wanted us to turn them over at the living islands."

"I know. Poor human. If only he'd reached us before all these bounties came about. We could have had a nice final voyage together."

"This is our final voyage," Tunik said. "Get a move on and get all those passengers off my ship." He looked at the fish man. "I want all your wizards to make sure nothing can breach the seal of the first deck, nothing."

The fish man nodded and led the others from the bridge room. The second the door opened, the crashing sound of the Fall exploded into the room. The fish men exited and closed the door behind them.

A frantic fish man returned. He threw the door open and jumped back in. His comrades and many more followed.

"Close the door!" Tunik yelled as he angrily gestured them in, and they did so.

"They are gone!"

Tunik's squinty eyes opened wide. "That human. That human! They'll try to sneak onto the city port. We must find them!" He grabbed one of the other sea kobolds near him. "Unleash Lovecraft to track them!"

The door swung open again. The sea kobold yelled, but they couldn't hear his muffled words. A crew member inside pulled him in, and they closed the door.

"Vessels approaching, Tunik,"

"Who?"

"The merrows."

"How many ships?"

"At least a dozen."

"Scout, commerce, war, what kind?"

"Warships, Tunik."

Lady Aylen never believed the confidence that Traveler had placed in her was justified until the moment she dived into the ocean. The feeling was strange. She floated in the bluish void, breathing as normally as if on land. She felt no pressure from the water around, no discomfort or effort in breathing underwater. Her eyesight was enhanced, her ears picked up even the slightest vibrations. She could sense every living thing swimming nearby. She stared at her hand. Her fingers elongated with webbing between them.

Someone tapped her shoulder. The caravan's mole-looking fae also swam effortlessly. She nodded and lifted her other hand with her war trident. She was the sole vanguard for the caravan, but she felt no fear in here.

The first magic bubble neared. The magic was from their two fairy sisters, Wildglow and Sunpetal. The two of them sat in the first bubble, in complete awe of the great ocean around them. The Tree Shepherd leader, Greenwig sat in the next bubble. The next three contained a Tree Shepherd each.

A secret underwater caravan of magic bubbles followed one after another led by Lady Aylen. No one was more amazed than Young Quillen, who smiled from ear to ear. The mole-man and the dog, in the form of a giant eel, swam alongside the procession of nearly ten thousand individual magic bubbles gliding toward the city of Titan's Fall.

They were dozens of feet down but the power of the Fall could still be felt. Just above them, the water violently churned. Below, the calmness of the great ocean remained for their silent escape from Tunik's ship.

"We have to travel by means that use the least amount of magic," Traveler had told them to explain why they used individual magical spheres of protection from the fairies rather than their pocket-realm. "There are fae who possess magic maps that can see a pocket-realm."

Lady Aylen flew through the water. She felt the presence of the ocean's fauna in her mind, but the only giant fish she sensed were many miles away. Her eyes noticed the many dark shapes passing above—ships. The city's port drew closer. One of the magic spheres rose from the others and moved to the front. Lady Aylen saw it was Traveler. He gestured to the surface.

She wondered if he meant they were surfacing. She looked up. The vessel above, constructed in the shape of a giant manta ray, was not on the surface, but sailing under the water. The vessel was not alone, but one of many. The caravan was like a helpless school of fish entering the shore city at Titan's Fall. Lady Aylen could begin to make out the hulls of an endless number of anchored ships in endless shapes and sizes.

All the magic spheres rose to the surface. Lady Aylen swam after them.

From the city's shore, a wall of water all along the horizon, fell from the heavens. To outsiders, the view of the City at Titan's Fall was hypnotizing. The city's own magic created an invisible wall to keep both the

Fall mist and the thundering noise of its water away. The port city rested behind the Fall, as not even its magic could shield it from the direct, daily assault of the heavenly waterfall. As Traveler had told them, the city was far larger than any they had encountered in Faë-Land Minor, Faë-Wick, Arion's Spire, or the elfin kingdom Fae'el in Faë-Land Major. The port, too, was more vast than they had ever seen. They saw city ships almost a hundred feet long down to one-man boats traveling in swarms of thousands. While many of the ships looked conventional, most looked like shells or sea animals.

Then there was the sheer number of people. There were water elves, fish men, toad and frog men, fairy-like humanoids, blue-skinned fae, white-skinned fae, lizard-like fae, occasional drows, and sea kobolds. Giants, birdlike fae, beast men, tall dwarves, and every imagined fae there could be walked the streets of the City at Titan's Fall. The styles of attire and the languages and dialects were as varied as the number of stars in the heavens.

Traveler moved slowly through the crowd with Dr'amal, the drow sorceress, and Ursi, the bear clan fae-blood, fresh from her own hibernation. Traveler had them replace their bluish cloaks for bright-yellow patterned ones. Especially Ursi, with her characteristic black clothing and necklace of brown stones, he wanted hidden. The dog had taken the form again of an aquatic, axe-beaked ostrich to follow them.

"I must commend you," Dr'amal said. "Never have I met a more cunning human than you. Did you pick up these traits from living with my people, or were you always so?"

Traveler gave her a look. "High praise from a drow. A bit of both, I'd imagine. And don't forget I lived with the darklings, too."

"Yes, I forgot about them, but that was intentional."

"What do we search for?" Ursi asked.

"Keep your eye on the port. You will know when you see it."

Traveler led them from one end of the port then back the other way. Ursi noticed at least a few other groups and individuals for the second time, meaning they were also watching the port, or them.

Traveler stopped, and the women did the same to see what he was looking at. Another fleet of giant ships coasted into the busy port. Tunik's crustacean ship was tied to the bow of a far larger lead ship like a trophy.

The ship anchored and gangplanks extended, a group of humanoid men clustered around it with large razor-edged tridents. The men had greenish skin, blue-green hair, visible gills on their necks, and pointed ears.

Elves began to exit the ship down the gangplanks.

"Do you know them?" Dr'as asked Traveler.

"The first ones, in dark blue clothing, are ocean elves. You can see the symbols of their kingdom on their chests and sleeves. Those after them are river and lake elves, likely a revered royal kingdom. You can tell from the sheerness of their dress, not thick at all. Sea elves wear greens and browns—the next group. The strange-looking elves in black are abyssal elves."

"They are strange looking. They are so tall and thin."

"They live very deep in the ocean and are rarely seen by land walkers. The city attracts many from far and wide, high above and deep below."

After the elves, a group of humans quickly ran off the ship, adults and children, but with no belongings or weapons. Traveler recognized three of them—the young woman and the two small children. Though many yards away, they somehow looked right at him.

"They saw us," Ursi said, distressed.

"Do not upset yourself. There's nothing to concern ourselves with."

"Who are they?"

"I don't know. We saw them only once, and it was brief before they returned below deck."

"Do you know what race they are?" Dr'amal asked.

"If I had to guess, maybe selkies."

"Selkies? Why would you guess that?" Dr'amal asked.

"The times I've been to the city before, I've seen parties like them. Identical to humans, no possessions, bare feet, children. Always they were selkies."

A flash of anger came over Dr'amal's face.

Dozens of green-skinned sea goblins, brawny, muscular frames in battle dress, flat noses, and large pointy ears marched off the ship as if into battle. But as sea goblins, their hands were webbed, eyes fish-like, and finned ridges ran from the top of their foreheads down their backs.

"The ones who shot at us?" Ursi asked.

"Not sure," Traveler answered.

Finally, they saw what they wanted; Tunik and his crew of sea kobolds, toadoids, and fish men were led off the ship by merrows. The green-skinned, green-haired female warriors were clad in battle armor, including helmets, and armed with long tridents.

"They've received what they deserved, your old friend," Dr'amal said. "The green-skinned men they're meeting are merrows too?" she asked.

"Yes."

"What will happen to them? It's not that they'll have any information to give."

"Merrows don't release prisoners, unless there's something to be gained. But they're klabautermann, so maybe they have mutual allies, or at least mutual interests."

"You're rooting for your old captain, even though he was plotting our capture?" Dr'amal asked.

"It's not as black and white for me as it is to you. Remember, they live here, we don't. I won't shed any tears for him, but I understand why he did what he did. He's a klabautermann sailor in an ocean empire ruled by merfolk, water elves, sirens, and elementals."

"We're being watched," Ursi whispered.

"We'll grab a meal before we head to the markets," Traveler said loudly.

He led them into the crowds. Ursi kept her eyes straight ahead. Dr'amal created a quick illusion spell to obscure her face.

The women had heard of ant men before but had never seen their race. The two humanoids were almost seven feet tall with four arms, red eyes, and mandibles that she knew had incredible crushing power. Without pupils in their red eyes, and at their distance away from them, there was no way to know for certain if they were watching them or simply looking in their direction.

Traveler walked fast for a human, when he wanted. Dr'amal continued to watch the two ant men as they moved deeper into the crowds toward the main city. The ant men maintained their stare in the same direction, as if they hadn't been watching them. But she still felt uneasy. She left her spell fade and looked straight up. The facade wall entrance to the City at Titan's Fall had to be well over two hundred feet tall. Even so, it was a tiny structure when compared to the Fall itself, and if the city's magic barrier ever gave way, the city would be swept away in the blink of an eye.

Ursi could feel herself shaking as she pushed through the crowds following Traveler and Dr'amal. There were so many people, too many people. She began to feel sick. She blinked uncontrollably then saw him, another fae, dressed in black with colored stones around his neck. Their eyes locked. They stood staring across the passersby between them. A hand grabbed her shoulder.

"Keep moving," Dr'amal said in her ear.

The drowess had to pull her away. The male fae-blood watched her.

"Which clan?" Dr'amal asked.

"One of the sea clans," Ursi answered.

"I take it they're not an ally."

"Fish don't like bears."

"Bears eat fish, don't they? Is it that kind of hatred?"

"In our realm, fish can eat bears too."

What disturbed the women more were the number of ogres, goblins, gargoyles, beast men, and other dark fae. They could barely keep up with Traveler, with his long strides. All the buildings around them were large towers, each with multiple shops or lodgings on the ground level. When their caravan master stopped, it was at an eatery packed with people.

As they sat at a table, Dr'amal watched Traveler eat. He seemed completely oblivious to their surroundings. There was no private seating or table in a corner. They sat at a small, round table near the entrance with people pushing past them every second. Ursi sat there fighting with all her might to remain calm; her clan hated large gatherings, even of their own kind. Traveler carried himself like a true resident of the city, as if he had always lived here. Dr'amal smiled as Traveler ate his meal, which looked like an extravaganza of octopus, crustaceans, and fish.

"You should eat," he said without taking his eyes off his plate.

"We're not hungry," Dr'amal said.

"Suit yourself."

"Here we are, but we are the outsiders, and you, the human, are the one at home."

Traveler looked up at her. "I've been here before."

"This eatery too."

"Yes. Many times."

"To have lived the life you have lived."

"What's wrong with you?" he asked Ursi.

The fae-blood glanced at him for a moment but returned her gaze to the center of the table.

"You know what's wrong with her," Dr'amal said. "Why did you bring us? You know neither one of us is suited for this."

"Our routine must be different for obvious reasons."

"Chose others next time. She saw another fae-blood."

"Yes, I saw him too."

"Which clan is he?" Ursi asked.

Traveler swallowed the last of his octopus. "Barracuda, I believe. I've seen them here in the city before. A few of them have a trading route here from Fae-Land. They trade with merfolk and water elves."

"Why are we here?" Ursi asked directly. The constant brushing of people at her back was increasing her annoyance.

"Someone could stab us in our backs, and we would never see it coming," Dr'amal said.

"Yes, I won't be taking you two along next time. We need to be moving about the city to see what there is to see."

"We need to leave," Ursi said.

"No, they know we're here."

The women looked around.

"Please don't do that," Traveler said. "You both already look like newcomers. No need to add scared newcomers to the list. I'm finished with my meal, and since neither of you will eat, we can head to the markets."

"I'd like to return to the lodgings," Ursi said.

Traveler leaned forward. "Give me your hand." He reached out and grabbed her right wrist. "You are in a state—cold, clammy, trembling." Traveler suddenly looked past her. Both women quickly looked back.

"Please don't do that," Traveler said.

"What did you see?" Dr'amal asked.

"I saw one of the children."

"Children?" Dr'amal asked. "The selkies?"

Traveler stood from the table. "We're leaving."

Dr'amal stood too. "When are we really leaving?"

"Ask them."

Dr'amal didn't turn as obviously as before. In the distance, she saw dozens of armed female merrows marching through the crowds to the eatery. There were far too many people for even them to pick someone out of the crowds. Besides, they were likely looking for a single elfess, humans, and a wolf-dog.

Adjacent to one large tower, a cluster of huts floated on a large pool. There were many such lodgings in the city. Two fish men strolled to them and dove into the pool to swim to their hut. Underwater, they passed through the entrance of their pocket-realm, and the illusion spell was gone.

Dr'amal and Ursi stepped through the other end of a short tunnel to be met by the Tree Shepherds' two nine-foot tree giants on guard. A literal army of elfin archers and berserkers, stood behind them, ready for battle.

"Where's Mr. Traveler?" Lady Aylen held her war tridents, Maiden Gwyness at her side.

Ursi didn't wait. She stormed off for the realm's huts in the distance.

"What's wrong with her?" Pangolin asked.

"She's exhausted. Her kind does not do well in such tight crowds. Mr. Traveler had an errand," Dr'amal explained.

The drowess laughed slightly at their gasps.

King Aereth approached the drowess, with her father, Dr'as.

"Did Mr. Traveler tell you what errand he was going on?" Lady Aylen asked.

"No. He simply said he'd return soon."

"Did he say when we'd leave?" Pangolin asked.

"We must have confidence in Master Traveler," Chief Ethor said. "He has gotten us this far. He will get us to our destination."

"One thing I can say about our caravan master," Dr'amal said. "He certainly has been in this city and many times before. He knew his way around exactly."

"What did you all see at the port?" Pangolin asked.

"Justice. That kobold captain of ours got what he deserved. The merrows they intended to turn us over to for bounty decided to arrest him and seize his ship instead. Also, we saw the passengers aboard the ship. We were sharing a ship with sea goblins."

"Goblins?" Lady Aylen asked.

"Any others?" King Aereth asked.

"Elves and other humanoids."

"Elves?" Lady Aylen asked.

"Yes, a few different races."

"We need to leave this city," Lady Aylen said emphatically.

Dr'amal shook her head. "We'd never make it. Mr. Traveler said they know we're in the city."

"They know?" the king asked.

"I didn't see anything but neither Ursi nor I knew what to look for. This city is also crawling with dark fae of all kinds, all the allies our enemies would enlist in tracking us."

"What does Mr. Traveler intend to do?" Lady Aylen asked.

"I agree with the elfin chief. Our caravan master is very drow-like in his cunning. He's been to this city before, sailed these waters before, traveled to Atlantea before, and has even lived in the fabled city. Who wishes a friendly wager? I say when our caravan master steps through the entrance realm that he will have our plan for escape and departure all in one. Who will bet me?" Dr'amal asked.

"Based on what nearly happened to us in the Great Forest, let's first make sure that whatever steps through the entrance realm looking like Master Traveler and his companion are indeed them and not some other creatures," Greenwig, the Tree Shepherd, said.

"And that our caravan master returns at all," Taylos, the desert elf, said.

The path from the port was but a single road through the city. It reminded Traveler of Caravan's Row in the Lands of Man. His dog was now a blue sea monkey hanging on his back as he moved through the crowds. Half of the people who lived in the city were those who had attempted to get to Atlantea and had given up. The other half were those still attempting the final leg to the fabled kingdom. Only a handful were such as he, who had successfully crossed into Atlantea.

As a port city, everything revolved around commerce. With endless ships to and from Atlantea and its surroundings, the business of trade never ceased. But it was a city without any central authority—no queens or kings, magistrates or elders. Codes of conduct and business was a collective pact agreed upon through the ages. One could do anything one wanted, even murder, as long as it didn't adversely affect the lucrative daily commerce. Fae could become very rich after a life of commerce in the city, which was why so many abandoned going to Atlantea after a certain number of attempts. Those who did enter and leave the fabled kingdom would invariably stop at the City at Titan's Fall.

Like Caravan's Row, the criminal class worked the streets. Pickpocketing was the common criminal practice. Outright robbery was far too dangerous a thing here with so many people always about and the fact that most were so individually dangerous.

Traveler blended in with the crowd. Nothing about him said newcomer to the ever-vigilant street thieves looking for an easy victim, but Traveler's eyes locked on one. The boy fae's head jerked up and the fishlike boy moved from his spot to follow Traveler.

Traveler stopped to wait for the fae-boy. The fish-like boy reached him and already had his hand out.

"You can hire me," he said with a smile.

Traveler threw a bag of coins to him. "There's more of that to come if you can do the task to my satisfaction. I'll walk through tomorrow at the same time. Find me."

The boy's gills fluttered as he giggled. "You won't be here tomorrow, human. But I'll do the task anyway. We don't like soldiers and assassins in our city. And we don't like those who bring them into our city."

Traveler smiled. "I like you. You will go far in your criminal career."

The fae boy giggled again and slipped back into the crowds.

Above the city, swarms of gargoyles circled, not behavior common to the race as gargoyles were not the most able flyers. They flew between destinations, but never remained afloat unless they had to—scouting. The key to life in such a city was to never attract attention, so his glance above appeared as casual as possible.

Traveler rode his striped horse through the crowd. He was far from the only rider in the city—beasts included griffin hybrids, lizards, turtles, and beetles. He would ride for hours through the busy streets. One could take months to ride through the entire city, but he knew his destination.

When he reached the open tavern across from the black tower, he dismounted and found a seat inside, back to the wall. Five cups of ale and three hours later, he was still seated. His horse had walked off, but now a large spider monkey lay on his table on watch. In the hours that had passed he saw male merrows come and go from the black tower prison. He saw no female merrows or any other races until a single sea kobold arrived in a long brown tunic with a large sack. They let the sea kobold in.

The metal door of the tower swung open again. Tunik stumbled out finally. He had been beaten savagely. Dried blood coated his face and clothes. Nifle and other kobolds from his crew trailed behind him. There were no fish men or toadoids from their crew. All the kobolds had been equally beaten. The new kobold in the long brown tunic followed after them after exchanging words with angry male merrows.

Tunik's battered head turned toward the open tavern. Traveler sat in the shadows, but he knew Tunik was scanning for him. The kobold's nose could pick up a scent, especially a human's, better than most fae.

The captain left his men where they stood as he struggled to walk. Tunik made his way across the street and through the crowd to stand at the caravan master's table.

"I never expected to see you again in my life."

Tunik collapsed in the empty chair at the table.

"Looks like I need a healer."

"You don't look like you have the money to pay a healer."

"Why are you here? Having trouble getting out of the city?"

"We got away from your ship, didn't we?"

Tunik's eyes closed. "My ship. The wretched females stole my ship." He opened his eyes. "You're going to help us get it back."

"That's your affair."

"If I had turned you in the moment the men wanted, this wouldn't have happened."

"It's my fault, is it?"

"Yes, it is. If you hadn't been such a good healer when you were part of my crew, I wouldn't have been so indecisive when it counted."

"Decisive in turning over a shipmate to be murdered."

"Murdered? I don't know that. And once you leave a ship, you are no longer part of the crew. You lose all standing and benefits of that family of the waters."

"Yes, I know. You told me before."

"I did warn you."

"Yes, and here we sit. Me sitting calmly. You beaten, penniless, and without a ship."

"What do you want, human? You are not the kind for gloating, so why are you here?"

"Time has come for me to use you for my purposes."

"How is that?"

"I need a captain for my ship."

A low guttural laugh grew in Tunik's belly. He tried to suppress it as much as possible as every part of his body screamed in pain. "I thought you didn't trust me, human."

"You'd do anything to get your ship back."

Tunik stared at him.

"I saw that you had sea goblins aboard too. Were they the ones who shot the cannon at my ship?"

Tunik said nothing.

"What's your arrangement with the merrows?"

"We are to leave the city."

"How do they intend for you to do that?"

"They don't care. They said if they see us again, they'll kill us."

"You know what I want. I know what you want. Make an offer. Whatever it is has to be done now."

"Maybe I'll decide to stay right here and not move one step."

"Then I will find another way, and we'll call this the end of our story."

"I can find others who will pay me a bounty."

"Hardly. You failed. Every one of them knows that by now, and they'd rather kill you on sight than listen to a word out of your mouth to redeem yourself. One gets only one chance with them, never a second. But do whatever you want. I don't care."

"You really aren't angry like a human would be."

"You simply did what your nature is. You're predictable just like every goblin I've ever met. You act like all your kind, according to your nature."

"I don't know if I like that description, human."

"I'm certain that you'll spend very little time thinking about it since you have to get out of the city with no money, no weapons, and no ship." Traveler stood and extended his hand. "Goodbye, Tunik."

"I do hate you, human." Tunik slapped his hand away. "You know my price."

"No, Tunik. I paid you already, remember. Three times the going rate."

"The merrows stole it."

"Not my problem."

"My men will never crew a ship for no money. You know that."

"It will be my ship. You'll captain it for me. With your capture by the merrows, you put off quite a few passengers who I'm sure also paid for no journey at all. Find them and find others. The others is where you make your money. We'll all get to the next sea city and we can go our separate ways from there."

"Won't your own people throw you overboard for this plan?"

"I know how to get to Atlantea."

"So do I. I can be their captain too."

"No. They'd throw you overboard."

"This is your plan?"

"The only plan for you."

"You're that desperate are you, human?"

"No, Tunik. I don't need you for my plan. I was going to hire another. The only advantage you pose is that you're not a stranger. Untrustworthy, but not a stranger. I'll take what I know for what I don't, but if that's not an option, I'll go with what I don't know."

"If it's my best and only plan, then you know my answer. I'll tell the men and we'll find our new passengers. Do I get to inspect my new ship?"

"My ship, and no."

"Then my answer is yes."

"While you're finding new passengers, I'd find a healer, too, and clean yourself up."

Tunik grinned. "I'll have to work through the pain, as all sailors do."

"Tunik, do understand this: I will throw you overboard or worse if you try to double-cross me again."

"I know that. I know all about you and your animal."

When Traveler stepped through the realm entrance, everyone was immediately relieved. For a second, the Tree Shepherds' two nine-foot tree giants, the elfin archers, and the human and fae berserkers relaxed. Then Tunik stepped through the realm's entrance.

The uproar was so loud, the royals and others couldn't get to the scene fast enough. Lady Aylen and King Aereth reached the realm entrance with Gwyness, Hobbs, and their royal guards. Pangolin and I'wulf had already arrived ahead of them.

On the ground was the sea kobold, Tunik, laughing so hysterically that he could barely breathe.

"I told you, human," he managed to say after a few moments. "See their faces. They do want to throw you overboard."

"Get off the ground, Tunik. You have work to do if we are to depart in the morning."

A smiling Tunik hopped to his feet. "Yes, Captain."

Never had so much been done in such a short span of time. Hobbs had the men break camp, and the sprites tucked all their huts into their magic bags. No one had time to argue or even fully think through Traveler's scheme. All anyone had to hear were the words "we set sail in the morning."

Traveler had the pech open up a magic bag that he tossed to them. The super-strong pech pulled out the caravan's ship purchased from the icarian. Everyone was happy to see it again, as it meant they would once again be in charge of their own journey.

Both Traveler and Tunik stepped aboard the ship, and all they saw were flashes of light. The ship grew larger. Compartments rose out of the deck. Their ship that looked like a dark silvery giant supine golem grew more arms to add to the dozen it had on each side, tucked in tight, fists clenched.

Their caravan master gave Pangolin the duty to get all the warriors aboard, while Hobbs saw to the nonwarriors. Both men smiled, as it was the division of duties they had been accustomed to all along the Trail. When every last human, fae, and animal was aboard, the remaining pech lifted up the ship and marched out of the realm.

They emerged from the realm entrance right at the giant port of Titan's Fall.

The work shifted to Tunik and his men, who were waiting on the docks. Titan's ship would have its own passengers, and Tunik's men had them board, every one of them walking up three separate gangplanks.

It was then that Young Quillen saw the girl step onto the main deck. He would have sworn they were human, a party of adults and children, clad in creme-colored loose clothing but not one of them wore shoes on their feet. The girl was among them. Her primary duty seemed to be watching over the smaller children of the group. Quillen realized that she was watching him too.

"Mr. Quillen."

Quillen turned to see their steward watching him suspiciously. "Yes, Mr. Hobbs?"

"Do you not have duties to attend to?"

"Yes, Mr. Hobbs." Quillen ran to the steps to the lower decks. As the passengers arrived, Titan's Crew was already below deck. A cloaked Hobbs and Pangolin were all that remained. The main deck would be manned by Tunik's crew of sea kobolds.

Titan's ship had two bridges now, the main one closest to the front of the ship and another behind it. The main bridge was where the leadership gathered, which now included Tunik as well as Nifle and his main men.

Traveler studied the list that Nifle had given him.

The bridges were identical. Here, Tunik and his own men would navigate the ship. A circular body-length mirror hung in the air at eye-level to show forward, smaller mirrors on each side to show port and starboard, with another large mirror apart to show the rear. Everyone kept one eye on the displays of the many fae and vessels in the port and another on the meeting. A large map table took up half the other side of the room.

"You see, Nifle, when you work for me, one day you'll become my captain, even if you're a human." Tunik cackled, and so did Nifle.

"The selkies are here, but what of the elfin parties you had?" Traveler asked.

"They found other transport the moment their webbed feet touched the ground and departed that same day," Tunik said.

"Fish men. Various water fae with names I can't pronounce." Traveler folded up the list and held it in his hand. "What of the sea goblins you had aboard?"

"What of them?" Tunik asked.

"You do know there's a city ship of them in the region."

Lady Aylen and King Aereth glanced at each other. Pangolin, I'wulf, and the lionoid fae berserker, Hax, also made note of the news. Greenwig, the Tree Shepherd, Chief Ethor with all three lead elfin knights, Dr'as and Dr'amal, Bragg, and Frog-Dor, who the men hadn't seen in so long, were all gathered in the room.

They noticed that Tunik wasn't surprised. "The sea goblins boarded the ship weeks before. They couldn't have been part of them."

"That would suggest at least one other goblin ship, then."

"Yes, it would. But we'll be sailing away."

"Were the sea goblins one of the parties with a bounty out for us?"

"No. Merrows, nereids, and tritons."

"Heard from either the nereids or tritons?"

"No, but I do expect to see them again before Atlantea. Am I sailing straight to Atlantea, or will you be throwing me overboard sometime along the way, when I've outlived my usefulness, Captain?"

"No, captain, no one is going overboard. We'll do it step-by-step, like you taught me. Kraken Wake is our first destination."

"Very good, Captain," Tunik said.

"What of the captain's gossip? What strange things have you heard recently?"

Tunik gave his men a wicked grin. "Like he's always been a captain of these waters. Yes, indeed, captain. Banshees!" he said with great emphasis.

"Gossip or truth?"

"I don't know. They said a ship barely escaped but not without massive death."

"Could such creatures be this far? And sirens wouldn't allow them into the region."

"I never got the chance to investigate or inquire further. Other matters came before me."

"Yes, that we know of."

"I'd spend no time thinking about banshees when its sirens we are more likely to encounter and that are the greater danger. But alas we travel away from the sirens' domain. Their archenemies, the merfolk and water elves, are not likely to allow them into this region."

"This is your bridge. We'll have ours."

"Which neither my men nor I am allowed to enter?"

"Correct."

"Then I will need Lovecraft."

"Lovecraft? I thought your serpent was gone."

"No. I wasn't about to let the merrows get him and eat him or worse. My men can find him."

"You want me to allow you to bring your sea serpent aboard my ship?"

"Lovecraft brings me luck, and with all the bad omens surrounding your party, we will need it. I will need it. Besides, my sea serpent is well behaved."

"If you can find your sea serpent in the next few moments, but we sail now."

Tunik laughed as he stared at the display mirrors. "Found, Captain."

Traveler and the others noticed several of Tunik's kobolds struggling to pull the sea serpent, in chains, out of the water and onto the dock. Traveler huffed with disgust.

"Don't be like that, Captain. Lovecraft is well cared for and loved by the men," Tunik said. "Our lucky charm."

"Tunik, what were some of the dark water fae that you told me any sight of was a sign of approaching doom?"

"Captain, don't say that," Tunik said. "Don't jinx the journey. I believe I taught you that, too."

"You also told me to beware of these dark fae too and not to sail if you saw one."

"Why are we talking about this?" Tunik asked.

"What are you referring to, Mr. Traveler?" Lady Aylen asked.

"Have any of you seen one of these dark water fae before?" Traveler looked at Tunik's men and the fae of the caravan.

"What are you talking about?" Lady Aylen asked impatiently.

Traveler pointed to one of the smaller display mirrors. The view changed when their caravan master waved a finger.

"What is that?" Gwyness asked, pointing.

"A crab centaur, Tunik?" Traveler asked.

Tunik's joking had disappeared. "That's as good a name as any. None of us can pronounce their fae name either."

"Get us out of here, Tunik."

"Aye, Captain," Tunik said.

CHAPTER FIVE

Open Waters

A nightmarish creature, from the waist up it was a sickly blue-skinned elf-like humanoid with seaweed-like hair down past its shoulders. Below the waist, its torso was a gigantic crab body. Its humanoid half had two arms on each side, one larger arm ending in a large pincer and a humanoid one holding a trident weapon below. The other three pairs of larger limbs protruded from its lower crab half.

Members of Titan's crew returned to their own bridge. They all gathered around the display windows. When the creature crawled out of the dark water, every fae on the port that saw it stopped their activities immediately and ran in fear. The creature kept its gaze on their ship though they were a mile away at least, and sailing farther away fast.

Traveler had Hobbs find Dr'as. The drow leader arrived with his daughter and several drow warriors. The staircase to the caravan's private decks was in their enclosed main-bridge structure. The drows joined everyone at the display mirrors.

"We have not seen its kind with our own eyes for quite some time," Dr'as said.

"Your people have experience with them," Traveler said.

"In the past, but not for some time. Our people encountered them when they came into our region."

"They're allies of the night drows though?"

"They are. But they have other centauroid allies that should concern us."

"Spider centaurs?"

"Yes."

"What are you two speaking about? Spider centaurs? Crab centaurs?" Lady Aylen asked. "I've never heard of their kind."

"They are dark fae, princess. Very rare but very dangerous."

"Even though your Mr. Tunik said the bounty was offered by only three races, could there have been others?" King Aereth asked.

"Or, sire, the three races were simply the intermediaries."

"How do these crab centaurs travel? Can they come after us?" Lady Aylen asked.

"They simply appear from the water. No one has ever seen a ship of theirs, only their evil forms. One or dozens," Dr'as said.

"Mr. Pangolin, how are you and Mr. I'wulf assigning the Cut-throats?" Traveler asked.

"I will spend most of my time here in the bridge with a team of them. Mr. I'wulf will see to the training, which will be daily."

"Mr. Traveler, what are your thoughts on this sole crab centaur?" Dr'as asked. "To appear as if to see us sail off. A city as enormous as this, how would it know?"

"It wouldn't, but if there was any weakness in our escape plan, it would be Tunik and his men. All it would need to do is maintain vigilance on him, if it was indeed searching for us."

"Your decision to retain him I completely agree with. Better we stay in here and he be the face of the ship to all outsiders."

"If the creature was at hand to see us sail, what might it do with that information?" King Aereth asked.

"Hopefully, we can get to Kraken's Wake without being delayed. We must stay hidden in our area, but if we are attacked in force, Tunik and his men will likely not be able to repel them alone. At that point, we must attack in force, not to repel but to utterly destroy. This is our only ship, and we won't get another."

"If it's destroyed, we're destroyed," King Aereth said.

"Yes, sire. It all comes down to that one hard fact," Traveler said.

The ship departed through the city's magic barrier and back into the thick white clouds of watery mist from the Fall. Again, visibility was gone, so they had to assume that Tunik and his men would be preoccupied with their ship duties. For Titan's Crew, they had much to busy themselves with.

Pangolin and his men sat on the floor helping Estus and two fae berserkers. The one had features of a boar and tusks. The other's mouth looked like a cat. They all had stacks of arrows, which they prepared by painting the tips with a magical concoction.

Lady Aylen rarely left the front of the main display window. Courtesy of the brownies, she and Gwyness had more comfortable chairs to relax in.

"What do you make of it all, Gwyness? Crab centaurs? I hadn't yet gotten over the other centaurs we met in Faë-Land Major. Winged centaurs and ones with bull horns, part hippogriff, cat centaurs, tiger centaurs, and panther centaurs."

"I would take any of them over this new one."

Pangolin joined them at the display mirrors. He would periodically check them, but they all knew that the only view to be seen for days would be thick white mist. King Aereth returned from the lower decks to join them in their daytime vigil.

"I agree. That was no creature, more like a demon, staring at us. What do you think of Mr. Traveler's plan, Mr. Pangolin?" Lady Aylen asked.

"I approve, Lady Aylen," the berserker said.

"Approve? I thought you'd be of my mind on this. Our ship is being piloted by a scoundrel who attempted to turn us in to our enemies."

"It's brilliant."

"Brilliant?"

"Lady Aylen, none of those enemies will think to look for us with such a fae, and a disgraced one at that."

"This fae is nothing but a pirate, a pirate with a sea serpent resting on top of his building," Lady Aylen said.

"It only eats fish, Lady Aylen." King Aereth tried to hold in a laugh.

"No sea serpent only eats fish. If anyone disappears, we know where to look—in its gut. What are your thoughts, sire?" Lady Aylen asked. "We are all glad to be on our way and in full command of our own ship again, but am I the only one ill at ease?"

"Certainly not, m'lady?" Gwyness said.

"I echo the maiden. But our caravan master has again taken the wisest course available to us."

"Mr. Pangolin said it brilliantly."

"Yes."

"There is still Mr. Traveler's invisible goblin ship," Lady Aylen said.

"And this crab centaur creature," Gwyness said.

"Demon. I heard the drows speak about it. I have a real sense of foreboding," Lady Aylen said.

"The danger is there but it has been with us for our entire time on the Trail," King Aereth said. "But our final port draws near. That is what's important, even if Oughtred is still out there."

"Yes, sire."

"We'll ask him if we can speak freely. I do not see why we couldn't since this section is secure from the rest of the ship."

Traveler appeared on the bridge off and on, busy with his own preparations. The other half of the room was taken up by the map table. Its magic map appeared as if it, too, were a mirror, but it displayed the frightening motion of the ocean as if seen from the heavens. Hours later, their caravan master returned with their five musicians, the Brothers Brimm, led by their man, Johnter. However, they were dressed for battle, no longer in their fanciful, colored dress. Around the waists of four of the men were thick belts with long pouches, but there was no dagger. Theirs contained white metal wind tabor pipes. Johnter had a satchel over his neck, and daggling at his side was a small lute. The string instrument was made of some opaque material. Traveler had them sit and relax at the map table.

Later, Traveler returned with the caravan's kilmoulis, Mr. Elman, and the other male half-elves. The half-elf Elman possessed the gift of magic sight and could see farther than other fae in the caravan. The caravan's sixteen kilmoulis, with their huge noses covering most of their faces, may not have been attractive, but their magical sense of smell made them invaluable. Their main bridge had two stories—the main room and a spire up to a smaller upper level. He led them up the spire's staircase to the second level.

"Putting Mr. Elman's talents to use, Mr. Traveler?" Lady Aylen asked when he came back down.

"Mr. Elman's and our kilmoulis, princess. He may see nothing. They may pick up no scent at all on the ocean breeze, but there's a chance they will. Sometimes survival comes down to luck alone."

When Traveler returned again for the noon meal, he was not alone. The royals and Gwyness's kirins followed. Traveler's dog also appeared, now in the form of a dog-like kirin with elements of all three. Traveler sat, and all four animals sat next to their masters. Hobbs and the food servers came up from below decks soon after with plates, trays, buckets, pots, cups, and more.

"The ship has another bridge of sorts on the lowest deck," Traveler revealed. The time went fast with the caravan master informing them of the protocols and duties of the ship. "There, many of Tunik's men will watch the depths below. Bottom-watchers is the term. Sounds lowly, but it is a very important role. Tunik will also have his own crow's nest to watch the skies and surface of the oceans as we sail out of the mist, just as Mr. Elman and his half-elfin comrades will do for us."

"Does Mr. Tunik have enough men for all the tasks?" King Aereth asked.

"We're manning the cannons, sire."

The king nodded. "That was my concern."

"Every last pech, sire," Hobbs said, who had joined them for the noon meal with the female half-elves, Quillen, and the fenodyree. The hairy sprites were never far away from the kirins.

"How long will it be before we are free of the cloudy mist of Titan's Fall, Mr. Traveler?" the king asked.

"Five days, sire."

"Do we risk attack while enshrouded by the mist, Mr. Traveler?" Gwyness asked.

"If at all, maiden, it would be from below, but I don't expect it."

"Here we are on the ocean, and we're still eating the meat from Mr. Bragg's Great Forest hunt," Lady Aylen smiled.

"Enjoy it, princess, while you can. We are land-walkers on the Oceanus Omnis and its ancient magic takes away from us. The ancient magic of the Great Forest gives."

"What of me, then, Mr. Traveler? A water elf raised as a land-bound human."

"You have the best of both worlds, princess. Did you not feel it when you were swimming free in the ocean during our escape?"

"I did. A strange feeling. As if I was home, but home in a place I had never been before in my life. I wish those water elves aboard your Mr. Tunik's ship had remained. I would have liked to speak to them."

"Yes, but you will have plenty of opportunities to speak to water elves. We will stop in at least two cities before we get to Atlantea."

"Kraken's Wake doesn't sound very inviting, Mr. Traveler," Gwyness said.

"It definitely is not."

"The other city?" Lady Aylen asked.

"The elfin city of White Waters."

"Then Atlantea?" Lady Aylen asked with anticipation.

"Hopefully, princess. Hopefully, there will be no other stops."

Traveler leaned over the map table. The image of their ship moved through white clouds on the magical map. Nothing else could be seen, but the caravan master stared at it anyway. Hobbs slowly neared him.

"Yes, Mr. Hobbs?"

The steward scanned the giant map table too. "Sorry to disturb you, sir."

"No problem, Mr. Hobbs."

"May I ask something of a more personal nature, sir?"

"Of course."

"One of our younger members seems quite smitten with a member of one of our passengers."

Traveler smiled. "Female?"

"Yes, sir. The party that looks human, what are they? Selkies? I am not familiar with that race."

"They can magically transform into seals."

"I see."

"They are a benevolent race, no danger. They spend most of their time in human form. The why of when they take seal form is one of much speculation. They are a people as private as our fae-bloods, so very little is known, other than the stories. I would not concern yourself with it."

"Very good, sir. I thought it wise to inquire."

"I'm glad you did. If one of the men were smitten with a mermaid, then we'd have reason for concern."

"Oh, sir."

"Men run off with mermaids all the time."

"Yes, you hinted at that back when we were in Faë-Land and we saw them for the first time."

"The mermaids here in these waters are far more powerful and plentiful."

"Sir, you seem very fixed on the map today, though there is nothing to see."

"I'm watching the movement of the mist. Ships may be invisible, but they are still solid. These watery clouds go around them, not through."

Klabautermann packed the forward bridge commanded by Tunik. He paced back and forth in front of the display mirrors, as all around him, sea kobolds polished harpoon weapons, painted the tips of crossbow arrows, ate raw fish while working, moved in and out of the bridge area to the main deck, stacked metal shields, and gossiped in the loudest possible voices to be heard over the rumble of the Fall.

"Do you believe him, Captain?" Nifle asked, watching the display mirrors.

"Don't be foolish. If Traveler said he saw a city ship of sea goblins, that's what he saw. He knows what they look like. We ran away from enough of them when he was part of the crew."

"City ships don't go away," Nifle said.

"No, they don't. It's out there. I can feel it."

"What are our chances of escaping it in the Fall's mist?" another kobold asked.

"Fifty-fifty. But then, they can simply wait for us to emerge from the mist." Tunik stopped pacing and grabbed one of the men. "Go to their bridge, and tell Traveler to make sure those cannons are ready to fire." He pushed the kobold toward the door. "Run!"

The sea kobold ran out of the command cabin. On the main deck, with the secure translucent covering above, armed kobolds were spaced every few feet or so to watch over the side. The ship was moving fast.

Something caught the eye of a deck sea kobold. He stared out into the thick, billowy clouds of mist. There was a brief distortion. "Impact!" he yelled.

Every kobold on the deck was knocked off their feet, but none lost hold of their weapons. The shadow of the city ship engulfed theirs as it came out of invisibility.

Battle cries erupted from above as sea goblin warriors dove from their own ship many decks above.

The kobolds were blinded by one flash from the side of their ship after another, then the explosive booms as the hull of the goblin ship was ripped apart. In unison, the large mechanical arms of their golem ship engaged, reached, grabbed the goblin ship and pulled up just as the goblin cannons fired. The only thing hit were some of the falling sea goblin warriors, others bounced off the ship's translucent covering.

Tunik's kobolds spilled out of their bridge with crossbows and let loose a volley of arrows, which passed through the covering. Arrows rained down from the goblin ship.

The explosion was so loud that kobolds dropped their crossbows to grab their ears. The goblin ship had been blown in two. Their golem ship cannons didn't stop firing. Tunik had joined his men on the deck to see the goblin ship disintegrate as in sank below the ocean's surface.

The kobold captain stepped back to the display mirrors in the bridge to watch the city ship disappear for good. The waters were littered with dead or screaming goblins and wreckage of their ship. Their ship lurched forward to speed away.

Tunik turned. Traveler entered with the royals and other members of his caravan such as the large berserker in the strange earthen armor and some of the elves with their long bows.

"Well, Mr. Traveler, I surely didn't teach you such savage cannon warfare like that. What kind of cannons do we have?"

"The biggest ones I could buy."

"That you did. My ears are still ringing."

"You did drill into me that a proper ship must have proper cannons."

"I think I understand you now, Mr. Traveler. Everyone wants to get to Atlantea for riches, but you lived there already and got your riches. While everyone used their riches for recreation and good age-old debauchery, you used yours to personally fund your travels and have the means to buy whatever was necessary to succeed, then you traveled to other realms and even other worlds with star elves. I can only imagine what riches you acquired from them."

"They gave me a sword. I had to learn how to use it."

Tunik smiled. "I'd say we'll have smooth sailing to Kraken's Wake. The only thing ahead are adaro, but after this display of force, I'm no longer concerned. You blow apart one of their ships, and they'll scatter in every direction never to return."

"That they will."

"Well, Captain, I'll continue with my duties," Tunik said with a nod.

"Thank you, Captain."

Tunik turned and yelled at his men to get back to work. Traveler took out his telescope from his cloak and watched the wreckage of the goblin ship that grew farther and farther away.

"Was it the same ship you saw before, Mr. Traveler?" King Aereth asked.

"It was, sire, so at least that danger will not trouble us again."

"What are these adaro he mentioned, Mr. Traveler?" Pangolin asked.

"A race of mermen archers. Think of them as marauders from our lands but no match for our ship." Traveler removed his telescope from his eye. "I'll return to my maps." Their caravan master walked back to their main bridge.

His dog, back in his aquatic form, followed.

A grinning Pangolin looked at the royals.

"Why are you so happy, Mr. Pangolin?" Lady Aylen asked.

"We have cannons that can blow apart city ships ten times our ship's size."

The royals laughed.

Traveler saw them first on the map table then announced it to the crew. News spread fast throughout the decks, and in moments, the main bridge room was packed with humans and fae. The Tree Shepherds cast a spell to expand the display mirrors for all to see.

"Mr. Hobbs, can't I stand on the deck? I'll be fine," Quillen begged, showing his magic sketch book.

"Leave it to me, Mr. Hobbs," Pangolin said. "I'll watch him."

Pangolin gestured to a few of the berserkers to accompany him. Quillen raced out the door to the main deck. A day had passed since they finally emerged from the white cloudy mist of the Fall. There remained a layer of light mist on the ocean, and if one listened carefully, one could still hear the rumble of the Fall's crashing deluge. But the beautiful open ocean was all there was with the sunlight beaming. Sea kobolds also lined the side of the ship for the coming view.

Members of Tunik's fae passengers eagerly waited. Quillen's eyes caught sight of her. The selkies were among the fae. The adolescent girl turned, saw him, and smiled. Quillen stood there, smiling back.

"Mr. Quillen, is something wrong?" Pangolin asked.

The boy snapped out of it. "Oh, no, Mr. Pangolin."

"No longer want to sketch anything?"

"No, I do, Mr. Pangolin."

Quillen ran to the side of the ship but then realized he was running toward the girl.

"You can stand here," she said as she made space.

The beasts appeared. A school of ophiotaurus moved by jumping above the surface, diving back in, and swimming fast. Their fish-scaled upper torsos were that of a bull. The other half was of a long-tailed fish. The sunlight reflected off them to give a flickering effect as they swam by. The ship sailed fast, but the noble beasts overtook them, hundreds of the animals.

The girl watched Quillen sketch them. She appeared quite impressed. Quillen managed to keep his attention on his drawing, glancing at the beasts, then rending a near-perfect likeness by pen.

"You're very gifted," an older woman standing next to the girl said. Quillen's sketching caught the attention of a few of the adult selkies.

Pangolin leaned over as well to look at the drawing. He looked at the two berserkers with him and pointed at Quillen. "If we ever need an artist to defeat a creature in battle, the boy is our man."

The berserkers laughed.

"You are passengers too?" the older woman asked Pangolin.

"Yes, we are," he answered.

"Human," the man next to her said. "You are far from your lands."

"We are."

"We are fortunate to have a good captain on this voyage," she said.

"He is."

"Not the klabautermann," she said. "The real captain. We were on the klabautermann's previous ship. He was not a good captain. We are grateful our circumstances changed."

Pangolin said nothing but smiled.

She leaned down to the younger girl. "That is enough for today. We have seen the beautiful ophiotauruses, and if you ever forget what they look like, you can look at this young man's drawings."

Quillen rubbed the page of the drawing, ripped it out, and handed it to the girl.

"Oh, no." She looked at the notebook. The image he drew magically reappeared on another page.

"It is a magic book," he said. "This is for you."

"Say thank you," the woman said.

"Thank you." The girl gladly took the page.

"We return to our cabin," the woman said.

The woman had her arm around the girl. The man walked alongside them and all the selkies followed them toward the steps leading below decks.

Quillen stood watching the girl until they were gone. He suddenly turned. Pangolin and the berserkers were watching him, then burst out laughing. He ran back inside the main bridge room.

Traveler spent most of his time at the map table in their bridge room. Often alone, he watched for the smallest sighting. The magic map could show even the movement of waves and sudden ripples. He sat sipping from a mug.

"Must you stare at your map all day, Mr. Traveler?" Lady Aylen had a plate of food in her hand and sat near him to see what caught his eye at the moment. Dots were appearing and disappearing at a dizzying pace. "How do you make sense of all this?"

"Years of training, princess."

Lady Aylen stopped raising her cup to her mouth. "What was that large shape I just saw?"

Traveler laughed. "I'm not going to tell you. Eat your meal, princess."

"I'm sorry we doubted you, Mr. Traveler."

"Doubted?"

"Your plan is working. We maintain command of the ship and a native to these waters is the face of our ship to fool any searching for us. Is this how it will be all the way to Atlantea?"

"I wish I could give you a certain answer, princess, but I cannot. Sailing these waters is one of constant change based on the circumstances. A warship or a creature or a storm from nowhere can change everything."

"Was Mr. Tunik right about you and Atlantea and your riches and beyond?"

"He is, but any good caravan master finds their own way to do the job, knowledge and one's bag of tricks, as the fae are fond of saying amongst themselves. Lady Aylen, you need to know that these sea cities we'll dock at are extremely dangerous. I wasn't boasting when I said you will need to take the lead. Kraken's Wake is a royal city divided into a matriarchal section ruled by mermaids and ocean nymphs called nereids. There is a smaller patriarchal section ruled by tritons and sea centaurs."

"Not more centaurs."

"And a third section ruled by no one. It has many names. I know it by the name the klabautermann use—the Kelp Lands."

"Shouldn't you tell the others about this?"

"I will. I know how much everyone misses our leadership meetings."

Lady Aylen laughed.

"I'm telling you because you will have the biggest burden of us all, and I know you struggle with that knowledge. You are not just a water elf, but one with water elemental powers. One of the races we will encounter will be the undines, water elementals. You will be key in helping establish an alliance with them."

"Why is that important?"

"Sylphs, air elementals, are allies to the celestial and star elves. They await us in Atlantea."

"What of the water elves?"

"They will be in the elfin city of White Waters. We must maneuver through the danger and politics of Kraken's Wake first. We do that, and everything else will be easy in comparison."

"I hesitate to ask, but why is the city called Kraken's Wake?"

"Because, princess, the city was built on the skeletal remains of an ancient kraken that was, according to legend, the only living thing on Pan-Earth that could slow down a marching Titan. Legend or not, the skeletal remains are real. But there's more."

"More?"

"The waters around Kraken's Wake are the largest kraken breeding grounds in all of the Oceanus Omnis."

"Krakens? There are more than one?"

"Forget the fable of our lands, princess, with the sole monstrous creature in all of Pan-Earth. There isn't only one octopus or squid in our oceans. The Oceanus Omnis has many of the creatures."

"Why would any people build a city there then?"

"Because it's also the safest place in the Oceanus Omnis when it comes to kraken attacks. The krakens actually protect the city from fleets of other races. We won't have to worry about them ripping us apart and devouring us one by one, or many at a time, but the same cannot be said of the fae empires who command the city and its surroundings."

Titan's Crew came to view Traveler sitting at the magic map table as a lone Titan looking down from the heavens to ensure their safety on their ocean journey. It gave everyone a sense of comfort because, despite the school of beautiful ophiotauruses, they knew deadly creatures lay ahead. After all, they headed to an ancient city known as Kraken's Wake.

Traveler even ate his meals at the map table, his dog always at his side. Dr'as came up the steps to the bridge room alone.

"Dr'as," Traveler greeted.

"Traveler." The drow leader stopped at the table. He saw the incredible movement of currents and fauna appearing briefly then disappearing on the map. "Am I disturbing you?"

"Not at all. I can watch and listen at the same time."

"How do you make any sense of this? Magic maps have been used by fae for centuries, but this map would be dizzying for an argus giant with its hundred eyes."

"I manage, but I doubt you came to praise my talents as a reader of magic maps of the Oceanus Omnis."

"Tell me about the magic of this ocean realm. The magic drains us land walkers, as these water fae call us, but strengthens all water-born like our Lady Aylen, though she was raised far from here. Are there any other aspects to this magic of the Oceanus Omnis?"

"Such as?"

"Such as..." Dr'as couldn't get himself to say the words.

"Dr'as, despite all my time in the magic lands, I am certainly not capable of reading your thoughts. You must speak them out loud."

"What race is Frog-Dor?"

"Mr. Frog-Dor?"

"Is he human?"

"Part human."

"Part human? He doesn't have pointy ears."

"Dr'as, humans and elves aren't the only two races who have married and had children."

"What then?"

"Possibly elemental."

"Elemental? He doesn't exude any such power to be part elemental."

"A grandparent?"

Drow thought for a moment. "Part human, part elemental, our Frog-Dor, the wizard."

"Dr'as, what are you trying to say? Has something happened?"

"Something's happened, but calm yourself. It's nothing serious to anyone but me as a father."

Traveler smiled then started to laugh.

"Is this realm enchanted?"

"Your daughter is helping Frog-Dor regain his confidence and get accustomed to regularly using his magic."

"As you instructed."

"What's happened, Dr'as?"

"My daughter must be enchanted by this realm."

"Are you soon to have a son by marriage, Dr'as?"

"As long as he is a full-blooded drow."

"Yes, the realm can have that effect on people. There are mermaids, water nymphs, and water fairies. But no such enchantment is needed here. We've been traveling the Trail going on a year, Dr'as. Such things happen."

"Not when it comes to my daughter."

"Does Dr'amal listen to you normally?"

"Yes."

"That means no. My advice to you is to ignore whatever feelings you imagine are growing between them."

"I'm not for imagination."

"Yes, you are, Dr'as. You're drow, and you're D'Shar. We need Frog-Dor to be at his best. From here to Atlantea we'll encounter more wizards, male, female, and animal, than you've ever encountered in your life. He's the only conjurer wizard in our caravan. We should have an army of them. Your daughter is helping Frog-Dor become that army. Please leave her alone."

"I'll leave her alone, but I'm going to keep a steady eye on the both of them. And animal wizards? I've never heard of such a thing."

"Fae with animal companions, have you heard of that?"

"Of course I have, but not one's animal companion being the wizard."

"We may encounter them."

"We have yet to speak about the crab centaurs we sighted."

"Yes, another ally race of night drows."

"If night drows await us, it will be in Atlantea."

"Yes, I agree."

"Night drows like sea cities no more than we do."

"I assume you have spells cast to detect them."

"Of course. They are our blood enemies, as we told you before, or that you know of since you've lived with drow-kind in the past."

"Cast a spell to located spider centaurs, too."

"Are you serious?"

"You're unable to cast one for crab centaurs since you've never encountered them."

"Why not scorpion centaurs? Those demons are as rare as spider centaurs."

"The rarity is the number of sightings not their number in existence. Cast the spell. Spider centaurs are blood allies of night drows and crab centaurs. It wouldn't hurt."

"Do you know what you're saying? If I was even to mention this to my men, it would cause panic amongst them."

"Then don't tell them."

"I can't cast such a spell alone."

"Then only tell your most trusted."

"All my men are my most trusted. I'll see to it. I regret now that I ever came out here to speak to you. Do you truly believe we would encounter such creatures?"

"No, but then we should never have seen a crab centaur or a Nemain in the Great Forest or a spell-talker in Faë-Land Minor, or undead minotaurs in the Centaur Fields."

"Yes, an evil pattern. I'll see to the spell."

Dr'as left Traveler and his dog to return below deck. Deep worry was etched into his dark-blue face.

The caravan's elfin races guarded the decks below, from Chief Ethor to the elfin questing knights and Bragg's comrades. Their Titan's Caravan controlled six decks, each with its own door to a pocket-realm.

The second deck held the training realm, which was in constant use. Gone were the days of marching to be replaced by constant weapons and battle training. The realm was a vast green field with mountains in the distance. I'wulf and Hax, the lionoid fae berserker, took turns overseeing the training of the four hundred Cut-Throats with their one hundred chamroshes. The men had to master fighting while in flight with their winged boots, firing with crossbows with one hand and defending with a shield on the other. They also had to relearn fighting as a unit with their eagle hounds because now both man and beast would be in mid-air for the battle.

The heavy weapons team was now commanded by Estus, their weaponsmith, as King Aereth had his own new duties. Dozens of teams of four to five men continued to master firing a variety of projectiles at rapid-speed to hit any target from miles away. Besides the one thousand men, Estus still maintained control of the caravan's armor golems. The moving suits of armor encircled the weapons team to protect them from any would-be attackers with swords and axes.

Maiden Gwyness had gotten her own talarian sandals and was growing in confidence with her ability to fly and attack with her slender dual war hammers.

"Very good, maiden!" Nirgund yelled.

The berserker had his own battle training routine, alternating between the use of his new crossbow and his trusty halberd weapon. He, too, practiced fighting with his alphyns at his side. Another straw dummy hoisted on a stake in the ground received the fury of his attacks and that of his thirteen reptilian hounds. Nirgund used his talarian sandals not to fly but move on the ground quicker.

Gwyness continued her attacks on multiple straw dummies. "Confidence, movement, speed" were the words Pangolin told her. The only word that flashed in her mind was "kill." That was what she would have to do, as they all would.

She noticed Bragg in the distance near a mountain. The dwelf didn't need talarian sandals to fly. His golem stood as his motionless target as the dwelf fired his arrows while sailing through the air.

The eighty or so fae human mercenaries also trained. For them, they practiced with the longest pole-arms and pick weapons they could find. Humans weren't stronger than fae so their style was to keep attackers at bay and protect themselves and any behind them, until their caravan's elfin archers could attack.

Gwyness stopped training when she saw Pangolin appear from the real entrance.

"Hello, Mr. Pangolin."

"Maiden Gwyness, you are becoming a natural at flying."

"Have you seen Lady Aylen? She's fearless and fast."

"You'll be able to match her skills soon."

"I hope so. Is it quiet above?"

"A quiet ocean for as far as the eye can see, even in Mr. Elman's eyes. Do you have your practice war hammers?"

"I do."

"Then practice with me. Try to strike me."

She laughed. "Strike you?"

"Yes, I will go to the mountain and back. I'll deflect your blows with my weapons. See how many you can land."

"I can—"

Pangolin flew off through the air toward the mountain. Gwyness fumbled with her war hammers but flew after him.

I'wulf dropped from the air nearby Nirgund and his alphyns. "Mr. Nirgund, is it me or does there seem to be a lot of amorous feelings in the air lately?"

"I would say so, Mr. I'wulf."

"There are beautiful mermaids in this Kraken's Wake, and mermaids are fond of humans."

"I like your thinking, Mr. I'wulf."

Tunik sat wedged in his captain's chair in front of the main display mirror. He drank from an oversized mug. His men stood around him doing the same. Nothing but blue waters to the horizon.

"Two ships aft!" one of the sea kobolds yelled from their map table.

Tunik pulled himself out of the chair and met him at the map table. Kobolds were all around it, some with spectacles, other with telescopes, watching everything that moved on it. He leaned to look at the two ships depicted on the magic map.

"Increase speed!" Tunik yelled back.

"Aye, Captain!" a kobold yelled from the display mirrors.

"They're moving away from us," a kobold nearest him at the map table said.

"Good. We're going to be as unsociable as we can until we get to the sea city."

Tunik returned to his chair.

"Where's Nifle?"

He asked at the moment his first mate entered the bridge room with another sea kobold.

"Saw the two ships?" he asked.

"They're moving away."

"Nothing else to report, then, Captain."

"Have you seen our masters?"

Nifle chuckled. "They never leave their bridge cabin and decks."

"What's to happen to us when we reach Kraken's Wake?" a kobold asked Tunik.

"We shall see."

"But what do you think, Tunik?" Nifle asked. "What do we do? We have no ship."

"We'll have a ship."

"When?" Nifle asked.

"Where?" another kobold asked.

"We should take this ship," a kobold said.

"There will be no foolish mutiny here," Tunik said. "Once we arrive at Kraken's Wake, it won't be long before all aboard are known to the city. Once that is revealed, it will spread across the oceans. When that happens, we don't want to be on this ship or anywhere near it."

"He ditches us, or we ditch him. What about a ship?" Nifle asked again.

"I'll get us a ship, Nifle. I always do. Then we'll sail back to Titan's Fall and find those merrows who stole ours and get it back, even if we have to slay every one of them."

"If that was your plan, some of us should have stayed behind in the city to watch the merrows," Nifle said.

"I did do that, Nifle. I haven't been a captain on these waters for so long by being a moron. We have many friends in the city. The merrows don't."

"I say, Tunik, we don't even go to Kraken's Wake," another kobold said.

"Why?" Tunik asked.

"You know why."

"We can keep that secret to ourselves."

Hobbs made his daily rounds, moving from the bridge room to the different pocket-realms below deck. All day most of the caravan trained for battle. The steward welcomed it, as they'd had little opportunity while marching through the Great Forest.

The two thousand lizard minders trained with the animal men in a yellow grassy-marshy realm filled with giant trees. Their giant lizards—blues, yellows, greens, and oranges—ran through the plains between the trees. The men had been building up their stamina to run with the reptilian stampede in exercises. The lizards on their own could run faster than any of the men, but they never left their crossbow-touting masters too far behind.

The several hundred animal men—frog men, lizard men, squirrel men, raccoon men, possum men, fox men, rabbit men, bird men, mouse men—trained with their giant animals, jackalopes, and enfields. To see giant crabs, turtles, ducks, cranes, and the mole-looking fae on his giant moose fight with flocks of the enfields and hopping jackalopes was jarring.

Hobbs's attention was drawn to a couple of Bragg's elfin comrades watching the Diomedian Mares run together in a circle on the edges of the realm.

One of his guards stepped through the realm's entrance. "Need help, Mr. Hobbs, summoning them for the noon meal?" Tyfer asked.

"No, thanks, Mr. Tyfer. I'll wait for a quiet moment to do so."

The man who lived for so many years in the magic lands stood next to the steward. "We have quite a fighting force here, Mr. Hobbs."

"We do."

"Mr. Traveler won't say it aloud, but I fear we may be in full battle soon."

"Let us hope it is on our terms and on solid ground."

"I concur completely. I don't relish the notion of being dumped in these waters. A simple fish the size of a horse could carry us off to its depths so that we'd never be seen again. But our place will be indoors, away from battle."

"Unless it is to repel intruders invading the ship."

"True, but we will be fine, Mr. Hobbs."

"Have you heard of this Kraken's Wake?"

"Not at all. None of us have ever gotten this far. We never even got to the Great Forest before."

"As long as we don't actually see a kraken."

Tyfer chuckled. "I hope not, Mr. Hobbs. I've heard some are so large that their tentacles can pull an elfin flying caravan from the heavens."

Far from the busy main deck and their bridge commands, the secluded circular room was in the center of the last deck of the ship. It was cold and dimly lit except for the display mirrors, which each had their own glow. The glass floor was for direct viewing of the depths of the ocean. The ship was moving fast and the aquatic life flashed by in one long blur. But Tunik's bottom-watchers, fifteen sea kobolds, sat in their shell chairs in front of the display mirrors or lay on the floor with their faces pressed against the glass. They were the look-outs for anything that came at the ship from beneath it.

They hated their job but it had to be done. It was a constant mental battle against the boredom and sleep. But for the sake of the ship and the lives of everyone aboard, the mundane task had to be done. In a way, they were as important as the ship's captain.

"Oh, no!" one kobold jumped up from his spot on the ground and grabbed his telescope.

Other kobolds in front of a display mirror saw the shadow deep below.

"Go tell Tunik, quick!" another kobold yelled, jumping from his shell chair.

Several kobolds opened the main door and bolted from the room.

"Hold on, this will be close."

King Aereth entered the forever-dusk pocket-realm of the väki with its wall of black volcanic rock encircling a black mountain with a cavernous interior. He sat at a table with volumes of books in the lonesome magic hut with the book vault of the lost kingdom of Rivermouth. Lady Aylen sat at her own table reading her own ancient tomes with elfin symbols.

"How are your language skills progressing, Lady Aylen?" the king asked.

"Sire, we will be in this Kraken's Wake soon enough. We'll see if all that Mr. Traveler has been telling me is true: I'll simply be able to speak elfish like I have all my life."

"I'll see if all this reading about royal protocols will be of the value we hope. Not sure how useful I'll be without being able to speak elfish."

"Have no fear, sire. Mr. Traveler can speak them all. He'll guide us."

"Lady Aylen, your ears."

She was on her feet at her table. "Something's...approaching us. From deep below."

King Aereth rose. "What do you mean?"

"I can sense it. Hold onto something, sire."

Lady Aylen moved so quickly that she reached the steps to the command room before King Aereth could react. She ran up two decks and leapt up the final steps to land on the floor in the enclosed bridge. She startled the Cut-throats but saw Traveler sitting in front of one of the display mirrors. Lady Aylen ran to the main door.

"No, princess, stay inside. We can see from here." Traveler leaned forward from his chair and waved his hand in front of the mirror. Suddenly, it was as if the walls and ceilings had disappeared. For the first time, they saw the half-elves, kilmoulis, and a couple of the bird men on the upper loft section, seemingly standing on the air, as their floor went invisible.

More Cut-throats came up the steps to the main bridge, then elfin archers, and King Aereth. A group of väki trotted up the steps. They appeared as always with their frowning faces, surly disposition, and charred-brown-and-orange attire. The ship lurched so hard to port that all had to brace themselves as the entire vessel tilted to one side.

The gigantic form burst through the surface of the ocean about fifty or so feet away, but it could have been fifty miles away. It would not have mattered. The giant snakish form was at least ten times the size of their ship. The head shot up into the sky toward the clouds. Its lucent dark-green body with a rough tan underbelly kept rising up. For a moment, day became night as its head blocked the sun. Then the head arched back downward.

"Everyone, brace for impact!" Traveler yelled.

It seemed like an eternity for the giant creature's head to descend and crash back into the ocean. First the head, then the rest of its colossal body followed, taking equally as long to disappear beneath the surface.

The ship fell like a stone, tipping off the edge of the newly created trough in the wake of the creature. A wall of water rose, and when it reached its peak, its tidal wave crashed down. The ship shot forward into the waters around it to avoid the violent crash of the wave. The vessel violently lurched and tilted but maintained its bearing to break surface and continue sailing.

They all gathered at the display mirror to watch the creature descend into the depths.

I'wulf looked at Pangolin. "*That* was a sea serpent."

Pangolin laughed. "Good for us that it wasn't hungry. I doubt our impressive cannons would have had any effect on it."

"None," Traveler said. "All the cannons would have done is make the creature angry."

"Does that race of sea serpent have a name, Mr. Traveler?" Lady Aylen asked.

"Jörmungandr. They are the largest sea serpents in the magic lands, and that was a small one."

They laughed.

"A small one?" I'wulf asked.

"We have a visitor, Mr. Traveler," King Aereth said.

Traveler saw Tunik at their main door. With the wave of a hand across the display mirror, Traveler reversed the spell, and the walls and ceiling were no longer invisible.

He opened the door to a smiling Tunik. Traveler stepped out onto the deck and closed the door behind him. Tunik noticed that the human's animal had exited and had taken a position next to him in its aquatic wolflike form.

"She was a beauty, wasn't she?" Tunik asked.

"A young one, I'd say."

"Yes, they still have some play in them. Jumping from the ocean into the sky so their head can taste some clouds. As long as one's ship isn't in the way on the way up or the way down."

"It means we're getting closer to Kraken's Wake."

"Still have to cross merrow and adaro territory, but that's not why I came. Some of our passengers have asked to dine with the human captain and his party."

"Human captain? They shouldn't know anything about me, human or captain. You're the captain to the outside world."

"Don't blame me. I didn't speak with them. Your men did. Besides, they are the passengers from the previous trip. The party of selkies. What should I tell them?"

"I'd tell them no."

"That's not very hospitable for a captain. Captains must mingle with their passengers."

"When did you ever do that? Not once did you ever socialize with any passengers."

"Just because you didn't see me when you were part of my crew doesn't mean I didn't. You were the healer down below."

"I still say no."

"I will arrange it. What time? They want to meet you, human. They said it's important."

"Important how?"

"Dine with them and find out, Captain. Not my business."

"What do you know about these selkies?"

"What's to know? They're selkies. They're humans like you, for all I care. They paid me."

"Humans can't transform into seals. They're fae."

"Humans, I say, who need to put on a decent pair of shoes. What time?"

Traveler sighed. "Hopefully, there won't be any more jörmungandr encounters."

"They're like trolls, solitary creatures."

"Unless you happen to be in Troll Forest."

Tunik chuckled. "I forgot about that forest. Never been there myself, but I'm certain one sea serpent is all we will see today or tomorrow—besides Lovecraft, of course. After that, we'll soon have to worry about krakens."

"Dusk is fine."

"I'll tell them and have them show up at your door. Am I invited, too, Captain?"

"No, Captain, you'll be too busy with your duties."

Tunik cackled. "Yes, sir. Hey, Lovecraft, wasn't she big?" Tunik yelled at his pet sea serpent lounging on top of his bridge cabin. The creature watched the kobold then closed its eyes again and rested its head again. "I think our Lovecraft missed the whole thing, lazy creature."

"I'll leave you to your duties and your creature, Tunik."

Tunik knelt to look at Traveler's animal. The dog snarled at him. "My animal does the exact same thing when I'm close."

"Bye, Tunik." Traveler opened the door of the main bridge cabin and stepped in. The dog jumped through, and the door closed.

Tunik stood cackling again, and waved. "Bye, Captain."

Quillen begged until Hobbs finally relented. He proudly carried his magic sketch book, following after the caravan's receiving party.

Traveler glanced back at the smiling boy. "Haven't you drawn the passengers already?"

"They might want to see my drawings, Mr. Traveler."

The forward cabin was a deck below. When they stepped into the cavernous realm, they saw Hobbs had teams of humans, pech, and gnomes set up a dinner hall fit for royalty. Hobbs had a place for everyone, with Traveler, the royals, and Gwyness seated at a main table. Nirgund, Gresham, and Young Quillen at another. They waited while the Brothers Brimm performed their music to dancing gnomes. Traveler allowed no others to attend, not even Pangolin or any of the other Cut-throats besides Nirgund.

"Are we under a spell, Mr. Traveler?" Lady Aylen asked as they waited at their table.

"What do you mean, princess?"

"Your Mr. Tunik plotted against us, a plot that could have led to us getting killed, but I don't seem to care anymore. Am I bewitched? It would have bothered me greatly for a good long while before, if we were in our lands."

"Not necessarily. Very few are totally good on these waters."

"And the malevolent do have some good traits?" Lady Aylen asked.

"Like this captain?" King Aereth asked.

"Yes, sire. Allies and enemies change all the time."

"Like good goblins and bad elves," Lady Aylen said.

Traveler smiled. "I wouldn't go so far as that with goblins, but yes."

"Like the white elfess," Lady Aylen said.

"Like the white elfess with her ancient spell-talker giant companion," Traveler added. "Our guests have arrived."

The simply dressed party of selkies arrived, about a few dozen. Assembled caravan members guessed that the middle-aged couple that led them in were their leaders. The woman was of average height with dark-golden-blond hair; the man's hair, mustache, and beard were dark brown. A girl around Quillen's age followed with two smaller children. Hobbs had them attended to immediately and sat them at the main table.

Other guests arrived. Fish men and many races of water fae—humanoids with fishlike features like enlarged fishlike eyes, webbed hands and feet, scales for skin, or toad-like fingers. When all had arrived, there were nearly three hundred in the hall. Hobbs had meals served as if they were in a royal court not on the deck of a fast-moving ship in dangerous waters.

The selkie couple noticed the axe-beaked ostrich sitting next to Traveler but said nothing as Traveler and the others at the main table rose to greet them. Lady Aylen sat at the head, with King Aereth, Traveler, then Gwyness. The selkie leaders were seated across from them. Hobbs had all the selkies sit at the same long table.

The selkies were good-natured but never initiated conversation. They learned the woman's name was Nori, and the man, Otari. King Aereth graciously led the small talk about their journey aboard the ship so far.

"Never thought I'd meet an elfin princess who wears as little jewelry as I do," the woman said.

Lady Aylen looked down at her golden Sirnegate ring on each hand. The selkie had a single ring on her left hand. "Beautiful ring," the princess said.

"Thank you."

"You have good fortune that you were able to continue your journey to Kraken's Wake," Traveler spoke.

The woman, Nori, had a distinct royal bearing, always calm but very gracious. She nodded. "Yes, indeed."

"We were at the city of Titan's Fall, and now you travel with us to another sea city. I had a distinct notion that when you departed Captain Tunik's ship, you took a great interest in our party," Traveler said.

"Selkies and humans are similar. We see so few of either outside our own city," the man, Otari, said.

"I heard that you sought us while in Titan's Fall," Traveler said. The royals and Gwyness took notice of the fact.

"We did," Nori said.

"And you asked to share a meal with us. Uncommon behavior aboard a ship. Parties usually stay to themselves."

"We know who you are," Nori said.

"Do you?" Traveler sipped from his cup. "If so, it could be worth a lot of money to you."

"We are not interested in bounties." Otari had perfectly groomed facial hair, both mustache and beard. If there was one among the peaceful selkie clan that was most warrior-like, it was him.

"Why haven't you taken advantage of the situation, then?" Traveler asked.

"Our ship was wrecked at sea. You must know, our people are not warriors, and we were set upon by mermen archers," Nori said.

"Adaro."

"You know of them," she said.

"They are dangerous archers, but they are known to our people for their use of harpoon weapons of specific magical properties and violent power," Otari said.

"We had to abandon our ship, and we had little defense. However, the vessel we were both on ran them off. The captain allowed us aboard but refused to take us any further than Titan's Fall. We agreed."

"When one of our little ones said they saw you, we saw it as a sign from the Fates themselves," Otari said.

"How do you know us, then?" Traveler asked.

"Our people are allies to those who know of you," the man said.

"Or you are allies to our enemies," Traveler said.

"No, sir. If you know we are selkies, then you know we never ally with evil forces," the woman said.

"We ask you to allow us to accompany you to Atlantea," the man said. "My wife is also a gifted sorceress."

Traveler nodded. "But how do you know us?" Traveler asked again.

"The Selkies of Therian are allies of Queen Mother Anelle of the Celestial Elves of Nimbus."

A look of surprise came over Lady Aylen's and Gwyness's faces.

"The queen maybe, but are you allies of the celestial elves of Nimbus?" Traveler asked.

"Again, selkies never ally with evil," Otari said.

"Are your spirits not lifted knowing that you have allies who wish for your success?" Nori asked.

"Would your spirits rise if you were I? Invisible enemies, invisible allies. Which is which?"

"Your suspicions are understandable," Otari said, "but we can assist you at Kraken's Wake when we arrive."

"In what way?" Traveler asked.

"Your ship alone will not make it," Nori said, "but as part of a fleet, we can sail into Atlantea together. There is strength in numbers, as the wise adage says, especially here on these waters."

"Fleet?" King Aereth asked.

"Yes, sir. They have been trapped at Kraken's Wake, trapped by their own mistrust and suspicions of one another, and warring with outside dark fae. Only a neutral race could lead them forward. Selkies are one such race, as are humans. But we are not strong enough to command such a fleet. We are a race of advisers, like the learned centaurs of Chiron."

"We know you carry their banner," Otari said. "We are their allies too."

"When we arrive at Kraken's Wake, we can introduce you to the fleet leaders directly," Nori said.

"No one thought you could make it this far," Otari added.

"No one? Who?" Traveler asked.

"All those who oppose the Four Kings of Xenhelm."

For the leadership, it had been so long since they heard another outside the caravan speak the name of the evil kingdom of Oughtred.

"All the more reason to avoid Kraken's Wake," Traveler said.

"You know that to be impossible," Nori said. "You assembled a caravan upon land to get here. You must join another one on these waters, or you will never get to Atlantea. Let us help you lead that alliance."

Hobbs had never taken a seat to eat but instead moved about the dining hall, overseeing all the duties of the food servers. He noticed the same golden-blond-haired selkie girl at Quillen's table. He was eagerly showing off his sketchbook. Other selkie youths were gathered behind them, and Hobbs could hear the children's gasps and excitement. Quillen's drawings of the fantastic beasts and frightening creatures that the caravan had encountered on the Trail amazed them as much as it did anyone else who saw them.

With meals done, Hobbs gestured to their Brothers Brimm to play music in the background. Water fae rose from their tables and struck up conversations with the caravan's gnomes and humans.

At the main table with the selkies, other than the selkie youth, all remained seated, intently listening to the conversation between the selkie leaders and Traveler. Hobbs slowly began to make his way to the table.

Traveler stood, and everyone did so as well. "You have given us much to consider," he said to Nori and Otari.

"Our people only wish to reach Atlantea," Nori said. "An alliance can ensure that."

"Have your people been to Atlantea before?" Lady Aylen asked.

"No."

"I would suspect such a journey to be a regular occurrence for those on these waters," Lady Aylen said.

"This realm is far more vast than I think you know," Nori said. "Many more times the distance from here back to your own Lands of Man. Our people have been traveling for nearly a year."

"We have as well," King Aereth said.

"Travel on these waters is far more dangerous," the selkie woman said. "For my people, travel to Atlantea is viewed as a once-in-a-lifetime event."

"Many races have claimed the waters outside Atlantea's domain," Otari said. "One must either fight their way through or pay them, if they allow you to do so."

"Fight those allied with the Xenhelmians or pay those who are not," Nori said. "We can speak more when we reach Kraken's Wake."

"We must cross the territory of the adaro first," Traveler said.

"Yes, which is why you will not see us until we arrive at the city," Otari said. "We will not emerge from our realm below deck until then."

"We bid you a beautiful night," Nori said.

The selkie leaders led their clan adults from the table. The selkie youth fell in behind them. The selkie girl gave Quillen a big smile as she waved. Nori and Otari said goodbyes to other water fae then exited the dining hall. As the door opened, Cut-throat sentries could be seen on the deck.

"Mr. Traveler, do you trust these selkies?" Lady Aylen asked.

"I do, princess, but remain cautious."

"I cannot help notice that our young Mr. Quillen seems to be smitten with one of the young selkie girls. Not to be indelicate, but do we need to intervene?" King Aereth asked.

"There's no harm in it, sire. We were both Mr. Quillen's age once. What would you have done if you were in his place and the old folks told you to stay away from a pretty girl?"

King Aereth did not hesitate. "Ignore them."

"Then there's nothing else to be said."

"Mr. Traveler, they are shape-shifters though?" Gwyness asked.

"They can transform into seals when in the ocean."

"Any other forms?"

"Only seals, but they can communicate with many sea animals and beasts, as our Tree Shepherds can communicate with the trees and animals upon land."

The leadership retired from the dining hall. Many of the water fae guests remained, so Hobbs stayed behind. Traveler returned to their command cabin and promptly marched to his map table, with the royals and Gwyness following.

"The woman, Nori, they said she was a sorceress," King Aereth said. "That could be a great benefit, along with this ability to communicate with the fauna of these oceans, like Lady Aylen."

"A skill I have yet to use, sire," the princess said.

"Yes, sire," Traveler said. "One of the truly benevolent races in this region, they are a diplomatic people too. They will defend their kind but never attack others. That is their way."

"We need allies who can attack when needed," Lady Aylen said.

"We need both, princess."

"Then we plan to join their alliance to Atlantea?" she asked.

"Alliance to Atlantea, indeed. We will know when we get to the Kraken's Wake."

"They knew much about us, though, Mr. Traveler," King Aereth said. "Far more than I would have expected, being so far away. You were right. Everyone does know about us."

"Yes, sire. But it has been handled. Tunik is the face of the ship. They know we're here—not exactly what our ship looks like or where it is, but they do know where we are likely heading."

"That's why you wanted to avoid Kraken's Wake," King Aereth said.

"But we are stopping there?" Lady Aylen asked.

"I'm still deciding. If we go, there is a possibility we could get trapped. It's why I have been so focused on watching for any clue from the maps."

"But the new allies, this fleet?" Lady Aylen asked.

"Nothing is assured, princess, but Mr. Bragg may have given us an advantage. I will make a final decision soon and let you both know."

"Could we really bypass all these sea cities to get to Atlantea?" King Aereth asked.

"We could."

The royals looked at each other.

"Then forget what the selkies want. Let's get to Atlantea," Lady Aylen said.

Traveler smiled.

"It's not that easy, is it?" King Aereth asked.

Traveler shook his head. "No, sire, not in the slightest. The selkies are correct. I know these waters well, and we can hide and evade most of the forces out there. But inevitably, as one nears Atlantea, there is only one true ocean path. We could be confronted anywhere along the way and would need to fight our way through. When that time comes, the only question remaining is this: Can we defeat a fleet with a single ship?"

"The answer is no," King Aereth said.

"The answer is no, sire. There are many convoys that travel to Atlantea. That was my original plan to get there undetected, but now I'm not so sure."

"Why is that?" Lady Aylen asked.

"I'm too good for my own good, princess. Oughtred has tried to destroy us since the Lands of Man. All attempts, all his dark forces, have failed. He is not a fool. Remember, he was waiting for us at Titan's Teeth...and had forces at Titan's Fall."

"There were no forces at Titan's Fall," Lady Aylen said.

"Yes, there were, princess. They left before we arrived because they were summoned away. They thought we were killed in the Great Forest. But now they know we're alive. Oughtred knows we're alive. We already evaded their bounty hunters on the oceans once. I've made my decision."

"You have. What decision?" Lady Aylen asked.

"We must do the opposite of what he expects us to do."

"I agree, Mr. Traveler, that you have developed a pattern for cleverness in the art of escape and a foresight to his treachery in addition to your superior preparation skills as a caravan master. But that does not mean we should walk into a trap because he expects you not to."

"No, sire. We must assume he will watch *every* possible route to Atlantea. He can't guess our path so he'll simply have his forces watch all of them. We will go to Kraken's Wake and get that fleet."

"Why this sudden change of strategy, Mr. Traveler? All this simply from speaking to these selkies?" Lady Aylen asked.

"No, princess. The map."

"What about it?" she asked.

"There's nothing. We know there's a bounty on us. Tunik confirmed as much. But where are all our pursuers? Such a massive ocean but not a ship or craft in pursuit. Quiet. Empty. Where are they? No. To Kraken's Wake we go."

"A great strategist after my own heart, you are, Mr. Traveler," King Aereth said.

The region surrounding Kraken's Wake was known for its dark night clouds, which made most nights pitch-black. In this night sky, the moon did peek out from the clouds, but the night had a dark-blue hue. Tunik's sea serpent resting on the roof of the quarterdeck lifted its head and screamed.

Tunik ran out from the cabin with Nifle and two other kobolds at his side. Each kobold held a pike weapon in their thick, fat hands.

"Lovecraft, what are you going on about?" Tunik asked.

They stared up at the sky. Nifle pointed. They could barely make out the translucent forms high above.

"Sylphs," Tunik said.

A flying caravan raced across the sky, invisible to the human eye, but to their fae eyes, they could make out the translucent forms of many flying chariots carrying the air elementals known as sylphs. One jumped from her chariot.

The sea kobolds on deck looking through the transparent covering over them perked up.

"Where did she go?" Nifle asked.

Lovecraft started to scream again from its cabin roof perch.

The sylph appeared alongside the fast-sailing ship, hovering in the air. Like their earthen cousins, the nymphs, all sylphs were beautiful women. Her long, flowing white hair hung down to her feet. She watched them with white-irised eyes. Both her skin and ornate dress were a pale white, but she was a being of pure youth, vigor, strength, and power.

Tunik smiled and waved. The sylph did not respond. She floated a moment then shot back into the sky after her flying caravan.

"Not very talkative," Nifle said.

"Suits me. They can all stay on their cloud cities, far away from me." Tunik looked at his sea serpent. "Why is he still in a state?"

His creature fidgeted on the roof while staring down into the water. The kobolds moved closer to the bow. The face of a bluish female descended into the ocean and disappeared.

"An undine!" one of the kobolds yelled.

"Air elementals and water elementals," Nifle said. "What does it mean, Tunik?"

"Nothing at all. A flying caravan above us, and she must be a scout for one traveling underwater."

"They didn't need to send a scout, Tunik. They can see long distances quite fine," a kobold said.

"They got close to see who we were," Nifle said.

"And they saw us—just a ship of klabautermann, nothing to concern them." Tunik rubbed his chin.

"But they didn't see our passengers," a kobold said. "What if they come back?"

"What if we see them in Kraken's Wake?" Nifle asked.

Tunik laughed. "Elementals don't care about bounties."

"The merfolk cared about the bounty, and the water nymphs are allies to the undines."

"That doesn't matter. Elementals don't care about humans or fae other than sky elves and the sky cities of cyclopes and centaurs, so don't worry yourselves. We are a lowly crew of the open waters to them."

"What if we see these elementals in Kraken's Wake?" a kobold asked again.

"Then our human captain and his party will have serious problem," Tunik replied.

Tunik's pudgy finger pointed to the exact location on the map. Traveler leaned forward to study.

Though not quite dawn, the day shift was busy with work. Nifle and other sea kobolds lined their map table. Nifle glanced at Traveler's side, and his dog had his eyes locked on the fae. Nifle grinned.

"What would that mean to you?" Tunik asked.

"Nothing specific. Air and water elementals are allies. Why wouldn't they travel together? Maybe these caravans are common among them. They are in Atlantea."

"You asked us if there was anything unusual we encountered on our voyage," Tunik said. "What of you and your caravan?"

"Have you heard any rumors of demons?"

"Demons? What demons?"

"Spell-talkers, for example."

"You encountered a spell-talker?"

"Yes."

"In the Forest?"

"No, back in Faë-Land."

Tunik scratched his head, his mind racing. "Why tell me this now?"

"Why not? We'll be in Kraken's Wake in a couple of days. I thought it best to mention it since we have already encountered the crab centaur."

"Yes, we did."

"I can see from your face that there's something. What did you hear, Tunik?"

"It's not important."

"But you have heard rumors."

"We hear a lot of rumors on the water. You know that. Did you kill this spell-talker?"

"We're here, aren't we?"

"I bet it was your animal."

"Actually, it was I."

"Our little human healer has become far greater since leaving my crew. Any others? Demons or the like? Tell me everything, human. I need to know what you've gotten me into."

"I've gotten you into nothing, Tunik. You've been hired to get us to a city and nothing more."

"You and your party are hiding. My men and I are the ones on open deck. What else did you encounter that we should know about? Were there others?"

"Yes."

Now, the rest of the klabautermann crew joined them.

"What others?"

"Tunik, they should pay us more than double," Nifle said.

"You should keep quiet," Traveler told him.

"Much more than double."

"Nifle, should I have my animal companion kick you into the ocean?" Traveler asked.

"Nifle does make an excellent point," Tunik said.

"And the other was a Nemain."

"The banshee creature that makes men kill each other?"

"Yes. We also encountered night drows. I'm not certain they are in league with Oughtred, but—"

"But nothing. They are. Night drows are in league with spider centaurs, and spider centaurs are in league with crab centaurs. You have gotten us into something bad. Have you ever seen a ship overrun by spider centaurs? They can swim, too, so land or water, it makes no difference to them."

"No, I haven't seen spider centaurs before."

"I have, and I never wish to see such a thing ever again in my life. They travel with hordes of spiders the size of dogs. I hate spiders."

"How can you hate spiders as a kobold?"

"We're ocean kobolds. We're not our land cousins, who keep them as pocket pets. I want to abandon the voyage this instant."

"Tunik, you need not worry about them because we have the perfect weapon against them."

"Elves are the best archers of the magical lands, but hordes of black spiders commanded by spider centaurs—"

"Which can be easily defeated by fairies with swarms of insects at their command. Have you ever seen a fairy-storm, Tunik?"

"I have. You have fairies?"

"We have two."

The sea kobolds laughed.

"Why didn't you say so at the start? Elves and fairies. Then we're fine."

"I'm glad your mind's at ease now. So the answer to my question is that you haven't seen anything else strange."

"No demons, and we just told you what we did see—sylphs and undines."

"When do we cross into the domain of the adaro?" Traveler asked.

"We already have, Captain, so I'd be careful returning to your command cabin. Like elves, those shooting mermen never miss when they let lose their arrows."

CHAPTER SIX

Mermen Hunters

The next day, Titan's Crew watched the display mirrors from the safety of their command cabin.

"Are those reefs, Mr. Traveler?" King Aereth asked.

Traveler looked up from his map table. "No, sire. They are actually the peaks of giant mountains rising up from the ocean floor. Millennia ago, they rose to the sky but have since been worn down by the oceans. These land masses mark the beginning of the territory of the adaro, merman hunters who are the only water fae race to use bows and arrows when they emerge and attack from their underwater ships."

"Attack why?" Lady Aylen asked.

"We have entered their territory, and we're not adaro or their allies, the merrows."

"Besides being an evil race, what is the difference between mermaids and merrows?" Lady Aylen asked.

"Physical appearance and customs. Your eyes would perceive the physical differences, but to the average human, the two races are indistinguishable."

"How far away now, Mr. Traveler, from the sea city?" King Aereth asked.

Something caught Traveler's eye as he stared at his map table. "Two days or less, sire. These mountain peaks that look like reefs are also known as Kraken's Fingers."

"What names. As long as they aren't actual krakens, that is fine," Lady Aylen said.

"What do you see on the map, Mr. Traveler?" the king asked.

"Trouble."

Traveler increased his warnings. By day, he wanted everyone in the caravan to be as careful as possible to not be seen. The ship had a translucent cover over the deck and was protected by a magic barrier, but he told them that the closer they got to Atlantea, the more the number and power of the sorcerers increased. One could cast a spell with a whisper to simply reveal the race of all aboard their ship. That knowledge alone would reveal their identity.

The drowess, Dr'amal, stuck out her hand from the cabin and threw a cloud of dark-bluish smoke. As Traveler and the royals exited their command cabin, the spell made the two humans and elfess appear as goblins.

Laughter erupted from the kobolds on deck.

Traveler looked at his form and back at the smiling drowess as she closed the door. Lady Aylen looked at her hands.

"What is the meaning of this? First human, then elf, now I'm a blue-skinned goblin."

"It's simply a mirage spell, princess."

Tunik stood doubled over at the entrance to their quarterdeck command bridge to calm his laughing.

"Ignore them." Traveler marched to the front of the ship.

The royals saw it immediately, a line of wrecked, burning ships.

"What happened?" Lady Aylen asked.

Sea kobolds already gathered at the bow of the ship.

"We have goblins aboard!" one laughing kobold said.

"Are you afraid someone will see you?" another kobold asked. "No one can see through our barrier unless we allow them to."

Traveler ignored them and peered at the wrecks as the ship slowly moved forward. The darkened ships had suffered a terrible onslaught. The damage appeared to be from a cannon attack, but the volley had come from above, not the sides.

"Where are you going, Nifle?" Traveler asked.

"Goblin, it's none of your affair." The sea kobold had a thick coil of rope on one shoulder. Other sea kobolds armed with pikes and tridents lined up behind him.

Traveler looked back at Tunik, who approached with more kobolds.

"Tunik, are you allowing this?"

"Why wouldn't I? If my men want to salvage a wreck, they can do so. You know that."

"Tunik, when did we ever come across wrecked ships floating in the ocean in this manner, damaged enough not to sail, but not damaged enough to sink to the bottom of the ocean and conveniently without any crew."

"The crew escaped or were captured," Nifle said. "Happens every day on these waters, and we're not going to let the adaro take the wreck from us. First to arrive, first to salvage."

"First to arrive, first to salvage!" the kobolds sang around him repeatedly and triumphantly.

"Surely you're not that simple to believe this good fortune is anything but a trap," Traveler said to Nifle.

"Goblin, you say it's a trap. I say the Fates have smiled upon us. I smell treasure, and we're going to salvage it."

"Wait here!"

Traveler marched off back to the command cabin while goblin-King Aereth and goblin-Lady Aylen waited.

"Who's he getting?" Tunik asked. "It's not going to discourage them. He's wasting his effort. You're wasting your effort," he yelled at Traveler's back.

"No one must leave the ship," Lady Aylen said. "I command you to sail on to the city. We have no time for this foolishness."

"Sorry, goblin-elf," Tunik said. Whispers and chuckles erupted from the kobolds as if Tunik uttered a blasphemous word. "Your human is the captain, not you."

Traveler returned with a few humans. Lady Aylen and King Aereth recognized them as their fae mercenary members.

The fae mercenaries recounted their story of the Dead City and how they, too, left the caravan to seek treasure, ignoring Traveler's strong objections. One hundred men left, eighty-six returned. The rest were killed by a manticore, and the survivors had to be treated for some time from the putrid magic of the creature. As Tunik had said, Nifle and his men were unmoved.

"We go before any adaro show," Nifle announced.

"Nifle, I won't say a word to dissuade you, but Mr. Traveler does have a point. I smell the treasure, too, but I am not stepping off this ship for anything until we get to the city," Tunik said.

"But I smell a huge hoard," a smiling Nifle said.

Tunik shrugged. "Sorry, human, looks like we're going treasure hunting."

"Leave them behind, then," Lady Aylen said angrily.

"We don't leave men behind, elf. We wait. They find their treasure and bring it back. We sail," Tunik said.

Pangolin stepped forward with a few Cut-throats. Their armor was distinctive, but their faces looked goblin. The ship pulled as close as it could to the first wrecked ship. Nifle jumped from the deck high in the air and landed on the deck of the other ship. All his kobolds followed, one after another. Tunik and the other kobolds remained aboard.

They watched Nifle and his men crawl over the ship, ignoring the diminishing flames, and disappear into the hidden decks below.

Pangolin shook his head in disgust. "So fae can be as stupid as humans in these matters."

Tunik chuckled. "Of course."

Pangolin looked at his two Cut-throats. "Get the men ready for battle, in case."

The two Cut-throat "goblins" raced back to the command cabin.

"I thought you were the captain," King Aereth said to Traveler.

"They're kobolds, sire, no different than dwarves. If there is treasure, minerals, gems, or the like, there is no reasoning with them. It's like telling a fairy to be still or a manticore not to eat someone. Impossible."

The second Traveler and the king stepped across the threshold of their command cabin the goblin illusion spell vanished. Pangolin and the two Cut-throats entered right after them, going from goblin to human. Dr'amal stood in front of the main display mirror but not alone.

Lady Aylen stepped through last but hesitated for a brief moment at the threshold. "Mr. Frog-Dor, there you are."

"You look well, sir," King Aereth said.

The man Frog-Dor looked like a royal himself with a long tunic under his blue cloak. He held a tall wooden staff, which rested on the floor in his left hand, though he was no longer hobbled.

"You don't need a walking staff, Mr. Frog-Dor. Have your legs not completely healed?" Lady Aylen asked.

"Not completely, m'lady, and thank you, sire, for the compliment."

"He will be free of the staff soon," Dr'amal said.

Lady Aylen walked to him and patted him on the shoulder. "We are glad to have you back, Mr. Frog-Dor. We will need your magical abilities."

"Yes, m'lady."

Traveler focused his eyes on the main display mirror, watching the wrecked ships.

Pangolin joined him. "Do you believe something will happen?"

"This is a trap."

"Did you see them on your map?"

"No, I didn't. Such a battle I would have seen, but there was quite a bit of cloud cover."

From the display mirrors, they could see kobolds appearing from the holds below jumping up and down on the deck, laughing and dancing.

"They found their treasure," Pangolin said.

"Can we force the matter?" Lady Aylen asked Traveler. "We need to leave."

"Are all your men ready for battle, Mr. Pangolin?"

"All I need to do is call. They await below with our archers."

"How formidable are these adaro, Mr. Traveler?" a Cut-throat asked.

"They are as fast as elves, but their arrows can do more damage since they're made not to kill people but to destroy entire ships. They aim for destruction, not precision like elves. But adaro don't set traps like these."

"Then who?" Pangolin asked.

"That's what I want to know. Princess, why did you pause at the door when you entered?"

"Pause?"

"Did you sense something?"

"Yes, but it's nothing."

"Tell me anyway."

"Your Mr. Tunik's sea serpent."

Traveler looked at her. "What about it?"

"It smells different. I hate being an elf sometimes. I've never smelled a pet sea serpent before."

"Princess, is it the same sea serpent? It's important!"

Lady Aylen was taken aback by his tone and stern expression. "I don't know. What does it mean?"

Traveler ran for the entrance. The dog transformed into a humanoid form, taking to two legs, and kept growing.

Traveler threw the door open. "Our reunion has come to an end!" The dog swung once, knocking Tunik and his two kobolds overboard and sending them crashing into the water.

Traveler returned to the command cabin and grabbed what first appeared as a stick from a cloak pocket. He flicked it once, and it extended into a staff. He stabbed it into the floor, and a ship's navigation wheel sprouted from the top.

"Close that door!"

Pangolin barely had time to do so before they all felt the tremendous speed the ship accelerated to. Those in front of or near the display mirrors could see the wrecked of ships quickly become dots in the distance.

King Aereth, the sorcerers, and the Brothers Brimm, who had been sitting eating at the map table, were violently thrown into the back wall as Traveler pulled up on the wheel. Pangolin and the Cut-throats had their talarian sandals on, so they were spinning around in mid-air.

Lady Aylen thrust her war trident into the floor and held on as her body whipped toward the wall.

Her mouth opened in shock at what she saw in the display mirror.

"Mr. Traveler!"

Tunik's sea serpent wasn't on top of the other command cabin but rather a dark-greenish crab centaur. It failed to grab onto the roof with its giant claws and fell off as the ship rose into the air. They saw it crash into the ocean below.

Their acceleration was so forceful, everyone screamed. Then the ship ceased its upward flight and spun around while tilting.

Suddenly, a giant flying ship came out of invisibility barreling forward as Traveler turned the wheel hard in the opposite direction. The giant vessel looked to be chiseled from blue metal, however, they were about the experience the true uniqueness of their magic ship. Their caravan master purposely crashed them into the city ship ten times their size.

Lady Aylen saw hundreds of shadowy figures peering over the side of the city ship but was unclear about who or what they were. Then long cannons pushed out through its hull.

"They're firing!" she yelled.

Boom!

The explosion did not come from an impacting cannon. Titan's Crew's ship had fired first, and the vessel shook so violently that pieces of their walls and roofs fell away. The next explosion blew a hole in the center hull of the city ship, shaking passengers loose. The caravan's ship dropped tens of feet into the ocean.

They did not bounce but dove beneath the waters. Traveler pushed the wheel so far forward the wheel was inches from the ground. They were traveling at an incredible speed again. The Brothers Brimm screamed out as their vessel sped downward. Frog-Dor, his teeth clenched, shot a ball of light at the king and the Brothers Brimm, and one enveloped him and Dr'amal. Three spheres of light to protect them as the vessel continued diving.

The vessel didn't dive straight down but arced. Its speed increased even as the ship flew upside down to continue its arc back toward the surface. The speed and force increased. Every inch of the vessel seemed as if it was about to rip apart.

Traveler flipped the ship on its ascent to the surface, and the shaking force subsided, but not the speed. When the ship burst into the air, floating in Frog-Dor's magical spheres, they could not believe what they saw—several city ships and a convoy of ships each smaller but longer than theirs.

Their caravan master gave them no warning. The ship bounced once on the surface of the water and crashed directly into the stern of the city ship in front of them. The fae on the deck saw them but had no time to react. Traveler yelled something in a language they did not understand.

Boom! Again and again. Multiple cannons fired simultaneously. Their ship burst through as the city ships upper deck came down on the lower deck; the entire middle deck had been obliterated.

The beating noises sounded like heavy rain. From the display windows, they saw for the first time the adaro, the shooting mermen, humanoids with grayish skin like a shark's, large gills behind their ears, tail fins for feet, and backs lined with shark-like fins. Swordfish-like spears rained down on their ship, puncturing one side. The first hole appeared in the side of the cabin with a swordfish protrusion.

Traveler sharply turned into their vessel with a violent crash. The many arms folded along the outside hull of their ship grabbed the adaro hunting vessel along the side and repeatedly pulled it into their vessel. With every crash, the adaro hunters were knocked about on their main deck, some thrown into the water, others crushed between the two vessels. Then the arms rose, flipping the adaro vessel into the air. The vessel flew and crashed into another adaro ship to the rear. Both vessels sank into the waters.

A screeching sound of metal on metal indicated that the ship's giant anchor had been completely released into another adaro attack vessel. Adaro dove from their ship as the anchor crashed into the bow, shattering the boat into pieces. Traveler yelled the same strange words again. Multiple cannons fired. Other adaro ships were blown apart.

Six blue-metal city ships bore down on them, their cannons all extended to fire. Light flashed from some, lightning from others. The display mirror turned white with a blinding light as all the ships fired on them as one.

The thunderous sounds were so loud that, for a moment, it was if existence winked out. Every particle of their being, the ship, even the air wavered, as if shook by cosmic forces. Lady Aylen screamed as she grabbed her ears. They could all hear elves and other fae screaming from below deck.

Then silence.

Lady Aylen looked up from the ground, still within the light sphere, curled up, hands pressed against her ears, tears in her eyes.

The caravan master was already through the cabin entrance with his dog right after him. The ship had stopped.

Another adaro rammed into their ship's stern.

"Release us!" Pangolin yelled.

The magic spheres disappeared, and all in them dropped to the floor.

Pangolin bolted from the room onto the deck.

King Aereth picked himself up from the floor. The Brother Brimm, Frog-Dor, and Dr'amal did the same.

"Mr. Mossberry!" they heard Traveler's yell.

All four Tree Shepherds appeared from the steps below decks.

Lady Aylen got to her feet and stumbled outside to the deck. She gasped, frozen in shock.

The deck was littered with corpses. Lady Aylen stared at the dead blue-skinned water nymph lying at her feet then a green body of a triton. She had never seen their race before but had heard of their description—mermen each with legs like a serpentine fish tail. The deck was awash with the bodies of nereids, tritons, and adaro.

She noticed Gwyness standing at her side, equally in shock. Other members of the caravan came out from the command cabin onto the deck—Cut-throats, the elves, the drows, Mr. Hobbs, Mr. Gresham, the healer, Mr. Estus.

Pangolin gazed out from the side of the ship. When Lady Aylen and Gwyness joined him, they could not believe it. The entire dark-blue ocean around them extending far beyond their line of sight, was red—an ocean of floating corpses. Every one of the city ships had already sunk below.

The ship's passengers also began to appear on the crowded deck, including the selkies who joined the royals. Everyone was visibly terrified.

Lady Aylen snapped herself out of her state of shock. Their caravan master, away from all of them, stood on the roof of the quarterdeck. He scanned the horizon with a telescope. The four Tree Shepherds had their eyes closed, and their hands glowed. She noticed the faint outline of a translucent magic dome covering the entire ship with a hint of rainbow colors.

"How is such destruction possible?" Gwyness asked, overcome by grief.

"Do not shed tears for them," Nori, the selkie, said. "They had but one purpose. To kill us all."

"Is our ship this powerful?" Gwyness asked.

Pangolin looked at her. Even he was overwhelmed by the magnitude of death before them. "They fired upon us but destroyed themselves," he said.

The dog jumped down from the quarterdeck, now twice its size, in its aquatic form but feral in appearance.

Traveler carefully jumped down onto the deck so as not to slip on any blood or bodies. He walked toward them.

"Mr. Hobbs, organize the men to throw every corpse overboard as quickly as possible and swab the deck thoroughly."

"Yes, sir. Right away."

"We will not be able to rest for a moment. Mr. Pangolin, see to the ship's defenses."

Their master-at-arms nodded and walked off, gesturing for other Cut-throats to follow him.

"How long was that evil centaur creature on the ship, Mr. Traveler?" Lady Aylen asked.

"What creature?" Gwyness asked her.

"Tunik's pet sea serpent was actually one of those crab centaurs," Lady Aylen said. "But when? For how long? Was it the real serpent before? When did it take the serpent's place?"

Despite the gasps and everyone looking at each other in fear, Traveler looked on with a detached, cold expression. "Since none of our magic detected it, who can say, princess? Only you sensed it because of your increased senses."

"I am sorry, Master Traveler," Frog-Dor said with a saddened face. "I should have detected the creature."

"No need to apologize, Mr. Frog-Dor," Traveler said. "Your spell was to detect anything breaching our magic barrier, not an unwelcome passenger already on the ship."

"What now, Mr. Traveler?"

"Sire, I sail the ship into Kraken's Wake at its fastest speed. We'll arrive by tomorrow. There, our fabled quest to Atlantea resumes. We must see to it that it does not end there too."

CHAPTER SEVEN

The City of Kraken's Wake

Not even a day. None of them would have even a day to recover from what had just happened.

They had endured much on the Trail but nothing compared to this, cheating death by their caravan master's miraculous sailing on the waters, below them, and into the sky. His sailing prowess matched his master swordsmanship. After all, he was a human who could best even elves with the blade. No one else could have succeeded in such a feat—sailing a small golem ship to outmaneuver a fleet of six city ships and countless other vessels—but he did.

They had almost died at the edge of the Great Forest because of the landvættir, the ancient beast, or "walking land mass," whose magic had rendered them all comatose. There they had experienced, seen, and felt nothing. Helpless, they would have been consumed by the creature, like countless others through the millennia helpless. No one ever would have seen them again or found even the minutest trace of them. There, Traveler's plan had saved them all, including himself. But here, he had directly saved them from their fate.

Then there was the enormity of the death they beheld, every adaro, water nymph, and triton gone. The adaro must have laughed to themselves, so certain they'd slaughter Titan's Caravan with no less than six city ships of their water fae allies to aide their own fleet in attacking without warning. But instead, their four-race alliance lay dead. Their ships were at the bottom of the ocean—or on the way to the bottom of the Oceanus Omnis.

No one knew how. The city ships had fired upon them with weapons far more powerful than anything they had witnesses before. Yet their enemies were dead, and they lived. As the bodies of their would-be murderers were thrown overboard to their watery graves and the deck was washed of their blood—dark red, blue and red, green and red—for some it was too much to comprehend. Even the Cut-throats and other berserkers who lived for the battle were at a loss for words. No one spoke as the work was done.

Traveler told them that everything in the Oceans of Faë-Land Omnis, the empires of mermaids, ocean nymphs, and water fae, was of magic more powerful and deadly than anything that existed in the lands of man or fae.

They would not even have a day to recover from what had just happened.

They had arrived.

The ship moved smoothly about twenty feet below the surface, in waters as clear as if they were flying through the sky above. The ocean floor was hundreds of feet below, where thick sea grass rose up, swaying underneath them. As they neared the sea city, the sizes and varieties of fish increased. Many of the curious fish around them were as large as the ship.

In the distance, the appearance of the city of Kraken's Wake filled many watching the display mirrors with apprehension. It did look like a giant kraken. A walled city structure sat on a colossal, ancient, desiccated octopean kraken, its seaweed-covered giant tentacles floating in the ocean for miles.

The first water fae appeared, a mermaid in armor with a long silver trident. She was joined by many others then humanoid mermen, not the ugly human-faced fish species they had seen back in Faë-Land Minor but blue-skinned men in armor with webbed hands and feet riding hippocampi—beasts with the upper body of a blue horse and the lower body of a fish. Fish-headed humanoids also appeared in swarms around them. Their ship moved slowly forward between two of the kraken tentacle markers to the main sea city, as growing numbers of water fae encircled them and followed along.

They passed through the mouth of an underwater cave in the mountain—or was it the kraken's mouth? The kraken's skin actually draped over a massive hollow mountain, and in the center floated the true giant city. One of the men described it as an upside-down castle, wider at the upper levels and funneling down to a single level below. As they neared the main entrance gate, the number of water fae increased even more, along with a burst of water animals. While the water fae contingent accompanying their ship were warriors, they could also see many fae nearest the city had to be residents or travelers swimming through the water, going about their business.

The entire city was underwater but Traveler told them it had a port for land-walkers. The ship emerged onto the surface and sailed to the port where an army of water fae awaited, armed with tridents, spears, hand-cannons in the shape of conch shells, and shields: mermaids, moving effortlessly on the surface of the dock like erect cobras, two-legged mermen behind them, light-blue-skinned ocean nymphs standing tall on two legs, then triton warriors arrived, marching on their two long fish-tail legs.

The ship's hull door opened, and a gangplank magically extended and rested on the dock. Lady Aylen stepped out first with a war trident in each hand. King Aereth and Maiden Gwyness followed on either side. Next came Frog-Dor with his staff, Traveler, and Dr'amal. Pangolin followed next with Lyre and the high elf archers on one side and Talos with his men on the other, bows and arrows in hand, fae falcons on their shoulders. Then the four Tree Shepherds appeared with three of the crawling trees, still in the form of tree giants. Other fae of the caravan followed.

The army of fae waited with their armor and weapons of blue, silver, or white metal. Their helmets bore fins, tiny tridents pointing up, or ornate entwined fish. A mermaid royal floated forward with armed mermaids at either side. Her face was flush with anger.

The princess calmly stepped to her and nodded. "I am Lady Aylen of Sirnegate and the lost city of Rivermouth." She turned. "This is King Aereth of the human city of Helm Earldom, King Dr'as of the D'Shar, King Ethor of the nomadic woodland elves of Faë-Land Major, and King Greenwig of the Tree Shepherds of Faë-Land Minor."

"Not a queen among you?" the mermaid asked.

"This is Queen Nori of the selkie clan of Therian," Lady Aylen replied as Nori and Otari also joined them.

"But Lady Aylen is my senior," Nori said.

"I am Queen Geneva of Kraken's Wake. Why have you landbound come here?"

"We carry the banners of the fairies of Chrysa, giants of Antaeus, centaurs of Chiron, elfin banners of Magica, Bravehowl, Nightshade, and Falconbright, human banners of Sirnegate, Helm Earldom, Strongbridge, and Eastmoor, and the lost elfin kingdom of Rivermouth."

As soon as Lady Aylen began listing the kingdoms, the chatter of surprise erupted from the crowds of water fae. Even the mermaid queen's disposition changed from rage to a more neutral expression.

"A fleet of oceanids and tritons was destroyed with no survivors. Yet, your ship is here. Did you kill our people?" the queen asked.

Traveler said something, but it was in an elfin tongue. Lady Aylen thought for a moment and pieced together in her mind what he said.

The queen was angered again and slid past Lady Aylen to him.

"That is a lie, human!"

Lady Aylen stepped between them. "Is it?"

"It is."

"Then I apologize, Queen Geneva," Traveler said. "The fleet opened fire on us without provocation, unless Kraken's Wake was in league with adaro hunters."

"Adaro? Why would our royal kingdom be in league with lowly scavengers? We are not," she snapped. "Neither would oceanids nor tritons."

"I would not think such a royal city would lower itself to act on bounties from humans."

"We would not. I don't believe you that they were in league with any humans, let alone the Kings' Caravan of Xenhelm. We know Oughtred well and he and his allies are not welcome in this city."

"We are glad to hear that," Traveler said. "In any event, our small ship could not have destroyed an entire fleet. They destroyed each other."

"You bewitched them somehow!" a mermaid yelled.

"We did not make them fire upon us. We were in battle with the adaro. They appeared from nowhere and attacked us."

"We do not know how you did your evil deed but we will find out." The queen squinted as she stared at him. "I know you."

"No."

"I've seen you before."

"You have, but you don't know me."

"You've been here to Kraken's Wake before."

"Yes, as a healer of fae."

"I recall now. You were a human among a crew of filthy sea kobolds."

"I was."

"How did our fleet destroy each other?" the queen asked.

"They aimed their cannons at each other and fired. You said 'our.' Your fleet?"

"Oceanids are our blood sisters, so yes 'our,' my sister fleet." The queen mermaid looked at Lady Aylen. "I don't believe you."

"It's true," Lady Aylen said, "and you already know that, or you would never have allowed us entry into the city in the first place, and we wouldn't be talking now."

"Was the fleet from this city?" Lady Aylen asked.

"You have no right to question our queen, elf!" a mermaid yelled.

The mermaid queen raised a hand to calm her entourage. "It was not. But all mermaids and our allies come to the aid of one another."

"You say they weren't acting under your direction. You say they were not working in league with the Four Kings. Then they must have been mad, and they paid for it with their lives. The matter is closed for us and is of no concern to you," Lady Aylen said.

"You'd have us believe you possess the magic to defend against a fleet of our kind?"

"We do," Lady Aylen said. "But again, since they were acting without your knowledge or blessing, it is of no concern to you. May we continue on?"

"Why should we allow you?"

"Is this not an open city?"

"Why would you land-walkers wish to be here?"

"We will stay on the island for land-walkers."

One of the ocean nymphs stepped forward. "Queen, do know that whatever you decide, we will seek vengeance against them."

Traveler moved right up to the nymph's face. "You will do no such thing. The battle was had, and both winners and losers were decided. It's over. You have no claim to vengeance."

"I can smell the charms around your neck, human. Be sure they stay there, or I'll command you to dive into the deepest ravine of the city. You'll be helpless to resist as you drown horribly."

Traveler ignored her and looked at the crowd. "None of you have claim of vengeance! Or has the royal city of Kraken's Wake become as ignoble as the Kelp Lands with its sea goblins?"

The caravan master returned to his spot between Frog-Dor and Dr'amal.

Queen Geneva turned to Lady Aylen. "We will not allow you to set foot in our matriarchal territory."

"And the patriarchal waters are forbidden to you as well!" an angry triton yelled.

"All that is left for you, elf, is the ignoble Kelp Lands with its sea goblins, but other than you, your people don't breathe underwater. And the island you refer to has no lodging available to you outsiders. I suggest you board your ship and sail elsewhere."

"We have made arrangements to stay on the island," Lady Aylen said.

"There is nothing for you there or here," the queen said angrily.

One of the nymphs cleared her throat to get the queen's attention. Rising from the water, a female humanoid, part fairy, part mermaid, flew from the water around the dock to the group. A tunic made of fish scales covered her chest to her navel. Her legs were clad in a skintight fabric. She wore no shoes on her webbed feet. Large insect wings fluttered wildly from her back but made no noise. In her hand was a large key.

"What is your business here?" the queen asked.

"A key for a lodging on the island, my queen," the fairy mermaid answered.

"Lodging? What lodging?"

"For the Castle Peak, my queen."

"None of their kind entered the city."

"The structure was purchased years ago."

Traveler stepped forward again and reached to take the key from the fairy mermaid. "Yes, queen. I was the one who purchased it."

The mermaid queen quivered with simmering rage. The other water fae looked at each other.

"The mark of a good caravan master is preparation," Traveler said.

"The inhabitants of the Kelp Lands will never let you land-walkers step into their region," the queen said. "Without one to give you safe passage, you'll find your stay in this city short. I'd leave now. White Waters is filled with elves. Go there."

Traveler pointed to the water near the dock. They all turned.

The yellow spider climbed out of the water and settled on the dock. It rose up and transformed as it grew in size. A smiling sea horse-headed humanoid hopped up and down.

"Phooka! Be gone!" a mermaid said.

"Phooka?" A look of disgust came over Lady Aylen's face. She turned to Traveler. "No. It can't be. The creatures exist in this realm too?"

Traveler grinned at her.

Suddenly, dozens of the caravan's own darklings poured out of their ship—black figures with frog heads and fat-bellied reptilian bodies. Dozens of yellow spiders jumped out of the water and transformed into yellow seahorse-headed, fat-bellied reptilian bodies. Both species of phookas greeted each other in an explosion of laughter, hugs, back flips, dancing, and throwing themselves onto each other.

Lady Aylen and Queen Geneva looked at each other. The Kraken's Wake's receiving armies and Titan's Caravan members were in shock. The entire area echoed with the growing ruckus of the phookas. Lady Aylen and the queen sternly looked at Traveler.

"What? They're my friends," Traveler said.

In the middle of the great Oceanus Omnis, in a sea city built within the mummified head of a gigantic kraken, they marched, on the surface, into a castle at the base of a long-dead volcanic mountain. Ten thousand humans and fae, with their animals, marched in the most unlikely of places for the first time in many weeks.

The castle itself reminded Hobbs of the days when he was in the employ of King Theogar's royal family, all but a distant memory since joining Titan's Caravan. Outside was a windblown white-stone wall nearly sixty feet high with towers at each end and a larger keep within rising above it all.

They walked up the path of smooth white stone pebbles—the island itself was made of black sand— and up the drawbridge, though there was no moat. First, they passed into the gatehouse, the outer defensive double tower of the main entrance, with the portcullis locked above their heads. The inside of the gatehouse was made to defend against a full attack with stone slabs rising from the ground to a foot from the ceiling. The caravan had to divide into separate single-file lines to pass between the slabs. The rest of the gatehouse was larger still but Traveler led them straight out into the open courtyard, where they saw the keep, about forty feet away, and the dead volcanic mountain rising farther behind it.

Their six Antaean giants had not been themselves since the caravan set sail, leaving land behind. Traveler's vapor had helped, but the giants were still weak and needed the aid of the brawny pech to help them walk. To the eye, they no longer appeared to be eleven feet tall but much shorter, shrunken, hobbling. But something had taken hold of the giants. They pushed the pech away and ambled on their own, moving past everyone, then through the keep's open main doors ahead.

When they reached the keep, Traveler led them through a long corridor. The passage was dark, with no torches, candles, or natural lighting from window or any other openings in the walls or ceiling. They marched to a bright light from an open door at the far end.

Even before they exited the keep, all four Tree Shepherds moved ahead of them too. Outside, was a blackish, ragged peak pushing up through the center of an open field with sparse vegetation. The giants were slowly climbing the nearly twenty feet to the top.

The caravan looked up and around. They were within a hollow mountain with no top, a dead volcano around a smaller mountain in its center.

Grakdar, Barg and the other giants grew larger in size as they climbed up. They moved quicker. There was a visible glow of light from their eyes and palms of their hands. The caravan watched. The mountain was much more to the giants. For the first time in a month, they had direct contact to Pan-Earth itself, and their elemental powers were renewed.

The three crawling trees rolled up the mountain too and reached out with their branches to pull their entire trunks to the base of the mountain. The three trees began to grow taller, wider, and their branches stretched out. A flurry of life passed by them; the giant lizards, in their individual colors of blues, yellows, greens, and oranges, ran to the giant crawling trees and up into the branches. Two thousand giant lizards went wild as the trees continued to grow. Their human lizard minders laughed and applauded.

The giants reached the mountain peak, raised their arms into the sky, and yelled. Their eyes, mouths, and hands beamed with light. The giants disappeared from view as the trees grew so large that they blocked the view of the mountain.

The hoofed fae's leader, Strag, moved to the crawling tree farthest from the other two, followed by the five hundred elaphine warrior archers with their antlered heads, the two hundred deerlike cervids, with small horns, and the docile rusines.

The Cut-throats let their eagle-hound chamroshes take flight for the trees, too, as did the desert elves, watching their falcons fly to the top of the still-growing trees.

The mole-looking fae burst forward on top of his giant moose. He led the nearly seven hundred humanoid animal men to another still-growing giant crawling tree. The frog men led their giant crabs. The possum men rode their giant turtles. The raccoon men followed with their giant porcupines, bird men with their large jackalopes, and others their enfields. Fox men, rabbit men, squirrel men, and mouse men led the rest of their animals—giant ducks and cranes.

As the caravan's hundred smiling gnomes and fifty gnomoids ran to the trees, Chief Ammon followed with his daughter Zefea and his four hundred fauns, all armed with tall spears.

Smiles returned to everyone's faces. They were home in a way. The most enjoyable part of their caravan was camp with its welcome familiarity.

"Mr. Hobbs, I suspect most of the men will wish to rest and sleep outdoors rather than stay within the castle's quarters."

"Yes, sir. I would agree."

"More room for us, then," Dr'as, the drow leader, said.

"Yes, Dr'as," Traveler said. "Your people can have an entire floor."

"They're here!" Gwyness cried out. Gwyness's magical kirin galloped forward to her. The beast, with its black fur and scales, head adorned with full antlers, and not unlike a lion, responded favorably to her stroking its forehead.

The other two kirins followed, King Aereth's kirin with its golden fur and scales and thick mane of hair on its dragon-like head. He patted the side of its powerful horselike body.

Lady Aylen jumped onto her kirin with its lucent-blue fur and scales. As it curved its long neck around to greet her, she leaned down to rub its forehead, adorned with a single horn. Around its nose and mouth were its long catfish-like whiskers.

Behind them, the four fenodyree minders appeared. The hairy sprites were quiet but in especially good cheer.

King Aereth's guardsman, Nirgund, allowed his thirteen reptilian hounds to run to the trees to play.

"Sire, will you stay outside or in the castle?"

The king looked at Lady Aylen. "What do you think, Lady Aylen?"

"Sire, I must confess I miss sleeping under the stars."

"Mr. Nirgund, our royal tents it is."

Lyre, the high elf, laughed. "The elves and drows of Titan's Caravan are in agreement again. We, Mr. Traveler, will be lodging within the castle. That is what we miss."

"You can have a floor all to yourselves too," Traveler said.

Swarms of colored insects flew by them all led by two fireflies. They heard the distinctive giggling of their two fairies as the swarms flew into the air above the towering trees.

The four Tree Shepherds knelt on the dirt, and within moments, the dirt turned green with grass, then flowers popped out from the soil then brush.

"Titan's Caravan seems at home," Lady Aylen said from her kirin mount. "We're in the middle of the magical ocean, on an island inside the ancient skull of a giant kraken, and relaxing in our own green pasture within a dead volcano. Only in the lands of magic. I wish this would last forever, but I know it won't."

"Such negative words are supposed to come from me, princess."

"Yes, Mr. Traveler, you have affected us," she said with a grin.

"How long will we wait here, Mr. Traveler?" King Aereth asked.

"Until we gain everything there is to gain from the city, sire. Then we can sail away unseen."

"Mr. Traveler, you didn't tell us you owned a castle. Tell us more about that," Pangolin said.

"Yes, Mr. Traveler, do tell," Lady Aylen said.

"The castle is a temporary purchase. It's not uncommon for caravan masters to have such sanctuaries ready and available for their party along the path of the Trail."

"I told you Mr. Traveler was royalty," Lady Aylen said.

"This is a *big* castle, Mr. Traveler." Pangolin looked around. "You do have a lot of money, don't you? But then, you've already been to Atlantea."

"Mr. Traveler lived there for years," King Aereth chimed in.

"Mr. Traveler, can you buy me a castle?" Lady Aylen asked.

"I think it's time for me to go," Traveler said. "Look! What's that at the top of the crawling trees?"

Everyone stopped. Lady Aylen jumped down from her kirin, and they all stared at the top canopy created by the three crawling trees high in the sky.

"What did you see, Mr. Traveler?" Lady Aylen turned and burst out laughing.

They all turned, and Mr. Traveler was gone.

"That's embarrassing," Pangolin said dryly. "Adults are not supposed to be fooled by that childish trick."

"Where did he go?" Lady Aylen looked around.

The fenodyree stood together chuckling under their breath.

"You're not going to tell us, are you?"

The four sprites shook their heads.

"What are we eating?" Grakdar asked.

The six Antaean giants had created their own campsite at the top of the inner mountain as the sun set. Sick giants when no longer sick became ravenous giants. It took all of the caravan's five hundred pech almost an hour of shuttling pull carts overflowing with food to feed them. But the food was not from the caravan's food stores.

"They call it squid." Barg stuffed more tentacle into his mouth.

"Never heard of it."

"It's like octopus," the giant Alebar said.

"What is octopus?" Grakdar asked.

"Grakdar, you know what octopus is! It's the sea thing with the tentacles and suckers. You're eating it," Barg said.

Grakdar looked at the food. "Is this meat? It's soft and slimy."

"It tastes good. I like it," another giant, Aronir, said.

"You'd eat an Erymanthian boar's testicles," Grakdar said.

The giants laughed.

"Look," Barg said.

The Tree Shepherd, Little Root, had reached the peak with the leshies' fourth crawling tree. The soul tree glowed bright.

"Oh, the bird," another giant said.

Their rarely seen magic healing Caladrius bird descended from the sky and nestled in the top of the soul tree's branches.

The giants stood. Several of the väki in their charred-brown and orange clothing and caps headed straight for them. Ignoring the giants and Tree Shepherd, they walked directly to the center of the peak and gazed out into the night sky.

"The fire väki can leave their small-realm to socialize," Grakdar said.

The giants joined the elemental sprites. The väki stood quietly as their hands and eyes flashed with fire for a few moments.

"We have three elements, Antaean," one of the väki said. "Our fire, the elfess has water elemental power, and you giants and the one human in magic armor have the earth elemental power."

"What does it matter?" Grakdar asked.

"It matters because we are in the realm of water elementals, too much power for even us without land."

"We are helpless without the land," Grakdar said.

"Then we must figure out a way to combine our limited power if the elfess is attacked by air elementals. This is their realm too."

"What can we do? The moment we sail, we will not touch land again until Atlantea."

"We must draw as much power as we can while we rest here, like the Tree Shepherds."

"What are you not telling us, väki?"

"Giant, we're not telling you lots of things."

"Tell us what we need to know then. You could have come up here while we were sleeping. You wanted to speak with us."

"If we should need to create a fire giant, be ready."

"Fire giant!" the other giants said.

"That is a legend."

"Antaeans and väki allied against the fairies. How do you think we defended against their fairy-storms?"

Grakdar looked at his comrades. "We don't know the magic."

"Then learn it. Ask the human, Traveler."

"Why would we need to ask a human about secret magic of giantkind? You tell us."

"We don't like you."

"We don't like you either."

"Is it true his magic sword is a piece of the ancient Titan's Star Slayer?" Barg asked.

"Väki don't care about rumors, but if true, then we have one of the most powerful sources of elemental magic—that of a star."

"As long as we do not encounter another time elemental. I did not know such a thing could exist," Grakdar said.

"It doesn't. The demon was created," the väki said. "But we did not come here to speak about that. Be ready. In this realm, undines and sylphs are not our friends."

"We know that. Giants live on the Oceanus Omnis too. We will be ready for your plan, väki, should we need to."

"Good."

"And we will collect so much power from the earth, the next time we combine our Antaean magic, we will be of a power never seen before. Be ready, little man."

Only their second day and Hobbs had his routine running like clockwork, as if he had also been the steward of Traveler's Castle as the men had dubbed it. With most of the caravan in the mountain courtyard, he'd spent half his time there overseeing the men's daily duties. During the day, one third of the time was for work, a third leisure, a third training. Everyone, whether domestic, laborer, or warrior, kept to the schedule.

From there he'd enter the castle interior with his bodyguards Tyfer and Oeric following but not too closely. Their caravan master directed everyone never to go anywhere alone, even within their castle. Hobbs liked to think he'd adopted the long strides of their caravan master. The night before, the brownies had fitted the corridors with torches, so they were always well lit. Cut-throat sentries were stationed along all corridors in pairs, armed with crossbows and shields, and wearing their talarian sandals.

The drawbridge remained down even at night but the main entrance was securely protected by the portcullis. Within the double tower was Pangolin himself and animal-like fae berserkers, led by Hax, the lionoid, large, tall, and bald, his face like a lion, with whiskers, but human ears on the side. The other fae berserkers were cat-like, reptilian, and boar-like with tusks. Their sorcerer on duty was their mole-like fae whose name Pangolin tried unsuccessfully to learn.

I'wulf managed the roving two-man patrol teams—Cut-throats with one chamrosh. The patrols traveled the main floor corridor, outside the keep in the mountain courtyard, and along the outer perimeter of the camp.

Down the corridor, before the exit to the courtyard, was a perpendicular corridor running the entire width of the keep. To the left were steps to the second floor, the main hall, and various storage rooms. To the right were spiral staircases to the tower.

The elves guarding the castle towers were under their own command. Hobbs still liked to visit with them. By day, the elfin questing knights, Lyre, the high elf, Talos, and the desert elves guarded with their falcons. At night, Shadu-mun and his moon elves took charge.

"Mr. Hobbs," Lyre said when the man appeared from the steps.

"Mr. Lyre, don't mind me. I like to take in a quick gaze from the tower roof."

The view from the gatehouse tower was of calm waters encircling their black sand island and a high reef miles away with rough waters beyond it. They sat in kind of a valley with the ocean around them like a giant wall in the distance.

"We did see a city ship earlier today," Lyre said. "It sailed by without stopping in the city."

"What is the reputation of this city of Kraken's Wake in your elfin kingdoms?"

"We care very little actually of mermaids, merman, and the like. If one is unlucky enough, they might meet up with one or more giant krakens. If not for Mr. Traveler's knowledge, it would be a city we'd avoid."

"Are you looking forward to visiting the elfin sea city?"

"Our kingdoms have no alliance with these water elves, so we are not expecting a cordial welcome. Elves are scattered far and wide in the magical lands. Not all are allies."

"That is, of course, true. I will continue with my rounds, then, and leave you to your day."

"Thank you for visiting, Mr. Hobbs. Do so any time."

"I will, Mr. Lyre, and do let me know if you require any supplies."

Hobbs had always been fascinated by the unicorn swords of the high elves. He had not seen any of the woodland elves with their leopard axex beasts, so he assumed they were being held in reserve.

As he ran down the spiral stone stairs, he heard metal-on-metal movement. He stepped out into the open courtyard to see Mr. Estus assembling row after row of his elfin armor golems to stand at the ready. Their weaponsmaster was busy with his task. Hobbs smiled and continued on with his rounds.

Traveler stood at the window of the ground floor meeting hall of the keep. Armor golems stood in formation as Estus inspected each one. Their weaponsmaster was forever the perfectionist.

"How close did we come to dying, Mr. Traveler?" Lady Aylen asked.

Traveler had his back to the group seated around the table: the royals, Gwyness, Frog-Dor, Dr'amal, and the fae-blood woman, Ursi.

"You've gotten a stark example of the importance of paying attention to even the smallest details. Such observations can mean the difference between life and death. City ships such as those, with the numbers of sorcerers onboard each—if I hadn't done what I did, we wouldn't have escaped. But it's not important."

"We did more than escape," Dr'amal said. "We destroyed an entire water fae fleet, or you tricked them with magic to destroy themselves."

"Were they in league with Oughtred, Mr. Traveler?" King Aereth asked. "The mermaid queen was convinced they were not, and weren't after any bounty. But they were out to destroy us."

"It could have been for any number of reasons, sire, including trickery. With their crew dead, there's nothing more to do but focus on our time here. Do you remember what I said of Kraken's Wake politics?"

"They have a royal city divided into a matriarchal section ruled by mermaids and ocean nymphs, a small patriarchal section ruled by tritons and sea centaurs," King Aereth replied.

"Not more centaurs," Lady Aylen said.

"And a third section ruled by no one called the Kelp Lands. An open market for trade, especially illegal trade in the rest of the city," King Aereth added. "All cities have such places, human or fae."

"Have no doubt of it. Kraken's Wake is ruled by women. They have the final say on matters that concern the entire city. The smaller patriarchal section has autonomy over their own affairs in their section alone. It's a reciprocal arrangement, as the main far away cities of sea centaurs and tritons have autonomous sections for mermaids and water nymphs."

"For now, we wait and prepare. The selkies will be joining us and we shall see about this alliance they spoke of. We will also seek out a few parties in the city, courtesy of information from Mr. Bragg."

"Mr. Bragg?" King Aereth asked.

"There may be other humans here from the Lands of Man," Traveler answered. "Kraken's Wake is no different than any other city in that regard. Parties may seek us out, and we can use them to our advantage for much needed information of what's ahead and the rumors of the ocean about us."

"What of the creature, the crab centaur?" Dr'amal asked Traveler.

"All you must do, Dr'amal, is notify me immediately if you or your father sense any of these creatures."

"I shall."

"How are you, Mr. Frog-Dor?" Traveler asked.

"Good, sir. I will be able to serve as the caravan's chief sorcerer, with Dr'amal's assistance."

"Yes."

Traveler turned his attention to Ursi, who like the other fae-bloods in the caravan had stayed hidden for a time while sailing. She appeared as she always did, in black clothing with her necklace of brown stones, but she, too, was a fae of land, and her clan was not comfortable near such vast waters.

"We are encountering more fae-bloods on our ocean journey," Traveler said.

"My clan is familiar with only two others: wolf and cat."

"We've encountered four other clans."

"What were the others?" Lady Aylen asked.

"Insect and fish, princess."

"Barracuda," Ursi corrected.

"Which insect?" Traveler asked her.

"There are too many of them to know for certain unless they use their magic."

"When we visit the queendom, Lady Aylen will take lead. You and Gwyness will be at her side." He looked at Lady Aylen. "You did quite well."

"Only because you prepared the king and me."

"Princess, again, remember you are not just a water elf. You have water elemental power. You can summon and use water as a weapon, and there is water all around us. An entire ocean, in fact. That makes you very dangerous. Show some of that confidence."

"But mermaids and water nymphs can do the same," Dr'amal said.

"Yes, but the princess's power isn't inferior to theirs."

Traveler noticed his dog rise to its feet. His dog stared at Frog-Dor. The sorcerer had his eyes closed with his hand to his temple.

"Do you sense it?" he asked.

Dr'amal also had her eyes closed. "Yes, at the main gate."

"Greetings, inside!"

The visitor was suddenly there, a tall, fair-skinned man in a hooded cloak. Behind the closed portcullis of the gatehouse, Pangolin and other Cut-throats watched him with suspicion. He appeared human except for his large webbed ears sprouting out from his hood. Beside the man floated a strange animal companion—a large milky-white jellyfish creature.

"I am Betta. May I approach?" the man asked.

"Slowly!" Pangolin called out through the portcullis.

The man approached the gate as the floating jellyfish hung in the air where it was.

"Where did he come from?" Pangolin asked the men in a whisper.

"He must have emerged from the water," one said.

"Did you see him, though?"

"No."

All the Cut-throats at the entrance shook their heads.

"Keep those crossbows on him at all times," Pangolin said.

"May I speak with your masters?" the man asked.

"For what reason?" Pangolin asked.

"Excellent craftsmanship, your crossbows. I can assure you I am no danger to you."

"The arrows are elfin forged," Pangolin said.

"Yes, but you are humans not elves. Such arrows would be of no benefit to you."

"We could hit you many times over with no effort, regardless," a Cut-throat sneered as he aimed the arrow tip of his crossbow through the portcullis gate.

A flash of light temporarily blinded the men.

Tentacles from the man's jellyfish pushed though the openings of the portcullis, knocking Pangolin and his three men hard into the stone slabs of the gatehouse.

"We're under attack!" Pangolin yelled the alarm, pulling his axe-mace from his back and swinging at the tentacles of the creature.

"Pangolin!" a man yelled, pointing.

From the water outside the castle appeared one blue-skinned woman after another in fish-scaled armor.

Cut-throats fired their crossbows but the humanoid with the large webbed ears waved his hand and all their arrows flew straight into the sky the second they passed the portcullis.

"A sorcerer! They've breached the magic barrier!" Pangolin swung and cut the creature's tentacles. The floating jellyfish grew twice in size, and its tentacles multiplied in number.

The gatehouse's defenders began arriving, ready for battle—Cut-throats and the mole-man. With one arm and a yell, Pangolin pounded a lever, and the portcullis rose halfway, severing the jellyfish's tentacles. As berserkers fired their crossbows in unison at the jellyfish, the sorcerer swept them away with a simple wave of his hand. Pangolin charged at him, the mole-looking fae following.

Suddenly, arrows from the tower ripped into the giant jellyfish, slamming it back into the water. The webbed-ear sorcerer barely had time to react and shield himself with a spell as Pangolin's axe-mace crashed down on him. An enraged Pangolin, his berserker fury welling up inside him, kicked the sorcerer so hard the man flew into the air and crashed into the water.

The blue-skinned woman reached them. One transformed into a blue orca whale and threw herself at Pangolin. Other women turned into several giant water snakes and one into a vicious hippopotamus to attack the Cut-throats spilling out of the castle's entrances. At that moment, a tidal wave rose behind the wall and swept the shape-shifters away like a giant hand. Pangolin turned to see Lady Aylen directing the water, a war trident in each hand.

Another female attacker rose from the water—a water nymph with the fairest of blue skin and a flowing dress of ocean flora. She raised her arms and a new tidal wave grew to tower higher than the castle wall. The volley of arrows from the tower elves passed right through her. Lady Aylen commanded a fist of water at the nymph, but it, too, passed through her.

The mole-looking fae ran, scooped up sand from the ground, and threw a ball of it at the nymph's face. She screamed as her head was wrapped in a magic sand paste, unable to see. Her tidal wave crashed back into the water. The nymph fought to free herself.

The caravan's own sorcerer, Frog-Dor came from the gate entrance and threw his own ball of magic at the nymph. All the water immediately froze to solid ice. The nymph's body shook then broke off from the icy surface of the water and fell into the cold depths.

More blue-skinned women rose from the water and the webbed-ear sorcerer reappeared holding a giant ball of blue light above his head. Lady Aylen violently swept them all away with another vertical tidal wave.

More of the caravan's warriors charged out from the castle as additional attackers arrived. Several female halflings with butterfly wings shot up from the water, antennae sprouting from their blue-skin foreheads, and shells in their hands. The water fairies blew their shells, and every man doubled over where they stood. A counter harmonic wave of such power rippled from the tower. The water fairies went unconscious and immediately plunged into the water below. Lady Aylen could see the Brothers Brimm on one of the two towers with large flutes to their mouths.

She turned and pointed her tridents, and all the water in front of the island receded, revealing a hidden army of mermaid archers.

"Fire!" Lyre yelled.

Elfin archers fired from the towers. Faun archers fired from the gatehouse. The ground rumbled but the giants were not Antaeans. Their own fire elemental sprites, the väki, rained balls of red fire down on the mermaids.

The mermaid sorceresses among them struggled to shield their armies from the onslaught. With a mere gesture, Lady Aylen lifted the water into a wall to shield the castle.

A brown seal swam to them and leapt onto the ground before the castle. The seal transformed into the humanoid Nori. A sea lion joined her, transforming into Otari. The selkies ran to the castle wavering their hands.

"They surrender!" Nori yelled. "We surrender," Nori repeated.

Pangolin raised his hand. "Cease fire!"

Lady Aylen closed her eyes, and the wall of water rushed back to the edge of the island swallowing the mermaid army below. But the mermaids slowly rose from beneath the waves, crawling onto the sandy shore.

Traveler stepped through the crowd of the caravan's warriors with his dog to face the selkies. He had his magic sword in hand. The mermaid army had fully gathered ashore.

The väki disappeared behind the castle walls as they shrank back to their normal size. In front of the castle were faun and elaphine archers. Drow warriors arrived, then King Aereth exited the gatehouse with Gwyness, Nirgund, his guardsmen, and a dozen other berserkers.

"What is the meaning of this, Nori?" Lady Aylen asked the selkies angrily.

"Another will explain," Nori answered.

The two selkie leaders turned to the water encircling their castle island. The army of mermaids parted as the bow of a ship pushed through the water. In moments, a huge, multi-level, seaweed-covered ship rose completely above the water, floated to the land, and sat on the edge of their island. A gangplank descended from the upper decks and rested on the sand as columns of people came down. A woman with a crown in green-and-red royal attire approached them with an army of men and women in armor, men in cloaked robes, and followed by eight-foot-tall-humanoid ant men with red eyes, crushing mandibles, and four arms holding a spear in each.

The webbed-ear fae was on his feet and took his place beside the human queen. There was a trace of blood on his mouth. She grabbed his chin to look at him.

"How badly were you wounded, Betta?" she asked.

"I will live a long life, my queen."

She laughed and let go of his chin.

"This is Queen Issaleth," Nori said. "She is an ally."

"An ally?" Pangolin asked angrily. "My allies don't attack me."

"We had to be sure." The queen stepped to them.

"Sure of what?" Lady asked.

"We wanted to be sure of your forces. Crude but effective," the queen said. "The rumors about Titan's Caravan are many. What is true and what is fable must be determined. You do have the means of defending against sirens, which is good. We are not in their domain but there are growing rumors of their ships traveling these oceans. They are carnivorous creatures, you know."

"You could have been killed," Pangolin said.

"Killed?" Issaleth asked. "If we were so weak as to be killed by you, then we have no cause to be on Titan's Trail. But it gave us a chance to observe your strategy—defense only. If you were powerful enough to kill any of us, and did, we would know categorically that you were evil, as our intention was clearly not to kill you."

"This attack was your doing?" King Aereth asked.

The queen took special notice of him. "King Aereth of Helm Earldom."

"Yes."

"One of the members of the Kings Elder, along with Kings Sigbard the Blessed of Westmoor and Eotell the Courageous of Bridgewater."

King Aereth laughed. "King Eothelm the Blessed of Strongbridge and King Sigbard the Humble of Eastmoor."

Queen Issaleth glanced at the selkies. "They are who they claim to be." The selkies nodded.

"What kingdom are you from?" King Aereth asked.

"King Aereth, I am the queen of Armathain."

"That is in Baltica, is it not?"

"Yes, it." She gestured to one of her knights. The knight handed her a letter. "A letter from your comrades."

King Aereth was taken aback but took it from her. He opened it and began reading. His face lit up, and the biggest smile came over this face. He looked at Lady Aylen. "Our kingdoms are safe! King Rol and the forces of Cirencester have been defeated. There were casualties on our side, but Western Avalonia is free again."

"Sire, this is incredible news. I feared we might never have known what happened," Lady Aylen said.

"This lifts such a weight from my heart. King Eothelm and Sigbard are well. Your city was undamaged. Our combined forces led by our chief sorcerers defeated them despite 'the many demonic beasts under their command.'"

"Demonic beasts?" Lady Aylen asked.

"It doesn't say more."

"We can well imagine what they might have been," Lady Aylen said.

"How did you come by this letter? Do the Kings Elder know of our whereabouts?" King Aereth asked.

"They know you made it to the Great Forest," Queen Issaleth replied. "We in Baltica have sorcerers too. They sent a parcel of letters in the magical form of a bird should we encounter you at any of the sea cities before Atlantea."

"How would you know of us, queen?" Lady Aylen asked.

"Know of you? Everyone here knows of you."

"Oughtred's bounty?" Lady Aylen asked.

"Bounty? No. I know of no such thing. We know of the destruction of the Four Kings' New Xenhelm in the heart of Faë-Land Major and the death of his entire army of war wizards. You don't know what has happened? How could you? You've been marching through the Great Forest. There is much to speak about."

King Aereth looked at the letter in his hand again. "Thank you, Queen Issaleth, for this."

"You are most welcome, King Aereth. I am happy to once again see others from our mutual homelands. I hope to form our own alliance and sail to Atlantea as one fleet."

"It would seem that you have more than enough of your own allies for your journey."

"No. There are more, much more, king."

"But you have an army of shape-shifters," Lady Aylen said.

"The nixes? No. The nixes and mermaids will not leave their city. This is their home. They protect here only. We're the wanderers along the Titan's Trail for Atlantea. You did not ask the question."

"What question?" King Aereth asked.

"How long have we been here in Kraken's Wake?"

"Then how long?"

"Three years."

"Three years?" Lady Aylen asked. The royals glanced at each other. Good news always followed the bad, and vice versa, on the Trail.

"We have been unable to get to even the city of White Waters. That is why we need a fleet. We've waited these three years, waited for an answer to prayers."

"Waiting for the next Kings' Caravan?"

"No, Lady Aylen. Out here, caravans to Atlantea happen every six months. You are the first outsiders to make it to the city in three years, no one else."

"What was that outrage then from when we first arrived?" Traveler asked. "You are obviously well-informed of our travels."

Queen Issaleth stepped toward him with a smirk. She carried herself with the bearing of a royal, but up close, her dark eyes, with the scar near one, and calluses revealed she was a warrior queen, probably trained and fighting in battles since she was a child. In the Baltica Empire, it was the life of noble and commoner alike. She looked down at the dog. "You are the human caravan master we've heard about."

"Anything good, queen?"

"And bad and everything in between. We had to be careful not to anger either one of you in our test. New Xenhelm found out what happens when either of you are angered.

"To directly answer your question, which you already know the answer to, the outrage of the leaders at your arrival was a performance for the sake of others. Kraken's Wake is one city, but it isn't a unified city. Women and men fight all the time in life. When they control their own sections of a city, that conflict is amplified a hundredfold. Then there is the Kelp Lands with its inhabitants. May I ask how a human knows sea phookas?"

Lady Aylen, King Aereth, Pangolin and others gathered around for their caravan master's response.

"I'll happily recite the story when we gather for our first meal together to discuss an alliance."

"A fair exchange."

"What of these Kelp Lands?"

"Have you ever visited them before?"

"I have, queen, and I doubt they have changed."

"Yes. One should be very careful about visiting the Kelp Lands without an army. I have never set foot there and would not. People disappear there. If you were under my command, I'd forbid you to go there, but you're not. You seem interested in the area."

"You seem to know why I am interested in the area."

"You both seem to know something we do not," King Aereth remarked.

Traveler suppressed a smile. "Queen, will you excuse us for a brief moment? Sire, princess, a word."

"Of course," the queen said.

Traveler led the royals back to the gatehouse while all watched and waited.

The moment they stepped in, Traveler reached into his cloak and threw something against the ground. The royals found themselves in an empty room that looked like a hut. They had passed into a small-realm.

"Should we tell them that Oughtred intends to conquer Atlantea?" Traveler asked bluntly.

"I still can't see how that's possible, Mr. Traveler, if they are a people more powerful than all humans, fae, and elementals combined," Lady Aylen said. "You lived there. But are you suspicious of her?"

"No, we can trust her, but we do not know who else is in this alliance we seek to join. And I would say it's impossible, princess, but the Four Kings have done too many things that should be impossible. I pose the question because they have given us important new information. Oughtred's forces have been defeated in our own human lands. We have destroyed his war wizard army. We have escaped all his efforts to destroy us. We have forced him to alter his plans, which makes him far more dangerous. I suspect he will take on more dark allies."

"The crab centaur?" Lady Aylen asked.

"Perhaps. But Queen Issaleth revealed something else. Kraken's Wake has been blockaded from Atlantea."

"Yes, I realized that too," King Aereth said.

"If they've been kept here for three years, it must be a force never seen before. The water fae of Kraken's Wake are extremely powerful. Since we've been reminded of our Lands of Man, the army of this ocean city rivals those of Avalonia and Baltica combined. It has many warriors and magic-casters."

"Then we must meet with them immediately," King Aereth said. "Keep the knowledge of Oughtred's plan—or boast—to ourselves for the present time."

"Agreed, sire. We should meet and be on our way," Lady Aylen said.

"Are we also to assume from your brief conversation with the queen that you will be visiting these Kelp Lands?" King Aereth asked.

"Yes, sire, and both you and the princess will be accompanying me."

The night guard was on duty. Sho was another fae berserker with cat-like features—cat eyes, whiskers, and retractable claws in his hands and feet. He usually worked during the day, but Pangolin wanted extra sentries for the castle perimeter. Traveler had told them that the water fae wizard had breached their magic barrier simply because the magic tip of a Cutthroat crossbow arrow had. None of the men would make such a mistake again. They had two magical circles around the castle, and everyone knew to not even touch the portcullis, let alone stick a weapon or finger through it.

But something was happening outside the castle. He could see the water bubbling in the strong moonlit night. His fellow Cut-throats and two of the drow warriors approached too.

A wave erupted and washed toward the entrance. Within its wave was a sea centaur—upper body of a human, lower front like a horse, with two legs, and the giant tail of a fish for the rear. The male sea centaur wore glistening fish-scaled armor on his chest and held a single trident.

"We request a meeting with your masters," he said.

Water flowed under the east wall of the castle to one of the rooms in the keep. As an ocean city, primarily for water fae, such a room would have been constructed with a pool in the ground but was actually an entrance for any swimming into the castle.

Hobbs and a group of men brought in tables and chairs. Brownies set magic torches, evenly spaced on the stone walls. Traveler and the royals had been woken, though Traveler hadn't been asleep long, as he'd been studying his nautical maps.

Three male sea centaurs and two male tritons made up the contingent of royal visitors with a half dozen hulking humanoid crocodile men in armor bearing long tridents.

"We were impressed by the fact that you carry the banner of the centaurs of Chiron. They do not lightly bestow such honors," the sea centaur leader said, moving from their light conversation of a short while.

"We were deeply honored by them entrusting us with their banner," King Aereth said.

"The banner of the Chiron and the centaur king Lyongriff," Traveler added.

"They are among the wisest sages and oracles in all the magic lands," the sea centaur said.

"My comrades saw other centaur species for the first time—cat, leopard, tiger, black and white panther, lion, including a winged lion centaur," Traveler said.

"We heard you will be meeting with the women," the sea centaur leader said abruptly.

The chairs and table were for the royals and Traveler, at the direction of the water fae. The royals realized that the sea centaurs and tritons wanted a physical barrier of sorts between them as the sea centaurs rested on the ground facing them with their strange bodies, while the tritons and crocodile men stood around their water fae comrades.

"Heard from whom?" King Aereth asked.

"We have our sources," a sea centaur said.

"Will you be joining their fleet?" a triton asked.

"We have yet to meet with them, so we cannot say," King Aereth said.

"Did they tell you they've been here for three years?" the sea centaur asked.

"They did," King Aereth replied.

"Did they tell you of the forces outside the city on the way to White Waters?" the triton asked.

"Why don't you simply tell us? Otherwise, we'll be here all night," King Aereth said.

"We would not follow the women, but if you have an agreement with them, we would be willing to join your fleet. But only your party would be in command," the sea centaur said.

"What is your problem with 'the women'?" Lady Aylen asked. "You live in the same city."

"We will not bore you with the details of the long tension between our territories," the sea centaur said. "We coexist, but we are not allies, unless it is to protect the city, which we've had to do many times over the years."

"Who are the adversaries?" Traveler asked.

"All that you'd expect, but their numbers and magic are greater, and their vessels more powerful," a triton said.

The sea centaur smiled. "A human caravan master. The Atlanteans are fond of humans."

"Because we never made war on them," Traveler said.

"Humans could not make war on anyone in the magical lands, but it is a fair point. We received the reward we deserved for the treachery of our ancestors. We hope to reverse that enmity with the Atlanteans upon our arrival."

"We were attacked by a fleet of merrows, oceanids, and tritons," Lady Aylen said.

"They were not from the city," the triton said. "All elfin races are not allies of one another. Some even make war on each other. It's no different here. There were rumors of them working together in the past and for enemies of the city."

"But it does not matter. They're dead. You're alive. We carry on," the sea centaur said.

"Your Kraken's Wake queen denied they could have been in league with the Xenhelmians," Traveler said.

"She's not our queen," the triton said. "We live in the city she rules."

"Of course, they were in league with them," the sea centaur said. "Your encounter proves it. Why the women denied it is the question you should be asking."

"I must press the question," King Aereth said. "What enemies out there have kept your parties from sailing forth to the city of White Waters? I cannot believe sea goblins, these merrows, or even disreputable members of your own kind could keep you confined for years. You are a powerful force in your own right."

"Sea goblins are not powerful enough. Maybe their land cousins are a terror, but here on the oceans, they are as formidable as Finmen. There are dark water nymphs like the melusine, who are part snake. There are other races. All are powerful. There is fear of ships of sirens. Elementals couldn't be bothered, and all water elementals are allies of the city. We are saying to you that we do not know. Those who have escaped have seen the ships but not the crew. Others have simply never returned," the sea centaur said.

"Ever seen crab centaurs?" Traveler asked.

The water fae men looked at each other.

"You've seen one?" the triton asked.

"We have."

"Centauro-triton, we must tell the others," another sea centaur said to their leader.

"When?" the leader asked Traveler.

"The same day we were attacked by the nymph-triton fleet and the adaro."

"What happened to the creature?" a triton asked.

"We let it fall off the ship in the battle."

"You didn't destroy it?"

"Mr. Traveler was busy saving our ship and all our lives from the nymph-triton fleet and adaro through sailing skill alone," Lady Aylen snapped.

"That is fortunate for you, but that means the creature lives," the triton said.

"As disturbing as your news is, crab centaurs are never seen in large numbers."

"That we know of," Traveler said to the sea centaur leader. "And what of their blood allies, the spider centaurs, who do sometimes travel by ship and in enormous numbers."

The sea centaurs and tritons erupted into heated conversation and yelling. The fae language spoken was unknown even to Traveler, but he had heard it before.

The emotions of the water fae were a combination of shock and anger, but they calmed themselves to return their attention to Traveler and the royals.

"You've revealed more to us in one sitting than all our many scouts," a triton said.

"You still know more than us," Traveler said.

"You have stumbled upon something quite profound without knowing it—the answer to our mystery here in Kraken's Wake," the sea centaur leader said. "Do you not know why crab centaurs are so feared?"

"Not their alliance with their spider centaur cousins?" Traveler asked.

"No. In your human lands, you have an old myth of what you call the Olympiads of Olympius."

"Mount Olympus," King Aereth said.

"Yes. They commanded a single kraken to exact retribution and vengeance upon disloyal human cities," the sea centaur leader said.

"I have never been one for fiction, personally," Traveler said.

The water fae were amused. "Not fiction," the sea centaur said. "It was the time you humans were new upon Pan-Earth. You were savage primitives not much different than your own animals."

"And the great fae races of Pan-Earth?" Traveler asked.

"We were one great alliance. There was no separation of elves, drows, and goblins, nor sprite, fairy, and giant. There was no fae of light and dark then."

"No good fae or dark fae? Said another way, then, you fae were as savage and primitive as your beasts and humankind."

Centauro-triton glared at Traveler for a moment. "Should I be proudly insulted by what you have said to us or marvel at your own self-praising wisdom for a human?"

"I have said what I would have said to any other—human or fae. Any civilization that makes no distinction between good and evil, kindness and cruelty, is not civilized. It is wholly savage and primitive."

"A less traveled...traveler would not have known that. Yes, our fae ancestors were no more uniformly noble as an over-race than we are now. But the Olympiads did exist, though the myth about them is completely distorted and mostly false. The one from the story called Poseidon did exist too, however. He was a crab centaur, or the race that spawned them and many others. Crab centaurs can entrance and command krakens."

"We are in a city called Kraken's Wake, in waters that are the breeding ground for the kraken species,"

Traveler said, as disturbed as the royals at the revelation.

"Now, you and I are equal in our knowledge of the plight of Kraken's Wake," Centauro-triton said. "But I would be very careful about who you share this knowledge of coming terror with."

"Why should anything happen? Nothing has in three years," Lady Aylen said. "That is what we've been told. The danger has been trying to get to the city of White Waters."

"Something has happened, water elf," the sea centaur said. "The crab centaur you dispatched happened. You, Titan's Caravan, have happened. You are the cause of Kraken's Wake's plight. But then, you know that already."

The moon hung like a giant pearl in the night sky directly above their castle sanctuary. Traveler walked with the royals back to their well-lit outdoor camp of men sleeping around campfires with only a blanket to cover them and in tents or giant-slippers. Drow sentries and patrols were at work, brownies at the campfires chatting away.

"What do we do?" Lady Aylen asked.

The image of a single kraken was horrific enough. Every human child had grown up with such stories. Those were stories, though, to scare children and make them behave. What they faced was real and not only one kraken. Traveler's refusal to tell them how many krakens existed in the waters around Kraken's Wake did not reassure the royals.

Traveler said, "We get a good night's rest, as short as it will be, and be ready in the morning."

"Anything of note on your maps, Mr. Traveler?" King Aereth asked, trying to change the subject.

"No, sire. Nothing at all. Clear waters for as far as the map goes. But based on what our visitors told us, that means nothing. Our enemies are hidden from the maps. Their magic is that powerful."

They had reached their royal tents.

"Good night, sire."

"You both as well." The king disappeared into his tent he shared with the berserker Nirgund, who had waited up. His thirteen alphyns were already asleep, clustered together.

Lady Aylen stopped at her tent. The women's tent was quiet. Gwyness and the female half-elves must have all been asleep. "I do mean it, Mr. Traveler. You'd tell me if something was wrong, right?"

"I would, Princess."

She touched his shoulder for a moment then entered the women's tent.

Traveler entered his and stood in the dim light for a moment. He glanced at the dog lying on the ground near his sleeping rug. He had his animal companion remain behind to keep watch over his tent and his maps. The princess had sensed something, and she was right.

Morning brought the change of guards at the gatehouse. When Pangolin arrived, Hobbs, with the aid of two of the caravan lads, handed out and helped men change their charm necklaces to guard against the enchantment powers of water nymphs and the like.

"You as well, Mr. Pangolin," the steward said. "I have yours here."

"Yes, Mr. Hobbs." Pangolin grinned as he removed his helmet. Most of the men never saw their master-at-arms without his helmet.

"I have news for you, Mr. Pangolin," the cat-like fae berserker said.

"What?"

"We had visitors last night."

"Here?"

"In the keep. They swam in."

"Swam in? Who?"

"Ichthyocentaurs."

"What are those?"

The berserker laughed. "Sea centaurs."

"Why didn't you say that before? We saw them when we arrived. I don't know how they move about on land or in the sea."

"They, in fact, can move faster than mermaids."

"That I'd have to see. What happened, then?"

"How would I know? I wasn't in the meeting. Ask Mr. Traveler or the royals."

"What about Mr. Hobbs? Mr. Hobbs, were you in the meeting last night with our sea centaur visitors?"

The steward looked at them and smiled. "Ask Mr. Traveler or the royals."

The crawling trees had grown even larger than the towering keep. From the topmost branches, Elman lay on his chest and watched the ocean around Kraken's Wake carefully. With his magical eyes, he could see farther than any fae in the caravan, most fae in fact, which was why Traveler gave him watch duty. The trees blocked only a small section of the panoramic view. From his vantage point, the half-elf could see that theirs wasn't the only island in the land-walker section of the city. The islands were enclosed in the gigantic lake within the dead volcano or head of the giant kraken of the city's namesake. Their island was the largest at the center and had the highest elevation.

A single black city ship slowly sailed by in the distance to the south of the city. Above the ship, circling, were strange birds. He couldn't see them clearly. *Did the oceans have harpies?* He peered through a telescope lens Traveler had given him. His eyes were able to finally cut through whatever concealing spell they were using.

"Gargoyles," Elman said.

"Yes," one of the kilmoulis said.

Humans and fae alike often forgot that the kilmoulis despite their strange appearances with their large noses covering half their faces and the fact that they spoke and ate through their noses, were sprites. They could fly when they wanted to, though they rarely did so. A few of them joined the half-elf, sitting together on a large branch. The rest of their members were at the base of the tree.

"Do you smell their scent from here?" Elman asked.

"Yes. We sensed them even before you saw them."

"Is the ship gargoyles only?"

"No," one of them said. "The waves and winds of these oceans make it harder, but if we focus long enough, we can complete the picture of many living things."

The castle keep was busy with activity. Traveler stepped through the door of one of the rooms with his dog. Elman was at the window watching the Cut-throats weapons training with his fellow half-elf comrades. The kilmoulis sat on the floor nearby talking.

"Mr. Traveler." The sprites smiled with their eyes.

"Mr. Elman and company." The caravan master joined them at the window. "Mr. Hobbs said you had news. What have you seen, Mr. Elman?"

"A gigantic black ship with gargoyles and giants." Elman motioned to the sprites.

"Giants?" Traveler asked.

"Yes, Master Traveler. One argus. Ten fomorians," a kilmoulis answered.

"A city ship for less than a dozen giants, Mr. Traveler?" Elman asked.

"More room for cargo on the way back."

"What kind of giants are fomorians, Mr. Traveler?"

"Sea giants with heads similar to those of goats."

"Goat-headed?"

"Yes, and quite dangerous."

"And an argus giant. I know of them. I was told they are rare."

"Yes, they are, and all far from their lands. Have you seen other ships of any size?"

"No others."

"Let me know of any ships entering or leaving the city. Have your comrades join you to help."

"Will I be in charge, Mr. Traveler?"

"Mr. Elman, you have always been in charge of your half-elf comrades."

"Please tell them that explicitly for me, Mr. Traveler." Elman grinned.

"Are you able to sense through water?" Traveler asked the kilmoulis.

The kilmoulis nodded. "We must be underwater to do so, Master Traveler."

"I have the perfect room, then. Half of you remain with Mr. Elman, and others will be in a special room for a unique vigil. I will have some of the animal men keep you company. In these waters, one must be wary of what may swim up from below."

Gresham, the caravan's healer, spent most of his day working alongside the brownies in preparation for their eventual departure from the sea city. Teams of humans, brownies, and pech prepared food provisions for the caravan's many animals, especially their giant lizards, created charms and magic torches, and worked on a variety of magical defenses for their ship. He was a laborer for the day, not a healer, which he gladly embraced. When a healer's services were needed, it often meant someone might die.

"Mr. Gresham."

Traveler appeared at one of the working teams seated in a circle, creating charms not for the caravan but to nail on the doors of the ship. The humans wondered what creature such charms would ward off but were afraid to ask, as they might get an answer that would keep them up at night.

"Yes, Mr. Traveler." Gresham jumped to his feet.

Their caravan master led him to one of the rooms of the keep with his dog at their side. Traveler closed the door behind them when they entered one of the smaller rooms.

"Mr. Gresham, I have another special task for you that will begin immediately."

"However I can help, sir."

"Before we stepped into the Great Forest, I made preparations for the centuries-old mystery of the Forest,' which we now know was a landvættir larger than ever before seen, and older than any even in fae history."

"All of us could have died and disappeared and no one would have known."

"Yes, my dog and I were as helpless as all others, except my plan saved us—a special small-realm for my darklings to occupy, Mr. Bragg's golem, and a gemstone. I had other means in place, in case all of us became incapacitated for any reason, but our salvation came down to them. We will do the same here."

"Are you saying such powerful beings exist in this domain?"

"I am, and more than one—beings both great and small, single entities and swarms of creatures. We must be ready."

"I will be separated from the caravan."

"Yes, but not alone. It must be done. You will be able to see all. You will be our designated savior should it come to that. I'm making similar preparations with others so it will not come to that, but I prefer to prepare for all possibilities."

"You have ensured our safe journey to this point, and we all are confident you will see us to Atlantea. Yes, sir. I will do what is needed to ensure our success. Besides, I will never be as good a healer as you."

"You don't have to be as good as me, Mr. Gresham. You just need to be as good as you can be. But you do need to be good at this task for now."

"I will accomplish my task, sir."

Elman sat on a chair on the roof of the keep's tower, staring out as he ate a large water fruit with his other hand. He often skipped his morning meal, preparing to snack most of the day. An explosion of rainbow colors blocked his view—a swarm of butterflies. Two eyes appeared in the center of them, scaring the half-elf.

"Boo!"

Wildglow, the larger of the two fairy sisters popped through, giggling. Her smaller sister, Sunpetal, flew up too.

"Why are you here, elf?" Wildglow asked.

"I'm not an elf," Elman said. "Half-elves are not elves."

"Half-elf, elf, who cares? Why are you here?"

"Where else would I be?" Elman asked.

"You can't see from here."

"I can see better than you."

"Grab him."

"Grab him? What do you mean?" Elman yelled as the swarms picked up the half-elf and carried him off.

As he flew through the air, he noticed that the view of the sky and ocean wavered as if he were looking through a clear barrier just past the castle perimeter. The swarms dropped him on the top canopy of one of the crawling trees. He was about to yell at the two laughing fairies when he turned his head. His mouth dropped open. Pushing across the wide-open ocean was a blackish mountain towering into the clouds above. Circling at the peak were swarms of flying gargoyles, some flying in one direction, the others in opposite.

Time had come for Titan's Caravan to visit with the queendom of Greater Kraken's Wake ruled by the mermaids and water nymphs. Gwyness prepared for their noon meal with the other water fae leaders and could not shake the feeling of intense dread. Traveler had told the royals that they would not be going into the Kelp Lands after all, which of course led to many questions as to why. But Gwyness did not join in. The only thing that raised her spirits was the appearance of her black antlered kirin at her side. She stroked the forehead of the magnificent beast.

Traveler led their party from the castle along the white-pebbled path then to the black sand to a waiting fish-shaped vessel, more like a chariot with rows of chairs for passengers. When all were seated—Traveler and his dog, the royals, Gwyness, the mole man fae, Frog-Dor, Dr'amal, Ursi, a dozen berserkers, and a dozen of Bragg's savage elfin comrades, with the kirins at the rear—the vessel submerged. A thin bubble covered the open chariot as it moved forward on its own power. The visibility underwater remained breathtaking. The ocean waters swarmed with aquatic life. Gwyness peered over the side of the vessel. Many miles away, the bright, vibrant waters just stopped, yielding to a barrier of blackness. All Gwyness could think of as they sailed underwater to Kraken's Wake proper was the saying that if one died in the Oceanus Omnis, it would take a century for their falling body to reach the bottom.

As they approached the main underwater city, they could see the area that was called the Kelp Lands more clearly. A multitude of hamlet-like buildings on coral hills enshrouded by giant green weeds rising from the ocean. Like the rest of Kraken's Wake, it bustled with water fae, animals, and underwater vessels, small and large.

They passed many castle townships until reaching the city proper with the largest of structures. Mermaid warriors, their chests clad in fish-scaled armor and wearing helmets, surrounded them, armed with tridents. The entrance to their main castle was in the center of the structure, a gate heavily guarded by mermaids and humanoid female fae riding majestic blue-white hippocampi—front half of a horse, body and tail of a fishlike snake. Among them were many leokampoi—fish-tailed lion beasts with their own mermaid minders. The beasts were hyperactive, ready to attack but restrained, their clawed forearms scratching at the water. Their vessel had to pass through a gauntlet of guards until they finally reached the royal tower. A large flag—with the symbol of a two-fish-tailed crowned mermaid holding an inverted squid above her head—hung from the ceiling

The passageways of the inner castle were giant tunnels flawlessly carved and polished and filled with guards and domestic staff that stood at attention. The nymphs on hippocampi led them to a giant hall, and they shot up to the surface. In moments, all the water of the hall drained out, and their vessel rested on an ancient white marble floor. Before them were a delegation of mermaids, water nymphs, and blue-skinned women. They recognized the blue-skinned women as the shape-shifting nixies, alluring like all nymphs but without weapons, like the others. Their armor was ceremonial, including the many different type of helmets adorned with figurines of fish, tridents, or water beasts.

Also, among them were the selkie clan and Baltican humans. The mermaids rose on their lower fish half, looking like cobras waiting to pounce. Then their fish tails became humanoid legs.

Traveler stepped out first and led their party to the mermaids.

"Welcome again," Nori, the female selkie, said with a nod. "You remember Queen Issaleth of Armathain."

The crowned human queen wore a new lucent-green battle dress. Her attendants were knights without helmets and men in cloaked robes. The formidable ant men she had before were not present. Queen Issaleth acknowledged them with a nod.

"Our hostess is Queen Geneva," Nori reintroduced the mermaid queen. "This is Queen Oluania of the oceanids of Kraken's Wake," Nori said of the tall queen.

Traveler's party responded with nods.

"We can dispense with all the formalities of exchanging names and titles. We should sit, eat, and get to the business at hand," Geneva said.

Queen Geneva noticed the three kirins and walked to the beautiful beasts waiting near the vessel. Both groups followed her.

"Dragon-horses," Geneva said. "This one is bred for the ocean."

"Yes," Lady Aylen said as she walked to her lucent-blue kirin with its catfish whiskers and unicorn horn.

"They are very far from their magical lands." Geneva looked at the golden and black kirins. She turned to her staff. "We shall eat."

Giant shell tables were brought into the hall by mermaids, in full humanoid form, and in moments, all were seated and plates of food were served, all the delicacies of the waters around them.

The largest shell table had both water fae queens at the head with Lady Aylen and Titan's Caravan on one side and the Kraken's Wake delegation on the other.

"We saw mermen in our lands, but they were much different in appearance," Lady Aylen said.

"Fish with human heads," Geneva said. "Lesser mermen to the eye but greater in their magic. They live here too. Most are seers and oracles. The mermen you see here in the hall are domestics and fighters."

"We were told that the men came to visit you last night," Oluania, the nymph queen, said. "Always so predictable."

"They did," Lady Aylen said. "They wish to join our fleet to Atlantea."

"Yes, as long as others do all the fighting and open the path for them to slither through," Geneva said.

"Queen Geneva, may I ask what has happened in recent years that has created the rancor between your two principalities of the city?" Traveler asked.

She stared at him. "Yes, you were in our city before. It must appear a very different state of affairs, indeed.

Briefly, they tried to seize control of the city from us when most of our warriors were occupied elsewhere. Parties hiding in the Kelp Lands aided their treachery. However, we dealt with the agitators in the Kelp Lands, and we lessened the men's section of the city by half. If we didn't need the alliances of triton and sea centaur king in general, we would have expelled them altogether."

"You are very forgiving," Lady Aylen said. "More so than I would have been, if I were in your place."

"We had no reason to press any further. Soon enough the city will face another crisis and all its residents will have to come to its defense. That has not changed and has been that way for millennia," Oluania replied.

"A wise and mature decision," Lady Aylen said. "Though I can't necessarily say I'm either."

The queens laughed first, then the other water fae women joined. The tension of the hall was finally broken.

The hall had dispersed into smaller groups of conversations as the royals and city leadership continued on at the head of the table. Aereth's and Lady Aylen's kirins sat on the ground behind them.

Off to the side, in front of the main table, Gwyness stood waiting with her kirin. Their two sorcerers, Frog-Dor and Dr'amal, and Ursi waited with her.

"The last time we were in a big city, we had to deal with a day-walking troll," Dr'amal recalled. "Trolls, wind elves, dark fae, and high goblins."

"Hopefully, this city will not be Fae'el." Gwyness stroked the side of her kirin.

"Do you believe we will leave this city or the next without a battle?" Dr'amal asked.

"Battle or no, we will get to Atlantea."

"If we were attacked here, we wouldn't have enough forces to defend ourselves," Ursi said.

"Mr. Traveler knows what he is doing, and his dog is our army," Gwyness said.

"Mr. Traveler is our army," Dr'amal said. "His sword and bag of tricks."

"You must tell me the meaning of this term 'bag of tricks,'" Gwyness said.

"It's not a term. It's a magic bag on your person, literally a bag of tricks."

Frog-Dor turned. "We're joined by another."

Mermen ran to the side of the hall and pulled a human from the water then another—Pangolin and Elman.

Traveler and the royals stood from the table and watched as their man-at-arms and half-elf scout joined Gwyness and her group. Elman spoke to them calmly and quietly with Pangolin looking on.

"Do you need to attend to your people?" Queen Geneva asked.

"We can continue our discussion." Traveler returned his attention to the water fae queens and selkie leaders. "What is your theory as to the hidden forces preventing passage to White Waters and beyond?"

"We do not know," Queen Geneva replied.

"The actions are deliberate and planned. Our ships cannot sail out, but unknown ships can, and there are plenty of vessels that sail from the Atlantean waters here," Queen Oluania said.

"What theories do you have?" the mermaid queen asked Traveler.

"My theories wouldn't hold much weight as you are the ones here and have undoubtedly used every means available to determine the true nature of these dark forces."

"You said this began three years ago?" King Aereth asked.

"Yes," Queen Issaleth replied.

"What is the significance?"

"The significance is that it all began soon after the last Kings' Caravan of the Four Kings of Xenhelm passed by our city for Atlantea," Queen Geneva answered. "A fleet of flying ships purposely flying above our city for all to see. The trouble began weeks after."

"Then it doesn't have anything to do with us," Traveler said.

"Why do you say that?" Queen Oluania asked. "His plans may have begun long before you met, but he is aware of you now and he knew of us then. The rumors are this human king Oughtred doesn't tolerate his enemies living, nor any threat to his goals."

"That is why we must have our own unified fleet to sail to Atlantea," Queen Issaleth said.

"Are the mermaids and nymphs of Kraken's Wake agreeable to this?" Traveler asked.

"We are more concerned with ridding our territory of whatever dark allies the Four Kings command in the region from here to White Waters. Whatever can break that hold on our territory, we will support. If that means sailing as a unified fleet, even with the men, then yes, we are in agreement."

"Then we shall sail as a unified fleet to Atlantea," Queen Issaleth said.

"The presence of the Four Kings has spurred other alliances too. In fact, one of our oldest allies is sending their own fleet to join us. You have arrived at the most opportune time."

The oceanid queen laughed. "We will make Oughtred dead again, but this time, he will not rise."

The look on Traveler's and the royals' faces showed their surprise.

"We thought you knew he was a fiend," Queen Geneva said.

"We do," King Aereth said. "We didn't expect you did."

"Dead but alive. Yes, we know," Queen Oluania replied.

"He's a lich," Queen Geneva said.

Traveler's face appeared especially upset.

"What is a lich?" Lady Aylen asked.

"You do know of what humans call zombies and ghouls?" Queen Geneva asked.

"We encountered them in Faë-Land," King Aereth said. "Minotaurs."

"Minotaurs?" Nori asked.

"Minotaur ghouls," Traveler added. "Princess, each is more intelligent and powerful than the other. Zombie. Ghoul. Lich."

"Why does this trouble you, Mr. Traveler?" King Aereth asked.

"Things are beginning to make sense. I had thought it was a dark spell to extend his life far past death itself, but this is different." Traveler looked at the queens and Nori. "This fleet of one of your oldest allies, which allies?"

"The cecaelia," Queen Geneva said with pride. "A fleet larger than all the ships Kraken's Wake will send. Then all we must do is reach the elves of White Waters. Our combined fleet will be unstoppable."

The royals, queens, and Nori noticed Traveler's pained expression.

"Mr. Traveler," King Aereth said. "What is wrong?"

"Queen Geneva, could Kraken's Wake withstand an attack from the cecaelia?"

"Attack? Why would they attack us? They are part of our fleet."

"Could you?" Traveler asked.

"What a question. Could you withstand an attack from your water elfess or your wizards? The question is nonsense. They are our allies," Queen Geneva said, irritated.

"We encountered a crab centaur before we arrived here," Traveler said. "We told the sea centaurs and tritons last night."

The queen's entire demeanor and expression changed. Anger turned to fear.

"What did they say?" Queen Oluania asked.

"Crab centaurs can mesmerize krakens," Traveler said.

"Our city is named after them, but the krakens spawn and travel many leagues from here," Geneva said.

"So do the cecaelia," Traveler said.

The queens just stared at him without a word. The selkies looked frighten.

"What are cecaelia, Mr. Traveler?" King Aereth asked. "Lady Aylen and I don't know."

"Mermaids but instead of the lower half of fish, they have the lower half of an octopus," Traveler replied, not taking his eyes off the two water fae queens.

"The legend isn't true," Queen Geneva said.

"Is that so? Two races that are said to summon and command krakens. With the Four Kings out there, I would wager the legend *is* true. Then you tell us you know him to be a lich," Traveler said.

"What did you think him to be, or his sons?" Queen Geneva asked. "Even your theory was without merit. Dead but alive means you can be only one of a limited number of dark creatures—if they walk under the sun, there are only three. Not a slow-witted zombie that can be found in your human lands or a ravenous ghoul. Only a lich has the presence of mind, and Oughtred has a treacherous one. Many fae have died by his hand in his Kings' Caravan and in the creation of his New Xenhelm, which we have you to thank for destroying."

"Do you not have these fiends in these oceans' regions?" Lady Aylen asked.

"No," Queen Oluania answered. "Our regions negate most of the dark magic that sustains them. The fear is of ghouls, though rare, and they are always created by others."

"How did you find out they were liches?" Traveler asked.

"A magic spell by a cyclops seer and wizard who encountered them years ago. You know that the magic of the Oceanus Omnis can drain those not of this realm. As you need magic and special preparation to resist it, such dark creatures must use more magic to sustain themselves. The cyclops was able to see this magic aura around them. With that suspicion, he sought out and discovered their secret, a secret hidden from many, hidden by many, but secrets cannot stay hidden forever on these waters. Whether magic or money, tongues can be made to talk," Queen Oluania said.

"Hidden by whom?" Traveler asked.

"Many," Queen Geneva repeated.

"Sky elves?"

"Perhaps."

"Elementals?"

"Perhaps."

"Who else?" Traveler asked.

"You do not need us to answer your questions. You are as knowledgeable of the powers of these lands as we. How else could you become the human caravan master you are?" Queen Geneva asked. "We hear you have walked the entire breadth of Titan's Trail from one end to the other more than once. No mermaid or oceanid, triton or sea centaur will ever be able to say the same."

"Mr. Traveler, this boast of Oughtred to conquer Atlantea takes on a new meaning with this news, does it not?" King Aereth asked.

"Sire, you are astutely correct. No living thing can pass beyond the barrier of our realms into Atlantea's domain without permission. However, the undead can, but have never been able to because Atlantea is forever in daylight."

"Oh my," Lady Aylen said. "What are you saying, Mr. Traveler? Oughtred can march into Atlantea?"

"I need to find out why Mr. Elman is here," Traveler said abruptly and left them.

The caravan master strode to the half-elf still speaking with the group of Gwyness, the sorcerers, Ursi and Pangolin. The mole-looking fae saw Traveler and left his group of berserkers and savage elves to join him.

"You weren't going to tell us, were you?" Queen Oluania asked. "About the crab centaur. But you told the men."

"We were being cautious, but we were always going to inform you," Lady Aylen said. "But what of what Mr. Traveler said about your allies on the way?"

"Whatever powers they have or do not have, they are our allies and would never betray us," Queen Geneva said.

"Were not the sea centaurs and tritons allies?" King Aereth asked. "But you had a sort of civil war within your city."

"What are we to do, sire?" Lady Aylen asked. "We come all this way. Could we be invaded here? Could Atlantea be invaded?"

"Impossible," Queen Geneva said. "Even the Four Kings are not that powerful, lich or not."

"I have never seen him worried, despite all the dangers we faced. Not once was he ever concerned or scared," King Aereth said.

"True, sire," Lady Aylen said. "When do your new allies arrive?"

"Lady Aylen, there is no chance the cecaelia would attack Kraken's Wake or be in league with the Four Kings," Queen Geneva said again. "Though the presence of any crab centaur is of great concern."

"We should notify the wall guards," Queen Oluania said.

"Yes, immediately," Queen Geneva said.

Oluania only had to nod her head for a few of the nixies to run toward the entrance of the hall. They dove into the water.

Traveler marched back with Pangolin and Gwyness.

"What is it?" Lady Aylen asked.

"King Aereth, Mr. Pangolin will take you back to our island. You are to close the main entrance, shore up defenses, and prepare for attack. Remain inside until I return. Let no one in, and let no one set foot outside.

"Lady Aylen, I will take you and a few others. We'll leave immediately."

"What?" Lady Aylen asked.

"What happened, Mr. Traveler?" King Aereth asked.

"Mr. Elman saw a giant mountain moving across the ocean, past Kraken's Wake, in the direction of Atlantea. Its peak was swarming with gargoyles. Magic kept him seeing it from inside our castle walls, but the kirins told the fairy swarms. They told the fairies, and the fairies took him from the tower keep to the top of the crawling trees outside the power of the gargoyles' spell. But it wasn't a mountain."

"A ship then?" Nori asked.

"Possibly, but a city ship larger than anything ever seen in these waters."

"But you believe it to be something else?" Queen Geneva asked.

"Queen Geneva, the size of the gargoyle swarm, the sheer number of them, means they were collectively casting a concealment spell of such power that only our kirins could see through a piece of it. The beasts are of a magic of a different realm in lands far away, so they were somewhat unaffected. Why cast such a spell? What was it they didn't want us to see? Mr. Elman said that after a moment, the gargoyles and the floating mountain vanished.

"I've been studying my sea maps and have never before seen maps devoid of any ships or life of any kind—not a fish, bird, or insect. I believe it is the reverse. A concealment spell is enshrouding the entire region from Kraken's Wake to White Waters and beyond. What are they hiding? A growing dark fleet of the Four Kings' greater than anything we can imagine? A guess, with no facts on my part, but they do, after all, plan to conquer Atlantea."

"The magic of our people is far greater than any swarm of gargoyles," Queen Oluania said, "no matter what their numbers are."

"Then where are these gargoyles and their floating mountain, which passed not more than a hundred miles from your city? Did any of your sentries report it? If you cannot see a mountain, what of a boat or evil creature or a crab centaur? Are you willing to gamble with the safety of your queendom and its people? If it were me, I'd assume that Kraken's Wake will soon be under attack."

Queen Geneva yelled out to the water fae. Conch shells appeared in the hands of mermen and they sounded the alarm. Water began to spill back into the hall.

"Mr. Traveler, take us where?" Lady Aylen asked.

"To the city of White Waters."

"Are you mad?" Lady Aylen asked.

"No one would expect such a small party, princess. We have no choice. If we cannot sail to the city of White Waters, we must go there and have their fleet come here before what I'm certain will be a massive attack."

"We must come, too, then," said Otari, the male selkie, looking at his wife, Nori. "We both will go."

Bragg and his elves created a camp not far from the Antaean giants near the top of their castle's inner mountain. He lay on the ground with his eyes closed, unable to sleep. His mountain, forest, and savage elfin comrades sat or slept around campfires. Mr. Glog, their metal golem, kept watch over the Diomedian Mares gathered together in the distance. The beasts had spent most of the day surveying the entire mountain area to pass the time.

Whispering among the elves made Bragg open his eyes and sit up. Traveler came up the mountain with his dog. The caravan master crouched when he reached Bragg.

"Mr. Bragg."

"Mr. Traveler."

"I need you to do something for me. But you'll need to take your men and leave our castle."

"Are we leaving the city, Mr. Traveler?"

"I am, but not you."

"I thought we were not supposed to separate for any reason."

"We shouldn't, but we will. I have a task specifically suited for your skills."

The dwelf sat up straight. "Go on."

"We may have hunters in the city, Mr. Bragg, hunting us. Who better to hunt hunters than the greatest manticore hunter of the magic lands and beyond? For these hunters may be as dark and crafty as any manticore."

The dwelf had the biggest smile on his face.

Most of the men had never seen King Aereth run as he did now. They had been ferried back to the island by mermen in the same chariot-like vessel. Pangolin quickly followed him with Gwyness, Frog-Dor, the berserkers, and Bragg's savage elfin comrades. The black and golden kirins trotted on the air after them.

I'wulf and Hax waited at the gatehouse, but they were not alone. Elves, drows, animal men, pech, fauns, practically the entire caravan behind them, lined up straight back through the corridor to the open courtyard. Expressions of worry to outright panic shone on all their faces.

"Mr. Traveler is gone!" I'wulf said.

"Yes, Mr. I'wulf," King Aereth said.

"What does it all mean?" the berserker asked.

"Mr. I'wulf, we will talk more, but this is not the time. It will be a late night for all of us."

"Would it not be wise to explain something?" Dr'as the drow leader asked. "My own daughter rushed in and away without answering any of my questions or even a word. Where would Mr. Traveler, my daughter, Lady Aylen, that dwelf, and the mole man be off to in the middle of the ocean without a ship?"

"Mr. Dr'as, I promise I will sit down and explain everything, but for now, we have to turn this castle into a true fortress."

"Against what, King Aereth?" Chief Ethor asked.

"Everything," Pangolin said. "Men, we don't have time for this. We need to barricade ourselves in until Mr. Traveler returns."

"We have visitors," said Hax, the lionoid berserker, pointing to the shore.

A giant red vessel slowly rose from underwater. The enclosed ship was three times the size of their own golem ship.

Queen Issaleth's men waited at their ship's gangplank, including her webbed-ear sorcerer. Pangolin and the berserkers waited on the path to the castle's entrance. King Aereth and Queen Issaleth casually strolled along the sand away from both parties. The queen glanced up at the castle towers behind them and saw the many elves watching them closely, watching her.

"King Aereth, Kraken's Wake has expelled all visitors from its main city, which sadly includes my people. Your island is the only sanctuary for us."

"You say people are fleeing."

"Ships are sailing or have already departed—not for White Waters because of the danger, but other distant sea cities. Our alliance must begin now, here. We must combine our forces at your castle. I have a wizard. I have battle-ready knights. I have my ant men. As your fae will tell you, they are as relentless in battle as gnolls. We also have our own water animals, all of which will be at your service."

"I have no intention of turning you away, especially when we don't yet know the extent of the danger. However, our caravan master instructed us to barricade ourselves within our walls. We always follow his instructions. The issue is that we would be taking in strangers within our walls. Sailing as a fleet of ships is one thing, but in the close quarters of our castle is another."

"I know full well that trust has to be earned, however, we do not have the luxury of traveling together over many months to establish that relationship."

"What do you believe the immediate danger is?"

"Your Mr. Traveler has panicked the mermaids and water nymphs. I have never seen them in such a state. Your Mr. Traveler fears an invisible fleet of giant city ships under Oughtred's control. My wizard tells me the matriarchs of the city fear an attack of krakens. If there is one crab centaur, there may be others. He should not have reminded them of the legend of the cecaelia possessing the same powers. They imagine and prepare for the worst—a kraken attack."

"Has that ever happened before?"

"No, not in centuries. I was told the last time a single giant kraken strayed from its spawning grounds, the eye of the creature was larger than the entire city. Many died in the battle, but the creature was driven off. That was one of the creatures. But as your caravan master suggested, more than one was controlled by dark forces, I fear what could happen. We have no time to delay or cater to the doubts of your men about us. Yes, or no? I have a duty to the safety of my people too. Do I need to make other arrangements? The Kelp Lands have no real defenses, so we would be forced to set sail too for maybe the distant sea cities of the water fairies."

"No need, Queen Issaleth. Bring your people into the castle. Whatever we may face, we'll make our stand together."

From the gatehouse's east tower, Gwyness stood watch with her black kirin at her side. She touched her amulet, now resting prominently on her chest as she was no longer in her hooded robe. The elves were busy around her bringing pull-carts of magic arrows. The same bustle of activity was happening everywhere throughout the castle.

On the ground below, she watched Pangolin lead his own meeting of berserkers, human and fae, in front of the gatehouse. The chamroshes seemed to sense the heightened tensions among all at the possibility of a battle. Their masters kept a firm hand on the winged eagle-hounds. Each animal had a chain leash. Some men were eager, but most, like her, were fearful. Traveler was gone. So were his dog and Lady Aylen, but Titan's Caravan remained formidable.

"It will be our duty to sense any evil magic that may come and warn the others," Gwyness said to her kirin, running her hand over its forehead.

The decision had been made. Queen Issaleth's tall, webbed-ear wizard in a hooded cloak, Betta, and five thousand knights would take charge of the gatehouse. Their army of four-armed ant men with red eyes and crushing jaws would be their reinforcements. They bore thick spears but could easily rip apart an adversary with their hands or mandibles. Inside, floating above the gate's entrance, was Betta's giant white jellyfish. Queen Issaleth and her men referred to the creature as a wizard too.

Pangolin and the Cut-throats took charge of the open courtyard with their chamroshes as the second wave of defense. The final wave was Estus's army of armor golems forming up column after column in front of the castle's keep. In the corner, the wolf-clan fae-blood men waited quietly together. Using their magical powers, they would fight wherever needed.

Pangolin instructed the pech to set up camp for the men.

"If a battle is to come, it could be tomorrow, or never. We need to keep all the men comfortable," Pangolin told the brawny sprites with their bulging forearms, who nodded.

The keep entrance was to be defended by Dr'as, his drow warriors, and Frog-Dor. Chief Ammon and his faun archers and Chief Ethor and his woodland elfin fighters, armed with large shields and javelins filled the corridors behind the drows.

Beyond the keep, Hobbs had command of the camp at the base of the inner mountain. If needed, Strag and all his elaphine archer-warriors would take to the crawling trees hanging over the camp to fire their arrows. Pech and humans would defend against any attackers with their catapults and giant crossbows. Their forces also had the fairy sisters and their swarms, the Tree Shepherds, and two thousand giant lizards with their minders. Hobbs felt assured that they could easily defend the camp. But he felt strongly that no force could get past the outside castle wall, let alone past Pangolin and the Cut-throats.

Then the entire island rolled, as if a giant wave had passed beneath it. Every human and fae looked at each other.

"What was that, Mr. Hobbs?" Young Quillen was at the steward's side.

Hobbs looked around at their forces. It was easy to forget that they were on the Oceanus Omnis and not solid earth.

The island rolled again. Hobbs could see the fear in the boy's face.

"Mr. Hobbs, can one of the ocean waves cause the island to capsize?"

"Do not say such things. Boats and ships capsize."

"But what if an island flips over? Can that happen?"

"Mr. Quillen, please do not say things to scare yourself, because you may also do the same to others. Remain calm."

They could all feel the island rise up then descend. The rolling wave was larger.

The castle wall was actually two—the solid defense wall and a connected three-story structure of rooms. The elves maintained occupancy on the top floor. The drows vacated the middle, and King Aereth gave Queen Issaleth and her people both bottom levels.

With his royal guardsman, the thirteen reptilian hounds, and a few berserker guards, King Aereth stopped by the queen's room on the middle floor.

"Queen Issaleth." The king tapped on an already-open door.

"Please come in, sire."

The queen's servants had turned the room into a war and map room. While she conversed with knights and what the king recognized as members of the selkies, he saw the room was busy with white bushy haired, bearded brownies with brown caps and clothing dusting, sweeping, and washing the walls. The caravan's own brownies had told him they were a cousin race known as domovoi. The king joined the queen and her knights at their map wall. Clearly visible on the magic map was a fleet of massive ships slowly sailing toward the city.

"They are the cecaelia." Queen Issaleth answered his question before he could pose it. "They'll be here in seven days with ten city ships, warships."

"Do you know what is causing the waves moving the island?" King Aereth asked.

"Not only this island, the entire city of Kraken's Wake. Look."

The waves on the magic map moved from south to north. The cecaelia fleet on the map rose up then back down with the giant waves.

"We do not know the cause."

"Queen Issaleth, we shall go into the city and be liaisons," one of the selkies said.

"Is that wise?" King Aereth asked.

"We will not be in danger, king. We are allies. None will harm us, and we know the city well."

A knight entered the room and joined them. "Queen, the waters around the island are rising."

"How much?"

"Betta says the water will likely reach the battlements, but he has extended the magic barrier around the castle."

"We lose all advantage if the water keeps rising," King Aereth said.

"Kraken's Wake is ultimately an ocean city. The islands are for our benefit but are of no real concern to the water fae."

The selkies took their leave of the room, and the messenger knight soon did the same.

"How do you think the others are doing?" she asked.

"I have full confidence in Mr. Traveler."

"But if he succeeds and brings the water elfin fleet here, avoiding whatever vessels may be out there, we will still face them here in likely greater numbers."

"I am not concerned. It is a sound battle strategy. We will have our fleet."

The queen smiled. "King Aereth, we are the humans here. We can't breathe underwater, and I don't know about you, but I'm not the best swimmer. Even if I were, I would not want to swim here. Seemingly harmless fish like to grab things and dive deep below to drown them. To them its only play."

"You have a good army here. How did you make it here from Baltica? Same path as we, through Faë-Land and the Great Forest?"

"Yes. Our primary caravan master was an elf. Sadly, we lost him and most of our elves at sea on our way here to Kraken's Wake. We were attacked by pirates. They sank one of our ships. We sank five of theirs. My sorcerer leads us to Atlantea as caravan master, now."

"Caravan master and sorcerer."

"Yours is caravan master, magic swordsman, and I'm told, healer."

"Tell me of Oughtred being a lich. What does it mean?"

"One that moves under the light of the sun and appears as human, like they were prior to their transformation. From your caravan master's recognition, he seemed to know much about it."

"Do you know how such a transformation comes about?"

"My sorcerer told me the transformation is carried out by a powerful necromancer, far greater than the average, either for another or themselves. Immortality and dark power in exchange for being a walking, decaying corpse or skeleton."

"But the Four Kings are far from being cadaverous."

"No, they are not. Did you meet them?"

"Not directly."

"I did once. Many years ago. I was a child. They were attempting to convince the kings of our region to join him. My father did, against my mother's warnings. My mother was a gifted seer. She told me there was a shadow of evil around the man. My father and other kings of Baltica rode off with them. All King Oughtred had to do was entice them with the prospect of having their own griffins and other beasts from the magical lands. My father and the others were never seen again."

"I'm sorry. Much death has followed them."

"There were many great kingdoms in Baltica before Xenhelm came through with their flying griffins. Our empire is but a shadow of what it was. That is why I lead my kingdom's quest to Atlantea. It's why we must prevail, no matter what. To restore us to our former greatness."

"We will prevail."

"I appreciate your caravan master's bravery—to lead a small party across the wide ocean, without an army, though I've already heard from your men about his animal shape-shifter. They destroyed New Xenhelm. But these oceans are another matter, filled with more dangers than even the ancient Great Forest. Much rests on his success."

"He has never let us down."

"Your elves said that the 'mystery of the Great Forest' is solved."

"You have learned quite a bit in such a short time."

"It is why I am queen in an empire of kingdoms ruled by men."

"Let us say that the 'mystery of the Great Forest' almost added us to its eons-long list of disappearances."

"Only in the magical lands. Flowers can eat you. Trees can eat you. The entire land you tread upon can eat you. Yes, he's gotten you this far. We must not let him down here. Protect this castle. Kill anything uninvited."

King Aereth grinned. "You are definitely a Baltican woman."

"I am my father's daughter."

Night had fallen on the camp. Normally, the men would have already been fast asleep but not so this night. At the campfires, men and brownies conversed. Gwyness sat alone outside the women's tent on a camp chair. She could hear the female half-elves inside also talking among themselves. Gwyness stared at the bright, clear moon high above. The rolling of the island had never stopped and the fear among all was that no one could explain the cause.

If only Mr. Traveler were here. Gwyness thought.

"Not joining the meeting, Maiden Gwyness?" Hobbs peeked out from the nearby king's tent, where a private night meeting had convened.

"Not this time, Mr. Hobbs. I'll remain here."

"They are fine and will return—Mr. Traveler and the others."

"Yes, Mr. Hobbs. I'm sure of it too."

The men inside the tent were in a heated debate. King Aereth stayed silent. He knew it best to let the men express themselves to get the fear from their minds.

The tent was filled with berserkers, Chief Ethor and his elves, Dr'as and a few drows, and Elman with all his male half-elf comrades. Their own wizard Frog-Dor stood beside King Aereth. Queen Issaleth sat in a corner, quiet. Hobbs came in and closed the tent's entrance. All thirteen of the alphyns with their master, Nirgund, stood nearby.

"What if Mr. Traveler and the others do not return before these creatures do?" a berserker asked.

"They are not creatures," the wizard Betta said. "Cecaelia are allies of the mermaids. They are, in fact, mermaids of a sort."

"Mermaid octopuses?" I'wulf asked.

"Mer-octopus!" Nirgund said, and men laughed.

"Believe me when I say they laugh equally at those of us who walk on two legs alone," Betta said.

"Mr. Traveler believes they are not the blood allies you say," Pangolin said.

"May I ask, Mr. Betta, can you tell me of the abilities of these cecaelia?" Frog-Dor asked.

"They move as if they are without bones, they are so flexible. As fast and as strong as any mermaid, they can dive far deeper than mermaids and their bodies can glow in the dark at will."

"What of these tentacles they have?" Pangolin asked. "I've heard many things."

"Yes, they can use them as one, or each can move independently as if having its own mind."

"What of the power to control krakens?" Pangolin asked.

Queen Issaleth jumped to her feet. "We do not know if the rumor is true. They can summon octopi and other water animals the way mermaids can. They can even mesmerize men with songs like mermaids." She saw the men's faces. "Sirens are not the only water fae that can do that."

"Mermaids too?" King Aereth asked.

"Yes."

"Men, we should allay fears not add to them," King Aereth said.

"Do you know if Mr. Traveler and Lady Aylen will return before these cecaelia, sire?" a berserker asked.

"I do. That is why he left so hurriedly."

"What of these giant waves, sire? What's causing them?" another berserker asked.

"No one knows," Betta answered. "The waves originate so far from us."

"What do we do if they become larger, sire?" Pangolin asked. "Will our magic barriers hold?"

"They must, Mr. Pangolin. Men, I know none of us is happy, but this is what we must do if we are to continue onto Atlantea. We are close, always remember that. Keep the men calm and focused on their tasks at hand."

The king gave Hobbs a look.

"That is all, men!" Hobbs called out. "Get a good night's rest for the long, hard day's work tomorrow."

He opened the tent's entrance fully to allow the men to file out.

"I bid you good night, sire," Queen Issaleth said.

"You as well, queen."

The queen left with her sorcerer. Pangolin waited to leave with I'wulf and the animaloid fae berserkers. Hobbs and Nirgund were last.

"Good night, Maiden Gwyness," Pangolin said as he passed with the berserkers.

"You as well, Mr. Pangolin," she said from her chair under the moonlight.

Hobbs walked past too. "You should get sleep, too, maiden."

"I will soon, Mr. Hobbs."

"King Aereth!" Nirgund yelled to wake the king well past midnight.

They ran from the camp to the keep and through its corridor to the open court. Moon elves and drows waited. King Aereth stopped and had to take a knee. The island rolled again, but it was far more drawn out than before. He saw Queen Issaleth's knights.

"Sire, follow us," a knight said.

They entered the rear of the gatehouse to one of the rooms where the queen and her knight leadership awaited. The wizard Betta had created a whirling spiral of gas that solidified to become a doorway to another place. King Aereth recognized the sea centaur leader.

"Centauro-triton, is it?"

"I learned that your caravan master has left the city."

"He has."

"Why would you allow such a thing? We could have given him protection to White Waters, at least a battalion of warriors."

"Time was of the essence," King Aereth said.

"We are leaving the city."

"Leaving? Why?"

"Do you not feel the waves hitting the city?"

"Do you know why? My sorcerer cannot see the cause," Queen Issaleth said.

"We know the cause," the sea centaur leader said. "We had to combine our sorcerers with those of the women. Something is throwing mountains into the ocean about three days from here."

"Pardon? Throwing mountains?" the queen asked.

"I don't understand either," King Aereth said.

"Am I not speaking in your human tongue? The words are simple. Rip a mountain from the earth and throw it."

"What could do that?" King Aereth asked.

"You have giants among your caravan, king. Ask them about a race called the Athos. Kraken's Wake can possibly survive the waves that are coming, but I doubt your island will. And it won't be just one wave but many. Not even your magic barrier can protect your castle from these waves for long. My fleet is departing."

"What of our alliance?" Queen Issaleth asked.

"What alliance? The caravan master is gone. The water elfin fleet is not here, and we cannot get to them. The tritons have already set sail. We will follow."

"We can still gather a fleet, King Centauro-triton."

"Thank you, King Aereth, for the elevation in status, but I am only Centauro here. The true King Centauro-triton is far from here, and he cannot help us either."

"But we can defend the city. The danger is not just us and the female fae but your people—" Queen Issaleth began.

"Queen Issaleth, the waves coming are going to wipe away you and everything else from your island.

You also need to know that the direction of the waves is significant. The women's worst fears are indeed true. The waves will dump more krakens on top of the city than any living thing, human or fae, has ever seen or imagined. The city of White Waters is not an underwater city, so it will likely be destroyed too."

CHAPTER EIGHT

The Elfin City of White Waters

ady Aylen swam through the water faster than she realized without the least bit of effort. Her eyes could see for many miles all around. Her hands were not just fully webbed, but her fingers had elongated to create a greater width.

A giant gulper fish four times her size followed. The larger lower half of its mouth was a giant pouch. All around them was a school of black-and-yellow frog-headed fish. Whenever she glanced black at them, they smiled at her with their human mouths. She rolled her eyes.

Only once did they see a vessel. A city ship passed right above them, but the gulper spewed out a dark-bluish cloud so they could not be seen.

After near two hours of swimming, the gulper fish grew tentacles as its size increased again. Lady Aylen grabbed a tentacle, and so did all the phookas with their new frog-like arms. The gulper fish octopus sped away with them holding on. Lady Aylen could no longer see around her. They were enveloped in the creature's wake.

When the dog in its gulper octopus form stopped, Lady Aylen let go of its tentacle and floated upward. She could see the ocean city in the distance and the many water elf warriors guarding the underwater entrances. The water elves saw them.

The castle city floated on the ocean surface with a network of ports. Every manner of ship was docked. The castle stood nearly seventy feet, and there was a smaller network of ports for flying ships above.

The grounds outside the main entrance were vast enough for a large ground army but were empty except for the dozens of warriors who had them surrounded with scimitars, crossbows, and tridents. All were in elfin armor with ornate helmets, both male and female elves, some with skin tones similar to Lady Aylen but others with bluish skin.

Lady Aylen studied them. Dr'amal, Ursi, the mole-looking fae, Nori, and Otari of the selkie clan were at her sides. Traveler and his dog stood behind them. The rambunctious phookas were not allowed on the docks. Hundreds of them floated in the water, laughing in the form of black-and-yellow frog-headed fish as another group of elfin warriors watched them closely.

The receiving contingent marched from the main gate. The lead elfess had a sour face at the sight of them. Her helmet had a fish's fin, and she wore a flowing vest over her armor. Two tall elfin males followed her on either side, two cloaked females behind them, then a full contingent of elfin warriors.

Lady Aylen stepped forward and extended a parchment to the lead elfess. She looked at one of the cloaked females, who nodded. The lead elfess took the parchment and read it.

"Queen Geneva and Oluania. You swam here from Kraken's Wake?"

"We did," Lady Aylen replied.

"Even I am not that brave, or foolish." The elfess handed the princess back the parchment. "I am Queen Firi and this is the elfin kingdom of White Waters."

"Thank you, queen. I am Lady Aylen. And this Queen Nori and King Otari of the selkie clan of Therian."

"Yes, we know the selkies. You're always welcome in White Waters," Queen Firi said.

"Princess Dr'amal, her aide, Ursi, our mole fae has no name. This is Mr. Traveler," Lady Aylen continued.

"And your shape-shifter," Queen Firi said. "See that it stays in its current form at all times here. We have shape-shifters too."

"Of course," Traveler said.

"The queens' note and the presence of the selkies has given you safe passage into the city, but why are you here?"

Traveler handed the elfin queen another note.

"We're passing notes today, are we?" She took it and read quickly. "Why do you wish to see them?"

"It's urgent that we see them, queen," Lady Aylen said.

"Why?"

"I can answer the question, queen," Traveler said.

"Why can't she?"

"When I explain, it will become clear."

"Proceed."

"We need to see them immediately so we can depart for Kraken's Wake to join our awaiting fleet."

"Why isn't your fleet here? Sailing would be preferable to swimming bare in these dangerous waters."

"We need their forces for ours to be able to leave Kraken's Wake."

"Queen, another one," one of the elfin sorceresses said.

The rolling wave in the distance came toward the city in the distance.

"We will speak inside. The swells are becoming larger. Possibly a storm day's away from us. You will need to answer my question, or you will not be speaking to any elfin royals here. Follow us."

"Queen Firi, our phookas," Traveler said.

The queen and her contingent stopped. "I was hoping you'd forget about them. They can come as far as the outer foyer only but I will hold you responsible for any of their mischief or damage. They are not to transform into any different forms either."

"Yes, queen." Traveler turned and gestured to the phookas.

They began to jump onto the dock in the forms of pot-bellied humanoid frogs.

"Princess, you know what to say," Traveler said to the Lady Aylen. "I need to stand back and manage them. The others will watch over you. Besides you are an elf among elves."

Lady Aylen sighed.

"Shall we go inside?" Queen Firi suggested.

Suddenly, Lady Aylen's dragon horse jumped out of the water onto the dock. The princess smiled and patted its side. The elves were amazed by the cat-fish whiskered beast with its single unicorn horn and lucent-blue fur and scales.

"I have seen most beasts of the magical realms but never its splendid kind," the queen said.

"I wasn't able to sense the beast at all, queen," one of the elfin sorceresses said. Her face seemed especially concerned, as if she'd done something wrong.

"Interesting." The queen turned and marched them all into the city.

Lady Aylen glanced back quickly. Traveler waited with the darklings and sea phookas.

Inside the city's entrance, two sets of elfin warriors stood at attention in a line facing each other, one group on the left of the path, the other group on the right. Queen Firi and her delegation passed through an opaque bluish magic barrier covering the main entrance and disappeared. The two selkie leaders followed right after and disappeared. With her kirin, Lady Aylen stepped through.

Lady Aylen stopped with her kirin at her side. The interior was a massive hall under a domed roof, thick columns on either side. Queen Firi led her delegation and guests to the other end of the path to exit the hall by turning a corner.

Nori and Otari were walking ahead of Lady Aylen and the others and froze in their steps at the sight of a single water nymph, as beautiful as all of her kind but sinister in demeanor. The entire hall was filled with an army of merrows—green-skinned, green-haired female warriors clad in battle armor, helmets, and armed with long tridents.

Lady Aylen realized they had walked into a trap. She glanced at Dr'amal and Ursi on one side, the mole-man fae behind her other shoulder. But Traveler, his dog, and the phookas had not crossed the barrier into the hall.

"Get behind us," Lady Aylen instructed the selkies.

A growing puddle of water formed beneath the water nymph's feet. The fae woman was not a water nymph.

"Have you met my kind before?" she asked Lady Aylen.

"You are an undine," Nori said. "We have no quarrel with water elementals."

"We are of, and wield the power of water, the essence of all life. Only the sylphs are more vast in power than we are," she said to Lady Aylen.

"You are the first one I have ever met directly," Lady Aylen replied.

"Tell me, Lady Aylen of the human Avalonia kingdom of Sirnegate, why are you so far from your lands in our domain?"

"You have me at the disadvantage."

"I am Aquaria. The name of my queendom is unpronounceable to your tongue. Its name is—"

The undine made a sound like splashing water.

"I doubt knowing its name or how to pronounce it would be of any use to me."

"Where is your human?"

"My human? Mr. Traveler is—"

"Not him. Your human aide, the one called Gwyness."

Lady Aylen's eyes narrowed with suspicion. "You know quite a bit about me."

"I know all about you, Lady Aylen Brytthony of the human Avalonian kingdom of Sirnegate, adopted daughter of King Beothor and Queen Meri, bred to be a slayer of the lost elfin kingdom of Rivermouth under the mage mother Queen Faylen."

Lady Aylen remained silent as she clenched her fists.

"The mages and warrior clerics of Rivermouth were supposed to be dead for a reason, slayers and seers. My sylphic sisters tell me you even have followers though you have no kingdom—faoladh, fae, and humans."

"I do not know what is happening here, but we're here to see elves, not undines and merrows. You are not the ruler of White Waters," Lady Aylen said.

"But I am. We conquered the city days ago to await your arrival. You were taking too long so we decided to destroy Kraken's Wake instead and wait here. You did as expected. Your human, Traveler, is quite an interesting character, but we are learning how to predict his methods."

"Should I summon him?"

"All good things come to an end, in time."

"I was about to say the same to you about bad things."

"You cannot defeat me. You are a lowly elf, a fact you only recently discovered since you were raised as a human, a lowly elf with water elemental powers you have barely used. I am a pure water elemental who has used her powers from birth. You cannot comprehend my power, a power that draws from the entire mother Oceanus Omnis itself."

"So powerful, yet you have to ambush me with an army or merrows."

"The army is for your compatriots. You will be killed by me alone."

"Why would you do this?" Nori asked. "You have allied with evil. The Four Kings are evil. They are fiends, transformed by the darkest of magic! We are fae of light. We are the ones who you should be in alliance with."

"You know nothing, selkie, so silence your tongue before we cut it from your mouth."

The opaque magic barrier behind them became a solid black wall.

"Your human caravan master and his shape-shifter will not be coming to your rescue." Aquaria became more like water shaped in human form. Water rushed into the room from every entrance.

The mole-like fae sorcerer slammed dozens of the merrows into the walls with a volley of balls of yellow magic. A hand of water picked him up and hurled him across hall. He disappeared into the rising pools of water beyond.

Another hand of water slapped Dr'amal and Ursi off their feet. Lady Aylen's aquatic kirin dove into the rising water and disappeared. Lady Aylen waved her hand, and a tsunami instantly formed, crashing over the undine and merrows. Only the merrows fell on their backs; the undine was unaffected.

Lady Aylen quickly raised a wall of solid water to protect herself as merrow tridents rained down on her. The selkies, in the form of a seal and sea lion, hid behind the columns of the great hall.

A roar cried out. Ursi's eyes glowed white as she appeared as two images—her humanoid one and giant bear rushing forward on four legs. She attacked the merrow army as their tridents passed right through her. Her attack felled every merrow she hit.

A second roar echoed in the hall. The mole-fae's giant carnivorous moose emerged from the sprite's magic bag and also charged the merrow army. Its master on the beast's back showered the merrows with more balls of magic as he flew in the air. Then every merrow warrioress dropped their weapon as their heads were being smothered by dark-bluish sacks.

The undine watched with slight amusement.

The fury and speed of the water cyclone lifted Lady Aylen, the mole-like fae, and the moose, slamming them into the ceiling. A dark bluish blindfold wrapped around the undine's face, startling her. They all fell to the ground in the rising water.

Lady Aylen made a pushing motion with her hands. Another tsunami slammed the undine, but only the merrow were pushed back.

The undine ripped Dr'amal's magic blindfold from her eyes. "I am water, Lady Aylen. Why would you think I could be harmed by it?"

The lucent-blue kirin emerged from the water in front of the undine and kicked her with its hind legs. Aquaria sailed backward and fell on her back. She quickly got to her feet and touched her chest; she was injured. The kirin dove back into the water and disappeared.

"What did Mr. Traveler tell me?" Lady Aylen asked herself. "Water. I can summon all water."

She made a pulling motion with her hands and the undine screamed. Her face was ripped from her head and fell into the water of the hall. The undine recreated her face. Lady Aylen did it again.

"I may be water, but you are flesh!" Aquaria yelled.

The kirin jumped from the water and kicked the undine with greater force. The elemental hit the wall with her back so hard she coughed up water from inside her body. The elemental dripped down the wall to the floor. Her eyes grew intense with rage.

"I will summon every drop of ocean water outside the city and kill you all!"

Some type of projectile burst through one of the walls, creating a giant hole as more pieces of the wall fell away. Immediately, a swarm of yellow frog-headed giant bees flew in through the hall, then giant black snakes shot in.

Traveler stepped through the hole, his magic sword in hand. His dog jumped in after him. The caravan master threw a pearl to the undine. The water elemental laughed, expecting it to pass through her. Instead, she disappeared.

"Where did she go?" Lady Aylen asked.

"Far, far away," Traveler replied. "Open the doors!" he yelled to the phookas.

The creatures raced to the main doors, groups of darklings versus sea phookas in the form of duck-headed gorillas. The doors swung open, and elfin soldiers rushed in. The elves surrounded the remaining merrows.

Queen Firi re-entered the hall with elfin knights and more sorcerers. "Put all of them in the dungeons!"

Through the open doors, they saw a city ablaze. The selkies had taken their human forms again. The mole-man walked to them with his shaken giant moose.

"What did you do, Mr. Traveler?" Lady Aylen asked.

Queen Firi marched to them with an angry expression. She looked directly at Traveler. "You destroyed my city!"

"You led us into a trap to be killed by an evil undine!" Dr'amal yelled at the elfin queen.

"We liberated your city from conquerors," he said. "There is a difference. May we meet with the elves we came to see, now that we finished our playtime?"

Large sections of the city were ablaze. The streets were in a panic with elves and water fae. Elfin warriors ran through the crowds or flew above them on giant flying fish. The city had indeed been invaded by merrow armies, but fire had laid waste to all their giant weapons, magic catapults and giant crossbows as well as all their flying city ships and myriad of giant sea shells used to fly individual soldiers into White Waters.

The two selkies had left Lady Aylen and the others to run into the city themselves. They told them they would find their allies.

"I wonder what creature the dog turned into to do this damage to the city," Lady Aylen said.

"It was big, whatever it was, and breathed fire," Dr'amal said.

Traveler still spoke with the angry Queen Firi. His dog stood quietly, but Traveler had the phookas jump back in the ocean around the city to watch for more attackers.

Nori and Otari returned and took them to an establishment near the dungeons. Merrow warriors were led in chains through the city's underground dungeons by scores of armed elves. Several elves, male and female, waited by the main entrance. They were elfin leaders who looked as if they had just been released from the dungeon themselves based on the condition of their clothes and grooming.

"Is this them?" an elfin male asked the selkies.

"Yes," Nori replied.

"You are the allies of Queen Geneva and Oluania?" Lady Aylen asked.

"We are," a female elf said.

"We were afraid you would arrive and they would sink your vessels to the bottom of the ocean," another female elf said.

"Is a single undine that powerful against your city?" Lady Aylen asked.

"It was not a single undine," the first female elf said.

"She was not alone, and they were not just elementals," the male elf said. "A flying caravan descended on us filled with sylphs. We were distracted by the merrows in the ships. The undines attacked from beneath the city, the sylphs from above."

"These elementals broke the centuries-old alliance between water elves and elementals," one of the female elves said angrily.

"I'm sorry to press you," Traveler said, "but we must all leave now."

"Leave?" the elves asked. "We were held prisoner in our own dungeon. We are not leaving. I, for one, will have a proper bath, meal, and rest," said one elfin male.

"Your fleet must sail to Kraken's Wake."

"Where is your ship?" an elf asked.

"We have none. We swam here."

"Swam?"

The elves looked at each other in disbelief.

"Do you have any idea what lurks in these waters?" a female elf asked.

"I do, so no need to tell me. My comrades don't need nightmares. We did it once and will never do it again."

"You are that human caravan master called Traveler," a male elf said.

"I am."

"How do you know about him?" Lady Aylen asked. "Do you know about all of us, as did this evil undine we defeated?"

"You defeated her?" an elfess asked.

"Yes. I did my best, but Mr. Traveler magically sent her far away from the city. But we must leave. Is your fleet still intact?"

"You swam all this way to have us sail back to Kraken's Wake?" an elfess asked.

"Yes, we believe the city will be under attack soon," Traveler answered.

"Did you all manage to destroy the pirates between our cities?" another elf asked.

"Nothing will stop us from getting to Kraken's Wake now. How many ships do you have?" Traveler asked.

"Seven city ships," one elfess answered.

"The mermaids and oceanids have ten, and if the tritons and sea centaurs send theirs, we will have an additional six," Nori added.

"What do you know about the race called the cecaelia?" Lady Aylen asked.

"Why?" an elfess asked.

"They're sending fifty ships to join us."

The elves all looked at each other.

"Have they arrived at Kraken's Wake yet?" a male elf asked.

"No, but they're on their way. Aren't these octopus mermaids allies of the mermaids?" Lady Aylen asked.

"Undines are supposed to be our allies," the elfess said.

"The cecaelia are allies of the undines," the male elf said.

"Mr. Traveler's instincts may be correct, then." Lady Aylen looked at her party. "The cecaelia are sending the ships to attack us."

Everyone stopped talking. They all felt the city rise up then roll back down.

"The giant waves are becoming more frequent," a male elf said.

"We must leave now," Lady Aylen said forcibly.

The city of White Waters was populated exclusively by water elves of different sub-races. Water fae of all races made up the steady stream of visitors for trade and commerce, but only elves ran the city. Even without the color cues of their attire, Lady Aylen could sense the different elfin races—ocean elves in blue attire, sea elves in their greens and tans, river elves in whites, and lake elves in bluish silvers.

Sorcerers had extinguished all fires and were dispatched throughout the city to magically repair any structural damage to buildings. Others strengthened the magic sphere that encased the entire city. Because it had been so weakened by the elemental invaders, every inch of the city had to be inspected for intruders or magical devices.

Lady Aylen remained eager to leave and waited at the docks with the group. Many more warriors stood watch, armed with swords, long spears, and crossbows. From the top of the castle walls, they could see many more elfin warriors and sorcerers ready for any battle that might come. A delegation of elves approached them from the main entrance. The lead elfess in royal white attire had silvery hair, braided down her left side.

"May we speak privately?" the elfess asked Lady Aylen directly.

Lady Aylen looked at the others.

"I can assure you I am harmless to you. Your party can remain here. It is your decision to share with them what we speak of, if you wish. But these are elfin matters alone."

Dr'amal nodded.

"My animal companion will stay with me," Lady Aylen said.

"Of course," the elfess said.

Lady Aylen followed the elves back into the city.

"White Waters was supposed to be impenetrable to the kind of attack we endured. Both this city and our sister city of Kraken's Wake were built centuries ago as outposts on the voyage to and from Atlantea. There is much history here."

"Why haven't your elfin kingdoms gone to Atlantea on your own?"

"We have, but you will learn that the Atlanteans don't take to elfinkind. Our ancestors tried to invade their kingdom in the ancient past, and we are still being punished for it. We are only allowed entry to their lands every six years, and then only for a brief time. Sky elves have circumvented the rule through their alliance with elementals."

"We saved your city, so we can have our own alliance," Lady Aylen said.

"I don't know what is more shameful, to be conquered or to be rescued by a human with a shape-shifter and pack of phookas."

"I'll happily leave the phookas, if you'd like. Mr. Traveler and the dog will remain with me."

"No, we prefer you keep the phookas too."

Near the wall sat a section of buildings. Lady Aylen assumed them to be used by city officials in the management of the city's affairs. They entered a room filled with more elves, all looked to be royals from their attire, grooming, and bearing. The elfess led her to the center of the group. The princess smiled when she noticed her kirin waiting at the rear of the room.

"Lady Aylen of the Titan's Caravan," the elfess announced.

"You do know of us," the princess said.

"We should," the elfess said.

"What are the banners you carry?" a crowned elfin male asked.

"Titan's Caravan carries the banners of the fairies of Chrysa, giants of Antaeus, centaurs of Chiron, elfin banners of Magica, Bravehowl, Nightshade, and Falconbright, human banners of Sirnegate, Helm Earldom, Strongbridge, and Eastmoor, and the lost elfin kingdom of Rivermouth. Our caravan also includes the drow king of the D'Shar and the king of the Tree Shepherds of Faë-Land Minor."

"That alliance will include all the water elfin kingdoms here, and the selkies have told us that the mermaids, oceanids, sea centaurs, and tritons have already agreed to our alliance," the main elfess said.

"Yes," Lady Aylen said with pride.

"Are you prepared to lead such a fleet to Atlantea?" the elfin king asked.

"We are," Lady Aylen replied.

"We?"

"Our caravan master, Mr. Traveler, is also a sailor. He will be our captain, and I have already experienced his superior sailing prowess and strategy in action on these waters."

"Who did he train with as a sailor?" an elfin male asked.

"Klabautermann. Years ago."

The elves nodded with satisfaction.

"Wretched fae but an able sea-faring race," another elf said.

"The human's knowledge includes both land and sea," the elfess said to all.

"He has been from the beginning of Titan's Trail to Atlantea many times. He has lived in Atlantea. Is there a reason for delay?" Lady Aylen asked.

"We assume that the mermaids and nymphs told you about that devilish human Oughtred?" the elfess asked.

"Yes, that he's some living-dead creature."

"No, that is not accurate. He transformed himself and his sons to be the fiends they are to gain its power, form his evil alliance with sky elves and elementals, and possess the uncanny ability to assemble dark creatures so rare as to be extinct."

"Such as crab centaurs."

The entire room hushed.

"What of them?"

"We saw one."

"When?"

"On our way to Kraken's Wake. We threw the creature from our vessel into the ocean."

"It lives, then," an elf said.

"I assume so, but we left it behind to arrive at Kraken's Wake. We don't have time for this. We must leave. Besides, Mr. Traveler is the expert on these matters. He has a fuller grasp of Oughtred's scheming than I. Also, Queen Geneva said fifty ships of the cecaelia sail to Kraken's Wake."

The elves looked at each other.

"They are supposedly allies, but we must arrive first," Lady Aylen said.

"Maybe we need to abandon this," one elf said.

"Absolutely not!" Lady Aylen yelled. "We have come too far, and Atlantea is within reach."

"Not if we are all sent to the bottom of the ocean," the elfin king said.

"What is the truth of these cecaelia? Are they allies of the mermaids or not? Can they summon krakens or not?"

"Who told you they can summon krakens?"

"Mr. Traveler."

"Yes, they are not just allies to mermaids; they are a sister race. Water elves have never trusted them, but their alliance with the mermaids spans the existence of both races."

"But when have we ever seen them with an armada of that size before?" the elfin king asked.

"If so many ships are on their way to Kraken's Wake, the mermaids may not have their full defenses ready," the elfess said.

"That is why we must be there," Lady Aylen said. "Why are you so reluctant to leave?"

"The sylphs who attacked the city are still out there and are powerful enough to easily destroy a fleet."

"Speak with Mr. Traveler. He can reassure you, but we must leave."

The room rolled. Everyone looked around then at each other.

"Has this city ever moved in this manner from the ocean waves?" Lady Aylen asked.

"No," the elfess said. "The city is made of magic, too, and is immune to any movements of the great ocean, even in the worse of storms—or it was immune."

"We will see this human, Mr. Traveler," the elfin king said.

Traveler stood hunched over a magic map table of the city with Queen Firi pointing and describing the peculiarities of the currents. A group of elfin officials gathered at the table too.

"Pirate raids have increased in the waters between our cities over the years," one elfin captain said.

"They are bold and crafty. Even with a large fleet we cannot be assured they will not try to attack," another said.

"I don't care about pirates," Traveler said. "Do you really believe these pirates have been able to cut off passage from Kraken's Wake to here for three years?"

"Yes, we do, because it has happened in the past," an elf captain said.

"What of the sylphs?" another elf asked.

"My ship has defenses against them, and I'm sure all of you do too. Air elementals are powerful but not indestructible," Traveler said.

"We appreciate that you have earth elementals and fire elementals in your caravan, and Lady Aylen, but that will not be enough," the elfess said.

Traveler stabbed the map table with his sword. He had moved so fast that not even the elves saw him draw it. They saw its translucent fire. "Star elemental power is greater than air elemental power. Are there any other concerns?"

No one spoke.

"Are we sailing, or do my party and I have to swim back to Kraken's Wake?" Traveler asked.

"No need for that," Queen Firi said. "I'd say the human has convinced us."

Lady Aylen smiled as elves around the table nodded.

"Another wave," Traveler said.

They all saw the giant wave on the map table as the caravan master pulled his sword, flicked the fire out, and sheathed it.

"The waves are not natural," Traveler said. He looked at the elfin captains. "What do you think they are from? Is what I'm thinking possible?"

The elfin captains watched the map. "What direction are they coming from?" one asked.

"The lands of the giants," Queen Firi said.

"But that's in Faë-Land Minor," the princess said.

"No, we have our own lands of giants."

"There are only two kinds of giants capable of doing such a thing," Traveler said.

"One is peaceful, and the other doesn't exist anymore," an elfin captain said.

Traveler looked at them. "How fast can your ships sail?"

"How fast do you need them to sail?" the elfin king asked.

"Fast enough to get to Kraken's Wake before a wave can destroy the ship." He turned to Queen Firi. "I am sorry to say this, queen."

"No need. We must be prepared to evacuate White Waters."

CHAPTER NINE

The Cecaelia

The kilmoulis had rushed up from their ground floor room with a pool to the tower. Elman had been joined by his half-elfin comrades on his lookout duties along with a couple of bird men with their enfields. The magic elf had the additional responsibility of watching the entire region surrounding their castle island. When Elman saw them, he wondered if the arriving big-nosed sprites had run or flown up to the room. However, they had gotten to the tower, their news would not be good.

Elman ran straight from the keep to the caravan camp and royal tents, where King Aereth was meeting with Hobbs and several Cut-throats. The reptilian hounds lay on the ground in front of the entrance, and all jumped up at the sight of the approaching half-elf.

"Steady lads," Nirgund the berserker said from his seat within the tent.

"Sire!" he yelled.

"What is it, Mr. Elman?"

"The kilmoulis sensed something approaching the city. They are very near, two or more of them that smell like mermaids but far different. Their scent is like a squid. Are there such mermaids, sire?"

"Where exactly?" the king asked.

"Under the city, sire."

"Mr. Hobbs, contact the mermaids and find out if it is these cecaelia they spoke of."

"Sire, what is a cecaelia?" Hobbs asked.

Kraken's Wake had been locked down, all entrances shut, magic barriers reinforced. The giant, rolling waves moving the city, most of it underwater, up and down, were now constant.

The thick, giant seaweed that made up the Kelp Lands swayed forcibly. All its underwater dwellings had been abandoned—fae had left in their own vessels or riding their aquatic animals hours earlier. The region was situated between the mermaid-water nymph matriarchal section and the triton-sea centaur patriarchal section, but its magical barrier was far less than the greater city. The Kelp Lands were no different than similar sections in any other human or fae city. The quarter was for illegal and indiscreet business not permitted in the main sections. Its emptiness was ghostly. Even the ubiquitous fish were nowhere to be seen. Animals always knew when danger was coming before people.

Bragg and his elfin comrades had staked out the forest-like region. The underwater ports of Kraken's Wake were closest to the Kelp Lands. Traveler had given Bragg a task in his absence, and the manticore hunter was not going to fail. Traveler's caravan could only achieve success in the final leg of their quest to Atlantea as part of a greater fleet. The fleet of Kraken's Wake was protected by a magic barrier alone. No other soul was on guard—except for Bragg and his elves. Bragg admired how the human thought, always anticipating the treachery of others from years and countless unsuccessful attempts on Titan's Trail.

Unlike on land, Bragg's ears and nose never sensed them. He saw the three figures floating toward the region with not even a disturbance in the water. Female. Long tentacles instead of mermaids' tails. But two of their tentacles were longer than the rest.

The trio of cecaelia stopped their forward motion. Bragg had learned every possible thing he could about the race of water fae, but even their sister race, the mermaids, rarely encountered them. He wondered if they sensed him waiting in the kelp somehow. *Could their eyes possibly see me?* The three figures just floated there in the dark water, waiting.

Bragg and his elves had another concern. The turbulence of the water worsened every moment. At some point soon, they would have to abandon their vigil to get to safety. They could swim well, but they weren't water fae.

He and his elfin comrades were magically breathing underwater, oh so quietly, by a translucent covering over the lower halves of their faces. Bragg held his breath. A dark cloud engulfed the three figures. Cecaelia could shoot ink clouds from their bodies for defense or deception. Bragg and his hunters knew their prey were aware of their presence.

Their weapons of choice were useless for fighting underwater. Most water fae could easily dodge or deflect an arrow even from an elf. Few land fae could strike with a blade weapon with sufficient force or speed to be effective. Magic weapons were the only option.

Bragg and his savage elf comrades quickly swam away from their hiding place. They would be the ones to breach the magic barrier of Kraken's Wake proper, and with the special trident in Bragg's hand, they did. Nearly one hundred of them passed through—one moment swimming through the water, the next, they fell hard onto the floor inside some kind of enclosure devoid of water. The dwelf and the elves felt a moment of apprehension. They'd been captured by water fae before.

"Elves," a voice said. "But the large one is not an elf. He's a different race."

"I'm a dwelf," Bragg said to the invisible speaker.

The three cecaelia appeared in the room. Attractive, bluish-skinned females with jet-black hair, wearing black fish-scaled armor stood on grayish tentacles. The one in the center held a shiny black gemstone staff.

"Why are you here?" Bragg asked.

"Were they guards or hunters?" one asked the other two, ignoring him.

"Why would they give such a task to mere land-walkers?"

"Why indeed? Their stench radiates for miles in every direction."

"We should see how they fight in battle."

"The elves are different than others. Bigger and they have fangs like us—clawed nails too."

"I could rip one apart with one tentacle alone."

"Yes, it would be amusing, but we have work to do."

"What is your purpose here?" Bragg asked.

"Their mouths make disgusting sounds."

Bragg raised his open hand. "Please, we are only sentries," the dwelf said with false submission.

"Their mouths lie."

An arrow pierced the pocket-realm and exploded in blinding light. Bragg's arm was grabbed by a tentacle, but more than one of his savage elfin comrades sliced it to pieces just as the tentacles began to crush his hand and suck out his blood. The wound to Bragg's arm would quickly heal, and the cecaelia's tentacle would grow back. Neither was distressed, only in temporary pain.

The water rushed in. Savage elves took advantage of the lack of water in the pocket-realm to throw their volley of javelins at the three cecaelia. Some of the javelins hit their mark, but others were blocked by magic or swatted from the air by their tentacles. The cecaelia dove into the water as the pocket-realm collapsed, and they were all again in the Kelp Land waters.

Bragg's metal golem, Mr. Glog, grasped one of the cecaelia firmly as the other two fired bright white fiery balls of magic at it. The automaton was unharmed as the elves fired their own magic weapons—magic javelins moving at lightning speed. The two cecaelia fighters raised all their tentacles and hands, magic balls of light forming at the tips of each. Bragg and the elves knew what was coming.

Mr. Glog shot up toward the surface like a projectile, dragging the one cecaelia by her arms. The other two screamed and ceased their magic attack and darted away after the golem.

The two cecaelia burst through the surface of the water after the golem. It was already high above in the dark overcast sky with their sister screaming and helpless. They both jumped up as high as they could about to use their magic to fly, when giant nets closed around them. Their bodies fell back to the water to be seized upon by many savage elves.

Bragg, floating in midair, watched with satisfaction.

"Too bad you can't fly like dwelfs and my Mr. Glog." He held up a rabbit-foot pouch. "The stench of fear that you whiffed from miles away was a bit of my magic, a trade secret that I've used often on the hunt. I'm not afraid of manticores, you, or anything else. I'll hunt everything I can fit in my bag."

One of his savage elves pointed in the distance. Bragg turned and saw the growing wave.

"We have little time. Put them in a cage where they belong, then find our sorcerer since they're witches of some kind."

CHAPTER TEN

The Wave

The sky above grew darker and darker, though nightfall was hours away.

"Mr. Bragg is back!"

The announcement wasn't what the island wanted to hear, but it was good news. Mr. Elman's voice echoed throughout as both Titan's and Queen Issaleth's caravans were in complete panic. Order had completely broken down, and Hobbs was helpless to do anything about it. No one needed Mr. Elman's magic sight to see the ever-growing colossal waves, one after another. Death was what the coming tidal waves meant to the men, and they wanted hope. They wanted to hear from Elman that Traveler and his dog had returned with the others. Nothing short of that would satisfy them. There would be no work, no rest until then.

King Aereth had convinced the sea centaurs not to flee, but instead they boarded their ships to submerge them as far below the ocean depths as possible.

A Cut-throat entered the King's tent. "Mr. Frog-Dor, Mr. Bragg summons. He has captives."

"Captives?" the king asked.

The entire leadership gathered inside were surprised.

"Mr. Frog-Dor, go. Inform us as quickly as you can."

Rare was it for the king to be at a loss for action but all they could do was wait.

"What we are doing is a serious gamble," Dr'as said to the king. "We have no guarantee that the magic barrier of the city will hold. Kraken's Wake is mostly underwater but not us."

"We couldn't escape even if we wanted to," Chief Ethor said.

The Tree Shepherd leader Greenwig stepped into the tent. "The crawling trees are at their most powerful to brace the circle around the castle," he said. "The wave could still wash away the island from under us."

"But we sit on a mountain," someone said.

"We sit on a mountain of sand next to a mountain of the earth. The mountain will survive. The sand likely will not, but our circle holds much of the island within in."

"If it does not, what will happen?" King Aereth asked.

"Mr. Traveler is here!"

King Aereth burst out of the royal tent with the elfin and drow leaders and his guardsman. Gwyness was already outside the women's tent with the female half-elves. Men and fae ran from the camp to the keep near the main gatehouse, but suddenly they saw their caravan master galloping to them on the back of a giant wolf-dog.

He jumped down. "Mr. Hobbs!"

The steward appeared from the crowd of men, fae, and animals. "Yes, sir."

"You'll need help. Mr. Tyfer, Mr. Oeric. Help Mr. Hobbs get the entire caravan onboard our ship immediately. Don't look at me. Go! Unless you wish to be here when the waves hit."

Hobbs began yelling orders.

Queen Issaleth walked to Traveler with her sorcerer and her knights.

"Queen, get your people on your ship and ready to sail," Traveler said.

"Sail where, Mr. Traveler?"

"Away from here as quickly as possible."

"What of the mermaids and oceanids? The others, the men?" the queen asked.

"That is where Lady Aylen and the others are. They're preparing them to sail too. Queen, I can't stress enough the size of the wave coming. If we're here when it hits, we will not make it to Atlantea because we will not have our vessels."

"Mr. Traveler, we must tell you something first," King Aereth said. "The sea centaur leader told us."

"Yes, sire. I know. Krakens. In fact, you can already see their tentacles rising from the waves. That's what I mean. We'll survive the wave but not the number of krakens in that school. The creatures will be in a murderous frenzy and will kill everything they can reach, including each other."

Hobbs's short legs had done more running in those short moments than he'd done in months. The lizard minders raced their lizards to the golem ship, anchored next to Queen Issaleth's red ship. Strag and his hoofed fae races galloped after them as a herd. Human laborers and domestics, pech, gnomes, and gnomoids filled up the gangplanks afterward. The brownies were already aboard seeing to the torches and amenities. So were Pangolin and his Cut-throats, on the main deck as sentries. Others were below deck, making a level-by-level, cabin-by-cabin re-inspection.

After the fauns, led by Chief Ammon, the animal men followed with all their animals. All the elves waited on the shore, bows and weapons ready. The four Tree Shepherds were at the island's mountain controlling the crawling trees, which had grown as large and thick as those from the Great Forest themselves. They stretched out, bracing the magic sphere over the island.

The royals, with their guardspeople and kirins, watched Traveler fly their six Antaean giants from the circle and out of view over the mountain on the back of the dog in the form of a giant griffin, but he returned without them. When they landed, the griffin became a dog again, and he joined the royals.

"Sire, get aboard to the command cabin. You will communicate with Queen Issaleth. Have her ship follow ours close. I'll be aboard shortly."

"Will Lady Aylen be here, Mr. Traveler?" Gwyness asked.

"Yes, she'll be here soon."

Traveler moved quickly to speak to the elves. The drows marched from the gatehouse, followed by Estus and the army of armor golems. They filed up the two gangplanks, then the elves followed.

Hobbs joined the royals. "We will be the last, sire, besides the Tree Shepherds, Mr. Traveler, and the dog."

"Let's get aboard then."

The configuration of the bridge was the same—the main room with the large map table, a spire up to a smaller upper lookout level, and an array of floating display mirrors. The moment they entered the command bridge, everyone froze when they saw the magic map. From the main deck of the ship, Pangolin saw the looks on their faces and stepped into the room too. He moved to the table and was aghast. The magical map recreated all that happened in the waters around the city, and they saw a giant wave that literally stood three feet from the map. But more shocking was the mass of tentacles flailing out from the approaching wave some five feet or more from the map.

No one could speak. No one could move. The terror was more than the coming wave. It was the sheer number of giant krakens being pushed to the city from the wave. They did not realize Lady Aylen had entered the room.

"You're back," Gwyness said, finally noticing.

Lady Aylen's attention, too, was on the magical depiction of the map.

The door closed. Everyone turned as Traveler walked to the main display mirror; his dog at his side. However, on each of his shoulders were the fairy sisters. Wildglow and Sunpetal were the size of tiny birds but they could all see the worried looks on their faces.

"Mr. Pangolin, tell your men that this will be the roughest departure of their lives. Keep them away from the sides of the ship and down. If one of them is hit by a kraken's tentacle, they will never be seen again."

Pangolin bolted from the room, slamming the door.

"Everyone, you need to hold on. This may be worse than when we escaped the water fae fleet that tried to destroy us."

"Do what you must, Mr. Traveler," King Aereth said.

They all moved to the display mirrors. Staffs rose from the floor.

"Magic can be very useful," King Aereth said.

They all had something to hold onto. The three kirins simply floated in the air above the ground. They were calm and unconcerned.

Their golem ship rose out of the water into the air and flew forward above their island castle. From the display mirrors, they could see both the crawling trees and the Tree Shepherds. Then they saw it—saw them.

At the peak of the island's mountain, the six Antaean giants knelt on the ground, heads bowed, lined up with their palms touching the rock, yellow light radiated from their eyes, ear canals, and closed mouths. The same ghostly form they had seen at Fae'el towered above the entire island, a composite of each of the giants but taller and more solid in appearance. It had to be nearly one hundred feet high.

The city of Kraken's Wake slowly descended to reach a distance to fully protect itself from the coming wave. Every sorcerer and sorceress within its closed walls would strain their magical abilities to reinforce the magic protective sphere of the city. Kraken's Wake had existed for ages, and it would exist many more after that day, no matter the damage.

The golem ship dropped into the ocean behind the sky giant as it faced the coming wave. On the display mirror, Queen Issaleth's red ship landed directly behind them. Then one city ship after another emerged from the water, lining up behind each other.

A giant tentacle ripped past the Antaean's ghostly titanic form. Their island castle was gone, scooped up like a toy and tossed into the ocean as if it had never been there. The sky all around them became black with tentacles.

A thunderous crash shook their golem ship. But the kraken's tentacle had not breeched their magical barrier. The rest of the fleet behind them was also besieged by the tentacles as krakens were thrown over them. The tidal wave had arrived.

With the Antaean giants touching Pan-Earth directly, no force could move them. The death wave was cut in half by their ghostly giant form of yellow light and rushed past the fleet at a speed faster than they would have imagined, taking all the krakens with them.

"Queen Issaleth!" Traveler yelled.

Her face appeared on one of the smaller display mirrors. "I am here. Our ships survived."

On another mirror, the faces of women appeared—mermaids and oceanids. On another, the water elves appeared. The third had the face of Centauro, the sea centaurs.

"Did anyone lose any ships?"

They all answered in the negative.

"The tritons will join us as we sail. They submerged their fleet," Centauro said.

"We sail as soon as the Antaeans are aboard," Traveler said.

"Will we sail past White Waters?" one of the water elfin queens asked.

"We are not sailing that way," Traveler replied.

"Why?" more than one asked.

"Look ahead."

On the main display, in the direction of the elfin city of White Waters and the way to Atlantea, was a wall of writhing, crushing, flailing krakens, so many in number and with tentacles so long that they created night beyond them. Already the creatures had set upon each other in a frenzy.

An animal scream echoed in the distance. Tentacles pulled some kind of giant feathered snake creature from the clouds. It crashed into the ocean below.

"What was that?" Lady Aylen asked.

"Cloud creatures, princess. Many clouds of the magical lands are filled with them. Flying caravans have their own dangers to contend with, even high above in the heavens. The path is closed to us," Traveler said.

"Closed to us?" one of the mermaids asked. "What is our plan?"

"Can we not go around the creatures?" the nymph queen asked.

"No," Traveler said.

"We survived, Mr. Traveler. What now?" Lady Aylen asked.

"That wasn't the wave, princess. This is it now."

The royals and Gwyness realized for the first time that the illumination of the command cabin mimicked the daylight outside the ship. The interior went completely dark except for the glowing magic of the display mirrors.

The wave was so tall it blotted out the sunlight. The ghostly form of the Antaeans raised its arms, and its torso widened. The wave didn't crash down but swept over them with increasing, pressing power, but not even its raw force could impact the Antaeans. A pocket of safety was created for the fleet behind the ghostly sky giant, almost like a waterfall with the waters spilling past them. The islands had been completely washed away, as had the krakens closest to them.

Strangely, the main wave was less of an impact than the wave before it. Their ship bobbed and swayed, almost capsizing, but Traveler managed the steering.

"Krakens will be in these waters for some time so we need to put as much distance between us and them as possible. We are not beyond the reach of their tentacles yet."

"Are they still a concern?" the water nymph leader asked.

"I'm not as concerned by the krakens as I am by the fleet waiting on the way to Atlantea. Consult your maps."

"Our allies, the cecaelia fleet, will join us," the mermaid queen said. "With them, we'll have an even more formidable fleet."

"I do have a request," Traveler said. "I need you mermaids to send your best sorcerers to the ship."

"Why?" the mermaid queen asked.

"To question the three cecaelia witches we captured trying to sabotage your city."

"Witches?" the water nymph queen asked.

"Since we will not be sailing directly to Atlantea from here, we will go with my original plan for when my caravan reached Titan's Teeth. Have your cecaelia fleet, if they are allies, instead, chase us."

"Chase us where, Mr. Traveler?" Queen Issaleth asked.

"To the Sirenic Seas," Traveler answered.

"Madness!" That was what erupted from all the water fae royals and Queen Issaleth.

"The tritons will never agree to your plan."

"Review your maps before giving us your final answer. You all have also forgotten the cause of the death waves. The mountains are still coming, so we are not free of their danger. Also, we are being prevented from seeing past White Waters. I'm not sailing one inch toward Atlantea until we have the full means to see our way there. Since our maps are not powerful enough to do so, prevented by whatever magic, we will go to those who have the magic and the maps to succeed."

"The cyclopes," Centauro said.

"Yes, we carry the banner of the centaurs of Chiron, their ally. Whether it's one of their seers or magical maps, we must have one. What we can see is more than the continuing death waves and the wall of krakens. I told you to review your maps before giving us your final answers because, besides the approaching cecaelia fleet, there is an unknown fleet approaching White Waters, and there's a third fleet moving in our direction. The only madness would be to ignore all these facts and sail forward. I am the caravan master I am because I am anything but mad. The Sirenic Seas are our next destination. We must sail away from Atlantea to be able to eventually sail to it. You can join us or not."

CHAPTER ELEVEN

They Come at Night

The three cecaelia swam around in circles within an oval prison, a giant transparent bubble floating in the center of a larger room, both filled with water. The witches shot sparks of magic at the transparent barrier enclosing them but to no effect. They ceased their swimming and floated together in the center the moment they heard the door unlocking to the room.

Nearly two dozen mermaids, oceanids, and water elves, including Lady Aylen, swam into the prison holding room. The mermaids approached the bubble, slowly swaying their giant lower-body fish tails to maintain their floating position.

Lady Aylen studied their prisoners. She had never seen their kind before. Bluish skin, jet-black hair, clad in shiny black fish-scale armor, they stood. However, it was their lower bodies that attracted her attention—eight gray tentacles longer than the length of human legs, if they had them, but in addition were two longer gray tentacles lined with blue suckers under one side. They were both mesmerizing and terrifying in form.

"Why do you invite others into our talk?" one of the octopus mermaids asked a mermaid.

"Questions will come from us, sisters. Answers will come from you," the lead mermaid said.

The witches smiled. "As you wish," the cecaelia said.

"Why did you trespass into Kraken's Wake?" the mermaid asked.

"We were sent by our fleet to make contact."

"That is a lie. The city was closed. All others fled the city because of the coming death wave. But you trespassed, nonetheless, to be captured like fish by others."

"We were set upon for no reason. Cecaelia and mermaids are allies. We have sent a fleet to aid you in your quest to Atlantea and battle any enemies we encounter. Why would you be suspicious of us? The city was closed, so we could not contact you through magic. All we could do was swim directly to the entrance."

"You were not captured at the entrance. You were captured by the ports," a water nymph said.

"We sensed others and went to investigate."

"You lie," Lady Aylen said.

The mermaids, oceanids, and other water elves flashed disapproving looks.

"Who is she? Clearly not of these waters. She smells like a human, more so than any elf we've ever encountered," a cecaelia said.

"Answer her charge," a mermaid said.

"There is nothing to answer. It is she who lies. We are your allies. She is the stranger. You best release us from your prison. Our fleet will meet up with you, and they will want us returned."

"We were sent to aid you in your hour of need against the death wave. Why else would they send spell-casters and not warriors?" another cecaelia asked.

"We will allow you to cast a truth spell on us to prove what we say is true," another cecaelia said.

"We may do that," the mermaid leader said. "For now, you will remain here."

"Is our fleet close?"

"Yes."

"We'll await their arrival, then. Let us not allow strangers to pit us against each other. Atlantea awaits us."

"Yes, it does," the mermaid leader said. "You will also refrain from any magic while you wait."

"As you wish, sister."

Most of their golem ship had empty cabins because Traveler wanted the entire caravan in one pocket-realm. Besides the command cabin, there were cabins with caravan members for specific key duties. The wall of one displayed the dungeon of the mermaid's city ship where the three cecaelia witches swam ceaselessly around in circles in their magic sphere prison.

"Congratulations, Mr. Bragg," Traveler said, watching.

"Thank you, Mr. Traveler. You did indeed assign me a task I was both eager to fulfill and had the skills to match," the dwelf hunter said, arms folded, next to him.

"Any real challenge?"

"None. They swam into my trap. I was not about to let them cast any magic on me or my men."

"What do you make of them, Frog-Dor?" Traveler asked the sorcerer, who watched the display mirror with them.

Dr'amal the sorcerer, the mole-looking fae, and Gwyness also looked on.

"I have never seen their kind before, Mr. Traveler. But the mermaids are powerful enough to contain them. Whatever magic they have is of no concern to us."

"We should be rid of them," Dr'amal said.

"They can swim as fast as our ship," Traveler said. "We cannot let them go at the present time."

"How are they in hand-to-hand combat?" Bragg asked.

"It's like fighting a ten-armed gorgon with their body's flexibility and agility."

"Gorgon? That's not a happy thought. Oh, I did forget to ask you about our new alliance, Mr. Traveler. We are in the presence of all the many fae who hate the Four Kings as much as we do, maybe more so."

"All from your list."

"Yes. Some have been their enemy for many years."

"I shared your list with Lady Aylen, and she made sure to influence the elves at White Waters as to who would join our fleet. The greater and more powerful the enemy of the Four Kings, the better and more likely a potential ally for us."

"We thank the time elemental demon for giving us the advantage."

"We can thank Oughtred himself for sending the time elemental to give us the advantage, but we are not in Atlantea yet."

"We are one now. He can hunt us all he wants, but killing us will be a fruitless endeavor."

"Perhaps. Being together is a positive, but it is also a negative." Traveler glanced at the others. "Mr. Frog-Dor is correct that the magic prison of the mermaids is sufficient to manage the witches, but we must still watch them at all times."

"I will see to it, Mr. Traveler," Frog-Dor said.

"Mr. Traveler, are these cecaelia an evil race?" Gwyness asked.

"No, maiden, they are not—or most of their kind is not. They are one of the oldest water fae races but, except for merfolk, are hardly encountered by others."

"But you don't trust them?"

"I'm suspicious of them for many reasons."

"Your suspicions are warranted," Bragg said. "I wonder myself if we captured them or if they allowed us to."

"I thought the same."

"Why would the two of you say that? If you believe that, we definitely must be rid of them," Dr'amal said.

"I agree with Dr'amal," Gwyness said. "They're witches. We don't want them on any ship on the fleet."

"We'll resolve the matter soon," Traveler said. "We still must meet our new fleet alliance leaders."

Every ship of the new fleet was busy with activity despite nightfall. They had left so hurriedly that all the organization of ship duties had to be done at sea. Titan's Caravan's golem vessel and Queen Issaleth's ship anchored adjacent to each other. Surrounding them in a circle, hull to hull, sat the rest of the fleet— ten of the mermaids' and oceanids', seven of the tritons' and sea centaurs', one of which was a new weapons cargo ship, and seven of the water elves'. The city ships were a true floating wall around them in the middle of the great ocean.

Hobbs strolled the main deck, happy with the arrangement of the water fae's ships to protect them. Pangolin, who remained on watch duty, was not happy. In his eyes, their security was entrusted to those they had known barely a week. He joined the deck security of Cut-throats and moon elves. However, both men were unhappy that they had to remain behind for the first, and likely only, gathering of the fleet's entire leadership on Queen Issaleth's red city ship. Neither man felt comfortable with its deck crew of giant ant men with their beady red eyes.

Other than the moonlight, nothing illuminated any of the ships. Fae could see fine in the dark but not humans. They had to resist the urge to lean against the side of the ship or, even worse, peer out over it. Traveler told them many times that a fish could snatch a man from the ship and be miles away before anyone noticed. Both men took a break outside the command cabin.

"I can't even smoke my pipe," Hobbs said.

"You should turn in, Mr. Hobbs."

"No, I have to wait until they all return. I'd never be able to sleep anyway."

"Did you think we could do it? Get everyone aboard and set sail so fast?"

"Did you think we could survive a giant wave *and* an ocean of krakens?"

"Mr. Hobbs, this is our fabled quest. A little excitement is to be expected."

Hobbs chuckled. "As long as we have no more for the night, so at least some of the men can get a bit of sleep."

"But will they? They'll be gossiping straight through into the morning."

"That they will, which means they'll be sleeping through their day chores."

"What do you make of these part-mermaid, part-octopus witches Mr. Bragg and his men captured?"

"I don't know."

"We should throw them overboard and be done with it and have nothing to do with their fleet."

"Fifty ships though. Nearly double all our ships."

"But can we trust them? Twenty-six is plenty, all city ships except for ours."

"It's the same as on the land trail, Mr. Pangolin. None of us can get to Atlantea without the other. And from what we've seen with our own eyes, there are many things larger than our fleet of city ships on these oceans."

The merman announcer was the species Titan's Caravan had seen in Faë-Land, a giant fish with a humanoid head. He had white eyes, signifying a fae seer of incredible power.

"King Traerio of the tritons!"

The triton king, seated in his floating chair, simply waved. He had an upper humanoid half with a lower half of two green-scaled fish tails for legs. Dozens of triton warriors surrounded him, or warriors and sorcerers indistinguishable from one another. The armor of their upper half, with matching helmets, was of the same fish-scaled metal that was the norm of the Oceanus Omnis races. Their skin had a blue hue and their ears were very elfin, sprouting out level to the ground. With the exception of the crowned king, all the tritons carried a nearly seven-foot lucent-green trident in each hand.

"King Centauro of the ichthyocentaurs!" the merman bellowed.

Like the cecaelia, sea centaurs had different names depending on the race. Their ancient name were ichthyocentaurs. Others called them merman centaurs. Land walkers, especially, called them sea centaurs. King Centauro rested on a type of small chariot. His fellow sea centaurs surrounded him, each with a single trident of yellow metal as long as eight feet.

"Queen Oluania of the oceanids," the merman announced.

The ocean nymphs rode in on their beautiful hippocampi. The oceanids looked like human females in every way, in silvery dresses with flowing hair down to their feet. However, around them were their sister race of blue-skinned women—the shape-shifting nixies. The nixies wore fish-scaled armor, but none of the nymphs carried weapons.

"Queen Geneva of the mermaids."

The queen had not planned to join the fleet, as she was the chief administrator of Kraken's Wake, but so angry was she over the treachery against it, she decided to lead the mermaids to Atlantea herself. Underwater, all the mermaids had lower bodies of giant fish tails with fins. They all carried blue tridents. Some also had shields.

"Kings Finlor, Elfred, Agis, Queens Amphitrite, Leena, and Eriana."

The water elfin royals of White Waters had been selected by Lady Aylen from many others. Unlike the other water fae rulers present, the elfin royals appeared to be more administrators than warriors. The fact that they had sent so many royals on the fleet could have been a boast of the great alliance of water elves they had created. Likely, it was proof that they were so divided behind closed doors that no kingdom trusted the other to travel to Atlantea to carry the banner of all.

However, no one doubted the skill or courage of the water elfin knights always ready for a full battle.

"Queen Nori and King Otari of the selkies."

The fact that the selkies were announced at all meant they had some standing with the water fae. Lady Aylen didn't know what to think of them since in her mind when the battle came in the city of White Waters, all they did was transform into seals and hide.

"Queen Issaleth of the Armathain Caravan."

The second human caravan of the fleet was a welcome addition to the humans of Titan's Caravan.

"King Aereth and Lady Aylen of Titan's Caravan. Prince Traveler as their trailmaster."

Traveler shot a look at the merman. "Prince? When did I become a prince? King, is this your doing?"

The royals laughed.

It was a unique meeting, as the grand hall was filled with clear water up to their chests—a compromise for land-walkers and seafaring races. The mermen floated in the open air above them. In the water itself, Lady Aylen was amused by the variety of fish swimming around them.

The ceiling of the room was a giant display mirror. Many eyes were fixed on it. A giant shadow passed beneath their anchored ships. The one visible eye of the giant kraken was as large as three city ships.

"This is why we didn't sail on," Traveler whispered to the royals. "They are attracted to moving shapes. Shapes not in motion are spared from their attacks."

"How many of the creatures are near us?" Lady Aylen asked. "I can't sense them."

"Most fae races can't. Only pure water fae can. Even water elves and mermaids came from land-walking fae races," Traveler said. "No way to know how many of the krakens are in the region now. It may take months or years for them to disperse to their previous habitats. That means water travel in this region will be severely restricted for some time."

"Mr. Traveler," one of the elfin queens began, "what is our grand plan to get to Atlantea?"

"Before I answer your question, queen, we should hear from the mermaids regarding our three cecaelia captives."

Queen Geneva looked to one of her mermaid sorceresses.

"We used a truth-seer and found they were not lying," the mermaid sorceress said.

"What is your name?" Traveler asked her.

The mermaid hesitated. Queen Geneva gave her a nod.

"Talise."

"Talise, I don't care about spells. Do you believe they were telling the truth? This is very important. Out here on the Trail, I have found more times than not that instincts can saves lives as much as spells or magic weapons. Everything we have, the cecaelia possess. If we meet them, and it is a trap, can we defeat them? Yes, but how many of us could be killed, and how many of our ships destroyed? We already know we will face Oughtred's forces at Atlantea."

"Are you certain of this?" Centauro, the sea centaur, asked.

"King, I am certain." Traveler returned his gaze to the mermaid. "Talise, if you have any doubt, then I would argue we should not risk joining with them."

"How can I have no doubt?"

"Then you have doubt, which means we cannot meet their fleet."

"But you want us to go into the territory of the sirens," an elfin queen said.

"We are going to the cyclops city. I don't believe we have enough of an advantage anymore. It would also confuse our enemies because it is an action that will make no sense. They won't know where we are or where we are going."

"It makes no sense to us," Queen Oluania said. "We all have seers."

"Not like the cyclops," Traveler said.

"No one will argue that they do not have the most powerful sight."

"I need to know clearly what's ahead," Traveler said. "I will not lead any caravan, or fleet in my charge into a trap, or to its death. Our magic maps have thus far been useless in the detection of multiple enemies around us. We must have the aid of a cyclops seer."

"But this fleet we have assembled," King Traerio of the tritons said, "is quite powerful. I don't believe you know how powerful we are."

"Can we defeat spell-talkers?" Traveler asked.

"Spell-talkers?" more than one asked.

"Where did you encounter such evil?" another asked.

"Nemains. Lampads."

"Lampads?" the nymphs asked.

"Are we not forgetting the undine?" Traveler asked.

"No, we are not," the water elves said.

"Then there is the crab centaur we encountered. In all the stories I have heard of crab centaurs, so often there are stories of spider centaurs. I've always wondered of the possibility that the two races travel together."

"You are not the only one who has speculated the same," the triton leader said.

"Then there is one more group."

"Which is?" Queen Issaleth asked.

"Sky elves, Oughtred's main allies in all this. And you told us something that we didn't know. Oughtred is a lich, one different than any other—transformed rather than created by another. It explains his ability to assemble all these dark creatures. The rumor is that a lich can summon and command hordes of living dead creatures."

"Has Mr. Traveler convinced us of the course of action?" Nori, the selkie, asked the group.

"I'd say he has," Queen Geneva said. "I am not pleased, as the cecaelia have truly been allies to my city for ages. But we'll sail to the cyclops city and keep the three in our dungeon."

"Good. We'll quickly decide on the arrangement of the fleet and division of duties in any encounter or battle."

"One more thing. What if we do all this and sail for Atlantea and Oughtred and his dark allies still await us?" Queen Geneva asked.

"No need to worry there. If they attack, the Atlanteans themselves will destroy them."

No one on Traveler's ship could see them lining the bottom of the hull underwater—tiny mouse-sized creatures with toad heads and the limbs and bodies of mice. Some were black, others yellow. The darklings were enjoying their time with their sea cousins.

They watched the giant kraken float underneath the ship miles away in the depths. If only they could see one rip apart a ship with all its people, as long as it wasn't theirs. Maybe an enemy would come by, and they could see the kraken attack then.

Their eyes could see quite well in the blackness of the water. They also saw fish and a shark or two. But it was the krakens they were interested in. Not even their sea phooka cousins had seen one in real life. But they realized something strange. They were positive that the same kraken had swam by before but now was swimming the other way. *Is it circling our fleet from deep below?*

A giant yellow eye passed right under them, and they all almost hopped out of the water in unison. Its body kept going and going, then its tentacles. The phookas watched for nearly an hour before the creature fully passed by. What they beheld wasn't a giant kraken but one so large that giant krakens were the size of a mouse compared to it.

The darklings led the way, crawling out of the water. Both black and yellow climbed up the outer hull of the ship.

The golem ship did sometimes travel by sails, and its mast reached up high above the ship. Not to use sails but to be a lookout post during the day.

"We find Master Traveler," a darkling said. "You climb the mast and see what's to see."

The darklings became black rabbits with webbed feet and monkey tails and jumped over the side onto the deck, startling the moon elves on duty.

"You damn goblins! I could have thrust my sword through you!" a moon elf said.

The sea phookas became mouse-headed bats and flew as a swarm to the top of the mast. They all returned to their toad-headed mouse form to hold onto the mast as they scanned the dark waters around the anchored fleet. They heard the moon elves on the deck, looking up at them, cursing under their breathes. The phookas cackled.

"Look," one said. "I see goblins!"

A shadowy boat was miles from them, but it was there.

"Tell Master Traveler," another one said.

One dropped from the mast, changing to a yellow monkey-headed bat and flew down to the command cabin.

The moon elf deck guards, armed with their bows and moon swords, saw all fifteen male fae-bloods emerge from the lower deck steps. Their elfin eyes noticed the wolf-like yellow-tinted brown eyes. As always, the fae-blood were dressed in black attire and cloaks.

"Why are you on deck?" a moon elf asked. Other moon elves joined him.

"There are goblins nearby," one of the fae-blood men said.

"Goblins? Where? No one has sighted a ship," the moon elf said.

"Maybe someone has," the fae-blood man said, pointing.

Traveler approached them with his special orange-hued armor under his hooded cloak. His sword was in hand, and his dog was at his side. Several black ram-headed gorillas followed them.

"Trouble, Mr. Traveler?" a moon elf asked.

"The fae-bloods sense goblins," another moon elf said.

"And there are giant krakens circling under us," Traveler said.

Panic came over the moon elves' faces.

"Should we sound the alarm?" a moon elf asked.

"That is what we can't do," Traveler said. "We need to find that goblin ship. The darklings said they saw only one ship in shadowy form on our starboard."

"One ship only?"

"That they can see."

"What do you advise?"

"We need to handle this quietly. Sea battles at night are to be avoided at all costs. Sea battles with giant krakens swimming beneath us are suicide. I have an idea. So fae-bloods to the bow, darklings up the mainmast."

"I'll wake Chief Ethor, Lyre and Talos," one moon elf said.

"Should we wake any others?" the other moon elf asked.

"No," Traveler said. "Tonight, less is more."

Traveler stood in front of the main display mirror of the command cabin. Chief Ethor, several woodland elves, Lyre, several high elves, Talos, and several desert elves crowded around the mirrors too. Each mirror showed the waters around the fleet—nothing to be seen in any direction.

"Master Traveler, how did your phookas see the ship, but now that we all search for it, we cannot find it?" Chief Ethor asked.

"They know we saw them," Traveler replied.

"If we had to fire our cannons, what would happen?" Lyre asked.

"If the krakens below sense it, they could rip our entire fleet apart. Krakens are primarily night predators."

The door opened, and Dr'amal entered with her father, Dr'as. Though instinctively uncomfortable in a room of mostly elves, the drows neared the caravan master.

Traveler turned to them. "Dr'amal, we need your assistance. There is a goblin ship hunting us. It is close and waiting to attack us, but there is at least one kraken below."

"Kraken?" Dr'as asked nervously.

The door opened again, and the elves allowed the selkie leaders to enter. Nori held her staff in her hand.

"You summoned us, Mr. Traveler?"

Traveler walked to her. "You are a seer?"

"I am. All the women of my people are."

"Stronger than those of the mermaids and oceanids?"

"My wife is quite a powerful seer," Otari said.

"Dr'amal, go with them to the top deck. Enhance her power if you can, or if needed. We must find this goblin ship."

"I will see," Nori said as she waved her free hand in a circular motion.

Wherever there were elves, there were goblins. In the realm of the Oceanus Omnis, it was no different. Traveler had encountered sea goblins before, but the pirates they saw on the mirror of clouds Nori had created showed sea goblins much larger than normal. Their green skin was similar to that of an eel's, both ridged and scaled. Their pointy ears were larger and so were their clawed hands. Their faces were obscured by the faceplates of their helmets. Both helmets and body armor were of a shiny black goblin metal of high craftsmanship completely opposite from the kind their land cousins wore.

The weapons in their hands were a type of spiked mace, while teams of others held large nets for capturing people, not fish. Shoulder to shoulder were goblins with three-bowed crossbows. The pirate warship was more manned than any Traveler or the water fae had ever seen, but their attention was fixed on the goblin's cannons. A glow emitted from deep within them.

"Can you determine exactly where on the ship they are?" Traveler asked.

"I am trying," Nori replied.

Dr'amal readied her own magic to help, but Nori's husband gave her a gesture to wait. Nori's staff began to glow.

"Why do you think they haven't attacked yet?" Taylos asked.

"Master Traveler," Chief Ethor said.

Everyone returned to the main display mirror. Giant tentacles rose from the surface of the water. A shadowy form of a giant ship appeared not more than a hundred feet away from the fleet. In moments, the shadow ship became solid in form. Their cannons fired at once, engulfing the creature's tentacles in streams of lava that began to dissolve the limbs.

The surface of the ocean exploded in violence. Calm waves became rising swells. The creature rose from the depths. Only a tip of its elongated head emerged, but they knew that its size easily dwarfed all the ships of their fleet combined.

Water splashed all around the magic protective sphere of the ships, as Lady Aylen came through the door with Gwyness. From another display mirror, the eye of the creature rose beneath the circle formed by all their ships. She saw Traveler grab the wand from his cloak pocket.

"Oh, no. Not again." Lady Aylen pulled Gwyness inside and slammed the door.

The wand became a staff, which he stabbed into the floor and became a navigation wheel at the top.

"Depart! Depart!"

Their golem ship jumped over the wall of city ships and crashed into the water. All the ships broke formation to follow.

On the display mirror, they watched the giant kraken rising from the ocean. One of its tentacles slammed the front half of the goblin ship while another pounded the other half, disintegrating it to pieces. Sea goblin bodies in black armor were strewn everywhere. The wreck erupted in swarms of bat-like creatures that flew into the night sky.

The goblins had done what no living thing, fae or human, good or evil, should ever do. They had angered a giant kraken. Even with a weapon powerful enough to burn away one of its tentacles, that still left nine more.

They were not away from danger yet, but Traveler slowed their vessel.

"We have company," he said.

Before them was another fleet of ships of a design he had not ever seen, appearing as giant floating hermit crabs—an elongated shell for the aft and appendages forged of metal made up the fore of the ships. Traveler had heard of the cecaelia ships from other fae in the past.

"Prepare to fire!" he yelled to the fleet.

"No, Mr. Traveler," a voice said from one of the smaller mirrors—the mermaids. "It's the cecaelia fleet. They're speaking to our queen now. They said they commanded the kraken to protect us."

CHAPTER TWELVE

Escape to the Sirenic Seas

The lead cecaelia ship left its fleet formation to dock with the main mermaid ship. Aboard Titan's Caravan's ship, all watched as the cecaelia leaders walked with their long tentacles, their bodies riding along. Dozens of them came aboard the mermaid ship.

The meeting, or shouting match, was well underway when Traveler and the royals were escorted to the ship's meeting hall. The same water fae were present from the meeting on Queen Issaleth's red ship, and the room was filled with water to everyone's chest—except the cecaelia. With their tentacles, their upper torsos hung well above the water. Their piercing black eyes fixed on Traveler the moment the mermen led them into the room.

"A human caravan master," a cecaelia said.

Besides their beauty, the cecaelia all had striking thick black hair that stood like a beehive on their heads and flowed down behind their backs to the water. Dark fish-scaled armor covered their gray skin. Their formidable tentacles had been gray but appeared bluer in color when Traveler and the royals realized that the new water fae's skin were chameleonlike—changing color at will or due to their mercurial moods.

"Whom do we address? I am Lady Aylen. This is King Aereth and Mr. Traveler."

"We have no interest in you, elfess, or your human king. We do have special interest in your human guide. I see your dog beside you is not a dog at all. We have shape-shifters too. Shall we fetch them?"

"If you don't move against me, you have nothing to fear," Traveler said.

"We were told you wanted to fire on my ships," the cecaelia said.

"Why wouldn't we? A dark fleet rising from nowhere in the darkness. For all we knew, you were in league with the sea goblins."

The mermaid octopus women laughed. "I am Queen Atopia, and cecaelia have never and will never be in league with goblins. If the kraken hadn't destroyed them, we would have. I will excuse your action as an understandable mistake. I will not, however, excuse you convincing our mermaid sisters to flee from us like we were enemies. Our peoples have been allies since before you monkeys climbed down from your trees."

King Aereth laughed aloud. "Monkeys?"

"Yes, sire. They call us primates. We call them ugly octopus women. Take no offense. It's what they call all land-walkers, human, land elves, sprites, all of us."

"Because it's true."

"When do you plan to claim your witches?" Traveler asked. "The ones you dispatched against your sisters at Kraken's Wake."

The cecaelia queen's tentacles thrashed in the water in anger. "They are not our witches and not even of our race!" She looked at the mermaids. "Why are you listening to these humans? We are octopus fae. The witches, from what you've shown us, are squid fae!" She angrily looked at Traveler. "Or can't monkeys count? Ten is not eight!"

"Queen Atopia, if I can step in," King Aereth said. "We have never seen cecaelia before. When you say it, it's obvious that there must be different sub-races of your kind, but we would not know that. I can assure you that we humans have barely grown accustomed to the many sub-races of elves."

"That I can understand," Atopia said.

"How many different sub-races does your kind have, queen?" King Aereth asked.

She paused. Her anger had subsided. "Hundreds."

"Are you allies to all?"

"No."

"There it is, queen," King Aereth said. "Further, we are a noble caravan and well-bred. None of us are in the habit of staring below a woman's waist to count the number of legs or tentacles."

The hall erupted in laughter, and for the moment, all of the cecaelia were smiling.

"We echo what the human king has said," Queen Geneva, the mermaid queen, said. "These witches described your fleet perfectly. They claimed to have been sent by you. Moreover, they hid their additional tentacles from our eyes."

"Lying witches. Turn them over to us. My mages will deal with them."

"Could they be allies with the Four Kings?" Queen Eriana of the water elves asked.

"Undoubtedly they are. Sent to sow distrust among us, and they almost succeeded. What is your plan, human," she asked Traveler, "since we cannot sail directly to Atlantea with so many krakens in the waters? We agree with your assessment there. Not even we have the power to enchant so many, and they are in a murderous frenzy, being displaced from their natural habitats."

"We sail for the cyclops city of Mímir-Spring."

"Why there?"

"To convene with their cyclopes seers."

"You think their noble clan would aid us?"

"Yes. We travel under the banner of their allies, the centaurs of Chiron."

"That will get you an audience but no more."

"I have visited the city before."

"So?"

"I studied there for a time."

The cecaelia queen smiled. "Do you know why Oughtred of the Four Kings tries to destroy you? You and he are the same. He has traveled many places for evil, you for adventure. Good and evil, your caravan and his."

"Others have said the same."

"Should we form this alliance of good?"

"Yet Atlanteans prefer us to you," Traveler said.

The cecaelia glared at him. "We don't need to travel to the cyclops city, Chiron, or any cloud city for our seers. We have our own in the safety of our deep underwater cities."

"Then why travel to Atlantea?"

"Our sisters and I have conversed fully on the situation. We will not allow the Four Kings to seal off Atlantea from us or any fae. The power of that city is not its untold riches, but you know that."

"I do."

"Then why waste time sailing away only to have to sail back? The shortest route between two points is straight. Even you tailless monkeys must know that."

"It's not the shortest route if you end up dead. We monkeys don't knowingly leap into the mouths of lions."

The cecaelia queen laughed. "We are not afraid of what's ahead. We may not be able to sail a direct course, but we can sail around the giant krakens."

"I must say that the powers of your sorceresses to control the giant krakens is impressive," Traveler said.

"We speak to them, not control them. Do you control your shape-shifter? No, you speak to him with respect. Regardless of our connection with the krakens, that doesn't mean we are in league with crab centaurs. I heard you planted that ridiculous lie in the minds of our sisters, too. Did you think that because of the design of our ships?"

"We have never seen one of your ships before."

"It's foolish. We are not the only water race that constructs our ships in this manner. They don't ally with demons either."

"Have you seen any of their allies on the waters?"

"You are beginning to anger me again, human. There are no spider centaurs in these waters. You speak of spider centaurs as if they are a daily occurrence. They are so rare they might as well be myth told by fae mothers to scare their children into doing their chores."

The cecaelia queen turned to the mermaids. "We brought our fleet of fifty ships, and we intend to sail forward to Atlantea, not run away to one-eyed giants no matter how noble they may be. We depart at dawn. Choose, sisters and elves. Accompany us, as planned, or go on a pointless voyage to the Sirenic Seas with the humans and their tiny boat of a ship."

The queen looked at her fellow cecaelia, and they all walked out of the hall on their tentacles.

The mermaids, oceanids, and water elves looked at each other then at Traveler and the royals. King Aereth and Lady Aylen had the same sinking feeling.

Pangolin watched from his forward post across the ocean, but it was more than just Cut-throats on the main deck. Word had already spread through the men. Humans, sprites, and elves watched their fleet sail away with the new black ships of the cecaelia—the ten of the mermaids' and oceanids', seven of the tritons' and sea centaurs', seven of the water elves', and Queen Issaleth's ship.

"How do you think it would be to fight one of those octopus mermaids?" I'wulf asked him.

"Clearly eight tentacles and two arms are better than two arms," Pangolin said. "I doubt we'd be much of a bother to them."

"Berserkers can adapt to any battle against any enemy," I'wulf countered.

"Our only chance in a battle against them would be magic." Pangolin patted him on the back. "But since they sail away, let's put it to the Cut-throats to devise strategies against them should we encounter them in the future."

I'wulf smiled, nodding. "As we have always done in the past to great success. Though I do wish we hadn't lost our fleet."

"We don't need them to get to Atlantea. We have Mr. Traveler."

Pangolin had never been emotionally invested in the new sea alliance, but he didn't need to look at the men's faces to know how demoralized they were. Before they could fully marvel at their new fleet alliance, it was gone.

Traveler stepped out of the command cabin. "Mr. Hobbs, please get all the men not part of deck security back below. There are still stray krakens about."

"Yes, Mr. Traveler."

Pangolin noticed that their caravan master was unconcerned and focused on his tasks of the day. The berserker had a slight grin, as he knew that was the expression that the men needed to see and would see—confidence.

"Mr. Pangolin," Traveler said before going back inside. "We may have only one or two full days free of danger if we're fortunate. Once we near the Sirenic Seas, then things will change. You and your men will need to learn to work without the benefit of hearing and to rely on your chamroshes."

"Siren songs," Pangolin said.

"One siren alone could incapacitate the ship. We'll encounter hundreds."

"Hundreds?" a Cut-throat asked, panicked.

"Get back to work!" Pangolin yelled.

Steering the ship was none other than Young Quillen. The boy had a smile locked on his face as he kept his eye on the main display mirror.

"Mr. Traveler, this cannot be wise." King Aereth stood next to the boy.

"I can do this, sire," the boy said.

"Sire, Mr. Quillen is more than capable and is the only one in this room immune to siren song."

The Brothers Brimm musicians sat near the map table, four wearing their same thick belt with a long pouch and Johnter with the same satchel over his neck and small lute dangling to his side. They sat on the floor busy at work writing music on parchments.

The royals' and Gwyness's kirins relaxed in a corner of the room, quietly watching it all, just as Traveler's dog did, lying in another corner. Traveler returned to the map table, where an upset Lady Aylen stood with Gwyness.

"But I thought women were immune, Mr. Traveler," Gwyness said.

Traveler looked up. "I'm sorry, Maiden Gwyness, but there are male sirens too."

Lady Aylen threw up her hands with a laugh. King Aereth joined them at the map table.

"I cannot say that I feel any less distressed than the men. For all that we did, and to lose every last ship of our fleet," King Aereth said.

"Don't be distressed, sire. Remember our original caravan didn't even involve you back in the Lands of Man. We have evolved to meet the challenges along the Trail. Titan's Caravan was built to get to Atlantea, alone if need be."

"We destroyed the Kings' Caravan, or you did with your dog," Lady Aylen said, "but we remain under their evil shadow. We do need a fleet to safely get to Atlantea, do we not, Mr. Traveler?"

"I had hoped that at least Queen Issaleth would remain with us," King Aereth said.

"Perhaps, princess, what we need most is the ability to see all before us."

"Will you tell us of this cyclops city, Mr. Traveler?" Gwyness asked.

"Yes, I will, Maiden Gwyness. Then you will know all that I know of the magic city. That is if Mr. Quillen can get us there without crashing into a giant fish or sea serpent."

"I hear you, Mr. Traveler." Quillen laughed.

Bragg entered the command cabin and closed the door behind him. Others had come up to join the Brothers Brimm for the noon meal. He could hear Mr.

Elman and the other male half-elves up the spire's staircase on the second level.

Traveler sat at the map table eating, with his dog behind him eating some large bone with meat. The royals, Gwyness, and their kirins were on the main deck for fresh air.

"When do you get any rest, Mr. Traveler?" the dwelf asked.

"When we get to Mímir-Spring, Mr. Bragg."

The manticore hunter joined him at the map table. "It would appear that my comrades and I didn't use our time being sent back to the past wisely after all. I found Oughtred's greatest enemies, those alive, only for us to lose them again."

"You did what you could, Mr. Bragg. You paved the way for our alliance."

"Do the others know how we contacted the water elves at White Waters?"

"No. They don't know you were the one who made the introduction to Queen Firi for us because," Traveler looked at him with a smile, "you worked for her mother."

Bragg laughed. "If I was going to be a hunter, I needed someone to pay me."

"It's not important."

"When one creates an alliance, it would help if it remains one for at least a little while."

"We'll get to Atlantea."

"I heard of this cyclops city but never got a chance to visit. How close is it to these islands of the sirens?"

"Very close. They are no match for the cyclopes, but getting to the city is dangerous for all others. However, I know the way."

"Will we be taking on another giant only with a single eye?"

"If we're fortunate. More likely, they will give us a seeing spell that will light our way to Atlantea, revealing all around us, above and below."

"Good. If Oughtred awaits at Atlantea, my Mr. Glog and my elves will be ready. Once on land, my Diomedian Mares will eagerly join in if there is any battle to be had against any dark forces."

"No need for all that, Mr. Bragg. Once we cross the threshold of Atlantea, the Atlanteans themselves will see that all violence ceases, whether by weapon or by magic."

"But you are still concerned."

"I am, but not for us, for Atlantea. Oughtred is not to be trusted or underestimated, though he has underestimated us countless times."

"Our quest is supposed to be traversing Titan's Trail to obtain the limitless riches of the fabled kingdom, but instead, it has become a competition, in a way, between goodness and evil."

"Have you become a philosopher, too, Mr. Bragg, with age?"

"Merely repeating words of fables. But it's true, don't you think? We get to Atlantea but will have to face Oughtred again directly."

"We will face him directly at Atlantea, and the Atlanteans will deal with him."

Frog-Dor and Dr'amal arrived and made their own base in the command cabin, sitting in front of the display mirrors.

"Boy, you cannot steer forever," Dr'amal said to Quillen.

"Yes, I can," he replied.

"Go eat some food. I can stand in for you," the drowess said.

"You can steer a ship too?"

"Yes, I can steer a ship and have done so since before you were born."

Quillen relented and ran out of the room eager to get back. The mole-looking fae stepped into the room, closing the door for the boy.

"When are you going to tell us your name?" Dr'amal asked the sprite.

He grunted and walked to the map table to see its ever-changing scenery.

"Friendly as always," Dr'amal said to herself. "I was looking forward to being part of the fleet," she said to Frog-Dor. "With them, we would have had an army of spell-casters."

"We can manage," Frog-Dor said.

"I'd rather not manage. I'd rather crush any dark forces that keep us from Atlantea. I wonder if we can find others at the cyclops city," Dr'amal said, thinking. She kept the wheel steady as the ship went through choppy swells.

"I don't think any wizards at the cyclops city have any interest in Atlantea, nor in any money we'd try to hire them with."

The door opened, and Dr'as the drow leader, peeked in, staring directly at them.

"Father? Did you want something?"

Dr'as grunted and stepped back out, closing the door.

Dr'amal shot a look at Frog-Dor. "My father hates you."

"Does he?"

"Oh, yes." She smiled.

"That amuses you?"

"It does." The realization came over her face. "I'm sorry. I'm so sorry." She moved to him.

"Dr'amal, don't take your hand from the wheel."

She returned both hands to the navigation wheel and her attention to the display mirror. "That was cruel of me, even by drow standards. I have not forgotten about your curse."

"It's like a long-distant dream. I can barely even remember the prison of my curse. I can't even remember what I did."

"You did nothing."

"I did something. I simply cannot remember. It was too long ago."

"The curse is gone, and we will never speak about it again, and I will learn better discretion. I am drow after all. We are a people of discretion and honor. Please do accept my apology, Frog-Dor."

"You have nothing to be sorry for. I took no offense because there was nothing to take offense at. Your father is being a father, as he should."

"I will speak to him."

"The best thing to do is ignore it. Ignore and he'll soon forget. Speak about it, and he'll always be suspicious of nothing."

Lady Aylen and Gwyness re-entered the room with their two kirins.

"Clear waters, Lady Aylen?" Frog-Dor asked.

The princess nodded.

"Our own seer has returned," Dr'amal said.

Gwyness joined them as she touched her amulet. "We should pray that my amulet never glows again on our journey."

"We could, but we know it would be in vain," Dr'amal said.

Chief Ethor oversaw the elves forming up on the deck. Dozens of high elves took their stations, lining the main deck under their protective barrier with long polearms tipped either by spears, curved blades, or tridents. Each elf would be guarded by a desert elf and his giant falcon. Elfin archers would stay in the other main deck cabin.

Lyre, the high elf, and Taylos, the desert elf, walked the deck to inspect their elves, ensuring everything was in order and ready.

Pangolin and all his deck Cut-throats had their talaria sandals on and crossbows in hand as they floated above the deck. I'wulf and other Cut-throats kept their flock of chamroshes in another deck cabin. They would feed and play with them to keep the eagle hounds' attention.

Traveler exited the command cabin for a rare time to observe the progress. Pangolin flew to him.

"A ship is approaching. A big red city ship," their caravan master told them.

Even Pangolin couldn't help but smile as Queen Issaleth's ship caught up to them. Their main deck was filled by her ant men sentries with a weapon in each of their four hands. Her own wizards set her down on Titan's Caravan's golem ship, greeted by the happy faces of the royals and everyone else. She was joined by her chief wizard, her knights, and the selkies.

"Queen Issaleth, you've returned."

"Yes, I have, King Aereth. Let's speak inside."

Traveler didn't seem surprised as they entered the command cabin. His dog, however, jumped up on his four legs, almost snarling. They all gathered around the map table. Pangolin stepped in and stayed near the door. A smiling Hobbs ran in too. He saw Quillen looking at the selkie girl and saw she noticed him too.

"Mr. Quillen, are you steering the ship, or should I?" the steward asked.

"I have it, Mr. Hobbs," Quillen replied sheepishly.

"See that you do."

Hobbs knew that during his rounds, all the men would ask about was the return of Queen Issaleth and her crew.

"You must be surprised to see us," Queen Issaleth said.

"We're glad to see you," King Aereth said.

"What happened, queen?" Traveler asked.

"Yes, Mr. Traveler. What happened? I am the queen of my caravan, a human queen. We've waited years at Kraken's Wake for the right people to arrive for us to fulfill my plan of a great sea caravan powerful enough to defeat the treachery of the Four Kings, and you did. Waiting a bit longer would be of no consequence if the kingdoms of both the Baltica and Avalonian empires could cross into Atlantea as one caravan. The selkies agreed and decided to remain with us."

"Thank you so much, Queen Issaleth," King Aereth said. "We can't express how happy we are for your return."

"Yes, Queen Issaleth. We thank you greatly. Mr. Traveler, anything to say?" Lady Aylen asked.

"So, Queen Issaleth, what happened?"

The queen stared at him. After a bit, the royals realized something was amiss.

She sighed.

"You are not one for niceties are you, Mr. Traveler?"

"I told you I'm not royalty."

"I'm not so certain of that, but I will answer without the customary royal niceties. We Balticans aren't known for it anyway. The cecaelia fleet—when we sailed, they led the fleet. Then they broke away from us, moving so quickly that they soon disappeared in the distance. As we approached the wall—"

"What wall?" King Aereth asked.

"Sire, past Kraken's Wake on the way to White Waters, there is a wall of kraken tentacles reaching into the heavens. The death waves are gone, but the creatures remain in the waters of Kraken's Wake killing each other. The cecaelia said they'd use their magic to let us pass. Their sorceresses encased all our ships in magic bubbles to pass. Balticans are people of strong emotions and deep instincts. While the mermaids, nymphs, and others were confident of the cecaelia magic, my instincts told me to trust their magic, but distrust their motives. I was not alone. I gave the command to turn our ship around, even if it meant leaving our allies behind. We did so."

"What of the others?" Lady Aylen asked.

"I don't know. They either passed through or were destroyed. I knew we made the right decision because my sorcerer was never able to magically speak to them again after we separated."

Traveler noticed on the map table. "Another fleet."

Everyone quickly moved to get an unobstructed view of the map, forming all around it. Rough swells rippled everywhere on the magic nautical map. The kraken wall described by the queen was seen as a shadowy black line, but beyond it, in the direction of Atlantea, was a fleet larger than any had seen before.

"Suddenly, our map can see past Kraken's Wake," Traveler said. "That fleet was not there before."

"That can't be our fleet, unless they joined with others," Queen Issaleth said.

"Could they be coming back this way?" one of her senior knights asked.

"Could they have reconsidered as you did?" King Aereth asked.

"I don't know. It's possible, but I don't know," she replied.

"We are definitely not waiting for them," Traveler said directly. "Mímir-Spring is our destination without rest. I'll create another homunculus bird and see if we can contact the mages of the cyclops city from here."

"Why use such primitive magic?" Betta, the sorcerer, asked. "We can create a bird of magic to do the same thing."

"Because I'm not a sorcerer and it cannot be traced back to us should it be captured. Can you assure me that would not be the case if your magic bird messenger were captured by, say, a siren witch?"

Betta shook his head. "No, I cannot."

"Sirens are found this far away?" the queen asked.

"Yes. Long gone are the days when they simply sat idly on reefs waiting for ships to come to them. They have their own ships to hunt for their food, and they're not timid about using them. Though not as common, those ships have male sirens able to affect females as effectively as their women do men, and far more common, those ships have their most powerful witches. Do not think of them as evil mermaids. They are far worse."

"Have you encountered them directly in the past, Mr. Traveler?" Pangolin asked.

"I have, Mr. Pangolin. I was aboard Tunik's ship, in fact. They chained me to the ship tightly, as they did with all the fae. You see what it wants you to see as its siren song overwhelms you. Even without ears, you'd be affected, as the song penetrates your skull and your mental faculties. Your singular thought is to approach the creature with a compulsion beyond lust. Men have severed their own limbs with daggers or pulled their arms or legs out of sockets to free themselves from manacled chains. Even as the creatures devour you, you smile and look at it with lust. They are not mermaids."

"Why would the cyclops city be in such a place, Mr. Traveler?" Lady Aylen asked.

"The mages were there long before the sirens. There was actually a continent there and their mountain city was located in the center. Over the eons, the great oceans claimed most of the land, and the sirens came. The city is impenetrable to the sirens and the inhabitants of the city never travel by sea. They have no awareness of the sea around them, as they travel always by the heavens. In a strange way, the sirens protect the region of the cyclops city. But I know the way."

"Yes, you trained there," King Aereth said.

"Are you certain safe passage to the city will be the same as when you last saw it?" Pangolin asked.

"I am. But we'll verify with the homunculus bird, then the plan is simple: escape to the Sirenic Seas as quickly as our ships can sail."

THE SIRENIC SEAS

The Empire of the Sirens

CHAPTER THIRTEEN

Voyage to the Sirenic Seas

When finished, they would not stop until they reached the port of the cyclops city. For now, the two vessels were anchored in the middle of the ocean. Traveler told them that they would all know when they had crossed from the freshwater ocean to the thick salt water seas of the sirens. Until then, the crew on deck could enjoy the fresh air with moderate winds and calm waters.

Inside the command room, Queen Issaleth joined the regular crew in front of the display mirrors.

"King Aereth, I was going to suggest we give our vessels names," the queen said.

"What name would you suggest?"

"We were in Kraken's Wake so long, we'd begun to call ours the *Red Kraken*. However, after seeing a real one, or many real ones, I'm no longer keen on the name."

"That I would agree with, queen," Lady Aylen said. "To think the cecaelia can command one of those creatures. I couldn't even sense them. I realize now it's because of their titanic size."

"Do you sense anything in these waters?" Queen Issaleth asked.

"Yes, many fish and water animals not unlike our Lands of Man, but larger and more...magical."

"My sorcerer said he saw a strange bird leave before dawn," the queen said.

"Yes, Mr. Traveler's homunculus bird, on its way to the cyclops city," King Aereth said.

"I do hope our journey will be our next to last," the queen said.

"We couldn't more strenuously agree, queen," Lady Aylen said.

At the map table, Queen Issaleth's knights and the selkies had joined Traveler. Frog-Dor and Dr'amal sat on the floor before the main display mirror.

"Mr. Hobbs, what happened to our new navigator?" Traveler asked from his post.

"The boy is entertaining our selkie guests below decks, it would seem. But he's young. Youth like to spend time with those their own age."

"But I thought we were young, Mr. Hobbs."

"It's good that you believe so, Mr. Traveler."

The caravan's weaponsmaster and forge, Mr. Estus, oversaw the work of the pech, and Queen Issaleth's chief wizard oversaw their giant four-armed ant men. The two ships were to become one. Through magic, Betta, the sorcerer, kept the two ships pressed together, stern to bow, so their super-strong sprites, the pech, could do their work of welding the golem ship to the red ship under Estus's eye.

Pangolin wasn't entirely pleased with the decision any more than some of Queen Issaleth's knights. It meant the security of half their newly merged ship would be in the charge of another party. But the benefits ultimately far outweighed any downside. With even the finest sailors, keeping two ships together in the Sirenic Seas was difficult at best. Violent swells, stray rocks broken off from reefs, wrecked ships drudged up from the sea's depths, and flash blinding rainstorms were all commonplace in the water territory to which they traveled.

The pech used the same magical metal forging instruments that Estus had used for the caravan's weapons. Fortunately, they had few battles with swords, so the need to repair elfin metal had not come to pass.

"I don't like that their ship will be larger than ours," I'wulf said to Pangolin. "Those beady-eyed ant men will be looking down across our entire deck the whole time. If their deck is ever invaded, the enemy will have a simple time leaping down on top of us."

"We'll be ready to join in any battle up there, too, should it be needed," Pangolin said.

"Look at those," Hax, the lionoid berserker, said.

All three of the men looked up to the lip of the overhanging bow of the red city-ship and saw three large cannons being extended.

"If we do have a battle, we'll have our ears ringing from cannon blasts above our heads too," I'wulf said.

"Or we'll be able to blast apart an enemy without delay," Pangolin said.

"Our ship already has powerful cannons that can sink a city ship," Hax said.

"We have more now."

"We should have our own lookouts on their bow," I'wulf said.

"Yes, good idea."

The berserkers watched as a few of the desert elves and their giant falcons flew up and landed on the same bow overhang where they had been looking.

"Elves and humans think alike, after all," I'wulf said.

The welding of the two ships did not take long. Pech returned to the decks below with Estus. Betta, the sorcerer, made it back to the golem ship command cabin. The ships were one. Once the wizard entered and closed the door, the combined ship burst forward with incredible speed.

"How long will it take to get to this cyclops city?" I'wulf asked Pangolin. "We're backtracking to Titan's Teeth, aren't we?"

"Yes, we are."

"A week then?"

"Mr. Traveler said less because we're not sailing along the shore near Titan's Fall. We're sailing directly across the ocean to their land, and we'll be sailing fast."

"A city of one-eyed giants, but then you've been to a giant city already."

"And fought their giant boars," Pangolin said.

"What giant animals do you think these cyclopes have?" Hax asked.

"We could ask Mr. Traveler since he's been there already." Pangolin made a face.

"What?" I'wulf asked.

"Speaking of giant animals."

"The jörmungandr?" I'wulf asked.

"The jörmungandr," Pangolin replied.

"You don't think we'd see another, do you?"

"Another? What about the same one?"

"I'd wager not even giant kraken would tangle with that gigantic sea serpent."

The routine of leadership meals resumed under Hobbs's supervision with the addition of Queen Issaleth and her chief sorcerer. King Aereth accompanied Queen Issaleth on her stroll along the deck of her red ship. She made the rounds every night before turning in.

"Has your caravan master-now-captain left the quarterdeck since we've arrived?" Queen Issaleth asked.

"No, but he'll get us to this cyclops city faster than anyone else," King Aereth answered.

"King Aereth, I do not know much about your kingdom and those of the Kings' Elder."

"Your news was like a gift from the Fates. Both my kingdom and colleagues know we have nearly reached our destination."

"King, may I ask about your wife?"

"You may. She died. But at least she was not alive to hear word of our beloved son's death."

"King, may I ask how? I only ask because of the shock of my own father's disappearance and death."

"He may still live."

"No, he is dead. My mother sensed his passing."

"Then you remember him as he was."

"He was fearless. He would have rallied all of Baltica against Xenhelm had he seen what they were doing."

"Queen Issaleth, my wife was not well for some time. Our own chief sorcerers tended to her."

"Was her death expected?"

Both of them had been speaking softly as they strolled the deck manned by her giant ant men, who paid them no mind.

"No."

"We are the last two enemies left of the evil King Oughtred of Xenhelm. The last two, now on one ship. No fleet. No other allies at our sides. I heard from your men about some of his treachery you escaped on the Trail."

"You fear a trap?"

"Don't you?"

"Our Mr. Traveler expects every step along the Trail or length we sail to be a trap, with or without Oughtred, but I will heed your words with earnest."

"We travel waters where there are no benevolent water fae civilizations. All are evil. Both mermaids and ocean nymphs avoid these sirens and their domain."

"Mr. Traveler knows the way. I am confident of that."

"I have no doubts about Mr. Traveler."

"If a trap was laid for us, where might you suggest it would wait?"

"The sirens are more carnivorous creatures than intelligent merfolk, so there would be no alliance with Oughtred or any of his dark allies. I have three guesses: at the border of the cyclops city, beyond Kraken's Wake and White Waters, or at Titan's Point."

"The final marker of Titan's Trail."

"At the very border into the lands of Atlantea."

"I'll speak to Mr. Traveler."

"I also did not mean to stir any sad emotions regarding your wife's death, but I had to inquire if there might be a similar pattern with others I've met over the years who have threatened the Xenhelmians in some way."

"I miss the queen greatly, as much as I do my son. Your inquiry was fully understandable given our circumstances. I am not troubled, so you shouldn't be either. We are doing what is required of us to ensure the safety of our people on this quest."

"I should also let you know, sire, that I made a blood-promise to my mother. Should any chance present itself, no matter the risk to myself, I will kill Oughtred. My kingdom spent a fortune to acquire a weapon that could kill even a lich. I carry it on my person at all times."

"I know of at least two others, and a shape-shifter, in our caravan that may beat you to it."

The waters got rougher as they sailed. Word spread, from Traveler, among both crews, that they were far enough from the sediments of the great Titan's Fall and the land mass of the Great Forest that the true splendor of the Oceanus Omnis would be visible to even the human eye for a time. Most were shocked by the view. They sailed not on blue waters but waters so clear that it was as if they were flying fast above lands whose bottoms were too far away to see. What could be seen were the many schools of giant fish and other ocean fauna.

King Aereth joined a sole Traveler at the map table before dawn. The king couldn't sleep and assumed correctly that their caravan master would already be in the command cabin. Other than the dog, several drows were on guard. The king was surprised to see that the mole-man fae was steering the vessel.

"Good morning, sire." Traveler sipped from his cup.

"Any news of interest, Mr. Traveler?"

"Clear sailing, sire."

"That is news of interest too. I've given some thought to Oughtred. You should not be the sole strategist of the caravan, though you have the obvious advantage of traversing the Trail more than once and living in Atlantea itself."

"What is on your mind, sire?"

"There is an intelligence to his insanity. He destroys all enemies, real or imagined, whether directly or not."

"I know of his kingdom of Xenhelm. His father was a great and noble man. His grandfather, on the other hand, was a bloodthirsty savage."

"Yes. Under the grandfather, Xenhelm grew in stature. It acquired territory through endless conquest. I don't know why I had pushed it from my mind, but my own father spoke of him, how vile he was but how every kingdom feared him not because Xenhelm could defeat them but because they knew Xenhelm would do anything to become powerful enough to defeat them. No deed was too evil or outrageous. We had all thought that Xenhelm would follow in the footsteps of the father not the grandfather. We were horribly wrong, and we should have seen it."

"What brought this on, sire?"

"You have always been suspicious of the events of my own son's death at the hands of the Four Kings. I've been conversing with Queen Issaleth about her kingdom and others. One cannot help but see a pattern. Her father's death and the circumstances to my own son's death also at the hands of the Four Kings is too similar to ignore. He used their weaknesses against them, to bring about their demise for the gain of Xenhelm."

Traveler took his eyes off the map.

"I'd say he also used their strengths against them, or he anticipated their strengths. Your strength is meticulous planning, Mr. Traveler, far beyond that of any average caravan master. This caravan has thwarted him more than any other. You personally have harmed him more than any other."

"I've always known he'd seek revenge upon me for what my dog and I did to his war wizards, his New Xenhelm, and more so for what I did to his son."

"You can't kill what is already dead."

"But fiends can be incinerated or the dark magic drained from them to reduce them to dust, sire."

"You said you saw them at Titan's Teeth. All four of them? They rescued the son from the Necropolis."

"Yes, sire."

"But he left you to die rather than do so himself. Why?"

"You mean to say he wasn't gripped by rage, sire. He wanted me to suffer in my last moments, knowing that I failed. His demon might have had the event repeat over and over again, if it had that power. He thought he had vanquished another enemy."

"Possibly he wanted you to live."

Traveler shook his head. "That would be too clever. His pattern of behavior is simple: destroy. If it were a plot, to what end?"

"That, Mr. Traveler, I do not possess the knowledge of the Trail nor Atlantea to answer. We know what Oughtred wants—to conquer Atlantea, or so he boasts. How would allowing us to continue on help his goal? What brought this on was a discussion I heard of the queen with her sorcerer about the nature of liches. They are such dark creatures with a mind for such malevolent scheming without rage. They are calm and patient. When their plot is realized it is often at the point where one is powerless to avoid it.

"All I'm saying, Mr. Traveler, is that you said it yourself that there is only one entrance to Atlantea and you once jokingly said that we may arrive in the city and find the Four Kings waiting for us. You had the forethought to devise a defense against the landvættir, which saved all our lives. I hope you are doing the same against Oughtred."

"I am, sire. It's why we go to the cyclops city despite the danger and delay."

"Good. I won't speak about it again, other than to ask, does our missing Mr. Gresham play a role in this plan?"

"He's central to it."

"Good."

Traveler stepped through the doorway of the caravan's main pocket-realm. Two tree giants stood guard with many woodland elves with bows at the ready.

"We thought we'd never see you leave your maps," one of the woodland elves said to him.

"I have to keep an eye out for sea serpents and giant krakens." Traveler grinned.

"Then, please hurry back," another elf said.

Traveler waited as two of the tree shepherds appeared to greet him—Greenwig and Mossberry.

"Do you remember when I asked if Tree Shepherds could swim?" he said to them.

"Yes, Master Traveler."

"Summon Thornbeard and Little Root. Our Antaean giants were able to convene with the earth at our island castle at Kraken's Wake. We will see if you can do so here."

The two Tree Shepherds gave him puzzled looks.

"Here, Master Traveler?" Greenwig asked.

"Yes, time for a swim."

Quillen had to see them with his own eyes. He peered over the side with a Cut-throat on either side to grab him away if need be. Several of the young selkie children were with him, the girl he liked standing next to him. She watched him sketch the forest rising up from the ocean floor, its large-leaved canopy of branches right below them. With the water being so clear, every detail was sharp, as if there was no water at all.

Every one jumped back as a gray sea serpent dove from the deck into the water, followed by Traveler, one Tree Shepherd after another, and all the phookas, black and yellow.

A laughing Lady Aylen ran out from the command cabin with Gwyness and the king following.

"Where are they going?"

Word spread fast as both crews watched the Tree Shepherds reach one of the giant branches of the underwater forest—blue-barked trees, green seaweed-like leaves. The four Tree Shepherds pressed their hands against the tree with their eyes closed.

"The tree is glowing," the selkie girl told Quillen.

"Glowing?" Quillen looked up from his sketchbook.

"Do you see it?" she asked with a look of wonder.

He looked down at the waters again. Their ship was magically anchored in place again as all watched and the phookas swarmed around the Tree Shepherds in the form of frog-headed fish. Traveler sat on the back of the sea serpent. Quillen stared, and for a moment, he saw not only the glow of the Tree Shepherds but of every ocean tree for as far as the eye could see.

"What does it mean?" Quillen asked the selkies.

"They can talk to the ocean," the selkie replied with a smile.

"Talk to the ocean?" Lady Aylen asked.

"Yes."

"I wonder what the ocean has to tell us, then," Lady Aylen said.

The contrast unnerved many aboard the ships. As the vessel sailed toward the cyclops city, clear waters became opaque and rougher. Fresh air was replaced by the smell and taste of salt in the stale breeze. Blue skies with billowy clouds were replaced by overcast, black clouds and flashes of lightning in the distance with no sound of thunder.

Men served the night meal to Traveler and the royals at the map table.

"When we reach the cyclops city, I want both of you to show your weapons to the cyclops mages. Though we weren't supposed to ever be here, we must not let this opportunity pass. Anything they can add with their knowledge and seer magic will be invaluable."

"Were the cyclops involved at all with Rivermouth when it existed?" Lady Aylen asked.

"I don't know, princess. I'd say not because the mages of Rivermouth were independent of all others. However, I wouldn't be surprised if Rivermouth sought the cyclopes counsel."

"Then Gwyness and I will be seer and slayer when we arrive."

"Mr. Traveler, was the meeting of the Tree Shepherds with the trees...?"

"The Great Underwater Forest of Green Fir. It was very informative, sire. The trees told us of every creature that could be a danger from here to the city."

"Any other ships, Mr. Traveler?" Lady Aylen asked.

"No."

"Is that to be expected, Mr. Traveler?" the king asked.

"Perhaps, sire. But I had expected something. We are the only vessel in these waters. Not even a single siren ship is nearby." Traveler looked at Gwyness's amulet.

The maiden touched it nervously.

"Is that not good news, Mr. Traveler?"

"The news is at best, sire, of interest. The cyclops city is impenetrable to the sirens, but the seas around them are the total domain of the sirens. The great underwater forest is immune to their siren song and could hear them from even here, but they do not. Sirens don't abandon their territory, never. So if they are not patrolling their seas, where are they?"

CHAPTER FOURTEEN

The Cyclops City of Mímir-Spring

The city stronghold rose from a mountain visible a full day before they reached it. A region of perpetual night hung over Mímir–Spring, filled with a sea of the brightest stars any had ever seen. However, a sky of black clouds encircled everything around it, with dangerous giant waves smashing against reefs at the base of the city's mountain.

Visibility was difficult due to the spray mist from the violent waves. Traveler ably steered the ship, maneuvering between reefs, pushing into waves to keep the vessel steady, and at one point diving the ship underwater. They moved underneath the reefs, which from their view on the display mirrors, were giant chunks of rocks bobbing in the sea. When the vessel surfaced, the turmoil of the waves was gone, and they found themselves within the mountain. Much of the interior was hollow except for a giant waterfall. But the waters were not pouring down. Rather the water was falling up from the sea. Traveler sailed to it, and their ship rode the waterfall up many miles—a strange sensation for all aboard.

From the many flashes of light, they knew they passed one magic barrier after another. At the other end, it looked like they were heading straight to the heavens from the growing sharpness of the stars. The vessel leveled off and landed at the top of the waterfall in a giant clear lake surrounded by a white marble pantheon-style city of temples, domes, monuments, and columns. The lake was not at the top of the mountain but some fifty feet below its peak. At the very top stood a fifteen-foot giant clothed in a white robe. The giant's bald head was covered with eyes.

"An argus giant," Traveler told the crowd in the command cabin. "A giant of a hundred eyes. The ultimate seer in a city of seers. He's known as the Argan here."

Their vessel drifted to the port on its own power and there waited a group of cyclopes in various colored robes. Each giant, some bald, some with well-groomed hair, some with mustaches and beards, some with no facial hair, each had a single eye in the center of his forehead. The giants were of the same general height as the caravan's own Antaean twelve-foot giants, but regal in bearing.

The party departed the combined ship with Traveler and his dog at the lead. Both Titan's Caravan's leadership and those of Queen Issaleth's with the selkies.

"Master Traveler," one of the cyclopes said, greeting him with a nod, "you should have saved your homunculus bird. We knew you'd be visiting us again."

"This is Isim, chief mage and leader of Mímir-Spring," Traveler said to the others. "Master Isim, you knew we'd be visiting without my messenger?"

"Yes, Master Traveler. We knew from the time you stepped from Titan's Bridge into the magic lands so many months ago."

For the first time they had entered a city in the magic lands where they felt completely safe. Traveler allowed the entire crew to disembark their ship to explore the majestic city of giants. Never would they have such an opportunity, as even most fae would never visit the famed cyclops city in their entire lives. Pangolin led his group of Cut-throats and Estus down one of the wide streets filled with giants.

"This is so opposite of what I saw at the giant city of Khury. That city was a mis-match of construction. This city is...beautiful."

Estus was equally in awe. "If this is how they construct a building, imagine how they forge their weapons."

That got Pangolin's and other Cut-throats' attention. "They make weapons?" I'wulf asked.

"Mr. Traveler said they are some of the best builders and metalsmiths in the magic lands. Let's ask one. They're friendly giants," Estus said.

Isim personally conducted the tour of the city for Traveler's groups.

"You also have Antaean giants among you, Master Traveler?" Isim asked.

"We do, and they're eager to visit your fine city. I almost forgot how much I enjoyed my time here."

"We enjoyed having you here."

"You said you knew we'd visit, which is news to me since my original plan was to lead our caravan straight from Titan's Fall to Atlantea."

"You've been a caravan master long enough to know that original plans on the Trail rarely are the final ones."

"True."

"I know you need nothing from our storehouses as you have all the provisions and weapons needed. How can we assist you in your journey?"

"We are unable to see to Atlantea on the maps past the water fae city of Kraken's Wake and the elfin city of White Waters."

"You are unable to see because dark forces do not wish you to see. A fleet gathers in the waters surrounding Atlantea."

"We did see a fleet for a moment past the wall of krakens, but they vanished from the maps again."

"No, not that fleet. Those are known to you. Another."

"Another fleet?" Queen Issaleth asked. "Of the human lich Oughtred and the Xenhelmians?"

The cyclops leader stopped his stroll to turn and address them. "I see our words have traveled far."

"Yes, and I have the means to kill him when I encounter him," Queen Issaleth said.

"Your weapon may have that ability, but I do not believe you have the power to strike such a blow, as you are merely a human. He is much more."

"I have sorcerers."

"He has war wizards and more."

"We will get to Atlantea no matter what," Queen Issaleth said.

"You may die there too."

"Die there?" King Aereth asked. "Our understanding from Mr. Traveler is that the Atlanteans are far more powerful than all fae and humans."

"They are, but they are not invincible. The human known as Oughtred has coveted their kingdom for decades. His Kings' Caravan were never for riches or to capture the beasts of our lands to display in his king's court. Always his aim has been to seize the city. First, hiring wizards of our lands then turning to dark magic himself with his sons."

"He said he was going to conquer Atlantea," Traveler said.

"Then he might."

"He will not," Lady Aylen said defiantly. "Impossible."

The cyclops laughed. "Is she the one you spoke of?" he asked Traveler.

"Yes, and Maiden Gwyness. They are the last of the lost kingdom of Rivermouth."

"Yes, I knew Queen Faylen. She was a powerful mage, an exceptional teacher, and a gentle woman, even as a warrior cleric."

"You knew her?" Lady Aylen asked.

"Did you know my parents?" Gwyness asked.

"Yes, I knew them too. I met all the warrior clerics, whether seer or slayer, of Rivermouth. Our city and the sylphs had the most contact with their city over the ages."

"Why didn't anyone help them in their time of need?" Lady Aylen asked.

"Why would we? They made the same mistake that we made and that Atlantea makes. They said they were invincible, and they were not. Remember, Oughtred of Xenhelm is not the first to scheme to conquer Atlantea. The fairies, elves, dwarves, giants, all the fae races did so and attempted to invade the fabled kingdom many times before they were all banned from its realm. It is why humans have always been favored. Your race was the only one that never attempted to conquer its city."

"Until now, it would seem," Queen Issaleth said.

"Until now. And if Oughtred attempts it, with his many fae allies, visible and secret, then all of Pan-Earth will be forever banned from Atlantea, human and fae."

"Master Isim, before the beginning of the last Kings' Caravan, there were rumors in the magic lands that Atlantea would bar all fae forever from its realm," the Tree Shepherd leader, Greenwig, said.

"Which is why your Mr. Traveler has assembled a caravan of fae of many who have never left Faë-Land, who have always been enemies of one another, and included fae that have been hidden from other fae for ages."

"To establish a cordial and benevolent agreement with the Atlanteans," Greenwig said.

"All which will be for naught because of Oughtred and his own alliance of fae and elementals."

"We know that his fae allies include sky elves," Lyre, the high elf, said.

"Some, not all."

"Elementals too?" the selkie Nori asked.

"To our dismay, yes. Sylphs and undines have spent centuries rebuilding trust with the fabled kingdom on the behalf of fae. To ally with Oughtred is to nullify everything positive they did."

"Why would they do such a thing?" Nori asked.

"Elementals are no different than fae or humans, differing and opposing factions with individual interests unconcerned with the consequences to others, or themselves, should their plots fail."

"Master Isim, the real question is do Oughtred and his dark forces have any chance of success in their evil goals?"

"I see many possibilities, Master Traveler, of which in one he does succeed in the conquest of Atlantea—perhaps."

Traveler grinned. "I've never liked dealing with seers."

"No, you did not."

"Since I thought I was accidentally coming here to seek the aide of your mages, but instead, we were expected, tell me, Isim, how is it that we can aid you?"

The cyclops patted Traveler on the shoulder. "Thank you, Master Traveler. You do understand. We will give you the magic to take to and help the Atlanteans. Even they do not sense the danger to them. Your fabled quest is about the riches of their city for some, but for others it's about saving the fabled city."

In the great coliseum hall of the cyclopes, virtually every member of Titan's Caravan and Queen Issaleth's leadership sat in row after rising row encircling the center, where two cyclopes took turns speaking and answering questions.

"We witnessed Oughtred turning to necromancy at first to secure the beings necessary to ensure the success of his Kings' Caravan. First, it was his desire to collect fantastic beasts from the magic lands to boast, then he grew tired of impressing mere humans. He wanted to impress fae. He wanted to become more powerful than all fae. But what human could best the most powerful of elves, the celestials? What human could best those more powerful than the celestials, the sylphs and undines, for their reach is more vast than all others? What human could best the most powerful beings on Pan-Earth, the Atlanteans themselves? First, dark magic, then he dabbled in necromancy. He went further than any human had dared."

"Yes, not one has gone so far since the ancient drows who walked down the path thinking that dark magic could be used for benevolent purposes. An internal war among all elfinkind almost destroyed the race but split it into elves and drows forever, and many sub-races of each. Oughtred felt he could succeed where those ancient drows had failed, and in a way, he did. But not without the help of others—celestial elves, night drows, and elementals, as they all covet the fabled kingdom with an equal, blinding intensity."

The cyclops had enraptured the audience by weaving a vivid story. Listeners could see the image of events in their own minds.

None had noticed Traveler had left with his dog to seek out cyclopean mages outside the hall. "Good day, mage," he greeted.

"Master Traveler." All the residents of the cyclops city knew him by sight.

"Master Isim said I should speak to the Argan about a peculiar occurrence my vessel encountered sailing into your port."

"What peculiarity?"

"There are no sirens within sight or sound of the city. They're gone."

"That is peculiar, though we have never had any contact with them. They have no power within our domain, and we are immune to their siren song. Yes, we shall speak with the Argan to see what he can see beyond."

Traveler and the dog followed the cyclops from the hall through a maze of paths, though the caravan master knew the way. There were few cyclopes passersby about. Mímir–Spring was a city for study, scholarship, and meditation. Its mages spent more time in reflective contemplation than magic–casting.

When they reached the open court, they stepped onto a golden carpet and were airborne. They floated above the city and flew to the mountain peak with its own waterfall spilling downward. At the base of the peak, a mountain on top of a mountain, water fell into a lake of bubbling spring water.

"The Argan is not there," Traveler said.

"We have visitors from the heavens then."

"How often do flying caravans visit these days?"

"Not often. Sadly, learned pursuits is becoming a rarer thing for fae, as has happened with humans. War and magic for war is what most seek. Forgotten are the philosophies and disciplines of logic, debate, reason, ethics, aesthetics, the mind, the essence of being," the cyclops said with sadness.

They had been hidden from the spell on the ground, but above it all, Traveler could see the flock of the city's main defense. Stymphalian birds were greatly feared by fae and humans. A race of carnivorous birds with beaks of metal and metallic feathers, the birds were the size of human men but flew gracefully and silently. In the wild, they were unrelenting predators of any who trespassed into their territory. Here, the cyclopes trained them from birth to guard the city.

The golden carpet landed on a plateau at the peak of the mountainous cyclops city. Traveler looked down, and the buildings below appeared as tiny dots. He saw another golden carpet following them.

"My friends never let me be," Traveler said.

"Good friends to have." The cyclops mage led them from the carpet and across the polished white marble plateau to a cavernous entrance.

Already, they could see the argus giant inside with his back to them and the brightness of the realm inside.

When they stepped through, the sky was gone. A vast void of space was above all around them as if they were on the surface of the moon. The stars, though eons away, looked close enough to throw a stone at. One set of the argus giant's eyes studied Traveler as he greeted the watcher. The other eyes were focused on what the cyclops, the dog, and Traveler were staring at.

The flying caravan had already landed through the portal. A series of connected flying chariots, miles long, filled with cloud and high mountain nymphs, stables of flying horses and flying unicorns, and endless stores of provisions. Humans always mistook sylphs for nymphs or fairies, but they were air elementals of immense power. Several sylphs approached the argus giant with a column of cloud elf warriors in armor and others in robes.

"Greetings," the Argan said. "Your weapons must remain here, then you can enjoy the hospitality of Mímir-Spring."

"Our stop will be brief, Argan," the first sylph said. "We depart shortly after I procure one of your historical works from your great library for my queen mother, which, of course, means I shall be the one to read the book on her behalf. This is unexpected. Who is the human?"

Traveler didn't see him until it was too late. A star elf stepped from invisibility as a second chariot simply appeared, filled with star nymphs and star elfin warriors. The star elf stood well over six feet in height with a slim, toned frame. His silver white battle dress, like the others, had a geometric construction. All the star elves had white hair to their waists, pale skin, and gray-white eyes.

The tall, fair-skinned, white-haired star elf that approached them had glowing elfin symbols tattooed on his forehead

"I know you, don't I?" The star elf stared at Traveler with angry eyes.

"Return to your place," another star nymph said.

All of them glittered with starlight and appeared more as slightly glowing mirage images rather than solid in form.

A third flying caravan appeared out of invisibility, floating above the other two. At the head of a long multi-seat flying chariot was a sole celestial elf with a contingent of knights in full white metal armor. The skin of a celestial elf looked like hardened glass. He was dressed in attire that seemed to be made of the night itself. The celestial elfin knights began to rise from their seats.

The true magic of Mímir-Spring was that the mountain city nullified the magic of all, except its cyclopes mages. But for some reason, that was not so presently. Both star and celestial elves had used a spell to conceal their caravans from even the all-seeing eyes of the argus giant and his cyclops mage guide.

The second golden carpet landed with another cyclops mage guide. Lady Aylen, Gwyness, and Pangolin were the passengers.

"Well, Mr. Traveler, did you think you'd keep this beautiful sight all to yourself?" Lady Aylen asked.

Her eyes widened in horror, and she tried to lunge toward him as he caught the reflection of a blinding ball of starfire about to engulf them.

CHAPTER FIFTEEN

Star Fall

An invisible shield of magic blocked the starfire. The hands of the cyclops guide were raised in front of him, but the power of the starfire was only deflected back at the star elf who threw it. The star elf absorbed the magic into his body.

"You should not have intervened!" the celestial elf yelled. The blast of magic from his hand threw the cyclops out of the realm and over the side.

A ram's horn appeared in the Argan's hand as he vanished into thin air. A volley of starfire flew past where he stood and shot away into space. Lady Aylen blocked one ball of starfire with her forearm and yelled out in pain as her arm temporarily caught fire.

The air thundered with the warning cry of the Argan's ram's horn.

"The Argan has alerted the cyclopes!" the celestial elf yelled.

The celestial elf threw a ball of black fire at Lady Aylen, but the caravan master appeared and deflected it with his sword before it could engulf her.

Within a second, the celestial elf fired another blast of magic that resembled the void of space from each hand into Traveler's chest. The caravan master was blown out of the pocket-realm, and the power of the magic began to shatter the entrance.

"No!" Lady Aylen jumped out of the collapsing realm.

Traveler's lifeless body lay on the ground. Lady Aylen stood there in shock, looking at him.

"Mr. Traveler!" Gwyness kneeled to shake him. She shook him several times, crying.

Lady's Aylen's eyes pooled with water as the rage in her grew. She turned to run back in, but an arm restrained her.

"No." Frog-Dor jumped down from a third golden carpet landing with the sorcerer and Dr'amal. "They are sky elves and elementals. You do not have your weapons or the power to fight them."

"I will." Lady Aylen ran to edge of the dock and dove off the edge to the pool below.

"Where's Traveler's dog?" Dr'amal, the drow sorceress, asked.

They all nervously looked around. Gwyness glanced back.

"Help Mr. Pangolin!" Gwyness yelled pointing, back into the realm.

Pangolin was thrown onto his back again by starfire magic. His earthen magic armor protected him, but the elves moved too quickly for him to land a blow with his axe-mace.

"Since I cannot match your speed in hand-to-hand combat, I will do the next best thing!"

Already his berserker rage raced through his body. His eyes became bloodshot as he yelled. Flying through the air with the aid of the talarian wings, he lunged at their flying transports. When he struck with his axe-mace, his battle cry echoing in the realm, all three flying caravan chariots were obliterated, sending elves, elementals, and animals everywhere, some even into the heavens.

"Die, human!" a star elf yelled. As he raised his sword, he was struck with a moon arrow and fell to the ground, lifeless.

Appearing from invisibility themselves, Shadu-mun led his moon elves into the realm, firing moon arrows as they ran at the star elves. When they reached them, a battle of star swords versus moon swords raged.

The celestial elf rose from the ground as arrows fired at him burst into flames then disappeared. Entering the realm, Lyre and his high elves immediately concentrated their arrows on the celestial elf.

The sylphs also rose into the air to fight. The male cloud elves wore battle dresses of grays and blues, their skin equally as pale as the star elves', their hair a range of black, brown, or blond. All of them stood on small clouds as they also ascended in the air. More star elves joined the battle.

"You are nothing!" a sylph yelled as they all lifted their hands in unison.

"It is unlucky you decided to attack us here rather than outside, where you would have had the full power of the air and the sky." Frog-Dor already stood in the realm. He clapped his hands, and the air around the sylphs and cloud elves began turning to solid ice.

Their screams reverberated throughout the realm, making every elf in battle on the ground wince. Sylphs fell to the ground and shattered in pieces. Cloud elves fell to the ground with thuds, frozen solid.

The celestial elf fired a blast of celestial magic at Frog-Dor, but it passed through him. The celestial fired another quickly. Frog-Dor and Dr'amal fell out of invisibility and crashed to the ground as the drowess's mirage spell faded away.

"Do you not know the power of celestial magic is of stars, comets, and worlds?" the celestial elf asked.

"You will die." Gwyness stood at the entrance of the realm, tears streaming down her cheeks.

"Who will kill me? You, human?" the celestial elf asked. "Look, there." He pointed with his long fingernails in the distance. "That is another flying caravan of my kind. If you cannot beat me alone, how can you defeat, or kill, an army of us? You are distressed, so I will put you out of your misery."

Every arrow fired at the celestial elf by the high elves failed to penetrate an invisible barrier of celestial fire. Pangolin landed in front of Gwyness.

"Stay behind me," Pangolin said.

"Can your earth elemental armor withstand a direct blast of celestial fire?" the celestial elf sneered.

"Stop!" Isim, the cyclops mage, stepped into the realm.

Several other one-eyed giants followed after him. "You have broken the sacred pact between Mímir-Spring and the sky elves that has lasted for millennia."

A single blast of celestial fire incinerated the cyclops mage. Even the star elves in battle with the moon elves were shocked by the act. In their hesitation, some of the star elves lost their lives to moon arrows and moon blades.

The cyclopes marched toward the celestial elf, firing blasts of magic from their palms. The celestial elf dropped to the ground and gritted his teeth as he strained to strengthen his magic barrier of celestial fire against them.

More cyclopes stepped into the realm to join the attack. Woodland elves and desert elves jumped in.

"Star elves!" Lyre yelled.

The combined might of the four sub-races cut down every last star elf.

A ball of starfire landed and destroyed the entire sky port. Above them was not one new flying caravan of star elves but three.

"Surrender to the celestial elfin kingdom of Black Nebula." The voice boomed all around them as the dust and silt settled and humans and fae picked themselves up off the ground.

Tree branches reached into the pocket-realm and pulled every human, elf, and fae of their caravan, as well as the cyclopes from the realm. They were pulled from the mountain peak port, over the side, and down the mountain to the ground, where the forces of Titan's Caravan, Queen Issaleth and the cyclopes waited. All six Antaean giants stood at the front. The air above them was black with raging stymphalian birds.

"Celestial elves have arrived to seize the city," Lyre announced when his feet touched the ground. The three crawling trees had grown to tower over them.

"Where's Lady Aylen?" Gwyness asked.

"Our Lady Aylen had summoned a hurricane of water to bring into battle. However, she saw that her only task was that." King Aereth pointed above.

The giant monstrosity clung to the top of the mountain peak. A mass of arms, mouths, eyes, and tails covered in dark flesh. Lady Aylen stood on a column of water with her arms outstretched. No one could name the creature the dog had transformed into, but it pushed itself into the pocket-realm. Then the entire mountain peak realm imploded, disappearing to leave an empty black crater.

Traveler's eyes opened.

Gresham knelt over him with a smile. Their glowing white caladrius bird flew off the caravan master's chest into the air.

"The bird should remain here as she will use her healing powers for you again," a cyclops said. "A flock of them live in our city's garden. She missed her kind and will be happy here."

Traveler sat up quickly but almost fainted.

"That was not very wise, Mr. Traveler." Gresham held him steady. "You must lie down and remain still."

"Yes, Mr. Traveler. After all, you were dead only a few moments ago." Lady Aylen stood over him, her arms folded.

A grinning Hobbs stood above him. "You want to be like me, sir."

"He's been dead before," a cyclops said, to the caravan's surprise.

"A story for another time, but it's how I learned of the caladrius bird," he said.

"Why did you do that?" Lady Aylen asked. Tears welled in her eyes.

"It was either that or have you incinerated, princess. I had elemental armor on, you did not. The magic of the caladrius bird can only work if there is actually a body left to be restored."

"You had your elemental armor on but it did little to protect you from the elf's magic," Lady Aylen scolded him.

"Yes, princess, because that was no normal celestial elf."

"No, he was not," Isim, the cyclops mage, said appearing from the gathered cyclopes.

"You are alive too," Pangolin said. "But you were—"

"I am a mage of some note. If I can't transport my body away from danger, then I should not be the city's chief mage. Yes, Master Traveler, the celestial elf was a mage of some note himself."

The Argan appeared among the cyclopes. "Master Isim."

Isim turned and approached their argus watcher.

"Do you have a headache, sir?" Gresham noticed Traveler touch his forehead with his eyes closed.

"The dog."

"Your dog, Master Traveler, is dealing with the celestial elves," Chief Ethor of the woodland elves said.

"He already has," Traveler said. "He's flying from the heavens to us, but there is more. Mr. Gresham, help me to my feet."

Gresham and Lady Aylen did so.

Traveler looked at Isim. "How many do you see?" he asked the cyclops leader.

"Ten celestial elfin city ships approach."

"How many aboard each ship?" King Aereth asked.

Traveler shook his head. "Too many, sire."

"My city ship carries two thousand," Queen Issaleth said.

"The city ships approaching us have crews of ten thousand, but as with your ships, there is no telling how many pocket-realms each ship has," Isim said.

"Why would they break your alliance and invade Mímir-Spring?" Traveler asked.

"Why indeed? Your animal has saved us the task of destroying our sky port to deny them entry to the city."

"What do we do, then?" King Aereth asked.

"Prepare for battle?" Pangolin asked.

"No need," Isim replied. "They will need to land from the heavens. We have time to prepare but not a lot."

"Do you believe the army is for us?" Traveler asked.

Isim hesitated. "We've never seen these celestial elves before. But it answers your question as to why there are no sirens in the region. Their magic surrounds the land. Magic powerful enough to breach our city's defenses."

"Master Isim, why would the sky elves and elementals do this? Even if they recognized me from past encounters, their behavior seems..."

"As if it were a pretense," Isim said for him.

"They couldn't know we'd be here. None of this makes any sense."

"Not at the moment, Master Traveler, but in the near future, it will."

"We need a seer, or the magic to see to Atlantea, then we will depart immediately."

"My mages will give you the magic you need. The city will need all its mages in its defense."

"Like Rivermouth," Lady Aylen said.

"Yes," Isim said. "The celestial elves were involved in the destruction of your elfin kingdom of warrior clerics."

"A celestial elfin queen also had her ancient one deliver the last book vault of Rivermouth to Lady Aylen and Maiden Gwyness. An ancient one who was, or is, a spell-talker," Traveler told the cyclops.

"If only we could spend the days in mediation and seeing to unravel this scheme together, Master Traveler, in all its many layers. But the time is not this day nor necessary. You have a ship and I a city to attend to.”

“We’ll sail immediately, then.”

“The celestial elfin mage contacted his kind. They know what transpired,” the Argan said. “The star elf did know.”

“I have a history with them.”

“We know,” Isim said.

“War wizards,” the argus giant said, bringing about nervous chatter among the gathered caravans’ humans and fae.

“I’ve dealt with them before.”

“If it were another, I would have said not to be overconfident.”

“We do need another caladrius bird as well.”

“As I told you in the past, the key to the magic of the caladrius bird is to avoid ever having to use its magic. But my mages will see to it, too, only because your previous bird spoke so highly of how she was attended to by your Tree Shepherds and their trees.”

“Thank you, Master Isim.”

“The celestial elves will pursue you until they destroy you.”

“Yes, I’m counting on it—as long as they are away from here, your great city. Master Isim, I expect to visit Mímir–Spring many times again in the future for profound conversation over hot ambrosia tea, as only you know how to make.”

Traveler shook the giant's hand, his was tiny like a newborn baby in comparison.

"The cyclops city will be here, Master Traveler. No matter what the dark plans of others, it will be here to the end of time. I look forward to your next visit and company. May the Fates protect you on your own dangerous plans."

Cyclopes, fae, and human looked up and could all see a dark spot falling from the sky. The same monstrosity—the dog—would reach the city in moments. But then ten other smaller dots appeared in the sky too.

CHAPTER SIXTEEN

Escape to Siren's Island

When Quillen was hired by Titan's Caravan, one of his main tasks was to make a record of every man or woman lost in battle. He had almost forgotten about the duty with his other self-appointed task of sketching all the fantastic beasts and creatures of the magical lands in his magic book. But he had his other book in hand—the death book.

Their elves had fought bravely, killing all the invading star elves, with the aid of Frog-Dor and Dr'amal, and the power of the cyclopes mages had sealed the realm to prevent any of the celestial or cloud elves, and sylphs from breaching the city. But that didn't mean that the star elves hadn't inflicted terrible damage upon them. Shadu-mun had been killed, and so had several other moon elves, and a few of Lyre's high elves.

"No one dies in Mímir-Spring," Riva, the selkie girl, told him.

The words helped lift his sadness a bit, but when he saw their bodies brought to the city's gardens to be attended by a flock of caladrius birds nesting in a tall, green tree he could see the fact himself.

Shadu-mun was revived first and sat up disoriented. Elves attended to his head wound where he sat. The star elf's arrow had penetrated his forehead and had to be carefully removed and attended to by magic.

The moon elf leader looked up at his fellow elfin questing knights, Lyre, the high elf, and Taylos, the desert elf.

"I learned the hard way why one wears helmets," the moon elf said.

"At least you were smart enough to be killed in a city where you can't be killed," Lyre said.

Chief Ethor joined them and knelt next to the moon elf. "Good to have you back with us."

"Glad to be back, Chief Ethor. Though I can't help but be ashamed of my behavior. I let my rage overwhelm my training. I heard the star elf and charged blindly," Shadu-mun said.

"We all did," Lyre said.

"Better to learn the lesson here," Chief Ethor said.

"The celestial elf almost killed our caravan master," Taylos said.

Shadu-mun looked at him in dismay. "Is he all right?"

"The caladrius birds revived him as well," Chief Ethor told him.

"The celestial elf was different," Shadu-mun said.

"Different how?" Chief Ethor asked.

The moon elf looked at his comrade elfin knights, about to ask them a question, but stopped. "You would not know the answer."

"What answer?" Lyre asked.

"Are there different races of celestial elves?"

"Why would you ask that?" Chief Ethor asked.

"The celestial elf was too much...like us. Celestial elves are elves but not like elves."

"I don't understand," Chief Ethor asked.

"They are aloof and detached from elfinkind from being in lands far from Pan-Earth for so long," Shadu-mun said.

"They view all fae, including elfinkind, as animals," Lyre said.

"Yes, that's what I mean. It's why their alliance with the sylphs was formed so long ago. Sylphs view us as lesser fae too."

While Quillen watched the magical work of the caladrius birds, King Aereth listening closely to the elves.

"Chief Ethor, we should get all elves aboard," King Aereth said.

"Yes, of course, King Aereth."

The woodland elf leader summoned some of his elves, but Shadu-mun waved them away.

"I can walk." He slowly got to his feet.

"You will need to rest until all your strength returns."

"We sail already?" Shadu-mun asked.

"Oh yes, you were dead," Lyre said jokingly. "The celestial elves will likely send more forces. No way to know how many sylphs or other elementals will be with them when they attack Mímir-Spring again. We will not wait here to find out. But that's only the good news."

"What is the bad news, then, my high-elfin brother?" Shadu-mun asked. "Or should I wait to hear it from Mr. Traveler."

"We board the ship first, then talk," Chief Ethor commanded.

"Who's steering the ship?" Traveler asked from his cot. His dog sat at his side with its muzzle resting on his chest.

"Not for you to concern yourself with, sir." Gresham mixed a concoction.

"What are you making?" Traveler asked.

The healer smiled. "I'm not going to tell you, but it's from the cyclops, Mr. Isim."

"Master Mage Isim," Traveler corrected. "Then I'll drink it."

The small-realm looked like the large interior of a tent. Lanterns hung from hooks in the ceiling. A smaller map table rested against the back wall in the corner. The interior was larger than his tent on the Trail, but he didn't care for the elevated bed.

"Is it true, sir, that no one dies in Mímir-Spring, sir?"

"Aside from their caladrius birds, which live freely in their gardens, the cyclops city has some of the best healers, as well as the best seers, in all the magical lands. It was the third reason I went to the city. The second was regarding my magic sword."

"I never did ask you about the power of caladrius birds to bring one back to life. It is a different magic from the dark magic of—"

"Not the same, Mr. Gresham. The force of life for a creature like a ghoul or lich is pure dark magic. The magic of the caladrius bird is to simply return your own life force to you as if it never left. One embraces death, twists it; the other, life. A caladrius bird or similar magic could never restore a fiend to its former self, as their life force cannot replace the dark magic once it takes hold."

"I'm so glad we did not lose you, sir."

"That should never have happened. I lost my focus."

"It happens to us all, sir."

"It will never happen again. What is all that noise outside the tent?"

Lady Aylen walked through the flap with a chair.

"Healer, I thought I needed rest," Traveler said.

"You are resting, Mr. Traveler," Lady Aylen said.

In followed King Aereth, Gwyness, Queen Issaleth, Pangolin, and Frog-Dor.

The caravan master closed his eyes. "Who's steering the ship?" he asked again.

"Mr. Quillen," someone said.

He opened his eyes quickly and looked at them. All he heard were chuckles.

"Actually, Mr. Little Root is," King Aereth said, "under the watchful eye of two Tree Shepherds."

"Mr. Greenwig, I didn't know leshy could steer ships."

"Not a particularly skillful chore," the Tree Shepherd leader, Greenwig, said. "We can smell the land even through the thick salt air."

The tent was just barely large enough for the leadership and visitors.

"What is the plan, Mr. Traveler?" Pangolin stood near his bed.

"We would have lost you if we were anywhere else," Dr'as, the drow leader, said.

"It's a reminder that we can all become complacent if we are not watchful. I spent too many days hunched over magical maps and not enough time keeping my wits about me, or doing the barest amount of training," Traveler said.

"Here, drink this, sir." Gresham gave Traveler the cup. The caravan master lifted himself up a bit to drink it.

"That can be said of all of us, Master Traveler," Chief Ethor said. "But we will remedy that immediately."

"We already have," Pangolin said. "Daily training."

"The plan," Traveler said.

"The plan," King Aereth said.

"Where are the celestial city ships?" Traveler asked.

"They are no longer visible," Dr'amal said. "None of us can see them anymore."

"Can they see us, even though we're invisible?" Lady Aylen asked.

"Possibly," Traveler said.

Maiden Gwyness handed Traveler a note.

"From Master Isim."

"I still don't know why the cyclops gave you the note," Lady Aylen said.

"He has his reasons, Lady Aylen," Queen Issaleth said. "He is a seer above all, so every action has meaning."

Traveler read the folded paper written in a fae language.

"Master Isim said the sky elves and elemental flying fleet gather above Mímir-Spring but have not yet attacked, at least at the time of this note. That suggests to me that maybe the city is not their objective."

"You mean we are, then," Chief Ethor said.

"Yes. Master Isim also says that days ago ships of giants began passing across the region. The Argan could see them. Enormous ships of Athos giants." He looked at the group. "Athos giants are mountain throwers."

Humans and fae broke out in chatter.

"The ones who threw the mountains in the ocean near Kraken's Wake to cause the death waves," Queen Issaleth said angrily.

Others said the same.

Traveler shook his head.

"No?" King Aereth asked.

"I don't think it was them."

"Why do you say that, Mr. Traveler?" Lyre, the high elf, asked.

"Where did the mountains come from for them to throw?" the caravan master asked. "And with such an endless procession? We experienced not waves but death waves."

Everyone was silent. Traveler kept reading the note.

"A month ago were ships of other giants—Fomorians."

"Sea giants," Nirgund said. "Evil sea giants."

"Yes, giants with goat-like heads. Very violent when provoked. They live not on a continent but underneath it. I knew of them already. We have different races of giants also sailing to Atlantea. Whether they are friend or foe of Atlantea, we don't know."

"Surely, friends of Oughtred."

"Just because they are evil, queen, does not mean they are friends of Oughtred or any of his dark allies. And speaking of evil."

"Yes, Mr. Traveler, we remember your description of the creatures well. Yet, we sail for their lands," Pangolin said.

"We should have waited at Mímir-Spring and fought the celestial elfin fleet with the cyclopes," Nori, the selkie, said.

"No. Celestial elves don't travel in armies and don't hunt enemies. They can fire their magic from the heavens at any enemy when they wish. Also, celestial elves are not the same as humans or other elves. They don't have petty emotions of revenge. They will defend or attack for specific reasons out of logic, but that is not this. Mímir-Spring is too important of a city to the magic lands. However, that one celestial elf was different, but still."

"Have we taken the role of quarry to lead them away from others to be slaughtered ourselves?" Queen Issaleth's wizard asked.

"Of course not. However, we must recognize that things have been happening around us that shouldn't be. We are no longer in Faë-Land or the Great Forest, where I can simply devise a path to elude our pursuers. There is no place to hide on the surface of these waters."

"We have the magic of the cyclopes to light our path through to Atlantea, Mr. Traveler," Frog-Dor said.

"We will need it. I am going to say something to all of you. It will sound mad, but I don't trust these celestial elf pursuers because they don't act like celestial elves for one. Also, celestial elves are far more powerful."

"More powerful? They almost killed you, Mr. Traveler," Lady Aylen said.

"I've never directly encountered celestial elves, only star elves. But I've heard of them. The fact that I never met them is proof again that celestial elves were not interested in the magic lands at all. Even when I lived in Atlantea, I never saw one. They were always elsewhere in the heavens, other realms far away, other worlds. It was their allies, the sky elves and elementals, that traveled to Atlantea. No, I don't know what these elves are. Maybe they are not even elves."

"What is this mad thing you wish to propose, Mr. Traveler?" King Aereth asked.

"We need to destroy their fleet, but we are one ship. We need an alliance. My enemy's enemy is my friend is the saying."

"You cannot be suggesting what I think," the king said.

"I did say you'd think me mad. We should form an alliance with the sirens to destroy them," Traveler said.

For the first time, the caravan was divided. Different factions yelled their opposition to the new plan. However, none could suggest a better one.

"Are sirens that evil?" Gwyness asked nervously.

"They are," Dr'amal replied. "It's not the fables you've heard. It's much worse."

Lady Aylen sat in her chair quietly watching a sleeping Traveler. His dog, however, kept an eye on her as the entire tent went on with their heated debates.

After a while, Mr. Elman stepped into the tent. "Mr. Traveler."

Traveler woke. Lady Aylen realized that he had been actually sleeping and laughed, as did others. He sat up as the half-elf moved to his bed.

"What did you see with the eye?" Traveler asked.

"Celestial elves, star elves, cloud elves, sylphs, and undines."

"Elementals or nymphs?"

"I know the difference, Mr. Traveler. Air and water elementals, not nymphs, or at least that I could see."

"How far from us?"

"Not far enough, Mr. Traveler, if I can see them."

"Following our path, or searching?"

"I don't think they know our exact location, but they know we're nearby," Elman answered.

"There it is. One sylph could destroy our ship with a storm. One undine could destroy our ship with a whirlpool. Sirens, in addition to all their dark powers, can control the weather."

"Was this Master Isim's plan too?" Chief Ethor asked.

"Yes," Traveler said.

"We are helpless, then?" Queen Issaleth asked.

"If we were on land, I would have full confidence against these forces, but not from a ship on the seas. The advantage is all theirs."

"And this is a better plan than having stayed in Mímir-Spring?" Queen Issaleth's wizard, Betta, asked.

"Yes, and I will not have the ancient city of the cyclopes destroyed on our account. The city is irreplaceable."

"Aren't we?" Betta asked.

"In a fashion, yes. But this is different. We can sail away. The city cannot, so we lead the pursuers away. Titan's Fall, Kraken's Wake, White Waters, Mímir-Spring. These are the four main cities on the way to

Atlantea. They never expected us to backtrack to the cyclops city. We must avoid them all now, as I believe they tried to trap us at Kraken's Wake."

"White Waters is not there, Mr. Traveler," Elman said.

"Not there?" Traveler asked as did many.

"What do you mean, sir?" Nori the selkie asked.

"I am unable to see it with the eye the cyclops gave us. I can see it nowhere, submerged or otherwise."

"Did you see Kraken's Wake?" Otari, the selkie king, asked.

"There is a fleet of ships surrounding the city," Elman replied.

"Ships belonging to who, Mr. Elman?" Traveler asked.

"I believe those mermaid octopus women, Mr. Traveler."

"The cecaelia!" Lady Aylen said. "Mr. Traveler was right. They were in league with Oughtred."

Queen Issaleth felt light-headed. "Does that mean our fleet is gone? The mermaids, oceanids, tritons, and sea centaurs, all our allies. They would have waited for us."

"I did not see their ship or any wreckage," Elman said.

"Wreckage disappears in the blink of an eye on these waters," Queen Issaleth said. "You saw that for yourselves in your battle before arriving at Kraken's Wake."

"Queen, don't despair about their fate yet," King Aereth said.

"Yes, exactly," Traveler said. "They'd have to catch them to destroy them. These are their waters, too, not ours. Even if what we fear is true, there would be many survivors, and they would have sent for help. There are many mermaid, triton, and sea centaur kingdoms. Nymphs have more sub-races than all of them combined, and they are all allies."

Queen Issaleth felt reassured.

The quiet lasted awhile, everyone looking at their caravan master.

"The plan it is, then, Mr. Traveler," Pangolin said.

Traveler looked around at all the human and fae faces. "Who would be perfect to accompany me when I send my message to talk to the sirens?"

Gresham sat in a strange small-realm of darkness. He crouched on the ground, a sledgehammer resting in his lap. Other than a single light source that hung above like a giant motionless firefly, there was nothing else in the pocket realm save one thing. He could not see the contraption anymore. He had seen it once when Traveler first led him into the small-realm—a giant melon, he thought at first, but it was a perfect sphere and hung from a cord directly above his head.

Since his view of it was brief, he didn't know what its texture was or what manner of object it was, but it either blended into the dark or was invisible. He thought to himself that while all others worked diligently or waited throughout the ship, he sat alone in a sort of dungeon. But their caravan master reassured him and said for him not to despair, as his role might be the most important one of all.

The healer heard a knock. A realm door opened and there stood the man Frog-Dor. He dressed in a dark robe without a hood, common among magic-casters. The sorcerer's legs were free from Estus's metal braces, but he still used a walking stick in each hand to move about. The door closed magically as the sorcerer neared the caravan's hired healer.

"Mr. Gresham, I am to keep you company."

The healer smiled. "Have a seat, Mr. Frog-Dor. You are a welcome sight."

"Mr. Traveler did say the solitude would wear on you. But he thought you'd be grateful that he chose me rather than the darklings to join you."

Gresham laughed. "I will thank him profusely when I see him. The creatures do seem to have a special bond with him. How could any human live with such things?"

Frog-Dor sat across from Gresham. The sorcerer looked up at the light above them once. He shifted his legs to get comfortable. "A very empty pocket realm we find ourselves in—no sky or sunlight, no trees or wooden lands, no lakes or streams."

"Mr. Traveler said all of that might distract me from my task, should the time come. The power of the sirens is strong enough to affect even pocket realms within their territory. Frightening thought, that such an important task would fall to the caravan's healer, and not the real one at that."

"You are the caravan's healer. The fact that you are not as able as Mr. Traveler only gives you a goal to strive for, and if you persevere, you can surpass his skills and knowledge, if that is what you wish."

"I do. Mr. Traveler has opened my eyes to what a true healer can do, to gain the respect of all races, human, and fae—goblins too."

"Yes, I heard the story. I told Mr. Traveler that the time has come for me to begin paying my debt to Titan's Caravan. He freed me from my curse and ultimately saved my life, so I must use my powers in every way to see us through to Atlantea."

"We know you will, Mr. Frog-Dor. Our caravan master has done more for us than any other could do."

"Yes, but it cannot be him alone. We are an impressive caravan. We must each be impressive individually as well."

"What is happening outside?"

"We have crossed into the territory of the sirens. Already we are feeling their enchantment."

"So it will be you and I."

"Yes. If all else fails, it will be the two of us to save us all."

Gresham swallowed hard.

"Don't be concerned, Mr. Gresham. I will move between this realm and the deck, but I will not abandon you. Do your task as instructed. My task is to protect you so that you can."

There was no warning. Their ship had crossed into the realm of the sirens and everyone—whether human or fae, humanoid or animal—felt it. Those within the pocket realms felt as if the air they breathed had changed somehow. Those on duty on the main deck described the phenomena as a sudden headache, at first mild but with the potential to grow far worse.

The Brothers Brimm were in full armor for the first time. The five of them stood together near the display mirrors in the command cabin with the human and fae leadership.

"Should we begin, Mr. Traveler?" Johnter asked.

Traveler drank the last of his elixir in the tallest mug one the brownies could find. The dog stood next to him in humanoid form, bulky and ferocious. The animal had grown even more protective of its master after the attack in the cyclops city.

Traveler shook his head. They nodded. The helmets the musicians wore prevented all sound from entering their ears.

Frog-Dor and Dr'amal looked around, both with distress.

Dr'amal swallowed hard. Drows did not know the emotion of fear, but that was what showed on her face. "Mr. Traveler, this may be beyond us."

"It is beyond us, Dr'amal. But we will use cunning to see our way through. We cannot defeat the sirens in their own realm with words of magic or weapons. Let us wait for them to contact us. I need to stress again, if you feel your will slipping away, turn from the mirrors immediately. Pride in this situation will get you killed. There is no debate about it. We are the lambs, and they are the lions here. Never forget it."

Every inch the ship sailed, waves of sound pounded the vessel's protective barrier of magic with the force of a gale. The overcast sky had a strange green hue, and all the clouds in the sky were black like smoke. The ship stopped and floated forward in the waters that grew as dark as night.

Miles away, the sky and sea wavered as if a grand illusion, then the island was revealed. But the sirens' island was no tiny thing. Kraken's Wake looked like a giant desiccated kraken floating just under the surface of the ocean. The sirens' island of black jagged rock poked up from the sea's surface staring out like a giant mummified female head with slicked-back hair cascading down into the waters.

Traveler had their caravan move all animals into a separate pocket-realm under the charge of the fauns. The caravan's animals were wild with panic, and fauns and animal men struggled mightily to calm them. No amount of magic from either their sole fauness, Zefea, or the mole-like fae, or singing of their bird men seemed to help soothe the animals. But there was nothing else to do.

The caravan's kirins were the only living things aboard completely immune to the influence of the siren song, but three magic dragon-horses could not save over ten thousand men, women, and beasts of the combined ship.

All the women seemed unaffected, but Traveler warned them all again. There were male sirens that would appear out of nowhere, and if not prepared, the women would be the first to succumb to the collective power of the sirens.

Traveler nodded, and the Brothers Brimm began to play their musical wind instruments of magic.

Beads of sweat streamed down King Aereth's face. They stared at the single display mirror floating in the middle of the small-realm. Traveler stood before it with the king on one side and Pangolin on the other. Lady Aylen and Maiden Gwyness stood at their sides.

Hidden behind the mirror were Frog-Dor and Dr'amal. At their sides were the Brothers Brimm with their magic wind instruments to their lips, ready to play if anyone began acting strangely.

Traveler felt himself sweating. He saw what he saw in the display mirror and quickly closed his eyes for a moment. He opened them and whispered to King Aereth, "What do you see, sire?"

King Aereth fought for with his own sanity to remain calm. "I see my late wife."

"Humans," the siren said with a wanting smile.

The siren that appeared from the darkness of the mirror far surpassed the beauty of any nymph they had ever seen. Fair skin, long, flowing hair, cleavage beneath a sheer dress, piercing eyes. Traveler surmised that each man saw a version of a female that most appealed to them. He would have to ask the females what they saw later.

Two other sirens appeared. Humanoid above the waist, serpentine fish tails below. The mermaid-like sirens floated in the air with the slight sound of crashing waves in the background.

"What news do you have, human?" the lead siren asked.

"We wish to trade the news of invaders in exchange for safe passage through your seas," Traveler answered.

"You are invaders, human."

"These are invaders from the heavens whose conceit of superiority knows no bounds. They attempt to claim all these realms for themselves alone. They attacked the mermaids and ocean nymphs, the water elves, they attacked the city of the cyclopes. They even believe they can wipe the seas of all siren-kind."

"Do they? Who are these invaders who chase you?"

"They are celestial elves and sylphs."

"Celestial elves have no interest in this world or our seas. Why would our beautiful air elemental sisters trespass into our seas to destroy us? They would never do so."

"They follow the human named Oughtred of the human kingdom of Xenhelm."

"We know not of such humans or human lands or human affairs, but come to our island and make your case for safe passage."

"We do not wish to offend, but we cannot do that. We must speak this way."

"Are you afraid, human?"

"I am."

"Honesty. Appealing."

"What if I could prove the sylphs and celestial elves mean you harm?" Traveler asked.

"Then I would do so quickly, for the only trespassers to our seas we see are you."

"We will do so, immediately."

"You must do one other thing."

"Which is?"

"You must give us some of your men. You decide which. A dozen to show us your good faith."

"We do have men in our ship's dungeons, pirates who attacked us—twenty or so of them. We don't care about them. You can have them. Will that suffice?"

"Human, are you attempting to be clever, attempting to delay, attempting to lie?"

"No lie. We have prisoners. We'd gladly give them up for safe passage."

"Who are your prisoners? Humans?"

"No. One is, but the rest are fae who are in league with the human who sent these sylphs and celestial elves after us."

"Neither of them takes orders from humans."

"What if the human were a lich?"

"The most powerful of living dead necromancers? We have met a few in our time. Appealing. How much of what you say is lie, and how much is truth?"

"Some lie. Some truth."

The sirens laughed.

"You amuse us, human. We haven't encountered one who has amused us in so long, but you are a single ship in our sea of sirens. Words alone cannot save you. Surely, you knew that the second you crossed into our seas."

"We wished to do the honorable thing despite the danger. We are humans after all."

"Humans are always interesting but so weak and foolish. Fae would have attacked us immediately, though it would prove pointless. You humans talk because you cannot fight."

"Our ship has more than humans."

"We know all aboard your ship. Every human, fairy, elf, half-elf, giant, leshy, faun, hooved fae, sprite, brownie, pech, animal man, ant man, giant animal—mammal, amphibian, reptile, and fowl, chamrosh, alphyn..."

Everyone felt a growing sickness in the pits of their stomachs as the siren recited every race and animal on their ship.

"There are some fae we are not familiar with, but fae is fae. An animal we're not sure, maybe a shape-shifter. Three animals that have the scent of another realm far from here. The lowly gobliny phookas are not even worthy of feeding to our pets. And yes, we can even sense your tulen väki in their deep hidden realm of your ship. Nothing can hide from us."

"Is there anything we can trade to avoid a conflict?"

"The only thing you have that we want is you. Lower your magic barriers, and accept your fate."

"Sorry, but no one aboard our ship will be eaten this day."

"What happened to your twenty imaginary prisoners that you wanted to sacrifice?"

"We'll let them go and put swords in their hands."

"Imaginary swords for imaginary prisoners. This will be a day that we will sing about for many, many years. Our siren island will feast on you all on your one ship, riding our waves in our seas, then we will pull the ten city ships above that come to our seas hunting you. We will hunt them for the insolence of their magic, driving us from our territory, even if only for a short time. It will be a feast for years."

"There is no place to escape," a second siren said. "All that is before you is more of our kind, more islands, many more of our pets, and the power of our storms. We want you all to ourselves."

"What of your beautiful air elemental sisters in the city-ship above?" Traveler asked. "You will feast on your sisters too?"

"We can lie too," the main siren said. "We hate them, as we do mermaids and nymphs. We'll embrace them, as we will embrace you with song and a sensuous kiss. You will experience the greatest bliss of your lives as you're fed upon."

Traveler ran. The humanoid dog ran after him along with all others in small-realm. His abrupt departure startled them all as he pushed through the door. When he came through the door of the command cabin, he rushed to the map table and saw what he suspected.

"What is that, Mr. Traveler?" Lady Aylen reached the table before all the others.

"Another fleet."

"Not the celestial elves or sylphs?" King Aereth asked.

"No, sire. Someone else we haven't encountered yet."

"We have two fleets after us, Mr. Traveler?" Pangolin asked.

"Mr. Pangolin, chain yourself to the main deck the same as the other Cut-Throats."

"What will we do? What will you do?" one of the high elves yelled.

"Kilmoulis! Who is the approaching fleet?"

The big-nosed sprites stepped down on the spiral stairs of the upper level.

"We believe them to be spider centaurs, Master Traveler," one of them said.

"The mysterious race that the cecaelia said was nowhere in these waters. Mr. Estus!"

Their weaponsmaster had been waiting as directed. "Yes, Mr. Traveler." He came through the door in full armor.

"Weld myself, the royals, our sorcerers, Gwyness, and our musicians to this floor. Do the same for Mr. Pangolin on the main deck, and get yourself into the realm, and don't come out again. Tell the Tree

Shepherds to seal it up to prevent anything from entering. Mr. Frog-Dor, you will do the same for us."

"What of us on the main deck?" Pangolin asked.

"You and your men, Mr. Pangolin, will both be in the most danger, but you must be our eyes."

"But what will we do, Mr. Traveler?" King Aereth asked for all.

"No more delays. I have the eye of the cyclops. We're sailing to Atlantea and won't stop until we arrive. I am truly sorry for what you all will experience, but there is no other way. I did plan for it before we even exited the Great Forest."

"You're going deeper into siren territory."

"Yes, Mr. Frog-Dor. A single ship cannot destroy three fleets but siren storms can. The trick is not to be swept away too. The trick is not to fall victim to its madness. Today, we find out if I'm as good a navigator as I am a caravan master. I'll find out if what Mr. Tunik and his crafty klabautermann taught me is worth anything."

Estus was already gone. Pangolin struggled to see through a blinding rainstorm that set upon their ship without warning. He gripped the chain of his shackles to steady himself with all his might, but his footing slipped. The talaria sandals were suddenly useless because of the dark magic of the sirens, their seas, or both. He and his men did not even have the gift of flight anymore.

The sea water still got through the barrier somehow. It was rancid to the taste. Pangolin rubbed his mouth and tongue frantically. For all he knew, the water might be poison.

He yelled. The headache ripped through his skull, making his eyes close. He felt his will slipping.

"No!" he yelled.

Delicate hands reached up from over the side of the ship, human hands of olive skin. A beautiful form of a woman floated up. She smiled at him—a wanton smile. Pangolin's eyes locked on hers. His body shook.

"I will resist you!" Pangolin yelled. He temporarily regained a bit of himself and closed his eyes again.

When he opened them, the woman was Gwyness.

"You made a good effort," the lone siren said. "You lasted briefly longer than most of your kind with the berserker magic in your blood, but you are still human. No need to fight. I am here for you. I want nothing more than for you to be happy in my embrace. We will be happy together. I promise. I won't harm you. I want to make you happy."

Pangolin's body shook more violently as he internally struggled against the enchantment with all his might. He tried to summon his berserker rage but couldn't. Tears streamed down his face. The siren in the form of Gwyness floated over the side of the ship and glided down before him, but her feet didn't touch the deck. She had passed through their magic barrier with no effort at all.

All you need to do is let her pass the line. The memory of Traveler's words flashed into his mind for an instant but not the meaning, then it was gone.

The siren pulled herself farther onto the deck, no longer concerned that its true form would be revealed. She smiled and leaned forward to kiss his face. Her eyes rolled completely around. With the whites of her eyes and mouth frozen, her upper torso inclined back. At her waist he saw the horror of it all. The upper human torso was a facade of a humanoid woman—an elaborate appendage capable of mimicking any beautiful female form—the part concealing its true giant mouth. The mouth opened wide, revealing teeth sharper than any sword, like a piranha's and shark's combined, pushing out from within the creature and moving closer. Other sirens crawled up the ship's hull through the magic barrier to land on the deck. As the first siren reached out to him, the invisible line on the deck broke.

The piercing sound seemed to shatter reality. Pangolin had his will back. The sirens screamed and threw themselves off the ship back into the seas.

The sounds repeated over and over. The air all around the ship echoed in screams of countless sirens.

Pangolin looked around at all the Cut-throats chained along the main deck. Some of the men had dropped to their knees. Some had tears in their eyes, or were crying. For a berserker, nothing was worse than being helpless. Even death was preferable.

They were themselves again, but the shock of what surrounded them made them ill. Sirens floated in the sea, standing on the water by the rapid flapping motion of their giant lower tails. The dark sky above was filled with flying sirens circling their ship. Sirens were not mermaids. They were fish-tailed serpent shape-shifters, whose true forms were only revealed to their victims upon death.

Boom!

Their ship fired. Pangolin and every man on the deck felt their breath taken away as the ship accelerated to a break-neck speed.

A city ship came out of invisibility the moment the cannon exploded on its magic barrier. Another explosion and the invisible magic sphere protecting the city-ship erupted in flames so intense Pangolin and his men could almost feel the heat, though the flying vessels were dozens of feet above them. It looked like a sun as it crashed into the sea. More of the city ships came out of invisibility, flying higher above but changing course to them. They began to fire their own cannons. Starfire rained down on them.

"Shield yourselves!" Pangolin yelled.

CHAPTER SEVENTEEN

Siren Storm

Gwyness stood shaking at the wall near the door. Dazed, she touched her forehead and looked at the blood on her fingers. She looked at the door and the small burning hole in the center.

"What happened? Why can't I remember what happened?"

She turned to see both Lady Aylen and Dr'amal unconscious on the ground as a giant two-headed snake uncoiled from their bodies then transformed back into the dog.

"What happened? What happened, Mr. Traveler?" she yelled.

Traveler navigated the ship through wave after wave slamming against their speeding vessel. More starfire shot at them from the city ships above. He dove their vessel just underwater to blunt the impact of the volley.

"Gwyness, calm yourself, and wake the women. I need you all."

Gwyness didn't need to move, as both elfess and drowess already woke.

"Will someone not tell me why I'm bleeding?" Gwyness yelled.

"A male siren jumped onto the top of the cabin. It mesmerized all three of you, and you ran to it before my dog could grab you. You may not run as fast as the princess, but you run faster than most humans. You slammed into the wall, head-first."

The Brothers Brimm were chained on the other side of the display mirrors and already looked exhausted.

"Our musicians ceased their playing for only a second, and that's all the time that it took. Mr. Johnter, you all do not have the stamina to play nonstop for the time we need. Three play and two rest."

The lead Brothers Brimm looked at his comrades and pointed to two. The two musicians stopped and both gasped for breath. Johnter and the others continued to play.

"What is the hole, Mr. Traveler?" Gwyness asked. "And I hear fighting on the deck."

Frog-Dor tapped the fingers of his left hand together, and the hole magically disappeared.

"I shot a hole through its head with this." Traveler showed her the hand cannon hidden under his cloak. "Mr. Frog-Dor, the women broke free of their chains."

"Yes, Mr. Traveler. There is magic from something else out there that weakened Mr. Estus's melds."

"We must warn, Mr. Pangolin," Dr'amal said.

"The door stays closed!" Traveler yelled.

The ship suddenly dove underwater again but at a steeper angle. The women returned to their places and Frog-Dor magically re-attached the chained shackles to the floor of the cabin as quickly as he could.

"Does our ship still have our magic barrier, Mr. Traveler?" Lady Aylen asked.

Traveler ignored her as he focused his attention on the main display mirror. Frog-Dor saw it too, a dark shape moving toward their ship. The sorcerer said nothing but he was as nervous as all of them.

They heard a noise that sounded like the closing of many rusty doors. The ship's golem arms extended forward.

The impact of the crash was so violent that their ship spun ninety degrees before Traveler corrected course. The strange vessel was in pieces, and the sirens they briefly saw on the display mirror, looked to be twice the size or more of the previous sirens they had seen.

The caravan's vessel shot quickly to the surface.

Pangolin and the Cut-throats were able to gasp for air as the ship shot to the surface of the sea and slammed down onto the waves. The men of the deck were met with stinging rain and high winds. Then they grabbed their ears and yelled at the screams of countless sirens but the sound was not to mesmerize them. Pangolin looked up.

Dozens of sylphs warred with flying sirens. The air elementals created small thunderstorm clouds to unleash streams of lightning at the flying sirens. Sirens in the sea commanded their own lightning strikes from black clouds expanding above the entire Sirenic Sea.

Another city-ship appeared out of invisibility, descending to their rear. A clawed hand reached out of the sea and seized the entire craft. The giant serpent rose out of the sea to grab the city ship with another hand and pull it downward. A ring of starfire expanded from the hull of the craft to set the sea serpent ablaze, but it was too late. The elfin sky vessel crashed into the sea and hundreds, maybe thousands of sirens swarmed over it, ripped it apart, and swum inside.

"Hopefully, that doesn't happen to us," a Cut-throat said to Pangolin.

They heard yelling from above.

The bow of the red ship still hung over the rear of their golem ship. They could see the knights, with their giant ant men, all chained to their deck, frantically waving.

"What do they want?" a man asked.

"These damn chains!" Pangolin said. "How do we communicate with them?"

The sky flashed. They all looked to the sea.

"If we are hit by a lightning bolt like that, there will not even be ashes of us or the ship left to be scattered to the sea," a man said to Pangolin.

The door of the command cabin blew open. Elfin archers spilled out and jumped clear across to the other side of the ship.

"What is it?" Pangolin yelled at them.

"We shall attend to it!" a high elf yelled.

"Attend to what?" Pangolin asked.

The elfin archers kept emerging from the cabin and disappearing with one leap to the other side of the ship. Then came Estus's armor golems with their shields.

"We can't see a thing!" Pangolin yelled.

"A real battle and we're on the wrong side of the ship," a Cut-throat said.

Pangolin's berserker rage exploded within him as he grabbed his axe-mace and swung. His weapon hit the ten-feet greenish creature as it came up from the side—an upper torso with dark-green skin, one set of humanoid arms, and another set of the giant crab claws, with a lower torso of a giant crab with all its appendages. He heard a large crack in its crustacean shell as it spat blackish liquid and leapt into the sea to disappear below the surface.

"Was that one?" a Cut-throat. "A crab centaur?"

"Yes, man! It wasn't a mermaid."

They heard the growing commotion on the other side of the ship.

"What are they fighting?" Pangolin yelled.

More elves came out of the command cabins.

"Is it crab centaurs?" Pangolin yelled.

The elves shook their heads: "No!" But none stopped. They ran into battle and he could hear arrows flying.

He signaled all the men on the deck to be ready.

"If not crab centaurs, then what?" a berserker asked. "Oh no!"

A second giant crab centaur jumped out of the sea onto the deck, breaking through their magic barrier as easily as the sirens.

Never had any seen such a ship, a blackened ship twice their size—even combined with the Baltican red ship—of common construction for the Lands of Man but with a mound of earthen soil that sat in the center of the ships deck. From a hole at the top, spider centaurs swarmed out. They were as described, upper torso of drow-like males with purplish skin, unkempt hair hanging in front of their faces, long, protruding elfin ears, and the lower torso of a giant black spider.

The spider centaurs fired their arrows as they crawled out from their mound. The numbers grew, crowding on the deck. From the deck of the Titan's Caravan's golem ship, high elves rapid-fired their arrows. The spider centaurs far outnumbered the elves of Titan's Caravan, all one hundred fifty high elves joined by all one hundred fifty woodland elves. But the spider centaurs in their rapid-fire volley shot only one arrow at a time. The elves shot magic arrows that split in two, and they split again in flight, far multiplying the power of their small numbers. However, neither side impacted the other. Arrows were destroying arrows but the volleys between the ships did not cease.

A catapult launched from the overhanging deck of the red ship. The magic projectile breeched the spider centaurs' magic barrier, landed, and exploded temporarily sealing the opening of the center mound and throwing the creatures off balance. Many of the spider centaurs were finally felled by elfin arrows but not enough to turn the tide of battle.

Suddenly, spider centaurs leapt the huge distance from their ship to the red ship's deck. Human knights fired their crossbows, but unlike with the arrows from the elfin archers, the spider centaurs easily dodged them. The ant men attacked, also swarming out of the center of the red ship. The spider centaurs fired their arrows. The ant men advanced, blocking with their shields and striking at them. Ant men fought with bladed weapons in their other three arms and their giant mandibles. Spider centaurs were losing to the ant men twice their size. The creatures discarded their arrows to spray nets of webbing on the advancing ant men, which only slowed them. The ant men, covered in webs, simply threw their bodies at the spider centaurs and, once in contact, ripped the creatures apart.

Catapults launched again from the red ship toward the spider centaur ship. Giant crossbows fired at the spider centaurs on the red ship deck. Queen Issaleth's knights fired their own magic crossbows at the spider centaurs on their deck.

Bragg and his elves joined the other elves in battle—all three hundred—with their magic crossbows. The tide of battle was now in their favor, as Bragg's elves attacked both the spider centaur ship and the creatures still leaping onto the red ship.

A blizzard of double-blades flew over the elves' heads cutting down whole sections of the spider centaur army at once. Dr'as led his drow warriors into battle alongside the elves.

The spider centaurs saw the drows and became enraged.

Dr'as quickly scanned the spider centaurs on the deck, who had altered their arrow attack from elves to drows. The spider centaur arrows still couldn't get past the never-ending volley of elfin arrows. The drow leader, Dr'as, saw what he searched for in the shadow behind the drows—a single spider centaur in a hooded cloak. The javelin left the drow's hand so quickly, broke through all arrows in its path, and hit the spider centaur's leader in the throat.

Every spider centaur on the ship screamed.

The screams were heard on the other side of the ship. Pangolin and the Cut-Throats had to release themselves from the chains despite the danger of being thrown overboard. They used long polearms to fight the dozens of crab centaurs leaping onto the deck from the sea. The berserkers attacked the creatures in a melee of violence—stab, slash, push the crab centaur back over the side. The mad fighting style of the berserkers seemed to confuse the larger shell-armored creatures, whose only attack style was to swing at them with the giant crab claws of their upper torsos and try to crush their weapons. Pangolin continued to fight in close quarters with his axe-mace, and every blow that landed shattered a crab centaur to pieces. The creatures realized that his weapon was of magic and fled from him.

Crab centaurs were also being killed with one shot from the giant crossbow of Bragg's metal golem, Mr. Glog. The automaton marched along the deck firing its crossbow and literally slapping crab centaurs off the deck and back into the sea with one swing.

The desert elves joined the fight, one hundred fifty elves firing their magic arrows at the crab centaurs, whose shell armor protected them for only so long before the damage made them collapse.

Pangolin knew it was too easy. The crab centaurs they fought were only the scouts, not the main warriors. The sound of hundreds of legs came first, then crab centaur warriors swarmed over the side, from under their ship, with thicker shell armor, larger than the previous creatures. Elfin arrows bounced off their armor, but Pangolin's axe-mace still delivered crippling death blows that the new creatures' armor could not withstand.

The entire ship shook once then again. Their cannons had fired. The ship rocked again so violently that all on deck were knocked off their feet. Even the crab centaurs swayed side to side. Another violent rock, Pangolin timed it to jump to his feet and attack his target at the right angle. His blow landed with such power the first crab centaur broke apart as it crashed into another and another. A dozen crab centaurs were felled with the blow.

A tentacle reached over and wrapped itself around Pangolin's waist. He felt himself being pulled overboard. A flurry of arrows ripped the tentacle apart, and he crashed onto the deck. The crab centaur that rose from the sea was gigantic and had tentacles sprouting from its back.

Boom!

The heavy weapons team on the deck of the red city ship fired, and the giant crab centaur was gone.

A portal appeared on the deck below. Nearly a hundred spider centaurs spilled out before an explosion sealed the opening. The Diomedian Mares raced out of the pocket-realm and pounced on the first wave of spider centaurs. Unlike most beasts, the carnivorous horse-like creature had no fear of anything and ripped at the creatures with their claws and teeth.

Waves of the desert elves' giant falcons flew out of the pocket realm to attack spider centaurs in flight. Moon elves came out of invisibility from the other end of the corridor to fire volleys of moon arrows at the spider centaurs from behind. The creatures were overwhelmed by elves, falcons, and Diomedian Mares.

The portal opening began to appear again, but Shadu-mun threw another magic orb. The explosion closed the door just as more spider centaurs tried to push through, severing their heads, arms, and legs.

From the display mirrors, the royals, Gwyness, and the two sorcerers watched Estus's armor golems marching from the below decks to join the battle that was already turning in their favor against the two evil centauroid races. The red ship's heavy weapons teams were firing steadily.

The golem ship's cannons also began firing.

"Who did you fire at, Mr. Traveler?" King Aereth asked. He stared at one of the mirrors as concern came over his face.

"Are those islands?" Lady Aylen asked, watching. "Moving toward us?"

Flying things rose into the air from the distant islands ahead of them.

"What are those, Mr. Traveler?" Gwyness asked.

They all could feel their headaches growing. Johnter returned to having all the Brothers Brimm play their instruments.

Another spider centaur ship rose from the sea to join the first, but far larger in size. A giant portal opened above all the ships, and flying vessels dropped down.

"Wildglow, Sunpetal!" Traveler yelled.

The two fairies appeared as yellow fireflies floating above his head. "Send the message!"

The fireflies disappeared.

Armies of sylphs flew from the vessels floating above them all. All nine of the remaining city ships of the sky elves came out of invisibility. A single giant ship rose from the sea alongside them, its deck filled with undines.

The musicians had their eyes closed and focused on their playing. Traveler had a look of singular detachment as he sailed the ship forward toward the islands ahead and a growing wall of water before it. Everyone else looked at each other.

"We have no escape," Dr'amal said.

A black cloud also moved quickly toward them—an unimaginable number of flying sirens.

The sylphs created a cyclone from the sky as the undines created one of water.

The screams were too loud for the ship's barrier to shield them anymore. Lady Aylen grabbed her ears first. In the top level, they could hear Elman, the half-elves, and the kilmoulis crying out in agony.

The music.

You are so beautiful. I do want to come to you. Gresham felt his own sanity being ripped away. From even the bottom of the ship, a realm within a realm, it was as if no magic at all separated him from them. He could see the images of the beckoning sirens in his mind.

He knew why Traveler had him wait in a small-realm of nothingness. The only thing he could see now was the sphere above his head. The glow pulsated. All around him, he could literally see the siren song shake the realm. With each beat, another piece of the realm fell away.

Gresham struggled to lift his sledgehammer. What was merely a few pounds before felt like a ton in his hands. He had to be ready. From the corner of his eye, he saw Frog-Dor, eyes closed and teeth exposed, biting down with intense effort. The sorcerer wanted to scream, but he stretched out his arms, his hands contorted, trying to cast a last spell.

"Now, Gresham! I can't hold our realm together any longer. There are so many of them."

The sphere fell to the ground before Gresham's feet. He swung at it with his sledgehammer. The power of the siren song was so powerful. His body rose in the air, about to be pulled from their realm, the very ship, into their embrace in the seas.

The sphere exploded. Gresham fell to the ground. Frog-Dor collapsed, too, and he was able to restore their realm to its appearance.

On the display mirrors, the power of the sylphs' cyclone grew as it expanded, but something was wrong with the undines. The water elementals writhed on the deck of their vessel in pain, but it wasn't the siren scream. The magic of the beautiful water elementals waned as the salt of the sea stuck to their bodies and encased them in a film. Soon they were being suffocated by the hardening salt thickening to that of stone. Their water cyclone crashed back into the sea, and in an instant, all the undines and their vessel became a growing whirlpool.

Their caravan's ship lurched to the side, and Traveler held the navigation with all his might and steered the ship into the whirlpool rather than try to escape it. The whirlpool grew larger and larger. The dark sky around them followed in rotation. The rain grew more intense, now a full-scale hurricane. The first spider centaur ship broke apart in the whirlpool, spider centaur bodies scattering into the water. The second tried to escape the growing whirlpool. The water literally reached up its many arms and ripped the ship apart. When the ship flipped, for an instant, they saw why one centauroid race was so often seen after the appearance of the other. Theirs were combined ships, too—the spider centaur ship above water and attached was the upside-down craft of the crab centaurs. Seemingly endless numbers of the spider centaurs were scattered to the waters. Then man-sized shells spilled out from the wreck and disappeared quickly. Crab centaurs?

More than one ship popped up from the growing whirlpool. The design they had seen before—cecaelias. But they were not mermaid octopus ships. They were distinctively squid-like, which Titan's Caravan confirmed by counting their tentacles. They were equally helpless and tried to use the tentacles of their ships to escape. The tentacles of a single giant kraken reached out to the sky but was swallowed into the center of the whirlpool, its funnel growing deeper into the depths which each minute.

The siren storm was so vast and powerful that it soon engulfed the storm of sylphs. Bolts of lightning crackled and set another sky vessel, hiding in invisibility, ablaze. It fell to the sea into the center of the whirlpool. The sylphs had the power to escape to the heavens and flew up as fast as they could. Their sky vessel broke apart in midair, and its pieces became part of the giant cyclone above the whirlpool.

The sky elf flying ships tried with all their power and magic to escape. One hit the side of the cyclone, now a mix of water and air, and was shredded. Another lost control and crashed into the water to be pulled apart by the whirlpool. Every remaining sky elf vessel fell and crashed into the whirlpool. In an instant, nothing was left of the vessels or their crews.

Sky ships fired their star cannons, destroying five of the approaching siren islands. However, there were many more. The remaining ships hung in the air, in a death struggle with the sirens.

At the eye of the siren storm, flying sirens floated above it all watching the sole ship of the Titan's Caravan remain. No efforts made to escape; it submitted to its fate. The creatures sang among themselves in revelry. A fine feast would be had but the power of their whirlpool storm would not be satisfied until all invaders to their seas were killed. All would have to die.

"Hurry!" Traveler yelled.

The last of the caravan—a final giant orange lizard in a frenzy from the noise all around it, then two human minders under the spell of siren song were magically pulled in midair through the portal. Frog-Dor flew into the portal. The caravan master gestured and the dog jumped through. Traveler and Gresham were the last two and jumped through the portal together. The teleportal vanished. Soon after their golem ship disintegrated from the power of the siren's whirlpool.

The spell was cast, and clawed hands of water rose from the surface of the spinning whirlpool, reached for the combined golem-red ship, and crushed it to pieces. Nothing of it remained, and the pieces scattered into the whirlpool and the Sirenic Seas.

But not one body—human, fae, or animal—was to be seen.

The sirens sensed the absence of all life within the ships. The storm exploded in intensity as sirens in the air and sea screamed in psychotic rage. The water cyclone consumed the entire sea and the darkness of the churning hurricane winds surpassed what even they could control. Sea and flying sirens were swept up in their own death storm while others dove to the deep depths as quickly as they could propel themselves. The madness of their own siren storm was beyond control and would claim many of them.

The throne room of New Xenhelm's royal castle was like the cold void of space. Display mirrors of every size floated in the air, showing every angle of the siren storm battle. A war wizard—elfin, gargoyle, high goblin, or human—floated before each mirror.

King Prince Wuldricar the Savage of the Four Kings sat on his floating throne. With his pale eyes he watched. The large and bulky man with his orange-dyed beard and silver-white hair had an anxious posture at the edge of the throne chair. He clenched his gloved hands then pounded a leg under his exquisite royal garb of Xenhelm's colors.

"I wanted their bodies!" he yelled.

King Prince Renfrey the Wily floated in the air nearby. "Are they dead?" he asked the wizards.

All the wizards turned to face the two kings. The brothers could see in their faces that they were not to get the answers they wished.

"M'kings." A hooded wizard ran into the throne room.

"What is it?" King Wuldricar asked.

"A message from Queen Chrysa, m'king."

"Who is that?" Wuldricar asked.

"The high queendom of the fairies."

Wuldricar laughed.

"Do not laugh, brother," Renfrey said. "The fairies nearly defeated the elves, giants, and sprites combined."

"Send the message," Wuldricar said.

"Brother, it's possible that the human named Traveler not only escaped us again but outwitted us."

"What do you mean?"

All the displays went black save one. The face of a single fairy appeared on the largest. She was tall with pale translucent skin, gaunt features, forehead antennae, insect–like slits for eyes, and two sets of arms. She wore a cloaked light–gray robe."

"To what do we owe this honor?" Wuldricar asked.

"Do you not know that Titan's Caravan travels under the banners of the fairy queens of Chrysa?"

"The question is do we care?" Wuldricar asked.

"My two daughters travel with this caravan as our emissaries. I learned today that the caravan has reached the final leg of the Trail to Atlantea, and you tried to destroy them, kill my daughters, my youngest and favorite daughters."

"Are you about to threaten retribution, queen?" Renfrey asked. "We can forego the back-and-forth of threats and instead agree to a mutually beneficial alternative."

Another face appeared on another display mirror. It was a golden-haired bearded man with an ornate golden crown. "I am Centaur King Lyongriff of the kingdom of Chiron. Titan's Caravan also carries our banner. We learned that you attempted to destroy our ages-old allies, the cyclops city of Mímir-Spring, from its chief mage master himself."

"The only mutually beneficial alternative we are agreeable to is your death," the fairy queen said.

"Death has no hold over us," Wuldricar said.

"Yes, we know," the centaur king said. "Your fiends infected the Centaur Fields and could have spread to the Centaurian Forests."

"We spoke to the elves and giants whose banners Titan's Caravan also carries. As far as we are concerned, they have made it to Atlantea despite your continued treachery. No, it has been decided. You have achieved the status you sought, to be feared by all fae and human-kind. You will die this day."

"You know nothing!" Renfrey yelled. "We have already won."

"Your Titan's Caravan is no more," Wuldricar said.

"They are not dead," Chrysa said. "The Four Kings are not the only caravan possessing the magic to teleport across long distances. They sail aboard a new ship, one that you do not know."

"They told us your plot," the centaur king said. "To conquer Atlantea. The plot will have to continue without the two of you."

"You don't know where we are, centaur," Wuldricar said.

"You shouldn't have used that teleportation spell in the Sirenic Seas. You should have let it be," the centaur king said. "Escaping by portal is one thing. Sending something by portal always leaves one vulnerable to those who know the right magic."

"Fairy mothers can be such evil beings when you try to kill their children. We will make a new fairy tale for Xenhelmian mothers to tell their own children so that they remain good and just. For if they stray, they will receive only horror in the wee hours of the night."

The crystal blue sky was as calm and serene as the water their ship rested upon. The few clouds hung as wisps of white. The men rested on the sides of their new ship, looking up, taking in the sun and the quiet. Nothing else could be seen, even by Mr. Elman.

The new ship was a white warship with eight cannons on the bow and four on the stern. Three masts with full sails shot up from the deck. The center one was the largest with a fortified crow's nest for lookouts. No one knew where or how Traveler had secured the vessel.

Traveler lay in his bed in his small-realm, not on an elevated bed but on his thick bear rug on the floor with another to cover him. His dog lay nearby.

Pangolin stood guard outside the tent personally with several Cut-throats.

"Did he say where we are, Mr. Pangolin?" Lady Aylen asked, leading the king, Queen Issaleth, and other leaders.

"No, he's still sleeping."

"Mr. Traveler, are you sleeping?" Lady Aylen yelled, causing everyone to laugh.

"No, princess. Not anymore," Traveler said from inside.

"Where are we, Mr. Traveler? I'll ask how we got here and how we escaped another time."

Traveler's head peeked out from the flap of the tent. "Half an hour from the fabled kingdom of Atlantea."

Everyone's mouths dropped open. Some had tears in their eyes, even Mr. Pangolin.

THE THRESHOLD OF ATLANTEA

Land of the Fabled Kingdom of Atlantea

CHAPTER EIGHTEEN

Titan's Point

The ship erupted in wild celebration. Hobbs canceled all chores for the day, and all the other leaders did the same. Brownies came out of their pocket-realms to serve drinks as all aboard drank, danced, laughed, and gorged themselves—a final gathering of merriment in their main pocket-realm, all under the blue skies with breezy, fresh air, vast green pastures, rivers, and waterfalls under the cover of the crawling trees. The darklings chased their yellow sea phooka cousins in the form of ram-headed monkeys. In the lake, the six giants splashed water at each other, but this time the selkie children swam and played in the form of seals. Queen Issaleth and her crew joined in. Even the ant men attended, standing apart, speaking to each other, amused by the behavior of all the humans and fae.

Shadu-mun had left with two of his fellow moon elves but returned soon after. He found Traveler with the royals, Gwyness, Pangolin, Estus, Hobbs, Gresham, and their two sorcerers, Frog-Dor and Dr'amal.

The moon elf handed their caravan master a note.

"Mr. Shadu-mun, if that is anything but good news, then you will be exiled from the festivities," Lady Aylen said.

"I do believe it to be very good news. Two of the Four Kings are dead."

Traveler's smile disappeared as he opened the note. Those that heard Shadu-mun's words gathered around.

"The note is from your cyclops mage friend," Shadu-mun added. "It flew onto the ship as a bird into the hand of a sentry on deck."

Traveler read it. "Master Isim says that our allies, led by the fairies of Chrysa and the centaurs of Chiron, destroyed a city built on a moon far from us."

"We sensed the absence of it in the heavens," Shadu-mun said.

"Even from here during the day?" Traveler asked.

"Yes, it was a large moon, one of the largest of another world."

"This realm or another?"

"Another."

Traveler continued to read. "The moon was destroyed along with Kings Wuldricar and Renfrey, and their entire army of soldiers and war wizards. Oughtred was building another New Xenhelm."

"We thought the Four Kings to be dead before," King Aereth said. "Dead in the way we understand it."

"Their inner evil found a way to cheat even death," Queen Issaleth said.

"Liches cannot survive what was done to them because they are beings of dark magic, and it was that magic that was destroyed."

"But can dark magic truly be destroyed?" Dr'amal asked. "It can be delayed or redirected but never destroyed completely. That is what my mage elders always told me, and we drows have had a more personal interest in such things than most races."

"True. Master Isim explained what they did, fully. When a star dies, it leaves an opening that pulls anything into it, even the smallest particle of dust, with the combined power of the cosmos. Nothing can escape its power, not even dark magic or the fiends that live by it. They were thrown into this dead star, the entire moon and all upon it, and will never be seen of again," Traveler answered.

"Oughtred now only has the son left you sent to the necropolis," Dr'amal said.

"Gervase the Fair. From what I saw in my last encounter with Oughtred, there is nothing fair about him anymore," Traveler said.

"Oughtred is alone," Queen Issaleth said.

"His dark allies remain."

"Another battle, Mr. Traveler?" Pangolin asked.

"No, Mr. Pangolin. Or I should say, battles of a different kind."

"You have the seeing eye from the cyclops," Dr'amal realized.

"I do, but we should enjoy our festivities. Thank you, Mr. Shadu-mun, for the good news. At dawn, we arrive at the statue of Titan's Point, and you will all see the outline of Atlantea with your own eyes."

"And what else, Mr. Traveler?" Lady Aylen asked. "We know how fond you are of shocking us."

Traveler shook his head. "No more bad news from me. We enjoy our festivities, princess."

They all let it lie because finally, after nearly a year, they would be in Atlantea. But what of Oughtred?

Traveler stood on the deck of the ship in his hooded cloak and orange-tinted elemental armor, his sword in the sheath hanging on his back.

"You need new armor, Mr. Traveler, for celestial elves," Lady Aylen said with her dual war tridents on her back and Gwyness at her side.

"Celestial elves are not known for fighting, princess. Star elves are another matter."

"Why is that, Mr. Traveler?" Gwyness asked.

"Partly, because they are too aloof for physical exertion with lesser races, such as most of us on Pan-Earth. The real reason is their tremendous magic abilities. The one we encountered at Mímir-Spring must have been a lesser celestial elf."

King Aereth arrived with Queen Issaleth, the selkie leaders, Nori and Otari, Chief Ethor of the elves, King Dr'as of the drows, King Greenwig of the Tree Shepherds, Chief Ammon of the fauns, and all six of the Antaean giants led by Grakdar.

The three kirins descended onto the deck and followed after their masters. Traveler's dog looked more like a dragon-horse with hooves instead of paws.

Queen Issaleth's sorcerers followed after Frog-Dor and Dr'amal the drowess.

"What do you see?" she asked Frog-Dor.

"Ships. Many of them."

"Behind them. Is that a mountain or the statue?"

"Must be Titan's Point."

Queen Issaleth stepped to the tip of the bow jutting her head out and squinting.

"Here." Traveler handed her his telescope.

"It's them," she said when she put it to her eye.

Traveler's dog nudged him, and he looked up at one of the clouds. The cloud looked exactly like the face of Oughtred but dissipated. Only Gwyness had noticed it, too, and looked at him but said nothing. All the kirins had also noticed the cloud.

No one had seen the fae-bloods in many days, but that was to follow Traveler's instructions. They appeared again now, but this time Ursi wore a small golden crown as she joined them.

Traveler smiled. "Is it Queen Ursi?" he asked.

"We do not use such titles but yes."

The male fae-bloods also appeared to join them.

"We sense other fae-bloods," one of them said.

"Which ones?" Ursi asked them.

"We're not sure."

"I'm glad you both learned to speak to each other."

A fleet of two dozen ships sat to their left and fifteen or so of the distinct cecaelia ships on the other. Their white ship drifted forward toward the fleet.

Queen Geneva of the mermaids and Queen Oluania of the oceanids came aboard first. King Centauro of the sea centaurs came next, floating on a cushion of water, followed by King Traerio of the tritons. The water elves Kings Finlor, Elfred, Agis, Queens Amphitrite, Leena, and Eriana came aboard together. Then the cecaelia Queen Atopia climbed aboard with her tentacles.

"Queen Atopia," Queen Issaleth greeted bitterly.

The mermaid octopus smirked as she joined the other sea fleet leaders. "You mustn't be so quick to hold grudges, human. We did not think sailing with you was our wisest, or safest, course. If it makes you feel better, we lost ships in battling the decaelia, the ones you can't distinguish from us."

"Yes, ten tentacles not eight," Traveler said. "Did Kraken's Wake survive?" Traveler asked.

"It did," Queen Geneva replied. "We submerged the city to fight the squid mermaids and the krakens under their control. We drove them off."

"Did White Waters survive?" Queen Issaleth asked.

"Yes, the ocean city sailed for our main water elfin kingdoms for safety," a water elf queen replied.

"We may not feel comfortable leaving Kraken's Wake as the only ocean city between Titan's Fall and Atlantea," Queen Geneva said. "Sadly, we may sail it back to our main seas too."

"Why did you wait for us? That is the real question," Traveler said.

"Yes, it is," Lady Aylen echoed with suspicion.

"Queen Issaleth sealed our fate when she abandoned us to return to you," Queen Atopia said.

"You need humans to enter Atlantea," Traveler said.

"We had no choice but to wait, but there is another reason," Queen Atopia said.

"We did make it to the cyclops city," Traveler said.

"You did?" Queen Atopia asked, as surprised as all the water fae. "Then we were wrong to split from you."

"No, queen, you were right. You did what was best for your crew, as I, or we, would have done in your place."

The mermaid octopus queen nodded. "Thank you."

"Others have joined us," King Elfred, the water elf, said.

Summoned with the wave of a hand, two others came aboard dressed very similar to the fae-bloods of Titan's Caravan. Both wore crowns, one male and another female. The male had eyes very much like a fish's with a necklace of blue stones, and the female had pupils like a fly's with a green stone necklace. They immediately took note of Ursi and the fae-blood men.

"The bear and wolf clans are now allies?" the man asked.

Ursi hesitated before answering. "Yes."

The man and woman nodded.

"The insect and fish clans are now allies too," the female said. "We can enter Atlantea together."

"Thank you," Ursi said. "We encountered bird and snake clans on the Trail."

"We encountered a cat clan too," the male fae-blood said.

"How many ships do we have now?" Queen Issaleth asked.

"Thirty," the selkie Nori replied.

"What is the other reason for waiting for us?" Traveler asked.

The Colossus of Titan's Point stood one hundred feet on a single flat island on the final route to the fabled kingdom. Some said it was the perfect likeness of the humanoid Titan known as the Maker of All Mountains, wearing a helmet that covered his head, with a sad face, clad in chest armor, dragging his fabled weapon, the Star Slayer, upon the earth. The giant golden statue looked ancient but still glistened in the sunlight.

After nearly a year of travel, on the horizon beyond the Colossus was their first sign of the fabled kingdom that had claimed countless lives of humans and fae seeking to cross its border over the centuries. An illusionary image of a white city floated in the distance.

But the excitement ceased.

At the Colossus, waited another fleet, a fleet many times the size of theirs with ships far larger than even those of the cecaelia.

"Mr. Traveler, it's him," King Aereth said.

"Yes, sire. King Oughtred."

CHAPTER NINETEEN

Oughtred's Fleet

A robed iguana man levitated across the water and set down on the bow of their ship. Unlike the iguana warriors their own animal men had encountered in the Great Forest, this humanoid lizard man was a wizard. A row of elongated yellow scales ran from the top of his forehead to his back. His green tail with a bright-yellow streak snaked out from the back of his robe.

Every arrow and throwing weapon was trained on him. Traveler stood quietly across from him, Pangolin and Lady Aylen on either side, three Antaean giants behind him. The iguanoid wizard glanced alongside the ship and saw water elves training their arrows on him too.

"May I speak, or will that make you nervous?" the wizard asked.

"Perhaps you should return to where you came," Traveler said.

"No one in our fleet will attack. We are all under the watchful eyes of the Atlanteans. King Oughtred merely wishes to speak with you."

"I thought he wanted me dead. He should make up his mind."

"That was the past and is now forgotten. He will await your lead ship."

"He tried to kill us all for a year but wishes to merely speak now?"

"My king realizes the profound error of his ways. He has lost much, and you very little in comparison. Revenge should be his desire."

"What of simple self-defense from an evil madman. He set the events in motion not us. Wise is to kill the one set on your death."

"My king is set on only one thing at this moment, entering Atlantea."

"Conquering Atlantea."

The wizard laughed. "Were you the one spreading these lies far and wide? If so, your own cleverness has doomed you."

"Doomed?"

"Yes. No one shall enter Atlantea for a thousand years."

"You lie."

"You shall see for yourself, Master Traveler of Titan's Caravan. An impressive fleet you have assembled, though not more so than ours. The two of us are not the only parties here."

"Who are the others?"

"Goblins, of course. They feel they must be everywhere humans and elves go but never quite knowing why. I will return to my ship. Please do not fire any arrows into my back. I have no weapons."

"You're a wizard."

"I have no weapons."

"You are in league with Oughtred."

"I'm still without weapons."

The iguana man smiled as he stared at Traveler. "May I go?"

"Go."

The iguana man wizard floated from the deck and back across the ocean toward the ship from where he came.

"A good thing you said not to talk," Pangolin whispered. "I had plenty to say."

"I can still impale him from here with a trident," Lady Aylen whispered.

"I have no weapons!" the wizard called out.

Gwyness felt a warmth around her neck. Her amulet hadn't glowed in many months on the Trail. Something supernaturally evil stirred within Oughtred's ships, all bearing the orange-and-white flags of Xenhelm with the symbol of their kingdom in the center—a majestic griffin.

"If we had encountered Oughtred's fleet on the open waters..." King Aereth began.

"Battling sirens, sky elves, and sylphs were enough, sire," Traveler said.

"Or siren storms of madness," the drow leader, Dr'as, said.

"And walls of krakens," Pangolin added.

Most of Oughtred's fleet sat upon the water with no sign of their crew. However, those nearest him were filled with races of the living they had seen before.

Traveler recognized the Gaean party of tall green-skinned dryad warrioresses dressed in wood armor, their queen with a crown of thorns, on one ship. All carried slender black-tipped spears with their packs of large green fae dogs around them.

Another ship had male centaurs with crowns, three in all. Their upper torsos were fully armored in fae metal, their heads fitted with crowned helmets without faceplates to allow both their faces and hair to be free. Six-foot-tall gnomes and large satyrs with their herds of giant bison and boars stood behind them.

Another ship was filled with male iguana warriors—ten feet tall, clad in green armor with long axes on their belts and quivers of javelins. They held thick pike weapons in their clawed hands. Like the wizard, a row of elongated yellow scales ran from the top of their foreheads to their backs. Their tails were green, like the rest of their bodies, with a bright-yellow streak. There seemed to be thousands of them.

Another ship had dwarves and land kobolds. The dwarves wore thick, nonreflective dwarven armor, carrying metal war mallets or piked double axes. The ugly humanoid kobolds were draped in hooded cloaks.

There were so many ships with crews of fae. They saw a ship of grayish goblins on dire wolves and another filled with beast men, another of gargoyles. No one knew what creatures were aboard all the ships.

King Oughtred stood on the deck of a flat ship of gold. His giant griffin was at his side with King Prince Gervase, his remaining son, on its back in black armor with no part of his face or skin showing. A sole elfin sorceress stood on his other side with many hooded humanoids with strange yellowish eyes behind her. Beast men covered in thick black fur with pale monkey-like faces and razor teeth, part-baboon, part-reptile, stood in formation behind them.

Oughtred rose in the air and floated toward their ship. They could see his elfin sorceress's hand gesturing in the air. When his feet set down, not a human or fae was not gripped by intense uneasiness. Some were scared, some ready to strike at any provocation.

King Oughtred stared at Traveler with a cold expression but without simmering rage. He wore his crown on his head and full knight's armor with a red cloak. His bright red-hair, mustache, and beard were unusual now, knowing that the man was a lich.

"I heard of my sons' deaths," he said to Traveler. "It would seem we both have powerful allies whose reach extend beyond this world."

"As you once said to me, you must learn to savor the horror."

"Yes, I did. Never have I crossed one to bring me so much destruction as you. I should have personally killed you at the time. But that time has passed."

"Has it?"

"It would seem that the Atlanteans have tired of the caravans into their lands, or so the rumors say. Neither of us, nor any other, will pass beyond their gates for a thousand years."

"What of your scheme to conquer the city?"

"You shared our private conversation with far too many, and it was said as a boast."

"Are you unable to pass through Atlantea's circle with your dark army?"

"I'm unable to pass even the final edge of the Oceans Omnis because the Imperium will not allow us. A barrier blocks the final path to Titan's Gate. This is our final stop, it would seem, after so much time and sacrifice. But I will not wait a thousand years, even though I can. You cannot say the same."

"Neither can your dark allies."

"True, but I am willing to wait—for you."

"Wait for what?"

"For you to approach the Atlanteans and speak to them for entry."

"How does that benefit you?"

"If they allow you, they allow me."

Traveler glared at him. Oughtred laughed.

"What does he mean?" King Aereth asked.

"I mean, King Aereth, that Atlanteans do not make such distinctions as friend or foe or rival fleets. We are all Titan's Caravan here."

The human lich king stared at Traveler for a long while, smirking.

"Titan's Caravan can enter Atlantea, but not without my Kings' Caravan too. How is that for horror, Mr. Traveler? You must lead me in too, or travel back the years' long journey the way you came." He smiled. "You, Mr. Traveler, will allow Xenhelm to conquer Atlantea, and that is no boast. What will you do?"

"You will fly off our ship, or we'll throw you off."

"Unwise, and you are not one for unwise actions. Such a battle would be catastrophic for each of us. Your caravan is too powerful for me to utterly destroy, and mine is too powerful for you to do so. We would simply kill most of each other's men, leaving a handful of us left. Under the watchful eyes of the Atlanteans, neither one of us would ever enter again, or better still, I would instruct my forces not to lift a finger in their own defense, so the Atlanteans would see you as the aggressor."

Oughtred laughed as he rose into the air.

"The irony of things. When we started out in Avalonia, you were part of my caravan to Atlantea with me as the lead. Here we are at the end, and I will be a part of your caravan with you as the lead. If only you had kept your mouths shut about my rebirth as a lich, you would have had the ultimate triumph over me, entering the fabled kingdom on your own terms. Instead, we will march through Titan's Gate together, and I will wait as long as is necessary for you to submit to your fate, whether today or a thousand years from now. This is how Titan's Trail ends for you."

His laughter echoed in the air as he floated away from their ship to his.

CHAPTER TWENTY

The Imperium

"How can the entire kingdom of Atlantea be closed? What does that mean? How?"

"Has this ever happened before?"

"No stories exist that it has."

"Why would they do this?"

"What does it mean?"

"A thousand years. It cannot be so."

"Titan's Trail has existing for eons. It cannot be closed."

"How could we survive all that we have to be thwarted so at Atlantea's door?"

"This is Oughtred's doing. Yes, the Four Kings did this!"

"Kill him!" a berserker yelled, echoed by other humans, drows, and sprites.

"Archers!" Lyre the high elf called.

Pangolin angrily gripped his axe-mace, readying to attack.

Traveler restrained them and gathered their leaders inside the ship, away from the men. Every leader of Titan's Caravan, Queen Issaleth's caravan, and the water fae stood in the command cabin for that final meeting on the Oceanus Omnis. The majestic Colossus of Titan's Point showed on their main display mirror, but no longer as a symbol of triumph to any of them. All of them felt sick because of their inevitable decision.

"There's nothing to say, and there's nothing else to do. Return to your ships, and follow us to the Gate," Traveler said. "We sail into Atlantea immediately."

No one aboard knew what to think. The fabled kingdom of Atlantea was closed to them. Or they would truly have to sail into the city with the evil Xenhelmians at their side. King Oughtred and the Four Kings had tried to destroy them so many times on the Trail.

"We are not the only ones on these waters." King Aereth watched ahead of them.

Oughtred's ships were ahead, which they all preferred. Farther away, they saw other ships, many more ships, waiting on the sea. As they neared, they noticed their banners flying high. The ships were all of royal kingdoms. Their crews were human, elfin, or others races.

"Do you recognize any of them, sire?" Lady Aylen asked. "The crews of some of the ships are human—royals. I see elves, and other races with whom I'm not familiar."

"Do you know them, Mr. Traveler?" King Aereth asked.

"The lead human ships are from the kingdoms of our Seven Empires," their caravan master replied.

"That ship is Gondwanan," Pangolin noticed. "My original home lands. Another is Laurasian, the lands where my magic armor was forged."

"Yes, and the farthest one is from Larentia. I see a ship from Oceania too," Traveler said.

"All Seven Empires are here, sire," Lady Aylen said.

"Representatives of every empire in the Lands of Man here," King Aereth said.

"And elves and fae, of land and ocean," Lady Aylen added, "both of light and dark since we have no choice but to include Oughtred's fleet."

Oughtred's golden flatbed ship slowed in front of his own fleet, away from Titan's Caravan's ships and those of the other humans and elves.

"Look above!"

The voice that called out was their own Mr. Elman, gifted with magic sight better than any human or fae in the caravan.

On a thick, billowy cloud hanging in the sky, they could see people standing along its edge. Some had to stare, while other used telescopes to see. The cloud obscured briefly a flying ship resting on it as its occupants of elves and bird-like fae stared down at them all. One waved, and soon most of the men of Titan's Caravan waved back.

"Do you know who they might be, Mr. Traveler?" Lady Aylen asked.

"A rarely seen race of flying elves, princess, but not aligned with sky elves," he answered. But already something else had caught his attention in the sky. "The official greeting herald of Atlantea is here. We shall learn if what Oughtred says is true."

The sun in the sky began to descend. As it came closer, all aboard the many ships knew it wasn't the real sun at all, but a ball of fire that became more humanoid as it neared. When level with the cloud ship elves and fae, it appeared as a fully formed humanoid head. It scanned the many ships and those on the cloud.

"I deeply regret what I must announce. The kingdom at Titan's End, the ancient city of Atlantea, will be closed to all for a time. Spread the news to your kingdoms and to all who would depart upon Titan's Trail for our kingdom. Return in ten centuries, when you can again be welcomed to our lands for adventure, recreation, and treasure. Our decree is final."

Every human and fae aboard the white ship fell silent, crushed, shocked. Oughtred had spoken the truth. Surely this could not be the end of their journey at the very border of their fabled destiny, denied entry while the kingdom lay within eyesight.

As had been habit from the very beginning of their deadly journey, all looked to their caravan master—a look, a word, gesture, any indication as to what to do or feel.

Traveler glanced back at the crew.

"Mr. Hobbs."

The caravan's steward stepped forward from the crowd.

"Yes, sir."

"I know many are watching from the magic mirrors below, but have everyone join us on deck, including all our animals. We shall all be in Atlantea in mere moments," he said in a matter-of-fact tone.

Hobbs smiled. "You are certain, sir."

"Mr. Hobbs, I didn't hire you as the first man of the caravan those many months ago in Hopeshire to come all this way to the threshold of the fabled kingdom only to march back empty-handed." Traveler raised his voice to announce, "Everyone! Behold your first member of a race whose kingdom we have traveled so very far to visit. The talking head in the sky is an Atlantean." A large grin came across their caravan master's face. "He knows me."

SIREN STORMS OF MADNESS
The Fabled Quest Chronicles concludes in Book Six:
The Kingdom at Titan's End!

CONTINUE THE ADVENTURE

<u>Get Your Next *Fabled Quest Chronicles* Books!</u>

- ❖ ***Through Titan's Trail*** (Fabled Quest Chronicles, Book 1)
- ❖ ***In the Shadow of the Kings*** (Fabled Quest Chronicles, Book 2)
- ❖ ***Comes the War Wizards' Wrath*** (Fabled Quest Chronicles, Book 3)
- ❖ ***The Forest of Ancients*** (Fabled Quest Chronicles, Book 4)
- ❖ ***Siren Storms of Madness*** (Fabled Quest Chronicles, Book 5)
- ❖ ***Kingdom at Titan's End*** (Fabled Quest Chronicles, Book 6)

Fabled Quest Chronicles Box Set (Books 1-3)
Fabled Quest Chronicles Box Set 2 (Books 4-6)

<u>Prequels</u>
- ❖ ***Quest Master*** (Prequel to the Fabled Quest Chronicles)

<u>Also by Austin Dragon</u>

See all my books in fantasy, science fiction, and horror: <u>http://www.austindragon.com/books</u>

GLOSSARY / BOOK FIVE

Quillen's List of Races, Beasts, and Monsters of Myth and Magic

<u>Adaro</u> - Commonly called "shooting mermen," these malevolent merman-like creatures attack in packs of small, quickly moving vessels, any who sail into their territory. Male humanoids in form, with grayish skin like a shark's, a shark's dorsal fin growing from their heads, gills behind his ears, fishtail-like feet, and their backs are lined with shark-like fins. They hunt and kill by shooting sailors in the neck with poisonous flying fish fired from special bows. Victims hit by those fish are killed by the paralyzing poison alone. Adaro weapons include swordfish-like or spearfish-like spears, depending on the clan. Adaro ships are able to submerge and travel underwater, or fly in the sky, hiding by appearing as rainbows.

<u>Ant Man</u> - A race of giant bipedal humanoid ants with four arms—two arms on each side—red ant eyes, and large crushing mandibles in place of mouths. They communicate telepathically with their own kind and other intelligent races.

<u>Aspidochelone</u> - Colossal aquatic creatures often mistaken for rocky islands thick with trees, other plant life, and wildlife such as birds. Actually, they are giant sea turtles or shell-covered whales, and the visible "island" is their back. They spend most of their life sleeping, and feed on fish and water life passing underwater beneath them. Malevolent ones have been known to lure sailors to land on their backs to drown or destroy their ships, but likely the rare behavior is to play, rather than any ill intent.

Bauk - An evil animal-like creature said to be made of darkness itself. Appearing as a type of humanoid bear with long fangs, it hides in dark places, such as caves, abandoned buildings, barns, or ships, empty closets, under beds, or even in cracks, waiting to grab and eat a human(oid) victim. Simple light or noise can scare them away, as they attack only through surprise.

Blatnik (or Blatnoi) - Colloquially known as swamp-men, these intelligent creatures are made of mud or slime and live in swamps, marshes, or bog holes. If anyone comes too close to their home, blatniks jump out and drag the victim into the water to drown them. Some fae believe they also live near buried treasure.

Cecaelia (also known as a Mermaid Octopus) - A sister race of the mermaids who also live in matriarchal civilizations deep underwater in cities governed by queens. They are beautiful female humanoids with large octopus tentacles instead of bipedal legs, with their upper torsos clothed in material tunics or battle dress. Their skin is luminescent light blue but chameleon-like, able to change color due to mood or to blend into their surroundings. Their hands are webbed, and their fangs may barely be noticeable but can elongate when angry or in battle. Their hands can also become claws in battle. They have long, flowing hair down their backs or kept in a beehive style on top of their heads.

Cecaelia are said to have bodies free of bones (though not true) because of their seemingly impossibly fast movements, flexibility, reflexes, and speed. Their tentacles can act independently, as if each possesses its own free will, or as a single unit. Since they live deeper in the waters, their night vision is superior to mermaids, and their skin can also glow in the dark at will. Their regenerative abilities are superior to not only mermaids but most water fae.

Like mermaids, cecaelia can summon and direct aquatic life, but a far more diverse range of species and those that dwell in the ocean, unlike mermaids.

Decaelia (or Squid Mermaid) - A sub-race of the Cecaelia who are squid-like rather than octopus-like, meaning they have ten tentacles, two of which are longer and larger, rather than only eight equi-length tentacles. They possess all the abilities of their mermaid octopus sisters and possibly more.

Dobhar-chú (or "water hound") - Resembles a dog-like otter with a large fish-like tail. A very curious, benevolent animal that lives in lakes and streams. Its fur has magical traits which protect the animal from most physical attacks.

Domovoi (or Domovoy) - A sub-race of brownies. Halfling sprites who look like old men with thick gray mustaches and beards touching the ground, wearing dark caps and clothes. There are both day and nocturnal clans, who spend their time keeping their home dwelling they share with human or fae tidy and clean and see to other housework. They are also protective of the children or animals of the household. Female domovoi are called domania.

Some are said to be able to foresee and warn of coming calamities that threaten the household. However, despite their unwavering loyalty and protection of a household, they can get angry or even leave if the family engages in behavior or language they view as unacceptable or corrupt.

Finman (or Finfolk) - A race of territorial fae shape-shifters who sail the sea from the depths of their secret ocean homes in search of human(oid) captives. Finfolk kidnap sailors, fishermen, or children playing near the shore and force them into lifelong servitude as spouses or laborers. They travel the sea aboard invisible ships but have the ability to create illusions of other smaller vessels. Their race is territorial.

The dark fae appear human—bald, extremely tall, lanky with a frowning, gaunt face, and mirrored eyes—and naked, except they have no genitalia. With their shape-shifting abilities, they grow their size to the size of giants or into any of the fauna of the sea. A finwife is a female finfolk and are rarely seen.

<u>Fish Man</u> - Humanoid fish or fish-headed humanoids.

<u>Giant</u> - One of the major races of fae who live in patriarchal societies governed by kings and chiefs. The majority of the giant races are warriors, all possessing great strength, but others have kingdoms of diverse occupations. Giants can range in height from ten to one hundred feet.

<u>Sub-Races of Giants:</u>

<u>Antaeans</u> - Members of the sub-race of giants regarded as great warriors, ranging in height from eight to twelve feet. Antaeans wear shining armor and helmets. Their greatest magical power is that when they directly touch the earth in a deliberate stance, no force in the world can move or harm them.

<u>Argus</u> - A sub-race of seer giants whose bald heads are covered in a hundred eyes. They are greater oracles than even the cyclopes seers.

<u>Athos</u> - A sub-race of brutish giants who possess the magical strength to rip whole mountains from the earth and hurl them great distances. Hence, their common name: "mountain thrower."

<u>Cyclops</u> - A sub-race of giants with a single eye in the center of their forehead. There are many different

clans, both civilized and savage. Some are gifted builders, craftsmen, and merchants. Others are scholars and artisans. Rare ones are seers and oracles, able to see what cannot be seen with the normal eye, or the future. There are also savage clans known for their ferocity and cannibalism.

Hafgufa - These sea monsters deliberately disguise themselves as islands or rocks in the sea to hunt ships and their crews. There are endless species of the giant predatory sea serpents.

Hippocampus - Aquatic beasts with the upper body of a blue horse and the lower body of a fish. They are the chosen transport by many royal water fae races.

Homunculus - Called a "living puppet" by fae, these miniature humanoids created by magical potions and ingredients act as spies by their creator. The creatures can even be made to magically transmit everything they see or hear to their creator, but if the link is too strong any damage to the homunculus could also harm the maker.

The creatures are most often made to be humanoid but a homunculus can be made into a bird, mouse, snake, or any other animal, though the human form is the simplest to create.

Ichthyocentaur - See Sea Centaur.

Jörmungandr - The largest sea serpents of the great oceans of the magical realms, said to have even existed in the age of the Titans. They are so large and long they can shoot up to touch the void of the heavens above. Since very few living creatures are large enough to even get their attention, any destruction they inflict is purely accidental.

Klabautermann- A race of water kobolds (sprites) that are larger than the average human, hunched over, thick bodies, ugly faces, and usually missing teeth. In the Lands of Man, they are known to assist sailors and fishermen, even rescuing them from sea wrecks or those who are washed overboard. In the magical lands, they command their own vessels, as they are exceptional sailors. Like all sprites, they are given to merriment and music, but are hard workers. Like their land cousins, they can sense treasure of any kind near them and eagerly seek it out.

Leokampoi - See Sea Lion.

Mermaid - One of the major races of fae who live in matriarchal underwater cities governed by queens. They are beautiful female humanoids with a large fish tail instead of bipedal legs. Their skin is an almost luminescent light blue. They have long, flowing hair, and their eyes can be similar to fish or human. The only clothing they wear are a type of brassiere—like cloth wrapped around their breast area several times.

Malevolent mermaids love storms and floods, and are present at shipwrecks and drownings. Also, like sirens, they can lure and attract humans and other humanoids with their enchanted singing, often to crash sea-going vessels onto rocks. Benevolent ones can help victims of natural disasters at sea and have been known to fall in love with humans, giving up their fae lives to live as humans.

<u>Merman</u> - There are two main species: Ugly male sea humanoids that look like a brown fish but with the head of a man—blue-green hair, unsightly teeth, and slits for eyes. They enjoy storms and being present at sinking ships. Despite their appearance, they can magically cure sickness and lift curses. Others are sages and oracles.

The other species look like attractive blue-skinned male humanoids. Like mermaids, they can appear in their true form, with their lower torso that of a giant fish, or transform them to be human legs to walk upon land. They have the speed, strength, and agility of mermaids but not the same level of enchantment as mermaids.

<u>Merrow</u> - A fae warrior race of humanoids with green skin and hair, and webbed hands and feet. Parts of their skin scaled like fish.

<u>Nix</u> (or Nixie) — A race of shape-shifting water fae, either nymph or mermaid. They are enchanting, beautiful women with long hair. They look human but have an angelic glow. They can assume many different forms, such as human, fish, and snake. Sub-races can either be malicious or friendly to others.

<u>Nymph</u> - One of the major races of fae who live in matriarchal societies. They are enchanting, beautiful women with long hair. They look human, but have an angelic glow. Human men are helpless to their powerful, magical attraction. Fae men can also be susceptible to their enchantment.

<u>Nereids</u> - Powerful water nymphs of the seas and oceans.

<u>Ophiotaurus</u> - Fantastic fish-scaled beasts with the upper torso of a bull and the lower half of a fish with a long tail. They swim and live together in packs (or schools), and sightings of the peaceful animals are seen as good omens by fae.

<u>Sea Centaur</u> - Cousins to merfolk and tritons, they are a race of fae with a bluish-skinned humanoid upper torso and lower torso of a horse's forelegs and the tail of a giant fish. Despite their strange form, they can swim faster than mermaids and longer than most water fae.

<u>Sea Goblin</u> - The seafaring cousins of land goblins. Stout and muscular, in frame, their green skin is similar to that of an eel, both ridged and scaled. Their noses are flat, and their pointy ears and clawed hands are larger than their land cousins'. They are the mortal enemies of water elves.

They are called sea goblins exclusively, but exist in the oceans, seas, and deep underwater in different sub-species.

<u>Sea Lion</u> (also known as Leokampoi) - A large lion beast with the lower half of a fish. The aquatic beasts are found in the wild or are often domesticated to serve in water fae kingdoms as guards and companions. They are fierce fighters, and their claws are especially deadly to skin or metal, leaving wounds extremely resistant to magical healing, though not impossible.

<u>Selkie</u> - A race of humans, also known as sealfolk, who can transform into seals or sea lions. Little is known of their people outside of fae-kind, but they are a benevolent race respected by all five main empires of the Oceanus Omnis—merfolk, water nymphs, water elves, sea centaurs, and tritons—as advisors and seers.

<u>Siren</u> - The feared dark mermaids of the seas who lure sailors with their enchanting singing to their deaths. Siren songs strip men of all will so they shipwreck their craft on the rocky reefs of their siren islands.

They are creatures with the upper torso of a seductive female and the lower torso a giant fish (like a mermaid) or bird, but accounts vary. Like malevolent mermaids they can create storms and floods. They are the blood enemies of benevolent merfolk.

<u>Stymphalian Bird</u> - A race of carnivorous birds, twice the size of storks, with beaks of metal and metallic feathers. They can be unrelenting predators of any who trespass into their territory, and are feared by fae and human alike.

Sylph - The beautiful nymph-like elementals of the air. In appearance, women with pale, almost-transparent skin, clear eyes, and long, flowing blue-white hair. With their immense power, they can manipulate air and weather at will, making them the most powerful of all elementals.

They live high above in the clouds and work closely with their sister elemental race, the undines, or water elementals.

Triton - A noble race of water fae with an upper humanoid half and a lower half of two green-scaled fish tails for legs. They are one of the five main races of the Oceanus Omnis along with merfolk, water nymphs, water elves, and sea centaurs. They have a main fin on their heads and fins along their spines, arms, and sometimes legs. Their skin is blue or green in color, and they have pointed ears like elves.

Their weapon of choice is the magic trident. They are also able to communicate long distances to one another with large shells, often conch, or use them to magically summon various water animals or beasts. Wizards use the same method to calm or create storms.

Tritons' main allies are the sea centaurs, the other patriarchal race of the five main races.

<u>Undine</u> – The race of powerful elemental beings of water. Beautiful tall, thin women, who wear sheer, flowing dresses of nature. They live in the oceans or in giant sacred waterfalls. They possess the ability to summon and control water in any way. As their power comes from the oceans of Pan-Earth itself, only the sylphs of the air are ultimately more powerful than they among all elementals.

<u>Water Leaper</u> – A giant limbless frog creature with a bat's wings and a long, lizard-like stinger. They live in swamps and ponds. Though the size of a small dog, they are wild and dangerous, jumping from their habitats to eat any animal or person who has had the misfortune of venturing by. Usually, it moves too fast to get caught but can kill with its stinger as it flees back into the water, if threatened.

ABOUT THE AUTHOR

Austin Dragon is the author of over 20 books in science fiction, fantasy, and classic horror. His works include the cyberpunk detective *LIQUID COOL* series, the epic fantasy *FABLED QUEST CHRONICLES*, the international epic *AFTER EDEN* Series, and the classic *SLEEPY HOLLOW HORRORS*. He is a native New Yorker but has called Los Angeles, California home for more than twenty years. Words to describe him, in no particular order: U.S. Army, English teacher, one-time resident of Paris, ex-political junkie, movie buff, Fortune 500 corporate recruiter, renaissance man, futurist, and dreamer.

He is currently working on new books and series in science fiction, fantasy, and classic horror!

http://www.austindragon.com/books